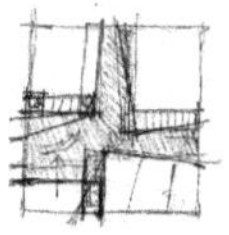

Secret Paths Editions presents

In Search of Lost Girls

The Boy & Girl Saga - Book Two
Revised 2020 edition

Alan McCluskey

Copyright Alan McCluskey 2014
Revised ebook cover September 2016
Revised edition 2020
Cover illustration by Alan McCluskey

ISBN 978-2-940553-21-1

Other books by the author

The Boy & Girl Saga
Boy & Girl - Book One
We Girls - Book Three

The Storyteller's Quest
The Reaches - Book One
The Keeper's Daughter - Book Two
The Starless Square - Book Three

Chimera
Stories People Tell

Coming soon
Local Voices

Thanks

Thanks go to the Geneva Writers' Group, in particular Susan Tiberghien and the other members of the committee, who continue to provide a stimulating context for so many writers to exchange and learn. Thanks go to two critiquing groups: the Basel Writers' Circle, which sadly has now disappeared, and the SCWI Switzerland YA group, both of which worked on critiquing parts of this novel. Thanks to Fred Leebron, who led a master class in fiction in Geneva during which the first three chapters of this book were critiqued. Thanks also to the participants of that master class. Special thanks go to my beta-readers Ginger Dawn and Michelle DiPietro for their hard work and constructive comments. The book has considerably changed thanks to their contributions. Particular thanks go to our piano tuner whose mother tongue is French, but who has read all my books. She insisted I publish another book as she wanted to know what happened next.

Thanks go to my children Zoé and Iannis for their comments and suggestions about the book cover. Above all, my gratitude goes to my wife, Huguette, for her continued support and encouragement. The other day, bless her, she asked me which of my books –all of which she has read– I advised her to re-read. I replied Boy & Girl, in preparation for the publication of In Search of Lost Girls.

In Search of Lost Girls

1.

"... One ... Two ... Three ..." Arthur W. Yong mentally paced out the empty cupboard. "That should be enough for the meddling brat." He'd teach her not to mess with his stories.

He glanced over the paper clipping. Girl maimed in car accident, the headline read. Yes. The perfect model for the tragic figure he needed. He remembered her well. As a young man, he'd met her once at a lunch-time concert during a visit to Switzerland. He winced. She'd stood out like a bright light in the midst of a drab, middle-aged audience. He was immediately attracted to her, but when he accosted her in the foyer, she'd snubbed him like the haughty brat she was.

He put down his pen, taking care not to smudge the ink, then raised the cup to his lips between trembling fingers. Since the attack, thirst was a constant companion, but drinking was a struggle. Being unable to control half his face, liquids sneaked out his mouth, ran down his chin and ended up on his shirt. His right hand, the only one that worked, ran nervously across his chin, checking. He breathed a sigh of relief. No tea had dribbled past his pinched lips.

Turning back to the manuscript, he reached for his pen only to have it slip from his uncertain grasp leaving a black blotch in the middle of the text. He cursed silently as he mopped up the ink, then painstakingly rewrote the lines.

So what remained to be done? The church held its own against unusually bleak weather for summer, its tower pointing bluntly at heaven. The cloister was in place. The nuns walked its wind-swept corridors. A hoard of ill-dressed girls cowered under a nun's watchful eyes, reciting lessons. To cap it all, the whole edifice bathed in a foul stench of burnt cabbage. Were he to close the pages, he was sure the smell would still linger.

He took a further sip, cautiously replaced the cup on his desk and closed his eyes. How would the story begin?

"Greetings Baron. Good of you to spare the time."

He was startled by the unfamiliar voice. Being called 'Baron' startled him too. That hadn't been in the story, but then neither had he. He'd written himself into other stories but never had he been unwillingly transported into one. He had no desire to be trapped in the dismal world he'd concocted for the girl. That was her hell, not his. After all, he was the author. She was a mere character.

"Baron?" the voice said tersely.

Opening his eyes, a tall, gaunt nun stood before him dressed in a black tunic over which she wore the traditional black apron. Her stern face was framed in a white coif topped with a black veil attached behind her head. Her lips were drawn in a tight line below a sharp nose. She was far more daunting than he'd described in his outline. Could this really be his story?

"Greetings, Reverend Mother."

They stood in a small, sheltered doorway cut deep into the thick wall that encircled the convent. Selecting a key from the keyring at her waist, the Abbess unlocked the door and ushered him into the guest house, a nondescript little building nestled against the convent wall. The interior was bleak and austere. He caught sight of a number of tiny bedrooms each furnished with a single metal-framed cot.

"I trust your little community is thriving," he said, placing his small holdall on a cot.

The Abbess winced, no doubt baulking at the word 'little'. From what he knew, the number of nuns continued to decrease. There were barely enough to maintain essential activities, let alone run the orphanage and school.

"And the girls?" the Baron enquired.

"There seems to be no end to the orphans and other down-and-outs that require the firm, helping hand of God," Abbess Johannes said, leading him out into the gardens that lay within the walls.

At the centre of the gardens, the buildings surged in a clumsy jumble. Parts were built in local grey-green stone, but most was wood, much of which was badly in need of repair. Having drafted notes about the convent, he knew the cloister lay at its centre and beyond, the church rose sullen and neglected.

The Abbess didn't make for the main buildings, instead she led him along a covered walkway that hugged the wall. Wind had blown dried leaves into corners and under benches, adding an air of abandon to the sinister scene.

A piercing scream ripped the numbing silence. A young girl dressed only in a tattered pinafore dress rounded a nearby building, running head down, her bare feet pounding the ground. Close on her heels came a nun waving a large stick, her robes girded up around her knees.

"How dare you," the nun shouted.

Intent on escaping, the girl hadn't spotted the Abbess who stepped out and intercepted her. The Baron wrinkled his nose. Not only did the kid look filthy, she smelt it too.

"Is this yours, Sister Helga?" the Abbess asked, shaking the girl.

Sister Helga came to an abrupt halt, one hand pressed against her chest as she struggled to catch her breath. When she'd recovered, she nodded greetings to the Baron then grabbed the girl by the scruff of her neck.

"This unholy specimen thinks she can mock us," the nun said.

The girl's eyes flashed, her fists clenched, her tall, wiry frame tensed to flee.

"What's your name, girl?" the Baron asked, forcing himself to take an interest.

"Tania," the girl mumbled.

For all her black eye, the livid bruise on her cheek and the scratches and cuts on her arms and legs, this one hadn't yet been broken.

"Where do you come from?"

"Nowhere, Sir."

"Her parents abandoned her in the hard times after the Second World War," the Abbess explained. "I'll talk to you later, Tania," the Abbess said, then she turned back to the Baron. "You must be thirsty. Why don't you join me for some refreshment?"

He followed the Abbess along the covered path till the walkway ended abruptly at a long, two-storey building. Halting in front of a low door, the Abbess pointed up at the building, explaining that it had once been the gymnasium, "the pride of the convent and the region," she said. The ground floor now served as a school for orphan girls and the first floor had been converted into a dormitory.

"Keep your head down," the Abbess warned, as she opened the door onto a dark, dank passage. The tunnel surprised him. No such passageway existed in his plans. He was relieved when they finally stepped out. They were once again outside the convent, close to the main entrance where the drive curled up in front of the church.

They skirted the library, which, according to the Abbess, would have housed many a treasure had it not been for the hoards of Protestants that had ransacked the place during the Reformation. Finally they reached the Abbess's House that lay between the library and the West Porch.

Holding the front door open, the Abbess invited him in.

On her knees in the hallway, a young girl scrubbed the tiles. Seeing them enter, she scuttled out of the way, hauling bucket and brush after her.

The Baron guessed she was twelve, but her skinniness and her hair cropped short made her look even younger. A tattered pinafore dress hung over her emaciated frame barely reaching her thighs. Like Tania, she was peppered with bruises and cuts.

"Clear that away, Suzanne, and prepare tea for two," the Abbess ordered.

The Baron followed the Abbess into the reception room. A small casement window let in a hope of light, most of which got squandered amongst the dark-stained furniture and dull drapes. The musty air hung heavy and suffocating.

The Abbess was boring him with the difficulties of getting extra money to pay for the children – apparently the local council had withdrawn part of their subsidies – when a timid knock came at the door and Suzanne entered carrying a tray bearing two cream-coloured mugs, a pot of tea and a small plate with two tiny biscuits on it. The Baron leaned away, overpowered by the smell as the girl moved around the table, transferring the tea things onto its surface.

"That'll do," the Abbess said, dismissing her, much to the Baron's relief. Before she could leave, however, someone knocked and entered. The Abbess introduced the short, chubby nun as the Prioress and sent Suzanne to get an additional cup.

"That won't be necessary," the Prioress said. "Reverend Mother you're needed. There's a problem with one of the girls."

The Abbess got wearily to her feet and apologised to the Baron. "I'll be back as soon as I can. If you need anything, just ask Suzanne."

The girl moved closer and poured him a mug of tea. Ignoring her, he took a bite of a biscuit and almost spat it out. Leckerli! He should have known. It was a local specialty. He couldn't stomach the mixture of candied peel that gave it its distinctive taste.

Replacing the half-eaten biscuit on the plate, he glanced at the girl. She'd returned to her position, leaning against the wall, her head hung, her hands clasped tightly in front of her. He wished the Abbess had dismissed her. He needed time to think.

Despite it being Summer, the room was cold. He clasped his hands around the mug, savouring its warmth, savouring also the ability to use his hand again, one of the few perks of being in a world of his imagination. Then he raised the mug to his lips, only to wrinkle his nose and put it down without drinking. It smelt so strongly of the girl that her odour masked any hint of peppermint. At the thought of her filthy fingers pawing the mug, he struggled to stop bile from rising in his throat. Getting to his feet, he took refuge by the window.

Outside the sky had clouded over and the threat of rain made the unpaved drive look all the more mournful. Somewhere in that direction, further down the hill, hidden by the folds in the landscape, lay the town, although he hadn't bothered to venture so far in the outline of his book.

When he finally turned away, hoping the girl might have left, he caught her staring at him, a troubled, almost calculating look. What could possibly be going through her shrivelled little brain? He didn't want her telling wild tales to the Abbess. He'd done nothing wrong, but girls of that age could have fertile imaginations. Better to win her over.

"Tell me Suzanne," he began, "how long have you been here?"

"For ever," the girl mumbled.

He let out a "Hmpf!" of frustration. Conversation was not going to get him far.

"Tell me about school. I'm intrigued."

She stared at him, her lips pressed in a firm line, her fists clenched. What had he said wrong?

"Dunno," was all she finally uttered.

"What do you do?" he asked, forcing himself to be civil.

"Lessons," she said, her expression full of disgust. "Mostly I'm the Abbess's special help."

It was then the door squeaked open. Both spun to see who'd arrived. The Baron's face flushed with guilt. Goodness only knew why. As for the girl, she stood stock-still, her complexion drained of blood.

A small head peeked round the door and surveyed the room, then Tania emerged. Her wild array of scars and wounds now included fresh red weals on the back of both hands.

"You all right?" she asked Suzanne, ignoring him completely. "Did this bloke hurt you?"

Suzanne shook her head, glancing fearfully at him.

The sound of the front door opening had Tania scuttling out, leaving them alone. The girl hastily gathered up the crockery and headed for the door Tania had used.

"Ah Baron, I'm glad you're still here," the Abbess said as she entered. Noticing that Suzanne was not there, she enquired after the girl.

"She cleared away the remains of tea."

"Well Baron, you haven't told me the reason for your visit. I'm sure you didn't come just for a social call."

"I have a favour to ask."

The Abbess frowned as if she'd been expecting as much.

"The twelve year-old daughter of acquaintances has fallen on hard times. Her parents were killed in a terrible accident and she was maimed." He was pleased at the note of sadness that infused his voice.

"In what way was she injured?"

"She limps badly and the accident has left her deaf and dumb." At least, she would be, as soon as he'd finished writing her miserable part in the saga.

"And what do you expect us to do?"

"Take her in till I can find a permanent place for her." Long enough to break the girl. "I'll pay you well. No special favours required. Treat her like the others." He had a hard time not smiling at the misery the girl would have to endure.

"And what's the name of this gem?"

"Kaitling, but most people call her Kate."

2.

The school corridor lurched sideways. Peter leaned against the wall and shifted the weight from his crutches. His hands and arms ached. Closing his eyes, he took a deep breath. The doctor had been right. It was too early to return to school. But he'd insisted.

"Are you all right?" someone asked.

He opened his eyes, hoping the world had righted itself, and saw a schoolboy standing in front of him, a worried look on his face.

"You dropped this," the boy said holding out a tattered copy of Wilde's *Picture of Dorian Grey*.

Peter propped one of the crutches against the wall and stretched out a hand. The coma had left him clumsy and their fingers touched momentarily as the boy handed him the novel. Seeing Peter flinch, the boy took a step back, his pale blue eyes fixing him. Like many others, the boy seemed to expect something of him, but Peter had no idea what.

"I'm Andrew. You must be Peter," the boy said, his voice soft and musical. "I heard you'd been ill."

Peter studied the slender youth. Andrew's tentative smile echoed the caution in his eyes. His lips were full and sensuous contrasting with a willful chin. He wore his short brown hair carefully combed. Yet no amount of combing could conceal his natural waves. Peter's hair in comparison was much longer and never looked so tidy. The boy seemed younger, his head barely reaching Peter's shoulders.

Mmmm, he's delicious, a girl's voice purred in Peter's head. It was Kate, the young girl's spirit that lodged in his mind. He'd offered her refuge when her spirit had been brutally severed from her body.

Cut it out, Kate. His silent words were laced with affection.

You may not like boys, but I don't have to pretend I'm not interested, she scoffed.

It's confusing enough having a girl in my head, Peter told her, *without you muddling my emotions.*

She burst out laughing, sending an unbearable wave of shivers down his spine.

That's unfair, he told her, trying to shield himself from her emotions.

He's talking, Kate warned.

"... do you like Wilde's book?" Andrew asked.

"Haven't begun it yet," Peter muttered, not wishing to get drawn into a conversation. Kate was right. He didn't like boys. They made him uneasy, with their bragging, their rough ways and their dirty habits. He preferred girls. Luckily his step-sister Fi came waltzing down the corridor, sparing him any further questions.

Fi reminded him of a pixie. She was short and slim, but strong, with high cheek bones, sparkling blue eyes and shoulder-length auburn hair. She'd ditched her school blazer and tie, donning an airman's dark brown leather jacket, a prize found at a jumble sale. She had such a way with clothes she could even make a pleated, bottle-green school skirt look fashionable with the right accessories. On her head was her green beret, aslant as always, matching the green silk scarf tied loosely around her neck.

Even Kate had to admit she looked good, although she did comment, *I hope the headmaster doesn't see her dressed like that.*

Peter chuckled. The headmaster was Fi's new step father and Peter's guardian.

Fi flung an arm around Peter's shoulders, almost knocking

him off his feet, and kissed him noisily on the cheek. Then she turned to greet Andrew.

"Hi Andy. You chatting up Peter?"

Andrew blushed bright red.

That was Fi for you, not an ounce of diplomacy in her. Every young man who took an interest in Peter, not that there were many, was his potential lover. She'd have been delighted if her 'pretty boy' as she called him finally found a boyfriend. She preferred girls.

"Oie Andy!" a burly youth bellowed from the end of an otherwise deserted corridor. "Quit keeping us waiting."

"Blasted brother," Andrew muttered under his breath, his smile replaced by a worried look.

Thick-set and muscular, the youth swaggered down the corridor. A typical rugby player, head down, ready to blunder into the scrum. He'd also removed his tie, but unlike Fi, it made him look scruffy. Planting himself squarely in front of Andrew, his back turned to Fi and Peter, he shoved Andrew against the wall.

"Are you deaf?" he shouted.

Peter sensed Kate readying for a fight. She was a genius at unarmed combat, the author of those spectacular moves people thought were his. How could they possibly know he mentally stepped aside to let her use his body?

I don't think my body'll hold up to a fight.

Don't worry. I'll take care.

"I wouldn't do that, if I were you," Peter warned Andrew's brother, his voice trembling slightly as he spoke.

"Who says?" the youth asked, spinning round to face Peter.

Andrew laid a hand on his brother's arm and tried to pull him back, only to be shoved away. "Come on, Brian," Andrew pleaded, "Let's go. Mum's be worried."

"You wait till Mum hears you've been hanging out with these pansies. She'll be furious." Brian spat on the ground, as if to underscore his words.

"Please, Brian," Andrew beseeched, tears forming in his

eyes.

Brian face twisted in rage and swore, "Poof!"

His fists clenched, he lunged at Andrew. Kate sprang into action. Taking over Peter's body, she slammed one of the crutches between Brian's ankles and twisted sharply. Catching him off balance, the move sent him sprawling across the floor, his arms and legs splayed in every direction. He slithered to a halt inches short of a row of filling cabinets.

"Leave him," Andrew whimpered, tears streaming down his cheeks. "You'll only make things worse."

Brian struggled to his feet and stood swaying for a moment. He glared at Peter, leaning unsteadily in Peter's direction then abruptly charged, growling like an infuriated boar.

Some people never learn, Kate thought.

Using the crutches as a lever, she hopped sideways at the last moment, causing Brian to collide head-first with the brick wall. A resounding thud rang out, followed by a muffled grunt and Brian sank in slow motion to the floor.

"Stop!" Fi ordered. "Stop, both of you!"

Brian knelt on one knee nursing the side of his head as Peter took back control and edged along the wall out of reach.

"Enough," Fi continued. "Andrew, take your brother to the infirmary. The nurse is still there. Get him patched up and go home, both of you."

Brian looked game to fight on. When Andrew tried to help him to his feet, the youth shook him off. Putting his hand to his head, it came away soaked in blood. "I'll get you back for this, poof," he said glaring at Peter and staggered off down the corridor ignoring Andrew who scurried after him.

Why did Fi have to stop me? Kate complained. Peter was alarmed at how shaken she sounded.

"Kate says you're a monster for spoiling her fun," Peter told Fi, trying to make light of what was happening.

No I didn't! Kate protested.

"I bet she didn't," Fi said.

"I wish we could still talk mind-to-mind," Peter said. "All

this would be so much easier."

"I agree. If Brian bears a grudge, which seems highly likely, not being able to call each other mind-to-mind could be a disaster," Fi pointed out soberly.

Oh no! Kate gasped.

Like thunder clap, a blast of vivid memories exploded in Peter's head.

A man dressed in black leather, his face masked, towered over Kate, an axe grasped in his hand. All around, a sinister crowd of priests robbed in black, pressed ever closer, their enflamed eyes boring into her. And over it all, a powerful voice rang out, "Kill her". Kate's head was slammed onto the chopping block and the deadly axe whooshed down towards her neck…

Horrific memories of his own clamoured for attention, leaving Peter struggling to keep a grip on his emotions.

It's all lost, Kate wailed in Peter's head sparking a searing pain between his ears.

She'd always been so level headed and dependable. Even confronted with her own execution, she'd remained stoic. Now the brunt of her accumulated misery crashed over him. His back slithered down the wall till he landed on the cold floor, his head gripped between his hands.

"What's the matter?" Fi asked, alarmed.

"It's Kate," he gasped. "The mention of talking mind-to-mind had her bursting into sobs." Better not mention the horror that had gone with it.

Fi knelt next to Peter and took him in her arms, pulling him tight against her. "It's going to be alright, Kate," she whispered in Peter's ear. "We'll find a way. We'll sort this out, I promise."

Fi's arms around him calmed Peter, even if they did little to assuage Kate's despair. Nothing could get her body back. What a horrid prospect! A life without a body! It was a wonder anyone could survive. They crouched a long moment in each other's arms until Kate's sobs finally abated.

I'm sorry, she told Peter. *It's so hard. I try my best … But the fight reminded me of all that violence…*

Peter shuddered.

What'll become of me? Kate asked, her words trailing off.

"I have a suggestion," Fi said, helping Peter to his feet. She removed her beret and placed it on his head. "Why don't you loan Kate your body for the weekend? What do you think Kate?"

"She'd like that," Peter said, relaying Kate's thoughts. The suggestion made sense, but he cringed at what it would entail. "As long as you don't go running the streets with me dressed as a girl." It was meant as a joke, but he shuddered at the thought of bumping into someone like Andrew.

"Wasn't that always your secret dream, my pretty boy?" Fi asked, her pixie face sparkling with delight and malice as she slanted the beret on his head and began undoing his school tie.

Come on, Peter, I'd really like that. Not that I don't enjoy being in your head, but it's claustrophobic. Peter couldn't help noticing her brave attempt at humour. *Just for me,* Kate entreated.

"OK," he conceded.

"Sorry to keep you waiting," Dr Grant, said as he hurried down the corridor. He was no longer wearing the dark university gown that many teachers draped over their everyday clothes, but he still cut an impressive figure with his impeccable grey suit, his sober floral tie, not to mention his greying hair and his stately handlebar moustache. Seeing the beret on Peter's head his smile fled. "I trust you won't make a habit of dressing like that, I might have to give you detention for breeching school rules."

Peter hastily pulled off the hat and handed it to Fi who took it with an exaggerated bow. Dr Grant gave them both a stony look.

Is he angry? Kate asked, sounding perplexed.

I'm not sure, he told Kate. *He knows full well I wear girl's clothes, even if he's never seen me do it.*

Of course, Dr Grant would be furious if he went to school dressed as a girl. More than that, Dr Grant would probably feel betrayed. Not that Peter would ever do it. The thought of being mocked by fellow pupils had him shrinking back in horror.

After all the emotions, Peter was exhausted on the way home and he'd willingly have slept, but he forced himself to tell Dr Grant about the fight. Unlike many adults who butted in with their opinions before you'd finished, the headmaster listened in silence, interrupting only when clarification was necessary. Peter went on to describe Kate's reaction. Dr Grant knew all about the girl in Peter's head. He'd made her acquaintance when Kate had first visited Peter mind-to-mind.

The headmaster listened, his face grim as he watched the road ahead. "I suspected Andrew was having problems, but he is a good pupil and always puts on a brave face. It would seem you have unwittingly unearthed the gravity of his situation."

"Is there nothing we can do?" Peter asked, his own solicitude surprising him.

"You might need to do something for us too," Fi pointed out. "If Andrew's brother decides to get revenge."

I'm so sorry, Kate moaned. *I started all this.*

"No you didn't," Peter replied out loud. "It's Kate. She thinks it's her fault."

"Andrew's brother started it," Fi pointed out.

"And what about you, Kate?" Dr Grant asked as he turned into the winding drive that led up to their home, a large mansion on the outskirts of town.

"She's really sorry," Peter relayed.

"I wish there were something we could do to make you feel better," Dr Grant said.

"Peter's agreed to let Kate borrow his body during the weekend. I'm sure that'll help," Fi said, brimming over with enthusiasm. "So you'll be gaining a daughter."

"I look forward to meeting you face to face Kate," he said, sounding a bit uncertain as he brought the car to a halt in front of the house.

Peter blushed. It didn't make any difference that John Grant knew about and tolerated him dressing up, Peter was still embarrassed at the prospect of parading in girl's clothes before his adopted parents, especially as John had never seen him dressed like that.

Dr Grant switched off the engine but made no move to get out, instead he turned to Peter, his face grave. "I know you are a cautious boy, but you need to be extremely careful. No one should know what happens here. We might be in 1960, but few people are as tolerant as us. Many would not understand if they knew we let you dress as a girl. They would probably be furious. Some might even call the police. And we can hardly use Kate as an excuse. She's as much a secret as your dressing up."

3.

"Do I really have to wear that," Kate asked, as Fi handed her a bra. When she'd agreed to borrow Peter's body, she'd never imagined being forced to dress like a doll. "It's hardly as if Peter's body needs it."

Fi laughed.

Tell her to quit poking fun, Peter grumbled.

I thought you always dreamt of dressing as a girl.

I did, but I never imagined parading in a dress in front of my headmaster. I'll never be able to face him again. What's more, it's not me that's dressing up, it's you.

His distress affected her deeply. *The last thing I want is to upset you. Let me hand back your body...*

No. Don't. I know how much you miss having a body. This weekend is for you, not me.

"Peter's upset," Kate said out loud.

"How come? I thought dressing up would make my pretty boy happy..."

"He's feeling a little…" and she paused, uncertain about the word to use, "dispossessed."

Get on with it, Peter told Kate. *We're going to be late.*

"Peter said hurry up."

Fi took the bra back from Kate. "I've got a remedy for flat chests," she said, pulling two round pads from her pocket.

Typical Fi, Peter muttered. *No beating about the bush.*

Fi helped Kate clasp the bra behind her back. Kate wasn't sure if it was her or Peter that shuddered as Fi slid the two pads in place.

"There," Fi said. "Look at yourself in the mirror."

The sight of herself in Peter's body in matching pants and bra made her uncomfortable. It was true, he could easily be mistaken for a girl, with his thin, pale face, his high cheek bones and his light brown hair, not to mention his slender hands and long fingers.

No, it was not so much seeing a boy dressed as a girl that disturbed her. She'd come to accept the ambiguity. What choice did she have? Rather, it was the make-believe. Where she came from, people were not continually pretending they were someone else. In addition, Peter's discomfort at being dressed up seeped through, even though he was trying to mask his emotions.

She turned her back on the mirror and picked up the dress that Fi and her mum had chosen. The two had bought the most feminine clothes they could find, as if that would help her forget she was in a boy's body.

Made of a silky material she didn't recognise, the dress was royal blue and reached to just below her knees. The long sleeves buttoned at the wrists and there was a rounded white collar below which a double line of buttons ran the whole length of the front of the dress to the hem. A belt pulled the otherwise loose-fitting dress tight around her waist causing it to billow over her chest. That it concealed Fi's padded bra suited her well. Even though she knew Fi's mum and Dr Grant were not dupe, she couldn't help imagining what they would think if they saw that she, or rather Peter, had sprouted breasts.

"Now the tights," Fi said. They were a paler shade of blue than the dress. Another article from Fi's mum's shopping spree.

Kate made a face. She'd have preferred more practical clothes, a full-length skirt or trousers and a blouse.

"You'll like them," Fi insisted. "They look so sexy."

Kate snorted in a very un-girlish way. She'd caught the habit from Peter. "I hardly think there's any need to appear attractive."

"Of course there is," Fi retorted. "Every girl wants to be attractive."

"Dinner's ready, girls," Fi's mum called up.

Kate sat on the bed and tried to pull on the tights, but kept getting them twisted. The effort exhausted her. In the end Fi came to the rescue. Kate was acutely aware of Fi's helping hand, all the more so that she felt Peter's embarrassment.

Being a girl is hard work, she told Peter, as she finally pulled the tights up around her waist and smoothed her dress in place. *I can't see why you ever bother. Next time round I want to be a boy.*

Good luck with that, Peter said, clearly still disgruntled.

Come on Peter. I know you're tired, but don't spoil my weekend by being in a bad mood.

Fi sat Kate on a chair such that her face was in the light and carefully applied lipstick and eyeliner. "Just a hint of colour," Fi said.

Kate took the court shoes from Fi and slipped them on. They were a darker blue than her dress and had flat heels. Fi's mum had managed to find a pair that fit Peter's feet. Kate was grateful she didn't have to strut around on high heels as she'd seen some girls do. She could barely manage to stay standing on her bare feet.

"You look wonderful," Fi said, walking around Kate admiring her.

When the girl stopped her turning and leaned closer, Kate panicked, imagining Fi was about to kiss her. Her feelings were heightened by Peter's alarm. But Fi just brushed the hair out of her eyes, then pulled back.

"You are such a tasty morsel," Fi said, licking her lips. "You make my mouth water."

She makes us sound like a meal, Peter complained.

"Peter suggests we go down and eat before you gobble us both up," Kate said, a wry smile on her lips.

Fi laughed and took Kate by the arm, helping her down the stairs.

"Ah, there you are, Kate. How good of you to come," Dr Grant said, emerging from the kitchen with a tureen of hot soup in his hands. "Shame both you and Peter can't be here at the same time."

The apparent ease with which he accepted her in Peter's body astonished her, considering that earlier he'd expressed his reserve about the business of dressing up. It was like a play, she thought, but unlike the one she'd seen at Peter's school, the actors and the audience were the same people. She was surprised how much they all seemed to love pretending.

"I am very glad to be here," Kate replied, hoping she'd got her lines right.

"Let's have a look," Christina said, as she followed Dr Grant from the kitchen. Kate had first seen Fi's mum shortly after Peter had fled his home and gone to stay with Fi and her mum. It was only later when Christina had met Peter's headmaster, John Grant, and fallen in love, that they'd all moved to his house.

Like Fi, her mum was short and slim, barely reaching her new husband's shoulders. She could have been taken for an older version of Fi, the same high cheek bones, the same sparkling eyes with a few added wrinkles and a hint of dark shadows. She even had auburn hair, although hers was longer than her daughter's.

And like her daughter, Christina was enthralled by the business of dressing up. She had Fi turn Kate round to get a good look. "The dress is so feminine. It fits well and those colours suit you." Running her fingers through Kate's hair, she added: "You could have done something with this, Fi."

Fi shrugged. "I like her hair that way. It makes a statement about being both boy and girl."

Of course. She's done you up to satisfy her own tastes, Peter complained.

Kate glanced at the mirror in the entrance hall. The neatly dressed young girl with short, chestnut coloured hair whose sparkling eyes stared back caught her by surprise. Could it really be her? It certainly wasn't Peter.

All four sat at the dinner table and Dr Grant bowed his head.

"Would you like to say grace, Kate?" Dr Grant asked quietly.

The prospect troubled her. She'd never had to recite a prayer before.

Think of something important that has happened for which you are grateful, Peter suggested.

"May those that are excluded because they are different find a home such as this in which they are accepted and appreciated as they really are."

"Amen," they chorused.

Amen, said Peter silently.

When the meal was over, Kate offered to help clear away.

Christina refused. "You've been ill and must be exhausted after a day at school. And it wouldn't do to dirty your lovely dress. Take a seat and rest."

Truth is she's worried we'll break the plates and glasses, Kate teased.

We're not that clumsy, Peter commented.

Kate smiled at the 'we'. *You've dropped things a lot recently,* she said, reminding him of several moments when things had slipped from his fingers.

Kate went slowly into the living room with its deep armchairs and the crackling fire heaped high in the fireplace. The added warmth was most welcome. The weather had turned cold since Peter had left hospital and wearing such a flimsy dress and tights didn't keep her warm.

How am I supposed to sit down in full view of everyone with such a short dress? Kate mused.

Keep your knees together, Peter suggested. *I think that's how it's done.*

How uncomfortable and handicapping, Kate snorted, imagining herself having to fight in such an attire.

Her thoughts had Peter giggling. Kate smiled too.

"It's good to see you smile," Christina said as they joined Kate. Dr Grant agreed.

"I was joking with Peter about wearing short dresses. They are such a handicap."

"But you look so pretty," Christina protested.

It was Dr Grant's turn to laugh. "Fashion has its limits."

When Fi returned from the kitchen, the conversation turned to Andrew and his brother. Peter's fear at the mention of the youth had Kate worrying too.

"What exactly did Andrew's brother say?" Christina asked.

"He said, I'll get you back for this poof," Fi told them, shuddering.

A desperate hammering at the front door halted their conversation.

"Who could that be so late on a Friday evening?" Dr Grant wondered as he got to his feet. The knocking rang out again. "Coming!" he called, leaving the room.

You don't think it's him, do you? Peter asked, trepidation in his voice.

Who?

Andrew's brother.

Surely he wouldn't dare come here...

Kate strained to hear as the front door opened. There was a heavy thud followed by a gasp and then a groan. Fi and Christina immediately got to their feet, but made no move to investigate. Kate would have got up too, but her legs ached from so much standing and walking.

No further groans came, much to her relief, but she was sure she could hear faint whimpers. Concerned, Kate struggled to her feet and took a step towards the door, but Fi's mum placed a hand on her arm to stop her. "You girls stay here," Christina said and hurried out of the room.

From the hall, Kate could hear the sound of scuffling feet.

It's a fight, Peter gasped.

No. It's more like something heavy being dragged across the floor.

"Fi, Kate," Christina called out, "come quick."

Fi rushed out into the hall, followed more slowly by Kate, only to find it empty. Urgent whispers came from the kitchen. A trail of blood smeared across the white tiles showed the way.

On the kitchen table lay a boy caked in half-dried blood, his chest heaving as he struggled to breathe. Twisted in pain, his face was almost obscured by the blood that flowed sluggishly from a gash across his forehead. Just above his right hip, his jacket and shirt had been ripped apart revealing an ominous red stain.

Christina was trying to staunch the flow of blood from the wound on his head, dabbing it gently with a wad of cotton wool.

"John's gone to phone for an ambulance," Christina told them. "Fi, fetch a clean cloth and some warm water."

Kate rounded the table trying to get a better look. The boy's face seemed familiar. Only when Fi returned with water and a cloth and wiped the blood from his cheeks and lips did she recognise him.

"It's Andrew," she gasped.

4.

The ambulance arrived in a whirl of noise and activity. To Kate's relief, the ambulance men announced that neither wounds was serious. All the same, they insisted he go to hospital. She didn't relish the idea. Hospitals reminded her of Peter's long stay and her being trapped in his unconscious mind, unable to do anything.

Dr Grant took the ambulance men aside and explained. "Taking Andrew to hospital," he said, "might put his life in danger." Finally they agreed, provided the headmaster called a doctor. Getting one to answer a house call at night wasn't easy, but the doctor who came was a friend.

"He was lucky," the doctor said. "Half an inch more and that knife would have caused serious harm." He stitched up the wound in Andrew's side and cleaned up the gash on his forehead. Then he rummaged in his bag and extracted several pills. "Painkillers. The boy'll probably need them." He slid the pills into a tiny envelope, handed it to Dr Grant and left, promising to return the next day.

What a strange world, Kate thought. These people come at the body from the outside with knives and needles. Even if pills did enter the body, they were still a sightless remedy unable to adjust to conditions inside.

Peter had told her about such behaviour, but seeing it first hand was surprising. If only they knew how to cure from inside, they wouldn't do so much damage. The two of them had become adepts at healing from the inside until ... Feeling Peter shudder in a distant recess of her mind, she broke off that train of thought.

Everyone was concerned how Andrew would react when he regained consciousness. Dr Grant, Fi and her mum all offered to watch over him, but Kate had insisted she do it.

"I'm not tired," she'd told them. "All I do is sit around in Peter's head." It wasn't true, of course. If Peter's body was tired then so was she. His body was hers, after all. And Peter was exhausted.

Peter was adamantly opposed to her spending the night with Andrew, but she managed to persuade him, pointing out that the boy would surely remain unconscious.

As everyone prepared for bed, Christina brought Kate a thick woollen blanket. "It can get cold at night," she said. "If you are too tired, fetch me and I'll take over."

At that moment Dr Grant, who came by on his way to bed, said, "Keep that blanket around you. Seeing you dressed like that might confuse Andrew."

I should say so, Peter muttered.

A distant clock struck two. Kate shivered, then yawned so widely her jaw cracked. She'd already drifted off several times. Wrapping the blanket tight around her shoulders, she rested her head on her arms. All were asleep, even Peter in her head.

Raising her hands to her face, she ran her fingers around her eyes exploring their shape and the feel of her skin. It was soft and firm. She let her fingers trail down the high cheek bones, stopping only when her fingertips reached her lips. Pursing her mouth, she pressed her fingers against her puckered lips. A troubling quiver stirred in her stomach and she hastily pulled her fingers from her mouth.

Peter's body had become familiar, but this was the first time she had control for an extended period. For twelve years she'd lived secure in her own body. It'd never crossed her mind she might be without. If you didn't have a body, you were dead, right? But she wasn't. She'd survived. It was a reprieve, but also a condemnation. She'd never have her own body again. Tears welled in her eyes. She shook her head to clear her sight and looked down at Andrew. The soft whisper of his breath, regular now, was the only sound in the silent house.

She laid her hand on Andrew's. It was far too warm. Concentrating on the feel of his skin, firm against hers, she repeatedly tried to cross the natural barrier that surrounded him to get to his mind. It had always been so easy. The trick was to make yourself tiny and not force a passage. The more you forced, the more the barrier resisted. Once inside, she'd be able to heal his wounds. But try as she would, she couldn't get in.

Discouraged, she closed her eyes and began quietly humming a song she'd heard on the radio, one of those silly tunes that irritatingly whirled round and round in your head. Snatches of the words came back and she sang softly: "...sorrows heaving around my head... Making me remember when... When I'm not able to remember at all... The voices say to me that this was meant to be... Love's unkind and love's untrue. Oh why did love pick out you?"

"Poor me," a voice said.

Startled, she sat up, hastily pulling her hand from Andrew's. Was she hearing voices again? It wasn't Peter, she checked, he slept on.

"It's the title of the song," the voice said.

She opened her eyes to see Andrew staring at her, his regard so intense, she had to look away,.

"How do you feel?" she asked, pulling the blanket tighter around her shoulders.

"I'm not sure. Everything is muddled." He made a move to sit up, but stopped with a groan. She sprang to her feet letting the blanket fall and almost fell over in her hurry to help him. Her head was spinning wildly.

"My head hurts. My side too," he said. "What happened? Where am I? What am I doing here? Who are you?"

Kate smiled as she gingerly made her way back to her chair. Picking up the blanket, she wrapped herself securely in it.

"Which answer would you like first, Andrew?"

A troubled look flitted across his face at the sound of his name. "Who are you?"

"Kate."

"Do I know you?"

"I don't think so."

"But you know me."

"Yes. I saw you once at school."

"Do you go to my school? I've never seen you."

"No. I don't. I don't go out very often." The ludicrousness of her words had her smiling.

He looked troubled again. She wondered if her smile had offended him.

"But why are you looking after me? Arc you an apprentice nurse?"

A giggle bubbled up inside her and burst from her lips. She had an irresistible desire to play with him. "No. I'm an apprentice magician."

He looked alarmed, but his alarm quickly changed to anger. "Are you making fun of me?"

She sobered immediately. "No. Not at all." How silly of her to mention that other life when it no longer existed. "I offered to watch over you."

Andrew's eyes roamed the room. "Where am I?"

"At Dr Grant's house."

He looked at her blankly.

"The headmaster," she said.

"Ah yes. Where Peter lives."

"Yes. When you staggered in, you were covered in blood ..." Seeing Andrew turn even paler, she halted. "You're not going to faint, are you?"

"No. I just remembered what happened."

Intrigued, she wanted to know more, but she wasn't going to badger him. "Would you like a painkiller? The doctor left some."

"Thanks. But I can get by."

There was a long pause during which neither spoke.

"Who are you, Kate?" Andrew asked, his eyes perplexed as they fixed her. "I mean, it's the middle of the night, and I find myself accompanied by a pretty girl I don't know who claims she's an apprentice magician..."

Kate blushed. Thank heavens Peter was asleep. Had he been awake, her chatting to Andrew might not have been to his liking and the boy calling her 'pretty' even less so.

"All that business with magicians was just make-believe," she said, hoping a little deceit might cover her blunder. This world was tricky and it was changing her. If she wasn't careful, she'd end up as muddled about reality as everyone else.

"Shame," he said. "I'd like to know a magician's apprentice."

Kate shrugged off the blanket, feeling too hot all of a sudden, then hastily pulled it round her again, uneasy at the way his eyes lit up at the sight of her dress. All this was far more complicated than she'd imagined. In her world she'd had little to do with boys. She'd been far too busy studying magic. And in Peter's world, judging from the few she'd met, boys reacted in ways she didn't understand.

To her embarrassment he continued to stare at her as if searching for an answer. "You remind me of Peter," he finally said. "You look so much like him you could be his sister."

"No, I'm not, although you could say we're close..." She had a hard time not giggling. He couldn't possibly imagine how close.

He looked away. "I see." His words were heavy with meaning, but what that might be completely eluded her.

"What do you see?" she asked, perplexed.

"You are his ..." The words seem to stick in his throat. She waited, intrigued. "Girlfriend."

She checked to see if Peter was still asleep. She was relieved to find he was. "Yes. I suppose you'd say that." She looked up at him to gauge his reaction. He looked in pain. "Are you sure you don't want a painkiller?"

"Maybe that would be a good idea," he said, his voice a

strangled whisper.

She rose in alarm and went to fetch water from the kitchen. When she returned, Andrew lay with both hands covering his face. Were those tears trickling down his cheeks? "Oh Andrew, does it hurt that much?"

He hastily wiped the tears from his face and took the glass of water and the pill.

"I think I'll try to sleep," he said, not looking her in the face.

"Sleep tight," she said and sat down, preparing to continue her silent vigil.

"They never did like me," he said after a long silence.

"Who?"

"My brother, my mother. I was the odd one out. The misfit. My brother liked football, I hated it. I liked reading, he hardly opened a book. I got good marks. His school reports were a disaster. He was always fighting and smoking and drinking. The very thought of it makes me sick. He'd hit me. When I didn't fight back, he got mad. He called me a pansy and hit me harder. He said he'd beat it out of me. Mum encouraged him. There was something wrong with me, she said. It was father's fault. Bad blood, she called it. Tainted, she called me. Weakling. Weirdo. Poof. Fairy. Never Andrew."

He struggled to silence the sobs that rose in his throat.

Kate leaned forward and placed her hand on his, squeezing it gently. "Cry," she said. "Nobody will hit you here." Seeing his distress increase, she lifted his hand to her lips and kissed the back of it.

He turned his tear-filled eyes in her direction, that unspoken question still strong in them.

"I used to lock myself in my room, to get some peace, but he broke open the door and took away the key. Meal time was the worst. They'd taunt me, refusing to give me anything. I didn't deserve food, my mother said."

"How long has this been going on?"

"Years."

"And you told nobody?"

"No. Never!" He sounded shocked. "If I complained, he'd have beaten me even more."

"Poor Andrew."

When she felt his fingers curl around hers she realised she still held his hand. Gently freeing herself, she asked, "What happened last night?"

"Brian was hopping mad, but to my surprise, he didn't mention it back home. Then at dinner he was horrible. He took away my food and when I complained, he handed me a bowl of dog food. When I refused to eat, he smeared the stuff around my mouth. It tasted foul, so foul I threw up all over him. He was furious, but I managed to escape and barricaded myself in my room."

"Much later, I heard him fumbling at the front door. He must have dropped his keys, because he cursed several times, his words slurred with drink. I turned out the light hoping he was too drunk to think of me. And when he headed for the kitchen I thought I was going to be lucky, but my relief was short lived. He burst into my room, sending my barricade flying, and staggered towards me brandishing a carving knife. 'Don't think you'll get away this time,' he said, then he lunged at me. I bit back a scream. I didn't dare wake mother. Instead, I rolled off the bed as the knife plunged into the mattress. Several times he came at me, and each time I dodged."

"I cowered in a corner with him towering over me. He staggered forward and took a wild swipe, getting in his first hit, slicing open my forehead. I muffled a scream as blood spurted everywhere. He let out a whoop of triumph and attacked with renewed vigour. He's not a good fighter, especially not when drunk. His hands and legs never go where he wants. I would've escaped without further hurt, but he tripped over my slippers, fell forward and cut through my jacket and shirt, leaving a large gash in my side."

"How did you escape?"

"In falling, the idiot knocked himself out. I was terrified he was dead. But, to my relief, he began snoring. It was a dreadful sound, like a wild animal. I was sure he'd wake mother. If she came, she'd kill me for hurting him."

"But he hurt you," Kate said, indignant.

"Do you think that mattered?"

"It must have hurt terribly."

He nodded. "I thought I was going to die. There was blood everywhere and my head and side throbbed dreadfully. I didn't know what to do. Then I thought of Peter. Had he not protected me at school? And he was staying with the headmaster who didn't live far away. Surely he'd protect me."

A strange tugging distracted Kate. She hadn't felt such a call since Peter summoned her from across the worlds. Who could possibly be calling her? The thought worried her. What if her executioners were dragging her back to finish her off? She tried to resist the pull, but it became insistent. She reached out to Peter, meaning to wake him, when everything went black and her link to him was severed.

5.

Peter fled as fast as his legs would go, panting wildly. Dark figures pursued him down murky, wind-swept corridors. Whenever he thought he was rid of them, another cloaked nun surged up, nails outstretched to claw his face. A strident chorus of female voices intoned a funeral mass to the sound of their steadily advancing footfalls.

"No!" Peter wailed, desperately trying to end it. His cry awoke him, but the nightmare played on and with it lingered the nasty smell of that other place.

Where was he? Certainly not in bed. To his surprise, fingers were gently raking through his hair. "Cut that out Fi."

"Are you all right?" a boy asked. "You sound strange."

Peter eyes sprang open in alarm and he looked up. His head was resting on the edge of a camp bed in which Andrew lay, a bandage wrapped round the top of his head. The boy looked confused and worried. Peter sat up abruptly and as he did Andrew's fingers fell from his hair.

Glancing down, Peter was shocked to see he was wearing a blue dress and pale blue tights. His hands flew to hide his face as he blushed bright red. Then memory flooded back. It was Kate's weekend. But where was Kate? He plunged into his head, searching desperately, but found no trace of her. Fear and panic coursed through his veins as he teetered on the verge of a gaping hole.

"She's gone," he wailed and sprang to his feet.

"What's the matter?" Andrew asked, dismayed, struggling

to prop himself up on one elbow. When Peter didn't answer, he repeated, "Kate, what's up?

"Kate!" Peter exclaimed and staggered towards the door, shedding one shoe as he went.

He hobbled up the stairs, hopping clumsily from shod foot to bare foot. Halting a moment to catch his breath, he shook off the lone shoe, then continued on in stockinged feet.

His shout had woken everyone. Lights flickered on and doors squeaked open. He hastened on up, not wanting to meet anyone. In the attic was a small, disused room that had once housed a maid. He headed there, wanting to hide. Inside, the door shut tight, he flung himself on the narrow bed and buried his face in the musty pillow.

Where could Kate have gone? Since that fateful day when she had been beheaded, her spirit had never left him. Without his body she couldn't survive. Unless, of course - he shuddered at the thought - she'd been given another body. The cursed Arthur Yong sprang to mind, a malevolent jester grinning insanely at him. Peter clenched his fists and bit back a scream of frustration. So that was it. The blasted author was meddling with her life again. Hadn't he done enough damage already?

Peter rolled over on his back and stared up at the sloping ceiling. Where did that leave him? Had his spirit not been lodged in Kate at the end? Could it have perished with her body? The thought terrified him. He might have become Kate's body, but had she become his spirit? With her gone, was he now spiritless? He didn't feel any different, apart from the seething anger, that is.

He closed his eyes and dug deep inside, frantically scanning the smallest neurons in search of anything that resembled a spirit. But what did a spirit look like and where would it reside? He might have been used to having another spirit in his head, but he'd always seen it as Kate, not as a spirit. As for his own spirit, even if he'd travelled in that form to Kate's world, he had no idea what it looked like. Hopelessness washed over him. He opened his eyes, searching the blank ceiling for inspiration.

If Kate had a new body, he might be able to call her. That was how they'd got to know each other across the divide between worlds. He tried. *Kate?* If she could answer, she would. But he felt no answering presence, no reassuring voice. *Oh Kate. Where are you?*

Downstairs people were calling his name. Couldn't they leave him alone? As he roamed his mind in search of Kate, the heavy weight of sleep tugged at him. He was exhausted. Not surprising, what with Kate keeping his body awake all night and the aftermath of the coma.

When he awoke, warm breath caressed the back of his neck and arms grasped him tightly around his waist. Someone was lying close behind him. Alarmed, he imagined Andrew had pursued him. The thought made him furious, especially as he was still wearing Kate's dress. He was about to break free when a sleepy female voice said, "Ah, you're awake."

It was Fi.

She pulled him in a tight embrace. "You make a lovely girl, you know," she whispered in his ear.

For someone who claimed to be so in tune with others, she could be very insensitive at times. He shook himself free and sat on the edge of the bed. "Stop that!"

She pouted. "Now that you've tasted being a girl, you no longer want my caresses? I knew it, you prefer Andrew."

The absurdity of her accusation had Peter wanting to lash out. It took all his control not to shout at her. "You don't understand," he said through clenched teeth. "Kate's gone."

Fi looked at him uncomprehending. "What do you mean 'gone'?"

"When I awoke she was no longer in my head."

"That's terrible. I didn't know she could do that."

"She can't. Not without a body."

"Could she have found a new one?"

"Found? No. Been given one? Maybe."

Fi looked at him blankly.

"You remember that bloke who wrote the story about Kate?

Well I suspect he's written her a new role."

"Why ever would he do that?"

"Revenge. We did mess up his story." He was going to remind her what happened, but she seemed distracted.

"Poor Andrew was worried," she said, straightening his dress. "He thought Kate ran away because he'd offended her."

"Who cares about Andrew! What about me?" he said indignant. "Not only has my other half suddenly disappeared, but there I was parading as a girl with a fellow schoolboy."

Fi was struggling not to laugh.

"It's not funny," he snapped. Anger threatened to overwhelm him. Was that the tribute he had to pay for the loss of Kate? Wild, uncontrollable anger.

A knock came at the door.

"Can we come in?" he heard Fi's mum ask.

"Who's 'we'?" he asked, irritated.

"John and I."

Peter took a blanket that lay folded on a chair by the bed and wrapped it around himself. As Kate he'd accepted to be with them dressed as a girl, but he was not ready to do so as himself.

"Come in."

Fi's mum took him in her arms and hug him tight. Dr Grant was more reserved, smiling from a distance.

"You lost this," Fi's mum said, handing him one of Kate's shoes.

Peter looked at the shoe perplexed.

"We found it on the stairs," John said.

"What happened down there?" Fi's mum asked.

"I awoke to find Kate gone."

"Maybe she just dropped out for a moment," Christina suggested.

Peter groaned and stamped his foot, causing the blanket to slip from his shoulders. He was fed up explaining. "She can't survive without a body." Better not air his suspicions about the author.

"You look worn out. Let's have some breakfast, then you

can have a rest," Dr Grant suggested. "We can talk about this later." Looking at Peter's dress that was now clearly visible, he added, "Maybe you should change before you come down. It might be a bit confusing for Andrew and we wouldn't want him gossiping at school."

Why were these people so worried about Andrew? What about him? Once the adults had left, Fi fussed over him, removing his makeup, chattering all the time. She was like a dynamo charged with words. She got on his nerves, something that had never happened before.

When she finally left, he took a long shower, hoping the warm water would undo the knotted muscles. Despite his efforts, his jaw remained clenched and his shoulders and neck were so tense they hurt.

Having donned his shorts and shirt, he felt uncomfortably underdressed. Pulling on long socks that reached to just below his knees helped. He pinched one of Fi's colourful kerchiefs and tied it around his neck. Glancing in the mirror, he had the impression Kate was looking back at him. Annoyed, he pulled off the scarf and tossed it on the bed. He ruffled his hair, pushed his socks down to his ankles and undid two buttons of his shirt. Showing off his chest was not his way, but it seemed like something boys might do.

Stepping cautiously down the stairs, in no hurry to arrive, he prayed Andrew would be too ill to join them. His prayers were not answered. Andrew sat at the table surrounded by John, Christina and Fi in quiet conversation.

"Ah, there you are Peter," Dr Grant said. "As you can see Andrew joined us while you were away. He's been in the wars, but he is well enough to eat with us."

Peter glared at Andrew. The boy was staring at him, surprise, alarm even, in his eyes. Realising that his mouth had fallen open, Andrew snapped it shut and looked away, embarrassed. Peter looked away too, furious.

"Is Kate not joining us?" Andrew asked, looking questioningly at Peter.

"She had to leave in a hurry," Dr Grant explained. "She asked me to say goodbye and to tell you to get well soon."

"What a shame," Andrew said, appearing more crestfallen than his words let on. "She was so kind during the night."

Peter shuddered at what Kate might have done while he slept. The boy seemed besotted with her.

"Whatever happened to your head?" Peter asked, deciding that, had he been away, it would be normal to enquire, but his words came out far harsher than intended.

Andrew shot him a troubled look.

"Did the accident damage your tongue?" Peter snapped before he could stop himself.

"Peter, that's not very kind," Fi's mum chided. "Andrew doesn't need you being unpleasant to him after all he's been through."

Peter stamped his foot in fury and was about to launch into a tirade against Andrew when the sight of Dr Grant frowning brought him up short. Tears brimmed in his eyes and threatened to overwhelm him.

"I'm sorry," Peter said, rubbing his eyes with his fists. Everything was such a muddle. "I don't feel myself," he managed to add through clenched teeth. "I am so angry..."

"It's because of Kate, isn't it?" Andrew blurted out.

Was the blighter trying to taunt him? Peter took a threatening step in his direction, but Dr Grant held up a warning hand, his face stern and forbidding.

"It must be really hard," Andrew said, his voice catching on the words, "when the one you love suddenly leaves,"

"Are you all right Andrew?" Fi's mum asked. "You should lie down."

Who cared about Andrew? He was the one suffering from the loss of Kate, not Andrew. Anger bubbled up again, red hot and eager to shout its mind. He felt like a little kid with a tantrum coming on. Feeling small and helpless only further fanned his anger. He had to avoid touching the objects on the table for fear he'd throw them at someone. Despite his efforts, the anger was getting the better of him. He kept his mouth shut in case he snapped at someone or worse, tried to bite them. He clenched the seat of his chair with both hands trying to get a grip on himself.

Dr Grant got to his feet, pulled up a chair and sat next to Peter, laying a hand on his clenched fists. "You are a good person, Peter. Things will work out," John said quietly.

It was just too much. Peter could hold on no longer. He burst into tears and buried his head in John's shoulder. The man put an arm round him and with his other hand patted Peter's back.

"There, there," he said. "Don't doubt yourself, Peter. You have done great things and you will do more. You'll get her back."

"But I feel so angry," Peter confessed. "I could smash everything."

"Anger is unpleasant, for all concerned," John said. "We'd prefer not to have anything to do with it, but it is the expression of a force that insists on being heard and we need to heed what it is saying."

Peter had no idea what his anger was telling him, but Dr Grant's words unravelled some of the knots that held him under pressure. "Thanks," he said.

6.

Sun was streaming through a crack between the curtains when Peter awoke. Chaffinches squabbled in the trees outside. He sighed. Term would soon be over and he had a mountain of schoolwork to catch up on.

All was quiet in the house. It was Saturday. Fi had gone to Guides and Mr and Mrs Grant must have gone shopping. Looking around the room, he spotted Kate's dress sprawled across the dresser where he'd abandoned it.

Kate! His heart sank.

He rechecked. No sign of her in his head. His only hope, if you could call it that, was that the author had spirited her away into a nightmare of his making. Peter strove to still his anger and frustration as he pushed back the covers.

He shook out Kate's dress and hung it in the wardrobe. Just in case she ever came back, he told himself, running his fingers appreciatively over the soft material.

He was about to leave, when a delicious sequence of notes wafted up from below like the thoughtful steps of a composer wending his way home through the lamplit night. He recognised the piece immediately. Eric Satie. Could Andrew be listening to an LP?

When the notes broke off, only to restart from the beginning, he realised it must be Andrew. Peter had no idea the boy could play piano. The heart-felt rendering of Satie was bewitching.

Peter loved music. He'd sung in the church choir for years and was now lead chorister. Sunday would be the first time he'd sung in the choir since what people coyly called his 'illness'.

When he reached the foot of the stairs he paused. The beauty of the music had him entranced. He stood for a long moment, silent and unnoticed, leaning against the doorframe watching Andrew play. The boy was oblivious to the world, engrossed as he was in Satie's score. Peter was fascinated by the way his fingers danced from key to key with such grace. He'd never noticed how slender, almost girl-like they were. He briefly imagined Andrew in one of Fi's dresses only to shove the idea away, annoyed at himself for conjuring up such a fantasy.

"Peter!" Andrew exclaimed, coming to the end of the piece. "Did you sleep well?"

Peter blushed. The sight of Andrew's slender face, his blue eyes beaming at him, his frail, almost fragile form leaning in his direction, had Peter thinking how pretty the boy was. The idea that Andrew might be a fellow soul was alluring, but above all it was troubling if not alarming. Colour rose in Andrew's face in response to Peter's embarrassment.

"You play the Satie well," Peter commented. "I had no idea you played."

"It's my secret."

Yeah. We all have secrets, Peter thought. "How come?"

"When I was six I first heard my uncle play La fille aux cheveux de lin." He spoke French with a lilting accent as if echoing the regal sway of Debussy's piece, the girl with the flaxen hair, his eyes lighting up at the memory. "It took my breath away, such was the beauty. I immediately knew piano playing was for me."

His face turned grim as he went on. "I got up my courage and asked mother if I could take lessons. I knew she'd hit me, she always did when I asked for something, but that was how much I wanted to learn. She did hit me, much harder than usual, telling me I'd end up like my uncle. The way she said it, the prospect sounded like a terrible threat, but I had no idea what she meant. Anyone who could play the piano that well couldn't possibly be bad. She must have known what I was thinking, because she forbad me ever to see my uncle."

"I bet you did, all the same."

Andrew frowned, then smiled wryly. "I did indeed."

"And he taught you?"

"You could put it like that."

Andrew's enigmatic reply had Peter wondering what else he'd learnt.

The boy turned back to the piano, saying, "You know this, I believe." He played the opening bars of Elgar's Lux Aeterna. Peter had sung it at church a few months earlier. It had been a great success with parishioners.

When Andrew played on, Peter crossed the room, as if drawn by the music, and leant against the piano. Without transition, Andrew returned to the opening bars and Peter joined in, softly singing the treble part. He loved that music. Singing it brought tears to his eyes and Andrew played the accompaniment so well.

When it came to an end there was a long silence, then Andrew looked up, his face aglow, his eyes sparkling. To Peter's surprise, the boy reached up and brushed a tear from Peter's cheek. The momentary touch sent shivers down Peter's spine. Instinctively, he took a step back, terrified at what he was feeling. Andrew's hand fell back, disappointment written all over his face, then he frowned like he'd done when talking of his uncle.

"I'm sorry. I didn't mean to frighten you. Your voice moved me..."

He looked so upset, Peter felt sorry for him. There was something vulnerable but endearing about the boy that made it hard not to like him. He wondered why he'd never noticed before. "You startled me," Peter said. It was only partly a lie. If Kate had been there, she'd surely have pointed out his lack of courage. He sighed.

Andrew must have misinterpreted his sigh because he closed the piano, got to his feet and headed for the door. Peter followed and laid a hand lightly on the boy's shoulder. "I didn't sigh because of you. I was thinking of Kate. I don't think she'll be back."

"You're very attached to her," Andrew said.

"You could put it like that," he said, aware that he'd used the same words as Andrew. "How about lunch?" he asked. "I'm famished."

Andrew agreed. They hadn't got far when the front door opened and Dr Grant called out, "Peter. Andrew. We're back."

Peter retrieved his crutches where he'd abandoned them in the corner of the room and the two stepped out into the hall only to realise that John and Christina were not alone.

"We've brought a policeman with us," Dr Grant warned. "We dropped by the police station to inform them of the attack. The Inspector would like to ask some questions."

As the Inspector stepped round Dr Grant, Peter immediately recognised the man. He'd had several brushes with the fellow, thanks to crazy Priscilla Wit.

"Ah you!" the Inspector exclaimed catching sight of Peter. His eyebrows rose at the sight of the crutches, but made no comment. "Always there were trouble's to be found."

"I could say the same of you, Inspector," Peter replied.

"As impertinent as ever, I see. Living with a headmaster doesn't seem to have improved you."

"You can hardly find fault with the Inspector for doing his job," Fi's mum pointed out.

That she should side with the inspector annoyed Peter. The last time Christina had seen the man, she'd all but thrown him out.

"You're right. I apologise," Peter said. "But that doesn't change the fact that he continually associates me with wrong doing."

"Well, if you want to combat evil, Peter, then you will invariably be there where wrong is done. That doesn't make you a bad person," Dr Grant said, ushering the Inspector into the living room. "But gentlemen, let's get comfortable before we begin the questions."

The Inspector seemed to have an unending list. After half an hour Andrew was beginning to wilt. Only the evening before he'd staggered into their house covered in blood. He must be tired and hungry. Using one of his crutches as a lever, Peter got to his feet and went to the kitchen in search of sustenance.

Returning, Peter interrupted the Inspector, much to the man's annoyance, as he handed food and drink to Andrew saying, "You must be exhausted." Andrew gave him a wan smile.

"You're right, Peter," Christina said. "Would you like something to eat and drink, Inspector?"

"No thanks. I need to be going," the Inspector replied, getting to his feet. "There is one last thing I'd like to mention."

Now comes the nasty bit, Peter thought, wondering what the Inspector had saved for last.

"It's your brother Brian," he said to Andrew. "We wanted to take him to the station for questioning, but he caught one of my colleagues off guard and punched him on the nose. In the confusion he managed to escape. A warrant is out for his arrest, but we haven't found him yet."

Peter glanced at Andrew who was seated next to him. The boy looked terrified. Peter sat on the armrest and put an arm round the boy's shoulders. Andrew burst into tears and buried his face in Peter's chest. The situation was vaguely familiar. Something similar must have happened to Kate while he slept. That would explain why he felt a surge of tenderness at having Andrew's breath warm against his chest.

"We questioned your mother, hoping she might tell us where he'd gone, but she was not very cooperative." The inspector chuckled, leaving Peter perplexed. Judging from the look on John and Christina's faces, they too were at a loss.

"I've heard some colourful language in my career, but your mother beats them all," the Inspector went on, shaking his head in disbelief. "She put all the blame on you, saying you were always taunting Brian."

Andrew pulled away from Peter and struggled to his feet. He was trembling with fury. Peter had a fleeting vision of him punching the policeman like his brother, but he did no such thing. Pulling his shirt over his head, not without difficulty because of the wound to his side, he revealed a mass of bruises that dotted his back and arms and chest. The only person that didn't gasp was the Inspector.

"If you call being used as a punching ball taunting, then I'm guilty."

"At least here there's little likelihood he'll harm you," the inspector said.

"You misjudge my brother. At school, at the shopping mall, on the playing fields, even at church,... Anywhere was good enough to hurt me. Being here won't hinder him. He might have been drunk when he stabbed me, but I believe him when he says he won't stop till he kills me."

"I see," the Inspector said. He glanced over his shoulder at the bay windows that opened onto the lawn and the small park that surrounded Dr Grant's house. "You might not be safe here," he added matter-of-factly.

Andrew struggled to pull his shirt on and, with Peter's help, finally managed.

"We could put a cordon round your house, but that won't stop somebody slipping by."

"We could go to my house," Christina suggested, although she didn't sound enthusiastic. The Inspector knew the place, he'd already been there.

"If this Brian is determined, he'll find you there. No. You need something much further away and less obvious," the Inspector said. "I'll have someone keep an eye on the house so you have time to think up a solution." The Inspector handed Dr Grant his card. "Give me a call once you've decided."

7.

Silence sneaked up on Kate smothering her. The hush was so intense she wished ardently for noise. She scratched her cheek, but her fingers made no sound. When she cried out, no words uttered from her mouth.

Alarmed, she sat up and forced her eyes open. To her dismay she no longer sat next to Andrew, but was completely naked on a small metal-framed bed.

Confused and distraught, her hands roamed the mattress for something to shield her from the bitter cold. A rough blanket was all she found. Pulling it over her shoulders, she rubbed her eyes and peered around.

Row after row of similar beds crouched in a large, low-roofed hall. A dim bulb hung naked in the far corner, shedding a meagre glow over nearby sleepers. The blankets, the bed frames, the floor, even the walls, all were grey and tern as if the last remaining colour had been wrung from the world.

A hand on her shoulder had her spinning round in defence. Looming above her stood a tall, wiry-framed girl, with a livid bruise on her cheek and a startling black eye. A fighter, clearly, her arms and hands all cuts and bruises. The sight was terrifying. She looked like an escapee from a war.

Kate got to her feet, meaning to fight or run, when a searing pain caught her unawares and her right leg gave way. She would have hurt herself had it not been for the quick reaction of the girl who caught her mid-flight.

Seated on the bed, Kate examined her leg. It was broken in

several places and had healed all wrong. No wonder it hadn't held her weight. What was this body she found herself in? Glancing down she found she was as skinny as the girl, although her skin was still unmarked by cuts and bruises.

She looked questioningly at the girl who sat next to her on the bed. The girl's mouth was moving as if she spoke, but Kate heard nothing. Alarmed, she tried to ask a question, but once again uttered no sound. Yet the girl put a finger to her lips as if Kate had made too much noise. Confused and frustrated, she wrung her hands.

It was then she noticed the smell. A foul mixture of rotting cabbage, filthy bodies and a hint of incense that reminded her of old churches in Peter's world. Peter! Where was he? The voice that had so long been in her mind was gone, leaving her empty and alone. She scanned her head, but found no trace of him. Bereft, she felt a dark veil settle over her.

The girl must have seen her waver, because she moved closer and laid a steadying hand on Kate's shoulder. Kate couldn't help wrinkling her nose, the girl stank. Yet for all her battle-worn appearance and her shorn hair, she seemed friendly. She took Kate's hand in hers and stroked it gently as if to reassure her.

Kate knew she should remain vigilant, but she was exhausted. She'd spent half the night at Andrew's side and finding herself handicapped in a strange world had drained the last of her energy. Heartened by the girl's touch, she lay back, pulled the blanket tight around herself and closed her eyes. The last thing she felt was the girl crawling under the blanket and cuddling up close, the welcome warmth outweighing the stench.

When she awoke it was still night. The girl was no longer there and the hall was bitterly cold. Kate pulled the rough blanket tight around her in clenched fists and forced herself to think. Her leg was mangled and she was stone deaf. How could that be?

Of course! The explanation was obvious. Blasted author! This was all his doing. He must have written her into a new story to get revenge. At least she had a body of her own, however messed up it might be.

A hand gently shook her shoulder. It was the tall girl. She'd shed her nightie and was wearing a pinafore dress that was far too small. It was as tattered and filthy as the girl herself.

She beckoned Kate to follow. Around the hall, other girls had donned the same uniform and were busy making their beds. Kate gingerly got to her feet and hobbled after, feeling the cold keenly despite the blanket wrapped around her shoulders.

The girls ranged from eight to fourteen. All were gaunt and shared cuts and bruises. They were as filthy as their uniforms and each was barefoot. Kate shuffled clumsily by, the girls turning to stare, some hostile, others curious, most indifferent. Judging from their reactions, she was as new to them as they were to her. Her part in their story had just begun.

She was led to a walk-in cupboard in which hung rows of uniform dresses. The girl unclasped Kate's unwilling hands from the blanket. It fell to ground at her feet leaving her completely naked and shivering violently. Putting her arms around Kate, the girl cuddled her tight. Kate wanted to pull away, but the girl's warm hands as they roamed her shoulders and back staved off some of the cold.

Kate dearly missed that warmth when the girl withdrew and went in search of clothes. She was relieved to see the smock-like dress she was offered was clean if a little tattered. The girl helped pull it over her head and shoulders. Kate expected to receive more, but that was it.

A tiny fragment of mirror pinned to the wall gave Kate a chance to see her new face. What she saw astonished her. She was so used to a boy staring back that the face that now studied her seemed all wrong. What's more, she looked nothing like she had as Kaitling. Her light brown hair was cropped short, barely reaching her ears. Her deep blue eyes looked tired, reflecting the pain she felt in her leg. There were dark shadows under her eyes and a frown on her forehead, but her cheekbones were high and her eyebrows arched gracefully. And then there was the fullness of her lips, curved in a small O of surprise. A bit of sleep and sun and she might even look pretty. She was so fascinated, it took the girl a while tugging at her dress to tear her from the mirror.

Back in the hall, the girls were lining up at the door, most still bleary eyed. Kate and her new friend, who held her hand and helped her walk, joined the queue. After a short wait, the door rattled opened and a tall, stocky nun shoved her way in, a large bunch of keys grasped in her podgy fingers. The woman barked orders, at least that was what Kate guessed it was. She heard none of it. In a column, two by two, the girls shuffled out, heads down.

As she squeezed past the nun, Kate ventured a cautious glance. The sister's hair and part of her face was hidden by a coif, but Kate could see piercing blue eyes scowling at her over a pointed nose and a tight-lipped mouth curled in disgust.

The girls filed down a steep set of wooden stairs, each girl gripping the banisters, till they were cramped in a small vestibule at the bottom. The nun lumbered down after them, not hesitating to shove girls out of her way. Once the door was unlocked, they tumbled out, shuffled along one side of a wind-swept cloister and stepped into an ill-lit church.

Left to themselves, the girls halted by a stone font, dipped their fingers in a small bowl of water and traced some form of hieroglyph on their foreheads. Kate imitated them. They then turned and bent a knee briefly making a strange curtsey in the direction of what she knew to be the altar. Her leg made copying them out of the question. Hopefully no one would notice. Finally the girls moved, heads bowed, into pews along one side of the aisle following what appeared to be a well-worn ritual. Her new friend led her to a seat at the back and sat down next to her.

Darkened windows lurked in the shadows like sinister stains. The sun had yet to rise. Scattered here and there, poorly dressed men and women were bent in prayer. A large carved screen divided the church in two. Beyond, Kate caught sight of cloaked figures shifting in the candle light. Periodically, the congregation got to their feet or knelt following cues Kate couldn't catch, but most of the time they were seated on the cold wooden pews. Kate shivered violently, her teeth chattering. She longed for warming arms around her again, but the girl's hands remained resolutely in her lap except when lifted in prayer.

The long, drawn-out ceremony was incomprehensible, but it left Kate time to think. There she was with a new body, all her own. But how had it happened? She hadn't thought it possible, lodged as she had been in Peter with no means of escape. Ok, he graciously let her take over from time to time, but it wasn't the same. His would never be her body. Now she had one of her own, albeit badly damaged. Not only was her right leg mangled, but she was deaf and possibly dumb. If only she had not lost her ability to heal.

Judging from the state of the girls and the behaviour of the nun, she wondered what other unpleasant surprises this new world held in store. If the author had cast her in a handicapped body, he probably wouldn't stop there.

In an attempt to stave off her worries, her thoughts turned to Peter. He would know what to do. She sent him a silent call for help. Even if she had little hope her message would reach him, it calmed her all the same.

When the ceremony was over, the girls got stiffly to their feet and filed out. Kate was frozen and her stomach complained bitterly at the lack of food. They didn't halt at their dormitory but continued round the cloister till they entered a large hall. Row upon row of wooden tables and benches filled most of the space. Here too grey was the dominant colour. A group of nuns were seated at a table by the window, eating in silence. All looked up and some even turned to get a better look at her.

Her friend led her up to a counter where a portly nun handed them a bowl of a soggy grey substance meant to be porridge. Kate turned to follow her friend only to find a nun towering over her, blocking the way. It was the same ill-tempered one who'd accompanied them earlier, her stern face twisted with disapproval. Judging from the way her mouth moved and her head shook, Kate imagined she was shouting. The nun grabbed Kate by the shoulders, her podgy fingers digging into Kate's skin, and shook her violently. Kate almost lost her balance on her rickety leg. As the nun raised her hand to hit her, Kate was startled to see her friend push between them and receive the blow.

The nun shoved Kate's friend to the floor and raised her hand a second time, taking aim at Kate. Her combat training kicked in, despite her damaged leg, as she swerved to avoid the blow. Initially surprised at Kate's reaction, the nun quickly regained her composure. Two nun's grabbed Kate's shoulders from behind and the stout nun took aim again. Her hand hit the side of Kate's face full force and Kate screamed or would have had she been able to, as blood spurted in her mouth. When the women hit her a second time she blacked out.

Kate came to, lying in the dark on a cold stone floor, her face pounding. She gingerly felt inside her mouth. One tooth had been knocked out, a second was loose and she'd bitten her tongue and the fleshy inside of her mouth. She spat a thick gob of blood onto the floor. *Oh Peter*, she pleaded. *Please! I need you so much.* Feeling utterly abandoned and unloved, tears rolled down her cheeks as silence was the only answer to her pleas.

She struggled to her feet. Her prison was tiny, the walls made of ill-fitting wooden planks between which the wind whistled unabated. There were no windows and the sole door was firmly locked. The ceiling, also made of wood, was too high to reach.

She slithered down the wall till she was seated opposite the door and closed her eyes. It was far too cold to sleep and hunger, not to mention the pain, ensured she stayed awake. She recalled a meditation her old friend and arms master Zhuru had taught her. It was a story she told herself in which she descended a spiral staircase to a beautiful land, her inner world. There she could search for her healing ability, lost since she had been cut off from her world.

Reaching the bottom of the stairway, she halted, confused. The lay of the land had completely altered. Parts remained recognisable: a strange sloping tree, a wooden bench painted brick red, a meandering stream that crossed the path. But nothing was in its rightful place and there were new things: a dour church the stones of which had blackened with time; a run-down herb garden enclosed by a fence; a small hillock breasted with firs and spruces. How could she possibly find her healing in that unfamiliar place?

The smell of sage caught her attention. She pushed open the rickety wooden gate and sat amongst the weeds that grew around the sage. Pulling a few leaves from the plant she slipped them into her mouth and chewed as she set about rooting up the weeds. The pungent taste was almost too strong. An infusion would have been better, but she chewed on. Amongst the weeds she uncovered other plants, the names and properties of which she didn't always know. The more she cleared away, the more delighted she was to see how beautiful the herb garden became.

Above the sky was blue, marred only by a smattering of puffy, white clouds drifting by. The sun shone brightly and Kate began to feel hot and tired. Stopping her labours, she looked at her hands. Through the earth and grime that clung to them, they glowed. Lifting one hand to her face, she held it against her sore cheek. Her touch was warm and comforting, as if the glow flowed into her face... Joy welled up in her as she realised she'd regained her healing. The thought broke her concentration and she found herself seated in the cold, dark cell opposite the door which had just opened.

8.

The noise struck Kate like a wall as the nun shoved her into the classroom. Not that she could hear it, but it was plain to see. Girls milled about, their aimless movements fuelled by boredom. Younger kids were crying. Nobody cared. Older girls gathered at the back, chatting, apparently unconcerned by what was happening. Although she did catch them glancing her way, but the moment her eyes met theirs they looked away.

A tiny, tubby nun sat at the teacher's desk almost lost in a tight knot of girls. The woman was engrossed in the illustrations on her desk. She paid no more attention to Kate than she did to the rest of the class. On the blackboard someone had scrawled: Flowers, God's gifts to man. Next to it was written: Sister Teresa. Kate took the name to be that of the teacher. At least she was able understand their language.

She looked for her friend, imaging they'd be able to sit together, but the girl was nowhere to be seen. Anxious, she hoped the girl was not floundering in a dismal cell.

Kate found a free desk near a window and sat down, but once she'd surveyed the room and everyone in it, she got bored. Imitating the others, she got to her feet and wandered. Girls skittered out of her way as if she had a contagious illness.

The classroom was a large hall with rows of small casement windows on three sides. In one direction she could make out the porch to the church. Judging from the light, it was early afternoon. She'd missed the midday meal, if there'd been one. Her stomach growled in confirmation.

Looking in the opposite direction, a small building nestled in the corner of the high wall that surrounded the convent. Beyond, fields gave way to hills then mountains, the tops of which were capped in snow. There'd been mountains on her island, but none as high or as majestic. A wave of nostalgia broke over her. She looked away. Below the remaining windows, a wide drive curved as it led to the main entrance of convent and the church.

Nearer the teacher's desk, Kate came across a shelf of books. She ran her index finger over the titles till she found one about herbs and healing. Pulling it out, she returned to her desk and began reading. There were many very good illustrations - she immediately recognised some plants from her secret garden - and the explanations were excellent.

She was engrossed in reading about a local plant she'd never heard of when the book was snatched from her fingers. At first she thought it was another girl, but looking up, she saw Sister Teresa, her mouth moving in that now familiar angry way that meant she was being shouted at. Kate readied for the blow. The moment it came, she shifted, setting the desk between her and the nun.

The nun, who was clearly unused to physical exercise, struggled to catch Kate, but was hampered by the closeness of the desks. Kate looked around in search of an escape. She was worried the girls might league against her. To her surprise they continued shifting aimlessly about the room, constantly getting in the way of the nun. Maybe she was not as alone as she thought.

Then she had an idea. She hobbled to the blackboard and picked up a piece of chalk. Checking the teacher was not close enough to catch her, Kate began to write: You teach botany. I am deaf. I cannot hear you. Can I not read about flowers instead?

As she turned back to see what had become of the teacher, she was amazed to find that the incessant movements had ground to a halt. Everyone, teacher and pupils alike, were staring, many with their mouths hanging open. The small group gathered around the teacher's desk looked frankly hostile. One of the girls, with fiery ginger-hair but a plain face, got to her feet and made a move towards Kate, but the others restrained her.

Sister Teresa finally made her way to Kate. Expecting a blow, Kate took a step back but instead the teacher held out her hand for the chalk. Kate gave it to her. The teacher wrote: You like flowers?

Medicinal plants, Kate wrote.

The teacher wrote no more but handed the book back to Kate and then abruptly lost interest. Left clutching the book, unsure what to do, Kate returned to her seat. All the girls, big and small, moved out of her way as if she were an alien. If only they knew! Their behaviour contrasted with the keen, almost greedy interest of the older girls.

During a pause in her reading, Kate examined her mouth and jaw. She'd forgotten all about them. They still throbbed, but, to her surprise, her tongue and the side of her mouth had both healed and the hole where her tooth had been was closing up well. Her trip to the garden in her head had done the trick. She vowed to try to heal her leg and her hearing at the first opportunity.

As the day wore on, she wondered how long they would go before they ate. Her stomach was past complaining, but she felt light-headed and was afraid she might faint. The thought of returning to the refectory, however, filled her with trepidation. What if that nun were to hit her again? Why ever had she got so angry? Kate resolved to ask. She got to her feet and went to the front of the class where she caught the teacher's attention and pointed to the board. The teacher nodded and Kate wrote: Why was I hit in the refectory?

Because you were impolite, Sister Teresa wrote.

Kate circled the word 'impolite' and added a question mark.

The teacher wrote: You didn't say thank you.

How could I? thought Kate.

Can you give me some paper and a pen, please? Kate wrote.

The teacher rummaged through her desk and produced a small notebook and a pencil.

Kate opened the first page and wrote: THANK YOU! She

showed it to the teacher, then tore off the sheet and slipped it into the sole pocket of her dress.

The ginger haired girl, who'd drawn closer despite her friends' attempts to hold her back, tugged at the nun's sleeve distracting her. Seeing that the nun was about to turn away, Kate wrote more on the board.

Is there a herb garden?

Sister Teresa nodded.

I would like to work there, Kate wrote.

The teacher nodded again and turned to deal with the girl who continued to pester her.

Kate studied the group of girls milling around the teacher. There were six of them, most Kate's age or older. Their dresses looked a little cleaner and they were slightly less battered than the other girls. If anything, the ginger haired girl seemed even better off. She had hardly a bruise or a scratch.

Kate had never attended a school, except briefly with Peter, and knew nothing of the workings of such places, but seeing the way that group of girls eyed her, she guessed she was in for trouble.

As the afternoon wore on there was still no sign of her friend. Kate began to worry serious harm had come to her. No one else befriended her. In fact, the girls seemed set on avoiding her, despite their furtive glances. When school was over, the girls filed out of the class, passing through the same vestibule as earlier. Judging from the stairs leading up, their dormitory must be above the classroom. They headed back to the church with Kate hobbling behind. She was the last to arrive at the side door to the church.

She sat alone in the back row just behind a group of older girls. If she wanted to find out what had become of her friend, she'd have to make contact. Pulling out her notepad, she wrote: Where is the girl who helped me? Checking to see no one was watching, she tore out the page and handed it to one of the girls. She looked at it blankly and passed it on to the girl next to her. Her note went the rounds and Kate was beginning to think none of them could read. Or simply they didn't know the answer.

One girl turned to her and pointed to the pencil. Kate handed it over. The time the girl laboured over the answer had her wondering. Maybe these girls could neither read or write. Then, folded, her note came back accompanied by the pencil. She read: Locked up!

Where? Kate wrote.

Stores.

Can we get her out?

No.

How long will they keep her?

No idea.

Can I get a message to her?

Too dangerous.

The girls stiffened at the sight of a tall nun walking down the side aisle heading in their direction. Kate bent forward in her pew so she couldn't be seen and slipped the paper into her mouth. It tasted vile after being handled by so many dirty fingers, but she chewed on it and swallowed the thing as soon as possible. The nun halted behind her. It was the same bitter lump that had hit her in the refectory. The woman held out her hand, no doubt expecting Kate to hand over the notepad and pencil. Kate shook her head. The woman was furious. Kate just hoped she wouldn't hit her while they were in the church.

She hastily wrote: I am deaf and dumb. I need the book to talk.

The nun glared at her and held out her hand to take the book.

Kate wrote again: Would God have punished the poor and weak?

She had learnt some things about the Christian church from Peter and Fi. Rather like the Syvan priests in the world she came from, what their god said and what the priests did were often two quite different things.

There was no knowing how the woman would react. She might not take kindly to being taught a lesson by a twelve year-old, but the injustice riled Kate and she couldn't let it go without a fight. The nun stood undecided for a moment then turned her back and marched away.

What's her name? Kate scribbled on her notepad once the woman was far enough away and handed it to the girls.

Sister Helga, the answer came back.

Kate was wary when the girls left, heading for the refectory. She felt vulnerable as she trailed behind the group. Just before they reached the corner of the cloister where it turned to run beside the refectory, a girl, by far the tallest of the class whose jet black hair was often visible over the heads of the others, slipped back to walk next to her and pointed discretely to a small door. Kate guessed that must be where her friend was locked up. She wanted to thank the girl but she'd already returned to her place.

A table full of nuns looked up when Kate entered, several staring coldly at her. She tried to ignore their unsettling presence. She was offered a bowl of some kind of pea soup that smelt like it had been burnt and a hunk of dry bread. Before taking the bowl, she pulled the note from her pocket and showed it to the nun serving food. At the sight of the words THANK YOU! the nun nodded her approval and Kate hurried to find a place to sit.

The tall, lanky girl with long, black hair beckoned her over. Hardly had she begun her soup, than Sister Helga came and stood next to her, prodding her none too lightly on the shoulder with a boney finger. Kate looked for ways to avoid the blows, should it come to that, although she continued shovelling soup into her mouth. She was starving and suspected the nun was set on stopping her eating.

Sister Helga pointed wordlessly at the notepad and pencil that lay on the table next to Kate's soup bowl, her mouth pinched in a grim line. Kate flipped open the pad and wrote: Please. I need it! The nun continued pointing stubbornly at the book. Giving way to her irritation at the woman's attitude, Kate wrote: May those who have ears to hear listen. She'd heard Peter talk of something like that quoting his bible. When the woman raised her hand threateningly, Kate realised she'd gone too far.

The tall girl next to her was talking now, no doubt taking

her defence like her other friend had done. Kate had no wish to see another girl punished because of her. She struggled to her feet, preparing to duck out of the way, but she didn't need to. Sister Teresa placed a restraining hand on her fellow nun's arm. There followed a long and heated conversation, judging from the gesticulations of the two. Sister Helga towered over Sister Teresa, but the tiny nun held her ground.

Kate made the most of the time to finish her bread and soup. Her stomach demanded more, but it hardly seemed the right moment to ask for extras. When finally the gaunt nun withdrew, Kate sighed. Her relief was short-lived, Sister Teresa held out her hand for the book. Kate handed it over, figuring she couldn't fight them all. She had to trust someone. The nun wrote in the pad and handed it back. After breakfast tomorrow morning you work with me in the herb garden, it said. Kate pulled out the paper from her pocket and held it up. THANK YOU!

9.

At the evening meal Kate sat with the same group as earlier. She was glad they welcomed her readily. Glancing round, she realised her friend had still not returned. The tall, dark haired girl told her her friend's name was Tania. She also gave her own name, Eileen. It was Eileen that had the others pile up their plates and carry them to the kitchen hatch. When it was time to leave, it was also Eileen that had the older girls help the young ones who'd dozed off.

Night had fallen by the time the girls were herded into their dormitory. Kate sat huddled on her bed, the blanket wrapped tight around her shoulders. Many other girls were similarly clad. The room was devoid of heating and the window panes rattled as they struggled unsuccessfully to keep out the cold.

Kate got to her feet and paced the room, worried. Why had Tania not come back? She examined the windows. They were nailed shut and there was a considerable drop to the ground. No escape could be had that way. The only door was locked during the night. A stinking bucket in one corner bore witness to their nightly imprisonment. Kate tried the door and found it unlocked.

She spotted Eileen talking to a small group. She hurried over and wrote: How long will the door remain open?

Eileen replied: Another hour.

I want to see Tania, Kate wrote.

Too dangerous.

I don't care, Kate wrote turning away to head for the door.

Eileen hurried after her and tapped Kate on the shoulder and, taking the notepad, she wrote: We'll help. The lanky girl who had spoken in her defence against Sister Helga earlier joined them, along with a skinny girl who seemed younger than the others.

As the group of four slunk out of the dormitory, Kate couldn't help noticing the sly look of the ginger-haired girl. More trouble, Kate thought.

The only movement in the cloister was the swaying of the trees at its centre. If the girls' bare feet made any sound, Kate imagined it masked by the wind swirling around the corridors and up amongst the rafters. Shortly after the arched walkway turned towards the refectory the girls stopped at a door. Kate tried it, but it was locked. The others turned to the skinny girl who grinned, pointing up above the door. Eileen stretched up, her hand fumbling along a high-perched wooden beam till she discovered a key.

The door gave access to the kitchens, an Eldorado for starving girls. Eileen and the two others began rummaging through cupboards and drawers in search of food under the guidance of the skinny girl who seemed to know her way around. Kate watched as they discovered delicacies that would never have found their way onto the girls' plates. She wanted to warn them not to touch the food - someone would notice - but she didn't have the heart.

She went in search of the storerooms. Through a nearby door lay a large, low-roofed, windowless building, its walls lined with shelves heavy with goods. There were piles of long, slender candles, row upon row of dark brown bottles covered in dust, rolls of tissue most of it dark blue or black but some white, immense sacks of flour with strange markings stamped on them,... There were even a great many shelves of blankets like the ones they used in the dormitory.

The lighting was so gloomy she didn't see the three low doors next to each other till she reached the very end of the storeroom. Two lay open, the third was closed, a solid padlock barring the way. Peering round one of the open doors, she recognised her earlier prison.

She didn't plan to break Tania out. That would have alerted the whole nunnery. Having seen what the nuns did to someone who couldn't say thank you, she shuddered at what they might do for such an act. No. She just wanted to check the girl was OK.

She examined the padlock. To her surprise it was simply threaded through the metal rings that held the door closed, but wasn't locked. When she opened the door, a terrible stench greeted her. Covering her nose with one hand, she searched for a light switch but found none so she felt her way forward in the dark.

Tania lay in a heap on the floor, unmoving. Kate slid her hands over the girl in search of signs of life. Her skin was stone cold and places were sticky. Blood no doubt. Please don't be dead, Kate prayed. Finding the girl's wrist, she felt a faint pulse. There was still hope.

She got to her feet and hobbled to the kitchen. The girls' improvised feast had an air of revenge. They'd be sick later. Kate pulled out her notepad and wrote: I need a candle and matches. Showing it to Eileen, the tall girl immediately turned to the youngest, who, despite looking a little queasy, set to work. Returning to the storeroom, Kate took several blankets from the shelves and headed for Tania's cell.

A gruesome sight awaited her. Tania's back had been stripped bare and was covered in bloody lashes. Someone had savagely whipped her. The girl must have rolled on the floor because dust clung to the blood. In several places the wounds were festering.

She set the candle down and returned to the kitchen for water. As she had suspected, the girls' faces had taken on a sickly hue, all three clasping their bellies. Fetching a sprig of chamomile from the storeroom, she instructed the skinny girl how to make a tea.

Enough of them, she told herself, Tania needed her more. Finding a saucepan next to the sink, she filled it with water and, asking the skinny girl for help with improvised sign language, had her heat it. Next to the camomile she had found dried sage which she added to the water. She let the mixture boil for a while then poured it into a jug.

Armed with warm water, a bowl, a pair of scissors and some cloth she had cut from a roll in the storeroom, she returned to Tania and began gently washing her wounds. The lashes must have hurt terribly.

Several times Tania stirred but did not regain consciousness. When she had finished cleaning Tania's back, Kate realised that it would not suffice. Without healing cream, the wounds would probably fester. She gently laid a blanket over Tania and returned to the kitchen.

The girls were mournfully sipping their camomile tea. Kate asked where the medicine was kept. In the infirmary across the other side of the Abbey, Suzanne told her. There was no way to get there unseen. Even if it had been possible, time was running out. Soon a nun would lock the dormitory door, Eileen warned her. Kate beckoned the girls to follow her and returned to Tania.

When Kate showed them the girl's back, several gasped, one even turned away her hand clasped over her mouth. Kate wrote on her notepad: I will stay. Lock me in and return to the dormitory.

Judging from the look on her face, Eileen didn't agree. The others weren't happy either. Suzanne mimed carrying Tania, but Kate shook her head. It wouldn't work. The girl was too ill. She waved them away. She had to do so several times before they finally turned to leave. As they did, Eileen refused to lock her in. Instead, she pushed the door closed and hid the padlock.

Kate slid down the wall and settled next to Tania, pulling a blanket around herself. She managed to shift the girl so that the blanket protected them both from the cold. She lay a hand gently on Tania's back and closed her eyes searching inwards and outwards for the place where their two bodies touched.

In her world she'd learnt to use her mind to heal from within. Although that ability now seemed lost, being able to heal her mouth and jaw was a hopeful sign. One of the difficulties with healing was getting past the natural defences that surrounded the body like a second skin. The slightest effort triggered strong resistance.

That she could feel the barrier delighted her. Only the day before she'd been unable to feel it in Andrew. The mention of his name set off a flutter in her stomach. The boy was what Fi would have called 'cute'. She'd even kissed his hand. She was imagining how Peter would react if he caught her kissing Andrew when the girl stirred.

Forcing her thoughts back to Tania, she tried several times to jump into the girl's body, but each time her spirit rebounded, leaving her frustrated. It was the annoying paradox to healing: desperately wanting to heal would only hinder doing so. After a while she gave up and let her mind drift, detailing ambitious plans to help the girls live better. Warmer clothes would be good, better hygiene too and meaningful activities to chase away the boredom.

As she was about to slip off to sleep a voice in her head startled her.

You came to save me, it said sleepily.

Had Tania awoken? Even if she had, Kate would not be able to hear her. No, this was in her mind or rather Tania's mind. She had unwittingly slipped across the divide between them. The voice she heard was not Tania speaking, but the girl's thoughts.

Now that she had managed to travel to Tania's mind, she had to make the most of it and heal the girl. In Peter's world, healing implied doing things from outside, like giving medicine or setting a plaster cast. The healing she and Peter did was quite different. They coaxed the body to heal itself. The task would have been daunting, but luckily each cell contained the knowledge it needed to right itself. Peter called it the body's blueprint.

The direct contact with that life-force was such a delight, it was hard to imagine how she'd managed to survive without it. She watched awed as the body, urged on by her, skilfully knitted together the skin where deep weals had been gouged. She checked there was no damage elsewhere and was relieved to discover that the bruises and cuts were all superficial.

Shortly after the healing was over, Tania was fully awake. Seeing Kate in the candlelight, she pulled her friend into her arms and hugged her.

"You came," Tania said.

Kate could not hear her words, but the thoughts that went with them were clear enough. She hesitated about talking to the girl mind-to-mind. Peter had warned that people would be terrified if they heard voices in their heads. It was said to be a sign of madness.

Tania, Kate said into her mind.

"You can talk," Tania exclaimed.

No I can't. Not like you. What you hear are the thoughts I send. In turn, I cannot hear your words, but I can hear the thoughts that go with them.

Kate could not have anticipated what happened next. She was bowled over by an immense wave of warmth and tenderness that flowed through her. She had a hard time not being driven out of Tania's mind such was the force of the girl's emotions.

"The moment I saw you lying naked in that bed I knew you had come for me," Tania said.

Luckily for Kate, she knew how to keep her thoughts and emotions to herself.

"But how did you get here?" Tania asked.

Kate guessed she was referring to the storerooms and not that miserable world. *Some of the older girls helped me,* Kate told her. *Eileen, Suzanne and a lanky girl with long brown hair and dark brown eyes.*

"That'll be Christine," Tania said. "She's our peacemaker."

Peacemaker?

"She sorts out quarrels and calms frayed tempers."

Well she's going to have her work cut out after the mess they left in the kitchen. We'll all be in trouble.

Tania cuddled up close, burying her face in Kate's neck,

saying, "Who cares?"

I care, Kate said placing a hand on Tania's shoulder and pushing her gently away. *A lot of girls will get hurt, not just those who made the mess.*

Tania was making so much noise, Kate was afraid someone would hear.

Instead of talking, send me your thoughts, Kate said. *Then no one will hear.*

The prospect clearly appealed to the girl, but she was at a loss how to comply.

It's like talking in your head, Kate explained.

Talking? Tania said and immediately burst out laughing when she realised she'd succeeded.

Shhh! Kate thought.

Tania sat up abruptly. "My back," she exclaimed, running a hand over her back.

Thoughts not words! Kate reminded her.

It was a bloody mess. Now it's all gone.

I healed you, Kate told her, wondering how the girl would react. *But tell no one. Say it must have been a miracle.*

Kate was inundated a second time with Tania's love and gratitude.

Do you think you can get up? Kate asked.

Tania answered by struggling to her feet.

Listen, Tania. Tell no one you can talk to me. People, won't like it. They'll imagine we're talking behind their backs. They might even start saying it's the devil's work. Then we'll be in for it.

Ok, Tania said chuckling. Kate could sense her bursting to break the news.

You must promise. It's important.

Ok. Promise.

Good. I think we have some clearing up to do.

10.

It was decided. They would flee to the coast. The cottage was in a tiny fishing village called Lettup Cove. An ideal place to hide, according to Dr Grant, who'd been renting the hideaway for years. A quiet retreat from the ruckus of work, he called it.

Dressing the boys as girls had been Fi's brainwave. A disguise to foil Brian's attempts to find them, she said. The suggestion caught Peter off guard. It was too soon and too much, especially with Andrew there. He suspected Fi sought to force his hand, just the sort of manoeuvre she'd try, and he didn't like it.

As headmaster, Dr Grant was not happy about them leaving school early, but agreed they'd be in danger if they stayed. When it came to publicly parading as girls, he was quite vocal in his opposition. Fi's mum however spoke out in favour, although she measured her words, taking care not to force her husband.

Such could not be said of Fi, who weighed in with all her enthusiasm. Peter watched Dr Grant's face as the girl extolled the benefits of her plan oblivious to the discomfort she was causing.

It was Fi's mum who averted a clash, packing Fi off to her room. The girl objected, till her mother said: "Why don't you prepare for your part."

Once Fi was out of earshot, Dr Grant turned to Peter saying, "I presume dressing up doesn't bother you."

"It does, actually." Peter could see his answer surprised more than one. "You're right, I like to dress as a girl," Peter went on, "but if it disturbs you, that upsets me."

Dr Grant shook his head. It was clearly not the answer he wanted. He looked uncertain how to reply. Instead, he turned to Andrew. "What about you?"

Peter could have sworn Andrew flinched. Certainly, his voice trembled as he spoke. "I'd rather be alive and disguised as girl, than dead as a boy." From the pained look on his face, wearing girl's clothes was in itself a form of death.

"It'll be alright, John," Christina said, putting an arm around Andrew's shoulder. "I'll see they don't get up to mischief."

John seemed poised to pursue, but reluctantly agreed. "Make sure you stay out of the public eye."

Fi came down at that moment dressed in a suit, having added a bow tie for good measure. To her delight, her mother made a show of admiring her, calling her "Very debonair!" Fi was clearly much less enchanted with Dr Grant's response, "Smart, indeed, but a tad conspicuous with that bow tie."

When Fi learnt that Dr Grant had agreed to her idea, she gave him a hug, which he graciously accepted, and then, linking arms with Peter and Andrew, she marched them up to her room, to "prepare the girls", as she put it.

Peter would have preferred to dress without Andrew present, but Fi overruled him. "It's no time to give yourself airs," she said. Had she always been so bossy?

Unhooking Kate's blue dress from its hanger, he cringed. Surely Andrew's eyes would be taking in his every move. After all, it was the very dress Kate had worn the night she'd been with Andrew. But when he furtively glanced, Andrew had had the decency to look the other way.

He hastily got undressed, donned the dress and was busy trying to pull on the tights when Fi offered to help. He refused. It was bad enough getting dressed in front of Andrew, without having Fi give him a hand with his tights.

When it was Andrew's turn, Peter retreated to the farthest corner from where he did his best to pretend he wasn't there.

Despite the distance, Peter felt terribly exposed in Kate's dress. Pretexting cold, he'd shrugged one of Fi's shawls around his shoulders and looked out the window at the wild array of flowers in Dr Grant's garden, warm and comforting in the early evening sun.

Despite his evident reticence, Fi finally managed to dress Andrew in one of her blouses and a skirt. They suited him well, making him look a "real pretty miss", as Fi put it. But at the sight of himself in the mirror, Andrew promptly broke down and hid his face in his hands.

The suddenness and force of his reaction shocked Peter. Fi's choice of clothes could hardly be called extravagant, without the slightest hint of pink or frills. Peter could only guess the boy felt humiliated. Silly really. He actually looked quite cute.

"Don't you want to look pretty?" Fi asked, uncomprehending.

In the circumstances, it was not a question Peter would have asked. There were things about others, he realised, that Fi just couldn't grasp.

"Oh come on Andrew," Fi said, loosing patience. "Think how lucky you are. You can be both boy and girl." She glanced meaningfully in Peter's direction having said something similar to him once. Andrew was sobbing.

The more Fi got annoyed, the more Andrew cried and the more he cried, the more she became irritated. Andrew looked on the verge of falling apart.

"Let me talk to him," Peter said, coming to the rescue. "Alone."

Fi gave him a filthy look, muttering "Cry baby" under her breath and stomped out.

Peter was not sure what to do. Had he been Kate, she would surely have taken Andrew in her arms. But he wasn't Kate and the idea of doing so made his stomach flip. He could imagine Kate coaxing him. Do it for him, she would have said. He's the one who's suffering, not you. He knew she was right. So he reluctantly stepped forward and took Andrew in his arms, struggling to quell mixed feelings.

At first, Andrew stood stiff as a board, but when Peter kept quiet and waited, the boy finally relaxed and laid his head on Peter's shoulder, sobbing quietly. Glancing at the mirror he saw two girls hugging each other, a sight that added to his confusion. Still watching his mirror image as if it were a separate reality that fascinated him, he raised his hand and ran it gently through Andrew's hair.

"Please, don't!" begged Andrew, straining to break free. "That's exactly how it began."

Andrew's words left Peter perplexed, but he released him and sat on the edge of the bed waiting.

"My uncle...," Andrew finally said.

There followed such a long silence, he wondered if the boy would say any more.

Andrew gave a shuddering sigh and continued. "He'd dress me as a girl. He had a wardrobe full of little girl's clothes. He had me parade in front of him, then he took me in his arms and ran his hands through my hair like you just did."

Peter, whose stomach sank at the thought of what must be coming next, struggled not to let his apprehension show.

"I told him I didn't want to be a girl," Andrew said through clenched teeth. "I refused to dress like one. But he was sly. He suggested a bargain. He'd teach me piano, if I agreed to dress as a girl at his house." Tears flowed down his cheeks again. "I cried then too and it wasn't the last time. I wanted so much to learn piano and there seemed no other way..."

Andrew paused as if wondering how to go on. "I finally agreed. For seven years, every time I went to his place I'd be dressed as a girl. He'd chose. Sometimes it was just underwear and stockings, sometimes it was elaborate costumes. Generally, he helped me dress. That was when he began to touch me..." He broke off, taking a shuddery gasp, his fists clenched. "I objected. I tried to fight him off, but he was much stronger and so good at getting his way."

Andrew burst into sobs.

"I'm so sorry, Andrew," Peter said, after a long silence. "I will let nobody force you to wear girl's clothes. Dress however you like."

"The silly thing is," Andrew said, wiping his eyes on the back of his hand, "I came to enjoy dressing as a girl." At which he blushed and looked away. "After a while, I couldn't do without it. I smuggled clothes home and dressed up in my room. That was when Brian caught me. He was furious and beat me till I was almost senseless, then he bundled up the girl's clothes and carried them away. I was afraid he'd tell mother, but he said nothing. Months later, rummaging through his cupboards for money he'd stolen from me, I found the clothes at the bottom folded neatly next to a pile of girlie magazines."

"Once, when my uncle was away, I imagined breaking into his house to dress up. I knew it was all wrong and I felt horribly guilty, but I longed to be a girl. When I realised I was looking at boys as if I were a girl, I got really worried. I'd heard of queers. It was a word reserved for those who were different, flawed. Nobody liked them. I was afraid I was becoming one. I would lie awake at night tormented by wild desires and through it all I could see my uncle standing over me, licking his lips, his eyes hot with desire."

Andrew sat on edge of the bed a few feet from Peter. "I knew you dressed as a girl," Andrew told him, blushing as he spoke. "I sensed it."

Had not the crazy Priscilla Wit said the same? Was his secret so obvious? Witless had wanted to kill him. What would Andrew try to do?

"I longed to befriend you," Andrew continued, staring at his hands in his lap. "But I was afraid I'd force you to be a girl at my service, like my uncle had me. I didn't want to be like him."

Peter finally understood the beseeching look that lit up Andrew's eyes. The boy wanted to be reassured he was not a monster, to be accepted and loved by someone, not by force, but through shared feelings and closeness. Peter could understand. He too had wanted to be accepted. How lucky he'd found Fi's mum and Dr Grant, even if the latter was still reticent. He shifted next to Andrew and pulled him into his arms, planting a kiss on the top of his head.

They stayed in each other's arms for a long moment, then Andrew pulled back saying: "How did you start dressing?"

"I was more fortunate. Nobody forced me," Peter said. He told Andrew about secretly dressing in his sister's clothes. He described the threats of Witless because she said he was queer and how her scheming had shattered his family. He described his adventures with Fi and how her mother had accepted he dress as a girl.

"But what about Kate?" Andrew finally asked.

"Ah Kate!" Peter said with a sigh. "That's a long story. I'll tell you in the car. Now let's get that makeup done."

Most girls of his age didn't go in for makeup. It certainly wasn't allowed at school. But his sister, who'd been a convenient model, and Fi, who'd been his initiator into the art of making up, both wore makeup whenever they could.

Before they left, Dr Grant, who was to join them at the end of term, warned Peter and Andrew to be careful. "People don't take kindly to being tricked about appearances, especially when it comes to gender. Make sure nobody suspects you are boys."

The world was full of contradictions, Peter thought. If people were so upset about boys pretending to be girls and vice versa, how come some characters in successful plays and books disguised as the other sex. Had not Peter in Peter Pan and Wendy been played by a girl? Contradictions apart, Peter appreciated the clear way Dr Grant went about things, even if he didn't always like the constraints.

The sun was setting when Fi's mum drove up to the main road and turned south. Fi sat next to her, still in a huff about being 'ejected'. The two boys sat in the back talking quietly.

"Wow!" Andrew said when Peter finished his tale about Kate. "I would never have imagined. So that was Kate in your body with me last night. I understand now why she said you were so close." He chuckled.

He was relieved that Andrew didn't challenge his story. The boy could easily have laughed, treating it as make-believe. Peter hadn't realised how much he needed to be believed.

"Where could she have gone?" Andrew asked. "Such a resourceful person wouldn't simply blink out of existence."

"You cannot survive without a body and she had no reason to leave even if she could. That's why I reckon that meddling author must have given her a new body."

"Author?"

"The one who wrote the story she was in."

Andrew looked troubled. "You mean she was a character in a book?"

Peter nodded.

"But we don't go around bumping into people out of stories."

Peter hadn't given it much thought. Listening to Andrew, the tale did strike him as beyond belief. "Well I did. I travelled to a world that turned out to be a story."

"And now you think this... What do you call him?"

"Old Man God."

"This Old Man God snatched her away and plunged her into another story."

"It does sound far-fetched, but it's the only explanation."

Andrew sat silent and thoughtful for a while. "If I were him, I'd want revenge."

It was Peter's turn to be thoughtful. Revenge did sound plausible. If Andrew was right, the author would have probably sent Kate to a horrible place. Poor Kate! He'd given up his efforts to contact her. He resolved to try again.

"Oh look!" Fi called out. "The sea!"

Peter and Andrew craned to see a narrow moonlit strip of blue between cliff tops and sky. Barely a few hours from home, Peter rarely got to see the sea. The sight always thrilled him, making him wonder why he'd stayed away so long.

"You girls bring your bathing costumes?" Fi asked, a wicked grin on her face.

"And you, young man, I trust you brought yours?" Peter shot back.

"I never wear a costume in the sea," she boasted.

Fi's mum snorted. "Fi!" she exclaimed. "The ideas you get! It must be the bad influence of these girls you spend so much time with."

"I doubt it, Madam," retorted Andrew. "We girls are the model of virtue."

Everyone laughed. Peter was pleased Andrew, or rather Andie as they'd decided to call the girl he'd become, had thrown off the miserable mood that had beset him.

When it came to Fi's name, Peter had suggested Ferguson because he was annoyed at her. "How about Fred?" Andrew said. Fi liked it, so she became Fred.

Finding a name for Peter wasn't easy. The others suggested Kate, but Peter refused. "Kate is not me," he insisted. He ran through girls' names that began with 'p'. None pleased him. He was tempted by Anne. When he said so, Fi stuck out her tongue. Apparently there was an Anne in her class she despised.

Finally he opted for Wendy which had Fi's mum laughing. "You've been reading too much Peter Pan," she said.

"Andie, Wendy and Fred," Fi said. "Two more and we can go on adventures."

"Who's been reading too much Enid Blyton?" Andrew joked.

"The Famous Five or Noddy?" Peter asked.

Fi struggled to get at the two who were splitting their sides laughing.

"Stop that Fred!" Fi's mum said. "You'll cause an accident."

Peter had to think a moment to recall who Fred was. He glanced out of the window trying to calm his mirth.

They were driving down a steep incline with cliffs towering on either side. As they turned a sharp bend, a bay opened before them and, nestling in the hallow at the foot of the incline, lay a small fishing village lit here and there by old fashioned street lamps. Judging from the lights in windows, there couldn't have been more than ten houses. The village had a tiny harbour in which a couple of boats were moored. At the entrance to the village, perched on slightly higher ground was a white-washed cottage, bright in the moonlight, with a shiny, slate roof.

"Welcome to Lettup Cove," Christina said. "There's the cottage."

<h1 style="text-align:center">11.</h1>

Once the excitement of exploring had subsided, Fi's mum shooed them out of the kitchen, sending them to pick their rooms, unpack and put away their things. "Do it properly," she insisted. "We could be here for weeks."

The cottage was small and there were only two bedrooms for them off the first floor landing, one with a double bed and one with two singles.

"I'm not sleeping with you," Fi said as she shoved past Peter into the room with the double bed and slammed the door on them.

Peter glanced at Andrew and shrugged. Andrew blushed.

Peter dumped his case on the bed below the tiny window and stared out. He could just make out the cove and the harbour with its boats bobbing in the moonlight. A familiar bubbling excitement surged in his belly. He hadn't been on holiday for ages. After his father's death, his mother had been unwilling to go away. Thinking of her had him feeling guilty. He hadn't visited her since before the coma. He preferred not to think about it.

He glanced at Andrew who had his back turned and was busy putting away his clothes. Unbuckling the case Fi and her mum had prepared, he laid each item out in neat piles. Wow! Had they been thorough. There was not a single shred of boy's clothes in it. He'd often dreamed of such a situation, but having no way out alarmed him.

While they unpacked, Fi's mum prepared a meal: granary

bread, smoked ham, pickles, mature cheddar and a few leaves of lettuce. To drink she made tea.

Throughout the meal, Fi did all the talking, drafting plans for their stay. Andrew looked tired and worn. He hadn't fully recovered and the bout of crying had left his face puffy. Occasionally their eyes met, only to look away. Did the boy regret having been so forthcoming? Recalling Andrew's story left a bitter taste. Peter tried tuning into Fi's twittering, but images of old man's eyes devouring his every move haunted him.

Clearing away the dishes offered a welcome distraction. Soon after, Fi's mum sent them to bed, saying, "It's been a long day and sea air makes people sleepy."

Rather than change in front of Andrew, Peter withdrew to the bathroom. Seeing his pink nightdress, he wondered if Fi had contrived to give Andrew a matching blue one. The boy must have hurried because he was in bed when Peter returned.

Once they settled in their respective beds, Andrew turned to face Peter and asked, "If Kate has been in your head all this time, it must feel strange without her."

Peter didn't want to talk about Kate. Not to Andrew. Especially not to Andrew. So he pretended to be asleep. Andrew didn't insist and Peter heard the squeak of bedsprings as the boy turned over minutes later.

Kate, Peter thought. *Where are you?*

No answer came. Where had that blasted author sent her? Andrew was right, he did feel empty. He tried not to think of her, but it was difficult. The numbness helped. As soon as they got out of this mess, he'd go in search of her.

He recalled her riding horseback towards the mountains as they escaped the invaders in her world. It was a warm, sunny day. The wind had been in her hair and the smell of wild flowers engulfed them. Safe in her mind, they'd talked long together. The memory soothed him and he finally fell asleep.

Peter awoke late. The night had been marked by disturbing

dreams leaving him frail and wary. Andrew had already gone down to breakfast. Peter donned thick woollen tights under his nightshirt, feeling less exposed, and descended the steep stairs cautiously.

In the kitchen, Andrew looked as washed out as Peter felt. Only Fi, in an outrageous combination of bottle green shorts, a checkered red and green shirt and a brilliant yellow silk scarf around her neck, seemed full of spirits and rearing to go.

Fi's mum treated them to full English breakfast. "It's Sunday, after all," she'd said.

They argued about what to do. Peter wanted to get out. He needed fresh air. Fi wanted to explore, but Peter was worried he wouldn't have the strength and both boys were reticent about being seen in public. Dr Grant's warning was uppermost in his mind.

When Christina reminded them they might have to stay several weeks and they could hardly spend all that time indoors, they finally agreed to go for a short walk.

A stiff breeze blew in from the sea as they set off to explore Lettup. Peter was glad Fi's mum had packed warm woollen tights. The wind was bitterly cold. It blew in gusts that constantly threatened to lift his smock. Despite the thick tartan shawl pulled tight around his shoulders and the tammy on his head, the biting sea air had him shivering.

Peter had decided to forgo crutches. "I'll look ridiculous," he'd said.

"Girls use crutches too," Fi's mum had reminded him.

But he was adamant. He took his time, savouring the fresh air, as Fi, who'd taken Andrew by the arm, strode on ahead.

He watched the two, Andrew walking tense and stiff in his austere dress and dark tights as Fi, a swirling mass of colours, leaned close and whispered in his ear. When she glanced back her game was clear enough. She thought he was enamoured with Andrew and hoped to make him jealous.

Houses were dotted along either side of the single road that sloped to the sea. One storey high, they were built of stone, weathered black by time and wind. The windows were tiny, but each window ledge was gaily decorated with flowers. Nets hung from washing lines and lobster pots were scattered here and there. Despite the apparent activity, no one was out and about.

Half way down the single street, the road broadened into a square. It was there Peter caught up with them as they stood outside the church, a squat construction, built of similar material to the houses.

Peter tried the door. It was unlocked. Glancing inside there were no choir stalls and no organ either. Instead, an upright piano stood next to a small pulpit.

Andrew opened the piano and played a few notes.

"It's been tuned," he announced, enthusiastic. Peter pulled over a chair and sat down as Andrew played the Satie. Once he'd finished and Fi had made a show of enthusing about his playing, Andrew glanced at Peter and began playing Elgar's Jerusalem. "You know this, I suppose?"

Of course he did. Who didn't? As Andrew accompanied him, he proudly sang the glories of a land full of hope.

When they'd finished, they were startled by clapping from the entrance. Peter spun round to see a vicar silhouetted in the open doorway.

"Wonderful!" the man exclaimed. "You girls must come to communion later and sing for us. Lettup hasn't had a choir in years. You're lucky," he chattered on, coming to greet them, "today we have parish breakfast. It happens so rarely these days. What are your names?" he asked shaking their hands. He was a short, thin man with a jovial face. His greying hair was windswept and his oversized hands were rough, making it look as if he regularly helped the fishermen.

"Andie and Wendy. What lovely names. And you young man?" he asked turning to Fi who looked put out at not being in the limelight. "Fred. Well hallo Fred. Your friends play remarkably well."

The girl was too polite to make a face, but Peter could see she was fuming. She pretexted having to buy bread and made her escape.

"Do you know any other pieces like that?" the vicar asked. "You could give a concert." The man didn't wait for a reply, he gaily made plans for a grand concert in which the two would be the stars of Lettup. So much for remaining incognito.

"I don't know about a concert," Peter said, seeing that Andrew was on the verge of accepting, "but we'll willing perform Jerusalem for you at communion today. When does it begin?"

"There's no set time," the vicar told them. "It depends on the tide." He gestured to the fishing nets strung up on either side of the altar. "But today it'll be at ten thirty."

"See you later, then," Peter said, taking Andrew by the arm and leading him outside.

"I like the idea of a concert," Andrew said, the moment they were out of earshot.

"Sure," Peter said. "If the vicar has his way the press and the radio will all be there. So much for keeping under cover."

Andrew looked disheartened. "Promise me," he said earnestly, "once we get out of this, you'll give a concert with me."

Peter didn't have the heart to say no and anyway the idea appealed to him. "We'll have to be quick" he said after a while. "Who knows when my voice will break?"

He wished his voice would remain treble forever, but there was no way that could be. What if his voice should break while singing dressed as a girl? He had nightmarish visions of being unmasked in front of the whole village. If God needed a reason to throw lightening bolts, surely that would qualify.

The baker's was across the street, next to the only pub. They found Fi chatting up the pretty girl behind the counter.

Fi might have called Peter pretty, but this girl really deserved the name. She was the same height as Fi, but unlike Fi she had long curly auburn hair that reached to the middle of her back. Her eyes were green under ample eyebrows and when she smiled, which she did now looking at Fi, dimples formed in her cheeks.

Fi didn't waste a moment. Hardly had she ditched them, than she was trying her hardest to make out with an unsuspecting beauty. He was half a mind to reveal her game, but he couldn't be that nasty to Fi and why shouldn't she run after girls if she wanted to?

"Can I help?" the girl asked in a sweet voice.

"I'm not sure," Peter said, looking around the shop, but ignoring Fi. "We are looking for a friend. We were supposed to keep an eye on him. His mother is afraid he'll get into mischief."

He could hear Andrew giggling. "Stop that, Andie," he said. "This is serious. Lord knows what Fred will do if we aren't around to keep an eye on him."

The serving girl shot a querying glance at Fi then looked back at Peter. "What does he look like?" she asked.

Peter described Fi, although he had some difficulty not bursting out laughing. It was then he pretended to notice Fi and exclaimed, "Ah there you are you naughty boy. Mummy will be very angry."

Fi took a swipe at Peter. She missed but sent Peter's tammy flying onto a shelf of freshly baked bread. The girl behind the counter looked confused, but fetched the hat and handed it back to him.

"Meet my cousins, Andie and Wendy," Fi said. "You see why I wanted to hide."

The girl giggled. "They sound fun to me," she said, intently eyeing Peter, or rather Wendy. "I like the name Wendy," she told Peter. "It reminds me of Peter, the boy who never grew up."

Peter blushed at the mention of his real name. Goodness knows what was going through her mind, but the girl blushed too. "Are you coming to church?" she asked, in an attempt to cover her confusion.

"Yes," Andrew replied. "The vicar has asked us to perform."

"Perform?" the girl asked, intrigued.

"I play piano and Wendy sings."

Peter could see Fi was hopping mad at being upstaged yet

again. She might be a bit overbearing, but he really liked her and didn't want to cause her pain. "Come on Andie," he said taking Andrew by the hand. "We've got to practice. Let's let Fred buy that bread. See you," he said to the girl and towed Andrew outside.

"Don't get too used to towing me around," Andrew warned once they were outside.

"Sorry about that," Peter said. "Fi's having a hard time. She really likes that girl and we were getting in the way."

Andrew stopped in mid-stride. "You mean..." He took a few steps and stopped again. "Fi likes girls," he exclaimed.

Peter grinned. "Always has."

"But you two... I thought you were ...," he said and scratched his head.

"Like I said about Kate, it's complicated. Sure Fi and I sleep together. We cuddle, we kiss, we talk a lot ... But we were never..." He hesitated over the word. "Physical."

"Oh!" Andrew said, looking like he might have drawn a winning ticket after all, but was afraid to believe it.

Like Fi, here was someone who lived in dreams and would probably get hurt because of it. Peter didn't want to be the one to hurt him, but it was hard to avoid.

"Listen Andrew," he said as they wandered up the deserted street. "I've never felt at ease with boys, but I feel at home with you." That wasn't strictly true. But he struggled on. "It's good to have someone to talk to. I've always been so alone. And we have things in common." He laughed, feeling self-conscious. Pausing, he was unsure how to go on. "But I don't think I want to be your…" He couldn't help blushing. "Well, you know."

Andrew walked on in silence. Peter was worried he'd upset the boy, but then Andrew turned to him. "It's true, a part of me wants you," he said with a sigh, steadfastly looking anywhere but at Peter. "You might not believe me, but I have dreamt of making love to you for ages." Seeing the desire in Andrew's eyes, it was all Peter could do not to take to his heels.

"But a large part of me doesn't want that physical stuff."

Andrew shook his head as if to rid himself of unwanted thoughts. "It reminds me of uncle and that disgusts me." Uncharacteristically, he spat on the road. "I would like to be your girlfriend, if you see what I mean," he said, holding out his hand.

"Girlfriends it is," Peter said, taking Andrew's hand and they sauntered up the road to the cottage with Andrew describing the clothes he'd like to wear.

"Ah, there you are," Fi's mum said when they entered. Peter could have sworn she shuddered at the sight of them holding hands, but if she did, she quickly hid it. The woman had always been opened minded, even if he and Fi had pushed her to her limits at times.

"I'm sorry our holding hands upsets you," Peter said, thinking directness might clarify things.

This time the woman really did shudder. "Peter, you have a disarming way of challenging people," she said trying to recover her composure. "Are you gay?" she asked, outdoing his directness.

"I'm not sure," Peter said. "It's tricky. We were just talking about it. Because I like to dress as a girl doesn't mean I want to be one. Nor does it mean I want to sleep with boys."

"Peter!" Christina exclaimed, looking dismayed.

He'd been too frank again.

"There's nothing wrong with two boys loving each other," Andrew put in. "What I find wrong is when one tries to force the other, I mean ..." He hesitated. "To make love or kiss or cuddle if the other doesn't want it. That's bad and does a lot of harm."

Seeing tears welling up in his eyes, Fi's mum opened her arms to Andrew and cradled him as he cried softly. She beckoned Peter over and put her other arm around him. "To think," she said, "I desperately wanted a son and instead I inherited two lost girls."

"You should be called Wendy, not me," Peter said.

"Why so?"

"Because you look after lost girls."

12.

The pretty girl from the bakery, whose name was Bonnie, must have been waiting for him, because the moment he entered the church she pounced on him, slung an arm round his shoulder, much to Fi's disgust, and planted a kiss on his cheek. Peter struggled to get free, but she clung on with the force of desperation.

She looked like a character from a fairy tale, although certainly not the sort you could trust. She had put on a green dress trimmed with white lace that barely reached her knees and wore white tights and dark green shoes. Her auburn hair was attached in a ponytail fixed with a silver clasp of a Celtic design.

Before Peter could get free, the girl seized his hand and pulled him to a seat saying, "Sit next to me, Wendy." Fi had threatened to come to church dressed as a girl now she knew Bonnie was more interested in girls, but her mother had overruled her. Seeing her hopes once again thwarted, Fi stomped off to join her mum who was looking for a seat elsewhere in the crowded church. He heard her mutter, "It's not fair."

The vicar hurried over to Peter who was squashed into a pew between Bonnie and her grandmother. Andrew sat on the other side of Bonnie. "You'll be singing at the end of the communion. I'll call on you," the vicar told them. He was about to leave but turned back to Peter. "It's Wendy and Andie, isn't it?" he asked, his forehead creasing in worry. "I wouldn't like to make a mistake." Peter nodded and the vicar ambled off, looking relieved.

"Where did you learn to sing?" Bonnie asked, placing a casual hand on Peter's knee. The temperature in the church shot up several degrees. Peter was so uncomfortably warm he longed to remove the shawl from his shoulders, but instead he clung to it like a rampart against a siege.

"I've always sung," he said, hoping she wouldn't insist on knowing where.

"Do you sing?" Andrew asked her, winking to Peter as he came to the rescue.

"Oh no," she exclaimed, giggling. "I dance." She turned back to Peter saying: "I'll show you later, if you like."

Why me? Peter wondered. He'd never had such success as a boy.

"Gran," she said, leaning across Peter such that he was pressed again the pew by the full weight of her chest as she spoke to her grandmother. "Can Wendy come to dinner?"

Peter kept very still not knowing how to handle this girl who took such liberties in full view of everyone.

Bonnie's gran agreed, apparently delighted her granddaughter had found a friend.

Peter spent much of the communion dreaming up excuses not to go. The ceremony was tern without a choir and the vicar's sermon had none of the moral fire of the Rake, the nickname they gave to their vicar at home. The only fire in the church, which was otherwise bitterly cold, was Bonnie's hand every time she placed it on his knee. She even managed to place a hand on his backside as he manoeuvred passed to get out in response to the vicar's call.

Standing next to Andrew, seated at the piano, it was a relief to be able to move freely without fiery hands groping at him. Concentrate, he told himself, or you'll be singing "Tyger, Tyger burning bright..." instead of Jerusalem. He smiled, mentally thanking Mrs Greengage, his English teacher, for his growing knowledge of literature. When Andrew began to play the opening bars, Peter took a deep breath, relaxed his shoulders and neck and prepared to sing.

Peter couldn't help it, his heart swelled at Blake's words and tears brimmed in his eyes. Had they not crossed England's green and pleasant land to get there? Luckily no dark satanic mills marred this part of the world. He glanced at the congregation as Andrew played the few bars that hailed the second stanza. Many were moved. When the piece was over, people got to their feet to applaud. Andrew stood, clasping Peter's hand, beaming as the two attempted a rather clumsy curtsey. Andrew's dream had finally come true: he'd played before an audience.

People clamoured for an encore. Peter whispered to Andrew who nodded and sat down at the piano.

"I know how much people like to sing Jerusalem," Peter said, smoothing down his dress. "I bet some of you found it hard to resist." A couple chuckled. "Andie and I will perform it again and this time you can sing along. And while you do, I'll try to improvise a descant."

The congregation stood to sing, an air of reverence and expectation filling the church. During the first stanza, Peter joined the people singing in unison but when it came to the second stanza he let his voice soar above them like a wild bird on the wing. He loved that voice, he loved that freedom as he reached up. "...I will not cease from mental fight, nor shall my sword sleep in my hand till we have built Jerusalem on England's green and pleasant land." On the very last note his voice slipped from under him and plunged two octaves making a dreadful rasping sound as he came abruptly to a halt. His voice had broken.

He burst into tears and hid his face, terrified all had noticed, but no one rushed to unmask him. Instead, people applauded wildly. Despite the ovation, he couldn't stop crying. He'd lost a treasured part of himself, for ever.

Andrew took Peter in his arms to console him. "My voice..." Peter whispered desolate as the congregation moved to congratulate them.

"I heard," Andrew whispered and kissed Peter on the cheek. "I'm so sorry." He pulled a handkerchief from his sleeve and wiped Peter's eyes. The crying had made a mess of his make up.

Their moment of intimacy was short-lived as people converged with their praise and thanks. Bonnie was foremost amongst them. Peter couldn't face another second of the girl's insistent attention. "I'm not feeling well," he told her, keeping his voice low in the hope it wouldn't break again. "Apologise to your gran. We'll have dinner another time."

Peter and Andrew had difficulty freeing themselves, but finally managed to leave. They found Fi and her mum deep in conversation. The girl was gesticulating wildly, her voice raised, but broke off as Peter arrived. Christina looked concerned when she caught sight of Peter's face, smeared as it was with tears and make up. "What happened?"

Peter didn't immediately reply, but waited till they'd moved away from the crowd surging out of the church. "My voice broke," he said quietly.

"Poor thing," Christina said, putting an arm around him.

"Serve's you bloody right," Fi muttered.

"Look here, you," Peter said turning on Fi, furious, his voice rising and cracking as it did. "You used to be one of the most sensitive and considerate people I knew. I loved that person. Whatever happened to her? You can have your damned Bonnie. I don't want anything to do with her. She's a nightmare..."

Fi's mum looked perplexed, her eyes shifting from one to the other, trying to understand. "It's complicated," Andrew said, shrugging.

The sound of steps following had them glancing back. A slight man with a thin, expressive face hurried along the road waving for them to wait. The last thing Peter wanted was more chitchat. He turned to continue, but Fi's mum stopped him, whispering, "That's rude, Peter."

The man looked Russian. His long fur-lined waistcoat hung loose in the breeze. On his head was a round cap like those Cossacks wore, he had a short goatee and his greying hair, pushed back behind his ears, hung to the middle of his back.

"I can help you with that voice son, if you want," he said,

addressing Peter without the least introduction.

That he had recognised him to be a boy had Peter alarmed. "Why do you call me son?" Peter asked, careful not to make his voice break again.

"You can't fool me lad," the man said. "For all your lace and ribbons, I know a treble voice when I hear one."

He glanced fleetingly at Andrew, then continued. "I may have strange teaching methods, but no one can handle a broken voice better than I." He handed Peter his card. "Come and visit me this afternoon, I live in that cottage over there." He pointed to a small house set aside from the rest of the village at the end of a steep incline half way round the bay. Then he turned and left without another word.

Peter studied the card. Dr Viktor Tchensenko. "I didn't know you could do anything with a broken voice," Peter said absently. The other choir boys all left the choir when their voice broke and stopped singing, often for ever. But for him a life without singing wasn't a life.

"I'd like to go," he finally said.

"Come in," a voice called out. As Peter, Andie and Fi's Mum (Fi had gone in search of Bonnie) entered the small cottage, Dr Tchensenko was seated cross-legged on a large cushion surrounded by instruments not all of which Peter could name. The man strummed a balalaika, humming softly.

He motioned for them to sit and continued singing, adding nasal sounds, words no doubt, but no language Peter knew. It might well have been invented. Then something extraordinary happened, the man sang several notes at once. Peter had not known it was possible. Harmonics rode high over a much lower note, singing a different tune. The moment was magic. Fascinated, Peter felt himself sailing up on that eerie counterpoint. It reminded him of his lost treble voice as he struggled to stem the tears that threatened to submerge him anew.

"The first step," the man said addressing Peter, his music at an end, "is to make friends with that break in your voice. Instead of avoiding it, like most boys do, you must plunge into it and ride it like a rough sea until it takes you where you want to go."

He paused to fix Peter with his bright blue eyes, tugging at his goatee as he did. "Do you have the courage to venture there were others are terrified to go?" he asked. When Peter didn't answer, he continued, "I suppose you must know something of courage. How else could you affront the world dressed as a girl?"

Peter was expecting him to ask why he was disguised, but he did no such thing. Viktor got to his feet and headed for the kitchen. "Tea?" he asked.

Once they were settled around the rough wooden table in the kitchen sipping the exceedingly sweet mint tea he'd brewed, Viktor continued, talking directly to Peter as if the others weren't there. "In my travels, I have learnt from singing masters and mistresses in many parts of the world, but above all in Switzerland. You'd be surprised how many talented people took refuge in that mountainous country during the war. They all taught me one thing: the voice is the key to the soul, both yours and those of others." He had a way saying the word 'soul' that made it sound like a rushing wind. Peter shivered.

"Learning with me is very hard work. Four hours a day, every day, even Sundays, two in the morning and two in the afternoon. If you accept, be warned that there will be times when you'll want to scream, when you feel like you're a hopeless wreck, a no-good who'll never sing again. But there'll also be times when you feel on top of the world and your voice will delight you and the people around you..."

"How much do you charge?" Fi's mum asked, as practical as ever.

"I don't charge for my work," the man said, still addressing only Peter.

"Why?" Peter asked, wondering what reward the man hoped to get if it wasn't money.

"I could say you have talent, and that would be true, but the real reason is that you need help and I am the unique person to

help you. There was a time, a long while ago, when I too needed
help and someone stepped up for me. I am immensely grateful.
In helping you, I honour the help I received."

13.

Crouched behind a low wall, Fi peered out at her mother, Peter and Andrew as they ambled towards the village. The boys were still done up as girls, but much to her disgust, they'd foregone their pretty dresses in favour of plain skirts and blouses. It was a long walk to the man's house, affording her sufficient time to carry out her plan. The very thought sent tremors rippling down her spine.

She'd had enough of being upstaged by Peter. To think she'd encouraged him to dress as a girl and now, dressed in one of the dresses she'd lovingly chosen, he stole Bonnie. She wasn't going for it any longer. She'd set things right.

Hurrying back to the house and up to Peter's bedroom, she shoved off her trousers and shirt, tossing them on the floor out of sight. Rummaging through the wardrobe, she picked a dress and pressed it against her body, admiring herself in the mirror. She looked ravishing. Bonnie wouldn't be able to resist. What girl could? If she tightened the belt around her waist it would accentuate her hips, an advantage Peter couldn't rival. A hint of lipstick, Peter rarely used it, and a dab of perfume behind her ears and she was set to conquer.

The next phase was more tricky. The baker's shop was shut on Sunday afternoons, but she'd overheard Bonnie tell Peter she went for a walk by the shore on a Sunday afternoon. Well, Bonnie would get her fortuitous meeting, but not with the girl she expected. Fi had to grin. She flung a shawl around her shoulders, glanced appraisingly one last time at her reflection and stormed out.

Down by the beach no Bonnie was in sight. The girl must have had enough of waiting for Peter, but Fi was pretty sure she'd be back. Bar the distant calls of gulls, the only sound was the whoosh of the waves breaking on the pebbles followed by the clink of stone rolling on stone as the receding water tugged them seaward.

Fi brushed the seaweed from a rock, laid down her shawl and sat on it, looking out to sea. A couple of fishing boats chugged out trailing a noisy cohort of gulls that swirled and swooped over the darkened bows and plunged into the waves. She inhaled deeply, relishing the fresh air. Mingled with the salty scent of sun-dried seaweed, she caught a whiff of creosote from a nearby shed.

She thought over the last few weeks. Much had changed since Peter surfaced from the coma. When his eyes fluttered open, she'd been so happy. Living together in their new home with her mum and new dad, she'd shared the newly married couple's bliss.

But the paradise wasn't to last. Things turned sour the moment Andrew arrived. She'd always known Peter would find a boyfriend, but when a boy did turn up, it wasn't like she'd imagined. Instead of becoming Peter's confidante, she'd been shoved aside by the boys.

Then there was Bonnie. What annoyed her most was she had suggested Peter and Andrew dress as girls. Little had she thought that, in so doing, Peter would get between her and one of the most delicious girls she had ever set her eyes on. Life really wasn't fair. As a consolation, she let her mind drift, dreaming of the delicious moments she'd spend with Bonnie once she was hers.

The warm hands that clasped tightly over her eyes from behind fit perfectly in her reverie. It was only when Bonnie exclaimed, "I knew you'd come," that she realised this was for real. The girl turned Fi's head towards her and planted a butterscotch kiss on Fi's lips. Fi, who wondered if she might still be daydreaming, responded with all the passion she could muster.

"You kiss like an angel," Bonnie said breathless as she finally opened her eyes. It was then that she screamed only to stop almost immediately. Glancing nervously around, she grabbed Fi's hand and dragged her along the beach.

"Who are you?" Bonnie asked once they were behind a disused shed, out of sight and earshot of the village.

The moment Fi had been dreading had come. Why couldn't they just kiss? Wasn't that enough? She licked her lips, savoring the lingering taste of butterscotch. How could she possibly explain, sworn as she was to secrecy?

"You look very much like that boy hanging around Wendy. Are you his sister?"

"That was no boy," Fi admitted. "It was me dressed up."

Fi had no idea how the girl would react. Disappointment? Shock? Anger? Disgust? Anything was possible. Hadn't Dr Grant said people could get very upset if you tricked them about your gender?

What actually happened caught her completely off guard. Bonnie flung her arms around Fi's neck and kissed her passionately. Fi had kissed a number of girls in her life, but only after cautious and often long and tortuous preliminaries. To kiss a girl she hardly knew with such a frank lack of inhibition, surprised and almost shocked her.

"Who cares?" the girl said when they paused for a breath. "We've found each other now. That's all that matters."

Fi had got what she wanted, her heart was beating wildly to prove it and her legs had gone shaky at the knees, but instead of being delighted she was wary. What had the girl meant by "who cares"? Would any girl do?

As if to confirm Fi's suspicions, Bonnie said, "I've been cooped up here for ages with not the slightest girl in sight. Imagine my relief when I saw you folk arrive."

Freeing herself from Bonnie's clutches, Fi leaned against the shed, looking intently at the waves as if they were the only thing that mattered. Out of the corner of her eye she could see Bonnie pouting. "Where do you normally live?"

"I live with my grandparents," Bonnie replied, reaching out to take Fi's hand. Fi shifted further along the wall, purposefully placing both hands behind her back. Undeterred, Bonnie changed tactics and snuggled her head on Fi's shoulder, her words coming as tiny wisps of warm breath on Fi's neck. "They have a house inland, that's where I go to school, but they insist on coming to this fish-ridden hole each summer. It's a tradition: they replace the baker during the holiday season. They are very easy-going and don't care what I do, but this village is torture." Bonnie planted a kiss on Fi's neck, sending shivers down her spine. Then the girl set about nibbling Fi's earlobe.

"Surely there are other girls here," Fi retorted, stepping away to prevent Bonnie devouring her.

"Not real girls, not like you and me."

Fi wondered why the girl avoided naming what they were. She had a mischievous desire to force her to say the word. "You mean girls who prefer other girls."

"You know what I mean."

"I'm not sure I do. What other girls are there than us."

"I'll show you," Bonnie said grabbing Fi by the hand and pulling her towards the village.

Fi dug her heals in, refusing to be dragged like a puppy. She might prefer girls, but she also knew that caution was needed. Walking hand in hand through the village was asking for trouble. "Where are you taking me?" she asked, shaking her hand free.

"Into town."

"But that's miles away," Fi said, shocked. She knew she could be wild and reckless, but the idea of heading for town so late on a Sunday afternoon was too much.

"There's a bus in a short while," Bonnie explained, as if it's existence made everything OK.

Fi had visions of being stranded for the night in some provincial town with bands of yobs loafing in the streets. "How do we get back?"

"Don't worry about that. It's easy to hitch."

Fi snorted in disbelief. Cars rarely drove into the village, especially at night. They'd deliberately chosen Lettup because it was secluded.

Bonnie tugged at Fi's arm again. "If you don't hurry we'll miss the bus."

"Listen, Bonnie," Fi said. "Kissing you was really great. I enjoyed it. But I hardly know you and I'm not running away with someone I don't know."

"But we're not running away," Bonnie exclaimed, exasperated. She constantly glanced towards the village. And, sure enough, a single-decker green bus came rattling down the road between the cliffs. The driver honked his horn at the entrance to Lettup, as if to wake the inhabitants.

"Come on," the girl urged, getting desperate as she tried to snag Fi's sleeve and drag her towards the square.

"Bonnie!" Fi said, her tone sharper than she'd intended. "I'm not going into town this late. Your grandparents will be worried and my mother will be expecting me back."

The girl stamped her foot. "You're so selfish," she said, tears of fury springing to her eyes causing dark rivulets of makeup to course down her pretty cheeks. "You're spoiling everything." In her despair, she raked her fingers through her hair, pulling at the strands till she looked like a savage.

Fi produced a handkerchief from her pocket, intending to wipe the smudged makeup, but Bonnie brushed her hand aside.

"We can go another time," Fi said, trying to be conciliatory.

"It's now that counts," Bonnie said, her words almost lost in her sobs. Then she turned and stomped off.

Fi was tempted to hurry after her and reason with the girl. But she stayed put. Why should she fix things? The girl was a complete stranger. What's more, she was visibly not right in the head. Ok. They'd tongue-kissed several times. Her stomach fluttered at the memory. But what did that prove? The cold detachment she felt alarmed her. Had she become so hard-hearted? She set off aiming to catch up with Bonnie, but the girl was nowhere to be seen.

In the distance, the bus was struggling up the steep incline out of Lettup, looking as empty as when it had arrived. Fi hurried to the bakery and knocked at the door. After a considerable wait, an old woman in a long white apron opened. "Yes?" she asked, wiping her floury hands on her apron.

"Is Bonnie at home?"

"No, love. She went for a walk down by the beach. Do you want to leave a message?"

Fi shook her head.

"You're one of those new girls in the house at the entrance to the village."

Fi nodded.

"It's really nice of you to call. Bonnie gets so lonely. I'll tell her to drop by when she returns."

"Thanks," Fi said and took her leave.

Back at the house, Fi hastily changed out of Peter's dress and, forcing herself to be tidy for once, hung it up in the wardrobe so no one would know. She'd just donned her trousers and shirt when she heard the front door open. The boys were chatting enthusiastically about what had happened.

"He was right," Peter was saying. "I was terrified."

"The way your voice squeaked and squawked, you sounded like a trapped bird," Andrew replied.

"I don't know about you," Peter said as they headed for the bedroom where Fi waited for them, "but I will be glad to put on a dress. This skirt is too tight."

The two abruptly stopped their giggling the moment they saw Fi lying on Peter's bed.

"So did the Doctor work a miracle and give you a new voice?" she asked.

"That's going to take time," Peter told her, unbuttoning his blouse.

Andrew left to change in the bathroom, but Fi stayed put. Getting to her feet she helped Peter out of his blouse, tossing it onto the bed and, when he struggled to get off his tight skirt, she gave him a hand.

Her encounter with Bonnie had left her confused and uncertain. The sight of Peter naked but for the white pants and bra, had her stomach fluttering anew. The Doctor might have worked on Peter's voice, but Bonnie had worked on Fi's emotions. Never before had she desired Peter as she did then.

She ran her fingers through Peter's hair, which was now shoulder length, and leant forward to kiss him gently on the lips. When he looked at her questioningly, she kissed him a second time, no less gently than the first. She didn't want to slobber all over him, as Bonnie had done with her. He seemed to appreciate her restraint, because she felt him relax. When he sighed, she pulled back and looked at him, saying, "We haven't kissed in ages."

"No, we haven't," he said and returned her kiss, more confident and less hesitant than she'd been.

Their kisses were interrupted by hammering at the front door. Fi helped Peter into a dress, the same one she had been wearing that afternoon. "That's odd," Peter said, sniffing the collar, "I never use perfume."

Oups! Fi thought, feigning surprise .

Luckily Peter was distracted by the knocking. "Come on," he said. "Who could that be?"

Fi was in no hurry to find out. She was afraid it might be Bonnie come to make a scene. But she was wrong. It was Bonnie's grandmother.

Seeing Peter, she immediately addressed him, presumably thinking it'd been him that had called earlier. "I can't find Bonnie anywhere," she said, distressed. "Then John at the pub told me he saw her climb aboard the bus for Bargeton. Do you know where she's gone?"

Peter looked perplexed and was about to say something when Fi stepped in.

"It was I that called earlier," she told Bonnie grandmother. "I borrowed Wendy's dress."

Both Peter and Andrew shot Fi a warning look.

"Bonnie wanted me to go with her to town," Fi explained. "But I told her I couldn't. I suggested we go another time, but she insisted and got upset."

"She's a fragile girl," Bonnie's gran said, wringing her hands. "Her doctor warned her not to do anything impetuous. That's why she has the pills, but she hasn't taken them today. I checked."

Christina arrived at that moment. "What can we do for you?" she asked.

"Help me, please," Bonnie's gran pleaded, clinging to Christina's sleeve. "Bonnie's run away. My husband has a bad back and our van has broken down. She'll listen to your girls. They'll persuade her to come back."

14.

An eerie, unsteady light approached their tiny cell, casting long, dancing shadows on the walls. Kate and Tania huddled under several blankets. Being found in Tania's cell had seemed better than sneaking out and getting caught elsewhere.

"What are you doing here?" the nun shouted, grasping Kate's shoulder in an iron fist, wrenching her to her feet and flattening her against the wall.

Kate heard the sister's words for the first time through Tania's mind. How nasal and unpleasant her voice was. The nun raised her free hand to strike Kate but Tania jumped to her feet and barrelled into the woman, shoving her outside the cell.

"Whip me again if you will, but I won't let you hurt my friend," Tania said, drawing her slender frame up to its full height. "Look what Our Lady thinks of your whippings," she exclaimed and let the blanket fall from her shoulders revealing the smooth skin of her healed back.

The nun gasped and took a step back, brandishing the cross than hung from her rosary. "This is Satan's work."

I told you she'd think it was the Devil, Kate said mind-to-mind.

"You are mistaken," Tania said, putting her hands on her slender hips. "If Satan did anything, it was the whipping. Our Lady in all her bounty did the healing."

The nun roared in fury, looking around for something to beat the girls with.

"What's going on here?" a voice called out from the dark.

Intent on rummaging through nearby shelves, the sister paid no heed to the voice. Finding a wooden axe handle, she brandished it at the girls.

Luckily the new arrival, still concealed in the shadows, banged on the wooden walls to get Sister Helga's attention. When the person finally stepped into the light, Kate was dismayed to recognised the Abbess.

"What's going on here?"

The woman was gifted with contradictory features making her hard to fathom. Her surprisingly fleshy, almost sensuous lips contrasted violently with her thin, sharp, accusing nose. Her forehead rose high, promising intelligence and insight above dark brown eyes that were dull and hooded.

"These girls have consorted with the devil," Helga replied, her features twisted in hate.

"How so?" the Abbess asked mildly, staring unseeingly at Kate.

The nun hesitated. Could she be afraid to admit she'd whipped the girl?

Tania was on the verge of spilling the beans, but Kate stopped her. *Let her wriggle out of this on her own*, she said mind-to-mind.

"Her back was bloody from a whipping," the nun told the Abbess. "It couldn't possibly have healed so quickly."

"Who did the whipping?"

"I did, Reverend Mother," Sister Helga admitted, shifting uncharacteristically from one foot to another. "She was foul mouthed and disrespectful."

"If her back is anything to go by," the Abbess said as if commenting the weather, "it looks like she has been pardoned." To Kate she added, "As for this one, a stay in a cell will do her good." For a brief moment, the mask that habitually shroud the Abbess's eyes fell, revealing a sharp look that sized Kate up.

Tania wanted to speak in favour of Kate, but Kate advised against it. *I look forward to enjoying some quiet*, Kate said, grinning mentally at her little joke. *I will try to keep in contact, at a distance.*

Tania got to her feet and followed the Abbess while Sister Helga, seeing the Reverend Mother had her back turned, shoved Kate causing her bad leg to give way, toppling her onto the floor. With a self-satisfied smile, the nun locked the door.

As the girl and nuns moved away, sound faded as did the light. Kate sat, shroud in silence, rubbing her leg. When she had no success alleviating the pain, she turned her mind elsewhere. Now that she was aware of the flavour of Tania's thoughts, it should be easy to reach her. Searching still took a while till she located Tania in the classroom with the other girls.

Voices wafted into her head over a background of noise and movement. Tania was telling Eileen, Christine and Suzanne about finding Kate in her cell and how she'd been healed. She even pulled aside her dress to show them. Thank heavens she didn't tell them what really happened. She waited till Tania finished, not wanting to startle her, then whispered, *Don't overdo it, that might get you into trouble. Sister Helga may have spies.*

Despite her precautions, Tania jumped, but no one noticed. Kate could hear them excitedly chatting about Tania's miracle.

You managed, Tania exclaimed.

Yes. I'm glad I did, but now I will withdraw and stay quiet. I don't want to disturb.

You won't disturb me, Tania thought, her feelings a muddle of pleasure and relief and yearning.

The girl had been lonely too long, an idea that Kate kept to herself. *OK*, Kate thought. *But I need time to think. Let's talk again when class is over.*

She should teach Tania to contact her, just in case, but that would have to wait till they were together.

Fortunately, Sister Helga had not confiscated the covers. Hidden under one was a small stock of food stolen from the kitchen. Kate scooped a handful of oats into a bowl, added a few raisins and poured water over the lot, then she let it stand till the oats had soaked up most of the water. The mushy mixture tasted good and she ate hungrily.

Wrapping several blankets around herself, she slid to the floor, her back wedged in one corner of the cell. The effort made her wince, her injured leg still throbbing from her fall. Yes! Healing herself would be her next challenge. She'd been able to heal her mouth but only by chance. Before she'd always relied on Peter when she needed healing.

Oh Peter, she thought, *I miss you*.

She remembered that time she'd been imprisoned and he'd accompanied her, in spirit at least. She missed their conversations. She missed his presence. She shook her head. Pointless dwelling on that. She closed her eyes and went in search of her inner garden.

A cacophony of voices drove her from sleep, leaving her confused and disoriented. Had she inadvertently cured her deafness? Reaching out, she felt the presence of Tania. She must have connected with her during her sleep. To her great disappointment, she was still stone deaf. Kate's hand went to her leg, hopeful her efforts had succeeded there at least, but it was as twisted and painful as ever.

The light of a lamp slanting between the ill-fitting wooden slats warned Kate that someone was approaching. Hiding what remained of her food, she braced herself, fearing it would be Helga.

To her relief it was Sister Teresa. The nun helped her to her feet and beckoned her to follow. When she entered the refectory, she couldn't help noticing the filthy look Sister Helga gave them both.

Sister Teresa motioned Kate to fetch something to eat, which she did willingly. When she pulled out her writing pad to say thank you, the nun took it and wrote: after lunch, come with me to the herb garden.

Kate went to sit with Tania, Eileen and Christine. Suzanne had already left. They welcomed her as a long lost friend. Tania's story had had its effect. Kate showed Tania Sister Teresa's note, keeping up the pretence they couldn't communicate otherwise.

It's cold out there, Tania wrote, a worried look on her face.

Are there no shoes and coats? Kate wrote.

Not for us, was all Tania replied.

Can any of the girls sew? Kate asked Tania.

Several can. Why do you ask?

We could make cloaks and slippers to keep us warm. And underpants too, Kate added as an afterthought, feeling the cold of the bench sting her backside. It was a wonder the girls didn't suffer from cystitis.

But we have no cloth.

There are tons of old blankets in the store, Kate pointed out. *They'd make excellent cloaks.*

The nuns would never let us.

Their conversation was interrupted when Sister Teresa came to fetch her. Access to the herb garden was via the kitchens. Kate stopped the Sister at the door, pointing to her feet then rubbing her hands together. When the nun looked back blankly, Kate pulled out her notepad and wrote: I need shoes and a coat. I'll get ill out there. Understanding, the nun pointed to an old pair of clogs by the door and then went to fetch a blanket from the storeroom.

The path to the herb garden meandered through flowerbeds below the refectory windows. She spotted Suzanne on her knees pulling up weeds. Surely she worked with the Abbess, not in the gardens. Her hands were blue and she trembled from the cold. Unlike Kate she had no blanket to protect her. Kate pulled off hers and draped it round Suzanne's shoulders, much to the girl's surprise.

In that brief touch she felt a rush of gratitude and affection and she caught smatterings of Suzanne's muddled thoughts. Apparently, she'd long been the Abbess's maid. For some reason she was now in disgrace. That Kate had unwittingly established a mental contact with the girl became apparent when she heard the roar of Sister Helga.

"Stop distracting that girl," the tall nun shouted as she strode towards them between the flower beds. "She's got work to do." The moment she arrived, Helga ripped the blanket from the

Suzanne's shoulders and flung it away across the garden.

Kate negotiated her way gingerly between the flowers to fetch the blanket. Both nuns watched her intently, no doubt wondering what she'd do. Kate bent down with some difficulty and picked up the blanket, brushing off the leaves that clung to it. Nearby lay a pretty rose that had dried in the none-too-warm summer sun. Returning to Suzanne, she handed the flower to Sister Helga and draped the blanket around the little girl's shoulders then hurried after Sister Teresa.

The nun patted Kate affectionately on the shoulder. Once again, in that contact Kate felt a swirl of emotions: approval for Kate mixed with intense disapproval of Sister Helga. Judging from the fragments of thoughts that reached her, Helga had a long-standing reputation for mistreating girls.

As they skirted a two-storey building, Sister Teresa used Kate's notebook to explain it housed the nuns' dormitory, washrooms and a parlour. The herb garden lay some distance away, bordering a low stone building which turned out to be the infirmary. It crouched beneath the massive wall that surrounded the gardens and boxed in a large part of the convent. Escaping would not be so easy.

Only part of the garden was used for herbs. There were also vegetables and fruit trees. The herb garden was surprisingly well tended, with many plants that Kate recognised and a lot she didn't. Sister Teresa set her weeding then entered the infirmary only to return bearing a rough coat. Despite its ragged appearance, it shielded Kate well from the cold for which she was grateful.

Kate began weeding, guessing it was a test. Would she pull up medicinal plants by mistake? Whenever in doubt she asked the Sister and had her write down the name of the plant. They worked side-by-side in companionable silence for a long moment, then gathered sage which was to hang to dry in the infirmary.

The distinct smell of cleanliness and the subtle mixture of herbs and chemicals in the infirmary, caught Kate off guard. It was in just such a place she'd worked with her father, so many good moments spent learning all he knew about remedies. She tried to conceal the tears that streamed down her cheeks, but the nun noticed and asked her why she cried.

I worked in such a place with my father, she wrote. He taught me about herbal remedies and healing. Now he's dead.

The Sister patted Kate on the shoulder almost affectionately then taking her notebook she wrote: One of the sisters has bronchitis, what would you give her?

Kate immediately thought of mullein, like a long finger pointing at the sky thick with tiny yellow flowers, but it would not yet have flowered. She searched through the sprigs of flowers hanging drying from the storeroom roof, but found none. So she wrote mullein on her notepad.

Good! the Sister replied and pulled out a jar of dried yellow flowers that had been concealed behind several other jars.

During the rest of the afternoon Sister Teresa quizzed Kate about remedies for the illness and ailments that troubled nuns and orphans alike. The more Kate showed, the more the nun expressed her delight. Several times Kate startled her with remedies she'd never heard of. When Kate wanted to describe plants that Sister Teresa didn't know, she sketched them. After a while the work bench was littered with sketches and notes about remedies.

You'll have to write them down and illustrate your work in a book, the nun wrote.

The idea appealed to Kate, but she had other priorities.

When the bell rang for vespers, Kate had one more thing to do. She'd used her new-found ability to sound out Teresa's thoughts and was encouraged by a strong conviction that Teresa would agree to her idea. She wrote on her notepad: Will you help us make cloaks? We need warmer clothes. We could use blankets from the storeroom and we could make them in class

The nun hesitated a long moment before writing, I'll ask the Abbess.

15.

Vespers was interminable. For the first time Kate heard the dreary singing of the nuns and girls. Most girls mumbled hymns and psalms off-key without the slightest enthusiasm. No wonder the few local people present fell asleep. It was hard to believe the girls couldn't sing better. Kate wondered if the nuns, busy accompanying the priest celebrating vespers on the other side of the Rood screen, were aware of this musical defiance.

Having trudged to the refectory, the meal was subdued, crowned by a particularly bland cabbage and potato soup. The girls talked little. The younger ones laid their heads next to their bowls and dozed. Kate too was exhausted.

Once the girls had put away their bowls and spoons, it was Sister Teresa and not Sister Helga that accompanied them. She led them to the classroom rather than up to their bedroom, provoking a stir of murmurs. On a normal evening, the girls spent the last hour and a half before lights out in their room, chatting or lounging about. Those who couldn't resist sleep curled up on their beds and closed their eyes. The prospect of more boring school had many girls muttering as they yawned and dragged their feet.

Kate's leg continued to hurt as she limped behind the others, accompanied only by Tania. The last to enter the classroom, she closed the door and went with Tania to join Eileen, Christine and Suzanne. Kate expected Sister Teresa to give an explanation. Instead, smiling, she beckoned Kate to join her. The little woman looked unusually flushed as she smiled at Kate.

Judging from the snatches of confused thoughts that reached her, the nun had had a heated conversation with the Abbess and Sister Helga. Kate guessed it must have been about making cloaks, but her sporadic connection made it impossible to know what the outcome had been.

Kate readied her notepad but the Sister indicated she should put it away. She beckoned Kate to follow and left the room. Kate turned and shrugged her shoulders at Tania and the others. The ginger haired girl, whose name she'd learnt was Jane, gave her a disgusted look as Kate hurried after the nun to the storerooms. Once inside, the nun handed Kate a pile of blankets and disappeared behind an immense pile herself.

Back in the classroom, seeing Sister Teresa and Kate arrive, Eileen had the girls push several tables together on which they piled up the blankets in precarious heaps. All the girls gathered round, clearly intrigued by this break in routine.

"Kate here," Sister Teresa said, motioning to Kate, "suggested you make cloaks to keep warm. I have asked the Abbess and she has agreed." Amongst the ill-defined thoughts Kate captured from the nun, she clearly perceived Sister Helga violently opposing the idea. "A sinful waste of time and money, you should be ashamed of yourself!" the nun had said. Sister Teresa had been cowered by the woman's violent outburst, but, much to her surprise, the Abbess had supported the idea.

Cheers broke out and a wave of friendly warmth flooded over her. It was as if she were connected to the whole class, emotionally at least. She was glad her ability did not extend to thoughts, or at least only sporadically, because she'd have drowned in the random thoughts of such an unruly mass. As it was, the sea of emotions buoyed her up and left her feeling light-headed.

Having announced what they'd do, Sister Teresa seemed at a loss how to go on. She stood, leaning with one hand on the table, staring blankly at the pile of blankets. Her indecision was catching. The excitement that had roused the sleepy group tailed off and restlessness rapidly set in closely followed by resignation and drowsiness.

Have you got a tape measure? Kate wrote for the nun. The woman, visibly relieved to be told what to do, went in search of one in her desk. Kate picked up a sheet of paper and pencil and, carrying the tape measure, she went to Eileen. A few scribbled words on her notebook were enough for Eileen to understand.

Eileen enlisted Christine's help, making the girl stand up straight while she measured the length from her neck to just below her knees and the distance from shoulder to shoulder. Eileen then drew three columns on the paper and wrote 'name' at the top of one, 'length' at the top of the second and 'shoulders' at the top of the third. Under length and shoulders she wrote the measurements and added 'Christine' in the other column.

Handing the tape-measure, paper and pencil to Christine, Eileen grinned at her then stood up straight so the girl could measure her. While Christine wrote the figures down, Eileen marshalled the rest of the girls into an orderly line and began taking their measurements with a flourish, calling them out to Christine who promptly noted them.

Which of the girls can sew? Kate asked Tania, mind-to-mind, once they'd both been measured.

Tania pointed to a short, mousy-looking girl, saying, *that's Claudia.*

When Kate approached, the girl looked alarmed and took a step back, her eyes darting round in a desperate search for an escape. Judging from the bruises on her neck, arms and legs, the girl had had more than her share of ill treatment.

As Kate lay a hand lightly on Claudia's arm, an onslaught of images rammed into her mind sending her reeling. Whippings, beatings and far worse flashed by, all carried out with calculated cruelty on a regular basis. Kate felt her stomach lurch. When she caught sight of Sister Helga, a long cane in hand, licking her lips in anticipation, Kate's knees gave way. Only Tania's timely action stopped her from crumbling to the floor.

Christine halted her measuring and rushed to Kate's side. "What's the matter?" the girl asked, her face pinched in concern.

Taking a deep breath to steady herself, Kate shook her head and tried weakly to smile. Christine still looked worried. *Tell her I'm OK,* she thought to Tania. *I had a shock, but everything will be alright.*

As Tania talked quietly to Christine, Kate got up her courage to look Claudia in her dark brown eyes. Beyond the pain, she saw distress and chronic loneliness. She saw intense wariness and distrust, but she saw no anger or hate. Kate's heart almost burst with compassion and affection for the girl.

She opened her arms and, when Claudia came to her, she closed them softly around her. The girl stood unyielding in her embrace, every muscle taut, ready to flee. Kate took long, deep breaths and waited, unmoving, struggling not to become tense herself. Finally, a succession of violent shudders rippled through Claudia's body and a sob burst from her lips. Kate cradled her gently feeling the girl's knot of tension cautiously unravel until she gave out an immense sigh of relief.

It's going to be alright, she whispered into Claudia's mind. *We'll protect you.*

At the sound of Kate's voice the girl's body became rigid again. *Don't worry,* Kate tried to reassure her, *it is only me. I can talk to you in thoughts. It's a gift I have. You will be able to do the same. I'll teach you. If ever you're in danger, you'll be able to call me.*

Looking up, Kate realised that all movement had ceased and everyone was watching them. There was both understanding and compassion in the eyes of the girls. They'd known, of course, but what could they do? Taking Claudia by the hand, Kate led her to Tania who hugged her. Others came forward and did the same, many with tears in their eyes, till there was a huddle of bodies with Claudia at its centre.

Someone, Kate didn't know who, began singing a lullaby softly in a lilting, soprano. It was taken up by the others, little by little, until all were singing but Kate. She couldn't help herself, the moment was too strong, she joined them singing the words softly in their heads. If anybody noticed or was startled, no one said.

When the song came to an end, the girls looked surprised at what they'd done. Fragments of their thoughts reached Kate: joy at singing, pleasure at being together, a feeling of strength, a sense of direction, love and affection, resolve,… and apprehension about the future

Standing at her desk, some distance away, staring out of the window at the mountains, Sister Teresa cut a sad figure. A lost girl, Kate thought, untethered and rudderless, excluded as she was from the strong bond that bound the girls together. Kate wanted to hug her, to prevent her from drifting away, but first she had to deal with Claudia.

You know how to sew, Tania tells me, she spoke in Claudia's mind. Sensing the girl's perplexity, Kate added: *Just think your answer and I will hear.*

Yes. I love sewing, the girl thought, her words coloured by pride and joy and sadness. *But I get so little chance.*

Can you make patterns for cloaks or capes for the girls? We'll use the blankets.

We'll need sharp scissors, a needle and some thread as well as at least one button per cape, the girl thought, enthusiasm getting her in its grip.

Ask Eileen. She'll help, Kate told her. Then giving Claudia a final hug she left the girl to cope with finding material for the patterns.

Kate turned to look for Sister Teresa. The nun was leaning on the windowsill, staring out at the fiery sunset that had the distant mountains aflame. Different shades of yellow, orange and red were reflected in the pale light of the nun's face, accentuating the impression of feverishness that Kate had noticed earlier.

Instinctively, Kate leaned forward to place a comforting hand on Sister Teresa's forearm, but she stopped short. Didn't nuns shun physical contact, Sister Teresa in particular? Instead she tugged at her sleeve to get her attention. The nun turned reluctantly, her eyes bright with unshed tears. Kate wondered if the woman really saw her, she seemed so distant and unapproachable.

A few minutes more and Kate had the impression the woman would be lost for ever. To hell with caution, taking the nun's paunchy hand, rough with work in the gardens, she was surprised to find it trembling. Far more startling was the mass of images that elbowed their way into her mind. Teresa's childhood, Kate guessed. A stern nun, hand raised to strike young Teresa. The girl flinching unable to avoid the blow that smashed her to the ground. Blood spurting from her nose as it hit the stone floor. A second blow breaking her arm, leaving her whimpering in a heap at the nun's feet. Had she not rolled over, she would probably have had broken ribs from a vicious kick.

Kate could stand it no more, she closed her mind to the onslaught and took the nun in her arms. Bereft of any will of her own, Teresa let herself be hugged and hung her head on Kate's shoulder, sobbing softly. Although Kate knew she was doing the right thing, the situation felt wrong. Who was the child? Who was the adult?

Come! Kate called softly to the girls. *Sister Teresa needs us.*

They came, even with her eyes closed she felt them, like a warm presence engulfing her. They formed a tight circle around the nun but, whether out of respect or fear, none came any closer. *She's a lost girl, just like us,* Kate told them. *As a child, she suffered as much if not more than us and her suffering continues even today.*

"Should we sing for her?" a girl called Clara asked. Judging from the jumble of thoughts that accompanied her words, she was the one who'd started them singing earlier. *Yes Clara, that would be lovely.*

Clara hummed the opening bars of another lullaby. The girls recognised it and hummed along. Then Clara began singing, her beautiful voice soaring high above those of the girls.

By the time the music was over Sister Teresa had stopped sobbing and stared in wonder at the girls grouped around her. "Thank you," she said, her voice trembling with emotion.

A violent crash had all heads turning in alarm to the entrance.

There, framed in the doorway, stood Sister Helga, her hands on her hips, her lips twisted in a snarl. At her side stood Jane. Instinctively the girls shifted away from Kate and Sister Teresa.

"What are you doing here?" Helga asked, her tone deceptively quiet, but deeply menacing. "You should be in bed. You too Sister Teresa."

The sight of Teresa looking completely deflated, her head bowed in shame, infuriated Kate. An idea surged in her mind. Yes! That would right the situation. She didn't care if it caused trouble. Peter had called it 'the voice of god'.

You will cease tormenting Sister Teresa and these girls, she spoke with grave authority into Sister Helga's head, her anger giving her the force to do what she had thought was no longer possible. *If you lay a finger on any of these girls or the sister, if you even so much as upset them, I will know and you will be punished severely.*

Suspended a moment in disbelief, Helga turned pale, her mouth falling open in shock, then she screamed and ran off, her robes trailing behind her like a haunting shadow, into the darkened cloister. Abandoned, Jane did her best to slink in unnoticed.

16.

Sister Teresa crumbled to the floor with a stifled gasp and lay unmoving at Kate's feet. She looked so small and insignificant as if the substance had been sucked out of her. Kate wondered if the shock of Sister Helga's dramatic sally had finished her off.

She was alone in noticing Sister Teresa's collapse. All the girls were so taken by Sister Helga's behaviour. "She's mad," one girl said. "She was pretending, to catch us out," a more cautious girl suggested. It was Christine that spotted Sister Teresa first and hurried to see what was wrong. As Christine and Eileen drew closer, other girls followed, little by little, until all were grouped in silence around the prostrate woman.

"Is she dead?" Jane asked, a look of satisfaction on her face. The girl's callousness shocked Kate. Did it not matter that this woman, who had so bravely tried to ward off abuse and violence and protect them, had possibly died?

Eileen can you get the girls to stand back, Kate asked mind-to-mind. *I need room to examine her.*

Talking to Eileen that way was risky, but the situation was urgent. In the heat of the moment, it was possible the girl hadn't noticed Kate's voice was only in her head, but if she had, she took it all in her stride.

Eileen was older and bigger and had been there much longer than her. She could easily have challenged Kate. After all, how could she possibly know the extent of Kate's knowledge about healing. But Eileen clearly trusted her and set to work marshalling the girls, co-opting Tania, Suzanne and Christine to put the younger ones to bed.

"Someone had better stay with them," Christine suggested. Turning to Claudia who had finished a rough pattern for the capes, and Clara, the singer, she asked: "Will you?" When they agreed, Christine continued. "The kids'll be upset. Try to reassure them."

Seeing that Eileen and Christine were handling things, Kate turned to Sister Teresa. Fears that the woman was dead were far-fetched. She was clearly breathing, albeit shallowly.

Kneeling next to her, Kate tired to straighten the woman's legs and arms, but it was not so easy. Tania, who returned at that moment, lent her a helping hand. Kate spread a blanket over the nun. Laying a cautious hand on the woman's forehead, she realised the nun was running a temperature. Tiny red spots had erupted across Teresa's face and arms.

If the woman had a contagious disease, their touching her could be a problem. *We need to get her to the infirmary*, she thought to Tania.

I'll ask the others to help, Tania replied.

No, Kate insisted. *Let's avoid them coming too close. If it's catching, we should limit how many are in contact with her.*

A wave of worried thoughts tumbled through Tania's head as she scuttled back. *You could've warned me,* she exclaimed, her thoughts razor-sharp.

I'm sorry. I didn't know. The fever tipped me off. We can protect ourselves, but first we need to get her out of here.

A noise at the door had both girls look up. There in the opening stood the Abbess and beyond her, hanging back were Eileen, Christine and Suzanne.

"What's going on here?" the Abbess asked.

"Sister Teresa collapsed," Tania replied, getting to her feet. "Kate thinks it might be contagious. You should keep back."

"What makes her think that?"

Tania looked questioningly at Kate.

The fever, Kate said, *and those little red blotches.*

"She's all hot," Tania said, "and she's covered in spots."

I think it is Chicken Pox, Kate thought.

When Tania told the Abbess, the woman looked grim. "Or something worse,…" she muttered. Turning to the girls behind her she shooed them away. "Go up to the dormitory. No. Wait. Christine and Eileen, go to the infirmary and fetch a stretcher." She pulled out a bunch of keys and removing one, handed it to Eileen. "Bring the stretcher here, but keep your distance." She nodded at Kate, Tania and Sister Teresa.

"It's dark outside," Eileen pointed out.

"Take a lantern from the kitchen."

As the two hurried away, Kate listed other things they'd need.

"Kate says we'll need oats, honey, carrots and garlic and a number of herbs."

"How does she know all these things?" the Abbess asked, sceptical.

"She's good at herbal remedies," Tania said, struggling to find arguments. Seeing that the Abbess still didn't believe her, she added: "It was Kate that healed my back."

The Abbess looked like she was about to say something, but stopped and shook her head. "Get the key from Eileen and Christine and have them fetch what you need from the kitchen and the stores when they return." She paused a moment staring at Kate. "But be warned girl, if you're having us on, you'll be in serious trouble."

She was about to leave when Sister Helga ran up. "What have they done to Sister Teresa?" the nun asked, pushing past the Abbess into the room.

"I wouldn't go any closer Sister, if I were you," the Abbess remarked dryly. "They are probably contagious."

The nun stopped abruptly in her tracks, fear and disgust battling to get control. In a rare moment of hesitation, she looked from the girls to the Abbess and back.

"Come with me, Sister Helga. We have to discuss what to do with the other girls. These two can take care of Sister Teresa." The Abbess left with Sister Helga stomping after her.

I hope they don't hurt the girls, Tania thought.

It's a worry, Kate thought. *Helga is capable of anything. I'll teach Christine and Eileen to speak mind-to-mind so they can keep us informed.*

But what can we do against the nuns? Tania asked. *They've been hurting us for years and no one ever ventured to stop them.*

Don't worry, Kate thought, chuckling mentally as she remember the nun's terror. *I have a couple of ideas.*

When Christine and Eileen returned with a stretcher, Kate sent them to fetch what they needed from the kitchen and stores. *Bring the things to the infirmary,* she told Tania, having her relay her words, *but don't come in. Call us from outside.*

She and Tania lowered the stretcher to the floor and rolled the senseless nun onto it. With much grunting and heaving they lifted the nun and carried her out into the night air having negotiated the hazards of the kitchens. As Christine and Eileen had already collected what they needed, the two accompanied them at a distance, lighting their way with a lantern.

It was a moonless night, although the clear sky was ablaze with stars. Whatever the circumstances, she always found the starlit sky profoundly moving. From what she could see, the constellations looked similar to those in Peter's world.

Kate shivered. Shame they didn't have their cloaks.

Once they'd negotiated the gardens and were away from the buildings, Eileen halted, whispering, "How did you do that?"

"What?" Kate asked, guessing what she was referring to.

"Put your voice in my head," Eileen pursued.

"Come off it, Eileen, that's not possible," Christine said.

"Unless she's one of those people who can talk without moving her lips, she sure did."

Eileen is right, Kate said. *I have lost my voice so I can't speak. But I can speak into your heads.*

"But how do you hear our words?" Eileen asked.

I hear them through your thoughts.

"That's extraordinary," Christine said. "I wish I could do that. It could prove useful."

"Typical," Eileen replied, giving Christine a playful shove.

With which both Christine and Eileen turned and continued lighting the way. As easy as that. Kate marvelled at their ability to accept what must appear impossible.

The Abbey was plunged in darkness, but as they rounded the nun's quarters light streamed from the ground floor windows of what Christine called the Chapter House. "That's where the nuns meet," she explained. "They're probably debating what to do with us."

"If Sister Helga has anything to do with their plans, it won't be good," Tania said. Kate could feel they all shared a deep-seated fear of the woman.

"What did the Abbess mean when she said the illness could be worse?" Eileen asked, after a poignant silence. "She sounded frightened."

Kate knew exactly what. She shuddered at the thought. Small pox. Similar in appearances, its impact was far more devastating. God help them if it was small pox. *I don't know,* she thought, not wanting to scare them.

Kate was relieved to reach the infirmary. The nun might have been small, but she was heavy and her leg hurt terribly. *Wait for us,* Kate ordered Eileen and Christine. *We need to talk before you return.*

Pushing open the door, Kate entered the infirmary and freed a hand to search for the light switch. By the dim glimmer of the filament, they continued down a short corridor into the single ward. The room had long been unused. Dust covered the tables by the beds and the air was stuffy and unhealthy. They placed the nun and stretcher temporarily on a table and pulled down the covers and sheets on the nearest bed.

Once Teresa had been rolled into bed, Kate made sure she was tucked in correctly and opened several widows.

Shouldn't she be kept warm? Tania asked.

No, Kate told her. *If she has Chicken Pox, she'll have a temperature and the spots will itch. Keeping the room cool will calm the itching. And anyway, the place needs a good airing.*

With that, Kate and Tania joined the two outside. They had dowsed the light and were leaning against the wall talking quietly.

As I told you, Kate said, *I can talk to you without speaking out loud. I want to teach you to do the same. Tania and I need to know what's happening, especially if Helga is to look after you.*

"It was you, wasn't it?" Eileen said excitedly.

Don't talk out loud, Kate warned. *Someone might hear. Think what you have to say to me.*

Both girls found it difficult. They constantly reverted to speaking out loud as they struggled to send their thoughts to Kate.

Just say the words in your head, Kate advised. *I will hear. What did you mean Eileen, earlier?*

Eileen hesitated, still convinced she wouldn't be able to do it.

It's easier than you think, Tania thought to her.

Eileen's face pinched in grim determination. She wasn't going to let herself be outdone by Tania. *You did something to scare Sister Helga,* she thought, her face lighting up as she realised she'd talked mind-to-mind.

Kate chuckled mentally. *Yes. I spoke into her head. A friend of mine, calls it ...* she was about to say 'the voice of God', but thought better of it. These girls were brought up from a very young age on religious precepts. Goodness only knew how they'd react to Kate pretending to be god. ... *The voice of authority,* she finished.

Whatever it was, Tania put in, *it scared the hell out of the old bag of worms. Serves her right. Is that what you plan to do if she hurts us?*

I told her I would keep an eye on her and if she hurts any of you I'll punish her. Careful, though, she doesn't know it's me. She just hears a deep voice. So keep it to yourself. If she knew, she'd kill me.

The girls were delighted that revenge was within reach and spent a long moment running through ways to get their own back.

Listen, Kate interrupted after a while. *If Helga let's you, you should finish the cloaks. You might even begin on pants. Get Claudia to make patterns. Whatever happens, protect that girl from Helga. The woman has treated her very badly.*

You can't begin to imagine, Christine said, a shudder of disgust and anger rippling through her thoughts. *The old hag had her do things no Christian would ever dream of. I know it is not right to think of revenge, but I can't help wishing we could make her suffer for all she's done to Claudia and the rest of us.*

She's a wicked woman, Eileen added, her thoughts almost a whisper. *How come God watched on so long and didn't punish her.*

Several girls had ideas on the subject. Kate listened to their thoughts in silence. She'd never believed in god. Her people counted on themselves and their limited magic to get things done. That was how she'd been brought up and there was no place for such a force in her life. It must be terrible to depend on a silent, unseen being to get things done. No wonder the girls felt helpless and hopeless. The inability to fend for themselves cultivated by the church had surely been convenient for nuns like Helga.

You should get back, Kate thought, interrupting Tania's tirade about god being unfair. *Keep in contact and let us know what's happening. And be wary of Jane,* she warned, *I don't trust her.*

You're right, Eileen said. *Jane's always been a favourite of the nuns, especially Sister Helga.*

I never could understand why Jane got on so well with the hag, Christine added.

If ever Helga tries to intimidate you or hurts anyone, let me know and I'll have a word with her.

Eileen and Christine giggled.

Keep an eye out for the signs of the illness, loss of appetite, nausea or headaches. Once it sets in there'll be fever and little red spots. Don't panic, with proper treatment the illness can be handled, but let me know immediately you suspect someone is ill. We can move the person here.

The girls said "Good night and God bless" and left.

Now, Kate said to Tania, *we've work to do. We should prepare medicine for Sister Teresa. Her skin is going to itch terribly.* That they would probably suffer the same fate, Kate kept to herself.

17.

Peter sat on the back seat, squashed between Andrew and Fi both of whom stared stubbornly out the window. The two had had a heated argument. Silly really. Andrew snapped at Fi because she'd stained his dress. Fi told him not to be such a sissy. What was wrong with them? Andrew was normally so gentle and Fi uncharacteristically resembled Witless, who hated effeminate boys.

Fi's mum was talking quietly to Bonnie's gran as she drove away from the cliffs and across the moors towards Bargeton, the closest town.

"... So you took her to a specialist?" Christina asked.

"We were at a loss what to do," Bonnie's gran replied, wringing her hands. "She got so upset when girls refused to befriend her. She'd mope around, not talking to us. She'd even refuse to eat."

"Did the consultation help?"

"She was calmer at first, but that may just have been the pills. Unfortunately, they made her sleep a lot, which didn't help. Then she became agitated. Aggressive and demanding, she blamed us for all her problems..."

Peter had heard enough. Finding Bonnie was not going to be easy. He closed his eyes and laid his head on the seat rest not wanting to lean on either Andrew or Fi. The session with Viktor had drained him. The man had him venturing into that no-man's-land in which his voice floundered and made such outrageous croaks and cackles. It'd been a real challenge, although it hadn't seemed physically demanding, but now he was exhausted.

... A dim light flickered in a grey, formless world. As the picture swam into focus, metal-frame beds lurched out of the gloom and congealed into what must be an old-fashioned hospital ward. Several times the scene drifted away then blinked abruptly back into existence. When the picture finally settled, Peter was lying on one of the beds, the starched linen and rough blankets chaffing his skin. Why was he so scantily dressed? The place was bitterly cold.

He counted five other beds but couldn't make out if they were occupied. Then a burst of coughing warned him he was not alone. He tried to see who had coughed, but his head refused to budge. Panic set in as he struggled to get control, to no avail. Then he remembered. The first time he'd been in Kate's head, he'd had the same experience.

Had he inadvertently found Kate? His delight was short-lived. He might have had a vague sense of touch, but couldn't feel the person's body. He could smell disinfectant, but had no other awareness of the person, let alone access to his or her thoughts.

Intuition told him it was a girl. She was probably ill or hurt because pain was coming from her hips or legs or maybe her feet.

A sharp crack had her sit up abruptly and turn to see a tall, stocky, tight-lipped nun, a heavy stick raised in her hand. The girl rolled over and jumped unsteadily to the floor as the stick smashed down on the bed narrowly missing her. Peter jumped too...

"Ouch!" Fi complained, shoving Peter onto Andrew. "Stop that!"

Andrew pushed him back towards Fi. Where they going to shove him backwards and forwards till their bad mood blew itself out?

For a moment, Peter struggled to understand, then he

remembered the nun. "It was Kate," he said, suddenly sure. "I've got to go back. She's in danger." He struggled to get free of Fi and Andrew till he realised where he was. Glancing forward he saw Bonnie's grandmother staring at him, a worried look on her face. "I'm sorry," he said. "Just a bad dream."

"Bonnie has nightmares too," she replied, sadness and resignation in her voice. "The pills make it worse."

It was at times like that Peter regretted loosing the ability to talk mind-to-mind. With Bonnie's gran in the car, he couldn't talk openly to the others. If he'd had a notepad he could have passed them written notes, but he had nothing. *Fi,* he thought, trying all the same. If he could reach Kate, why not Fi?

Yes, he heard a distant voice reply.

"Oh!" he exclaimed, forgetting himself. "It works."

"What works?" Andrew asked perplexed.

Peter put his index finger to his lips, then returned to his experiment. *Can you hear me?*

You sound so far away, she replied.

We need to get Andrew in the loop, Peter thought to her. *Andrew? Can you hear me?*

Judging from the alarmed look on the boy's face, he could.

Don't say anything, Peter thought. *Just think the words and I will hear.*

Andrew tried, but didn't succeed.

Well at least both of you can hear, Peter said. *I'll teach you later, Andrew.*

So what was that about Kate? Fi asked.

In a dream, Peter said. *It was terrible. She was in a hospital bed and a nun tried to kill her. She only narrowly escaped.*

Are you sure it was her? Fi asked.

She felt different and the contact wasn't the same, but I'm sure it was.

Fi was overjoyed, a broad grin stretched across her face, but Andrew looked sad and downtrodden, tears forming in his eyes.

Talk to me, Andrew, Peter insisted. *Whisper the words in your head and we'll hear.*

Tears were now flowing down Andrew's face, smearing the little make-up he had put on. *I'm going to lose you,* his thoughts a distant whisper.

No you're not! Peter insisted. *You're going to get Kate back. Think rather of that.* He cradled Andrew in his arms, planting a kiss on the crown of his head.

There you go, the two of you, Fi complained. *If you're going to be glued together, I'm keeping Kate to myself. Boys! I've had enough of them!*

Boys maybe, Peter said, his thoughts tinged with humour, *but sissy boys, never! How could you possibly get by without us girly boys to look after you, you delicious tomboy?*

Fi must have blushed because Peter could feel it in her thoughts. *Come on silly,* he said, giving her a hug. Unlike Andrew, she didn't cry, but he felt her relax, a bit.

"I hope you three are not getting up to mischief back there," Fi's mum said. "We'll soon be in Bargeton."

"Mischief, us? Never!" Peter said. "We were just making up."

"I'm glad to hear it. I don't like it when you fight."

"Young people are so strange," Bonnie's gran told Christina. "They don't see the world like we do."

If only she knew, Peter said mind-to-mind to the others.

They began their search at the bus station, if you could call it that. It was little more than a few stops one after another along a narrow pavement. There was a small cabin that served as an office cum sales point, just the place they needed, but it had long been closed and was boarded up. A few yards away in a run-down bus shelter a band of youngsters had set up camp. The boys, who were barely older than Fi, were shabbily dressed and looked tough.

Empty beer bottles lay abandoned around the bench on which they lounged. Discarded newspapers, soggy with the recent rain, clung to the broken flagstones and a cloud of cigarette smoke hung sinister over the shoddy shelter. The boys spotted what they took to be a group of girls and rose to greet them with whistles and catcalls.

Trouble, Peter thought mind-to-mind. Fi's mum and Bonnie's gran had gone to find the police station.

Should we run? Andrew asked, clearly scared.

No. That'd only make things worse, Peter said.

I wish Kate were here, Fi said. *She'd deal with them.*

They tried to skirt the group, but the tallest of the boys strode in their direction. "Now there's a tasty sight," he said halting in front of Andrew. "How about a kiss?"

Andrew took a step backwards, petrified. He would have tripped over the curb had Peter not caught his arm.

"No kisses, tonight," Peter said. "We're looking for a friend. Maybe you've seen her."

"Why don't you come and sit on my lap and tell me all about it," the boy answered, leering at Peter.

The rest of the group had joined him forming a tight cordon around the three of them. A dirty looking specimen with greasy hair and a spotty face, grabbed Andrew by the shoulder. Andrew screamed and tried to struggle free, but the boy put his arms around him, blocking his arms as he held on tight. A second boy got to work on Andrew, snaking his hand up his skirt.

Behind him, Peter heard Fi scream. He dared not look because the tall youth was edging closer. *Oh Kate! Wherever you are, we desperately need your help,* he called out. In that fraction of a second the brute was on him, shoving him back against a lamp post as he groped at Peter's chest. The youth stank of beer, cigarette smoke and stale sweat. Peter was afraid the youth would discover he wasn't a girl, god knew what violence that might spark, but flat chests didn't seem to deter him, on the contrary. He pressed with all his force against Peter, trying to wedge a knee between his legs.

As Peter struggled desperately to resist, he abruptly lost control. Someone had taken over his body. His alarm was short-lived. Whoever it was was on his side. Peter's knee jerked up in a sharp blow to the youth's groin. He relinquished his hold and collapsed to the ground, his hands clutching his crotch.

Peter watched as his body spun round, kicking the feet from under an unsuspecting boy who stood nearby, startled to find his friend writhing on the ground. The boy barely had time to cry out as he crashed to the pavement than a swift blow to his head had him out cold.

Two boys were trying to drag Fi backwards towards the shelter. Both had cuts and scratches where Fi had lashed out, but together they were too strong. Rather than attack directly, Peter tapped one on the shoulder. When he spun round, Peter's clenched fist drove upwards hitting the boy in the stomach with all his force. The boy doubled up and let go of Fi.

Making the most of her free arm, Fi swung her hand in a wide arc and slapped the other boy hard on the nose. In the mean time, Peter turned back to the boy he'd punched and gave him a sharp kick just below the knees causing him to crumble gibbering with pain. Fi seemed to be OK, but Peter had no further time for her.

Only two youths remained. They were hurriedly lugging Andrew's limp body across the wasteland behind the bus shelter towards a derelict house.

Follow them, but don't attack, Peter said to whoever was in control. *I need to know where they go.*

The boys were so busy carrying off their prize, they didn't notice Peter, fleet-foot, following them. The three-storey building they were heading for had once been a fine residence, but now its windows were smashed, many of them boarded-up, and the front door, at the top of a short flight of steps, hung precariously from its hinges.

The boys didn't climb the steps, instead they followed an overgrown path round the house and entered by the kitchen door. Making their way cautiously across the glass-littered floor, puffing and panting, they lugged Andrew down a long, dusty corridor and into what must have been an impressive reception room. Peter followed close behind.

The mirror over the fireplace had been smashed, although

shards still hung in place, reflecting fragments of the room in disturbing patterns. Dismembered chairs rose up at all angles and the bookshelf had been overturned onto the dining table scattering books everywhere. The only furniture that remained intact was a shabby canapé. It was there the boys dumped Andrew and began pulling at his dress, no doubt planning to undress him.

Peter made a noise as he entered, causing one of the boys to look up and see him. The boy grinned, baring a set of cigarette-stained teeth, and nudged his colleague, who turned to look. He too grinned.

"Now ain't that a pretty sight," the first boy said, getting to his feet.

Peter wondered how the visitor in his head would handle the two. He didn't have long to wait. He beckoned the two over and, with startlingly rapidity, grabbed their hair and bashed their heads together with a resounding crash. They fell unconscious in a heap at his feet. It was at that moment the person relinquished control and abruptly quit Peter's body without a word, leaving him both exhausted and bereft.

18.

The creek of a floorboard startled Kate from sleep and her troubled dreams about Peter. The moment she awoke, the familiar impenetrable silence engulfed her. In the darkness, it was difficult to know if anyone was there.

A sharp crack resounding in the silence had her sitting bolt upright. Turning to the source of the sound she saw Sister Helga, a raised cudgel in her hand. Kate rolled to the far side of the bed and jumped unsteadily to the floor as the heavy stick crashed down on the bed.

Awoken by the noise, Tania sprang from her bed and came to stand next to Kate, clasping her hand in fear. The Sister raised her heavy stick again and took a step forward till only the bed separated them.

"You horrible little monster!" she spat, her face twisted with rage as her eyes bored into Kate. "I knew you were no good the moment I set eyes on you."

Kate and Tania took a step back, but they were boxed in by the next bed. Kate ripped the sheet from the bed behind her and flicked it forward like a whip against the Sister's face. The woman roared in fury, bringing her stick down on the sheet just as Kate pulled it back. Caught off balance the nun fell onto the bed. Letting go of her stick, she flung her hands out to grab Kate who tumbled backwards onto the next bed. The nun's fingers clawed at Kate's dress trying to stop her escaping. Her nails gouged deep, blood-filled furrows in Kate's thigh.

Tania clawed at the woman's hands with her nails till the

nun let go and Tania was able to help Kate clamber over the bed. Sister Helga floundered, grasping her bloody hands. When she managed to get to her feet, she upturned the bed and clambered over it. The next bed behind Kate and Tania was not empty however for it was there that Sister Teresa lay ill.

Helga grasped the bed between her and the girls and was about to heave it out of the way when a feeble voice asked, "What's going on?" Kate heard it thanks to Tania. It was Teresa. Both Tania and Kate held their ground meaning to stand between Helga and the poorly nun. Uncertain, Helga paused in her onslaught, letting the bed fall back to the floor with a metallic thud.

"Help me up," Teresa insisted, getting shakily to her feet next to the girls.

Kate and Tania held her by the arm to prevent her falling. Kate could feel the nun burning with fever and her habit was damp with sweat.

"What are you doing, Sister Helga?" Teresa asked. "Have you gone mad?"

Sister Helga glared at her. "Don't get in my way, Teresa," she said.

"For the love of God," Teresa pleaded. "These girls are good. Can't you see it?"

"Good? Sure! I see how they've beguiled you. You always were weak and influenceable."

"Don't do this, Sister, I pray you. God is with them," Teresa mumbled, the fever getting the better of her. She would have moved forward had the two not held her back.

"God? The devil, you mean," Helga said and she heaved aside the bed then threw herself at Teresa, closing her chubby hands around the sister's frail neck. Teresa screamed as did the two girls. Both rained blows on Helga's head trying to stop her. When their efforts forced Helga to let go, the ailing nun fell to the floor in a heap. Furious and terrified, Kate played her last card.

Stop! a deep rumbling voice echoed in Helga's head, causing her to abruptly cease throttling Tania. She took a step back, her hands flying to her mouth. *Those hands that killed this woman will be forever cursed,* the voice boomed. *You felt her sweat, her fever and the puss-filled swellings. Her plague is now your plague. Run and hide woman for you are no longer welcome in my house.*

Helga looked at her hands in horror. She looked at the unmoving heap that had once been Teresa and finally she looked at Kate and Tania. Then she turned and, girding up her robes, she fled.

Get a candle, Kate said to Tania and knelt next to Teresa. Poor woman, she may well have been weak, but she'd tirelessly done what little she could to help the girls and in the end she'd stood up for their interests even against the Abbess.

Kate took one of the nun's hands in hers, not bothering about the risk of contagion. She'd seen far too much death. She thought of the friends, relatives and servants who'd accompanied her into the mountains only to be slaughtered before her eyes. She'd even witnessed her own be-heading. She'd had enough.

She lowered her head till it met Teresa's, brow against brow, feeling her last courage ebb away. It was then that a thin stream of desperately tired thoughts seeped from the nun to Kate.

She's alive, Kate called out to Tania who'd not yet returned.

Overjoyed at Teresa's miraculous escape, tried to make the nun as comfortable as possible. The ward was in chaos. Several beds were overturned and sheets and pillows lay strewn across the floor.

The aftermath of Helga's attack washed over her, leaving her exhausted. She shuddered at the thought of the crazed woman. Her leg smarted from the bloody gouges. All she wanted was to lie down and sleep, but she pushed aside her feelings and wearily cared for Teresa. When she got to her feet and was about to fetch some medicine from the apothecary's store she noticed a large group of children filling the doorway, all eyes fixed on her. It was the girls headed up by Christine and Eileen.

"Are you all right?" Christine asked.

Kate nodded.

"Tania ran to fetch us," Christine said. "Did Helga really try to kill you?"

She was out of her mind, Kate spoke to all of them.

"It was really weird," Eileen told her. "Sister Helga ran through the cloister screaming that the devil was at her heels. She woke everyone. The Abbess tried to calm her, but there was nothing she could do. Her cries rang through the convent. The last we heard was her voice in the distance as she ran down the road away from the convent accompanied by a chorus of frightened nuns."

It was Sister Teresa that saved us both, Kate told them.

"Is she dead?" Tania asked, pushing her way to the front.

No. But she's really poorly.

When the group moved closer, Kate motioned for them to step back. *There's no point in all of you getting ill,* she told them. Then turning to Tania who'd joined her next to the nun she said, *Give me a hand to get her onto a bed.*

Once the nun was comfortably in bed, Kate sent Tania to get medicine and then spoke to Christine and Eileen. *Can you get the girls back to bed? You all need a goodnight's sleep. Who knows what tomorrow will bring?*

Kate was worried Helga might return and seek revenge. *Do you have a key to the dormitory?* she asked.

"No. But there's one in Teresa's desk in the schoolroom. Why do you ask?"

You might do well to lock yourself in just in case some crazy nun tries to harm you, Kate said.

When Tania returned, Kate shooed the others away. *See you tomorrow after breakfast,* she told Christine and Eileen. Then she turned to Teresa.

Kate was exhausted when she finally lay down and pulled the covers around her. Involuntary shivers ran up her back as she tried to get warm. Even an extra blanket was not enough.

Good night Tania, she said, trying to relax her clenched jaw.

"Are you cold too?" Tania asked.

Freezing.

"Can I get in bed with you?" Tania asked.

The idea was appealing, but the beds were so small. *One of us would end up on the floor,* Kate replied.

"Not if we push them together."

Kate dreaded having to get up, but she agreed.

The cast iron beds were heavy. It was a wonder Helga had managed to upturn one. Finally, they managed to push two together and cuddling up under a heap of covers, Kate finally began to feel warmer.

"This is paradise," Tania whispered, putting an arm around Kate and pulling her even closer.

Paradise? Kate had mixed feelings about that. Her leg continued to ache despite the cream she'd applied to the wounds and she was worried how they'd manage if they too got ill. She'd have to train one of the girls to help, just in case. Suzanne would be a good choice, she was sensible, she was good at cooking and had already showed an interest in brewing herbal teas.

Her thoughts were interrupted when Tania's hands slid around her waist, lingering a moment on her stomach before cupping Kate's chest.

No, she thought, hoping the girl wouldn't feel rejected. *Not now. You might think this is paradise, but we've still got a lot of trouble ahead.*

"I'm sure you feel warmer now," Tania said, not heeding her refusal. "I just wish you'd do the same for me. I'm still very cold."

Tania had snuggled up cheek to cheek and it was clear the girl was grinning. Kate playfully tapped Tania on the backside with the flat of her hand. *Stop that, you naughty girl.*

Tania giggled and would probably have continued, but Kate turned over and pulled the covers tight around herself. *Goodnight Tania,* she said. *Sleep tight.*

Tania shifted as close to Kate as she could with her mouth and nose pressed against the nape of Kate's neck. It was to the accompaniment of tiny kisses that Kate drifted off.

A heart-wrenching call awoke her. Opening her eyes, she saw a youth coming at her, fists raised. She swung round expecting her bad leg to give way, but it held. She was surprised to discover she was wearing a short frilly dress that hampered her movements, but many of the attacks and counter attacks she'd long forgotten came back as she dealt with the youth and several others who were attacking a girl. Once she'd knocked them out, the girl turned to look at her. It was Fi. What on earth was Fi doing in the convent?

A deep feeling of concern had her looking for further trouble. Staggering across a nearby waste ground two youths were lugging a girl between them. Her thoughts were confused and her body didn't always do what she wanted, but instinct told her to protect the girl.

Follow them. Don't attack them yet, a distance voice spoke in her head.

She did as she was told, following the youths into a derelict house. They had bundled the girl onto a filthy canapé and were starting to undress her when she caught up with them. Spotting her, they abandoned their prey and sprang to attack. In a movement, the swiftness of which surprised even her, she dodged their outstretched arms and bashed their heads together.

The moment they crumbled to the floor, she felt her body lurch sideways as if she were being wrenched through a tiny hole and she found herself back in bed next to Tania who was like a furnace next to her.

19.

Peter tried not to look at the broken mirror over the disused fireplace, but every time he moved it caught his eye. A splintered vision of the room reflected distorted fragments of himself and Andrew, ripped apart and jumbled together in quite the wrong order.

He was seated on the filthy canapé cradling Andrew's head in his lap. The boy was unconscious, but, as far as Peter could tell, not seriously hurt. His assailants were less well off. They lay unconscious, sporting nosebleeds, sundry cuts and shiny bruises. He'd trussed them up with cords found in the kitchen.

Going over the confrontation, he marvelled at how he beat them when the situation was so desperate. It could only have been Kate. No one could fight like her. She must have answered his call, but why had she not spoken? It was as if she'd been there against her will or something stopped her talking. Rather like in his dream, the contact had been fuzzy and incomplete.

Peter studied Andrew's face. Despite a bruise under his left eye and traces of dried blood on his upper lip, he still looked pretty with his slender face, his high cheekbones and his finely pencilled eyebrows. Peter ran his fingers through Andrew's hair, comforted by its softness. It was beginning to curl as it grew. Sometimes it took so little to turn a boy into a girl.

Was he in love with Andrew? The awkward question came unbidden. He had to admit that, even if he wasn't, he felt a great deal of affection. They had so much in common: the girlishness, the dresses and the makeup, but also their ambivalence about wanting to be a girl, not to mention the struggle to be what they wanted in a world that would have them otherwise. There was a strong bond between them; sisterly seemed the best word for it. Compared to his feelings for Fi, Andrew had never excited him physically. He'd never wanted to kiss the boy passionately as he might Fi. He'd never wanted to merge with Andrew as he'd often wished he could with Fi.

"You look thoughtful," a familiar voice said.

He look down to see Andrew peering up. He hastily removed his hand from the boy's hair and asked, "How are you feeling?"

"Better ... now." Andrew sat up and glanced round the room. "What happened to them?" he asked pointing to the youths tied up on the floor. "Last time I saw them, they were..." His face twisted in a look of fear and disgust. Peter could feel the boy trembling. "To think that I dreamed of ..." He lowered his head, his two hands cupped over his mouth as if to stop the unsaid words escaping.

"It was Kate," Peter said, trying to avoid further embarrassment.

The boy looked at him, perplexed. "What do you mean?"

"Kate saved you, not me. From time to time, before she disappeared, she'd take over my body and use it to fight."

"But how could it be Kate?" Andrew asked. "I thought you'd lost all contact."

"I had. But it felt like her. Only she could best those boys so easily."

"Did she talk to you?" Andrew looked hopeful.

"No. It was as if she were only partly here."

After a thoughtful pause Peter was about to suggest they leave when the sound of glass under foot warned someone was approaching. What if the other youths had recovered and were coming to get them. Peter looked for another exit, but there was none.

"Peter?" he heard Fi call out.

Is that you, Fi? he asked mind-to-mind.

Yes. I'm here with mum, Bonnie's gran and two policewomen.

Peter heaved a sigh of relief. "It's Fi," he told Andrew. *She's with the police,* he added mind-to-mind. *Better not let them know we're boys.*

The moment Fi's mum saw the two, she hurried over and hugged them. "Are you all right?" she asked. "I was so worried."

"Andie got knocked out," Peter told her, remembering just in time to call Andrew by his girl's name.

"Actually I fainted, I think. Everything suddenly went black," Andrew said.

"How about you, Fi?" Peter asked.

"I'm OK, thanks to you. You were spectacular." She grinned at him. *It was Kate, wasn't it?* she asked mind-to-mind. He nodded. "I saw you following the others so I went to look for Mum," she went on. "I found her at the police station."

"Excuse me, miss," the taller of the two policewomen said looking at Peter. "We need to ask some questions."

Peter sat up straight, and shifted to leave a safe distance between him and Andrew. He'd had some bad experiences with policemen and didn't trust them, but maybe policewomen were better.

"According to your friends here, you got the better of seven youths, all bigger than you, all on your own. I'm intrigued," the taller woman asked moving closer.

"Wendy is very good at unarmed combat," Fi explained.

"Is she really?" the policewoman said plunging abruptly forward and grabbing Peter by the arm. He was terrified and offered no resistance. She pulled him up off the canapé, spun him round and twisted his arm behind his back forcing him face down into the filthy canapé. It stank. There was no way he could defend himself without Kate's help.

"I thought as much," the policewoman said, smiling as she pushed Peter even deeper into the canapé.

It took a moment for Fi, her mum, Bonnie's mum and Andrew to get over their shock.

"Have you gone crazy?" Fi shouted flinging herself at the policewoman. She didn't get far. The other policewoman, the short, skinny one, held her back.

"Stop that immediately!" Fi's mum shouted.

Peter felt the pressure on his arm let up. It had never really hurt, he realised. Finally the policewoman released him and stood up.

"You couldn't defend yourself against a fly, let alone beat seven youths," the policewoman said. "So how do you explain what happened?"

"You wouldn't believe me if I told you," Peter replied, searching desperately for a plausible explanation.

"Try me," the policewoman challenged, balancing backwards and forwards on her distinctly masculine boots.

"I have a guardian spirit. Sometimes, when there's real danger, she comes to protect me."

"And what would her name be?"

"Kate."

"I don't recall there being a saint called Kate."

"She may not be a saint, but she's really good at unarmed combat."

The woman snorted in disbelief and went to stand next to the two youths tied up by the fireplace. They had come round and were looking wide-eyed at the policewoman. She prodded one of them with the tip of her boot. "What's your version of the story?"

"We ain't done nothin'. That bitch there set on us 'nd beat us up," one of the two boys complained.

The policewoman barked a laugh. "You expect me to believe that," she said, prodding him a second time.

Her colleague came forward aiming to release the two boys, but Peter had learnt a thing or two about knots from Kate and they weren't so easy to undo. Finally the policewoman had to use her penknife to cut them free.

The taller policewoman laid a heavy boot on the back of one who tried to make a break for it, flattening him to the muck-ridden floor. "There's no hurry. We still have some questions. What were you doing with this young girl?" she asked, pointing to Andrew.

"...just innocent fun..." he mumbled, avoiding the policewomen's eyes.

"You knocked her out and lugged her here," Peter pointed out, furious. "That's neither funny, nor innocent."

The youth tried to scramble to his feet to hit Peter, but the policewoman forced him to the ground with her boot.

"I wouldn't if I were you," Peter said, an edge in his voice. "Remember what happened last time you tried."

"Now that interests me," the taller policewoman said, dragging the youth up off the floor and holding him at arms' length as if he were a bundle of filthy rags. "How exactly did she 'beat you up', as you put it?"

The youth looked shame-faced. "She bashed our heads together."

"And you let her?"

"She woz lightnin' fast!" the other youth said. "I ain't never seen the likes."

"This is all very well," Bonnie's gran interrupted, "but what about Bonnie?".

"Surely finding her is more important than proving Wendy didn't beat these boys when clearly she did," Fi's mum added.

The taller policewoman looked questioningly at her colleague who shrugged.

"You got any more girls hidden here?" she asked the boy.

He shook his head, trying to look unconcerned, but the fear etched on his face belied his words.

"We may never know whether this girl, against all odds, beat you up, but at least we can check if what you say is true," the tall policewoman said, pushing the youth ahead of her as she headed for the door. She was followed by the second policewoman pulling the other youth after her.

"You lot wait here," she called over her shoulder.

They could be heard making their way through the glass-littered kitchen.

"Bonnie'll be terrified if she sees them," Bonnie's gran said, her voice full of worry. "Shouldn't we go with them?"

If only he could locate her as he once used to be able to, Peter thought. "Hold on a mo'," he said. One hand rested on the mantelpiece for balance, he closed his eyes and stretched his attention outwards searching for the girl. He was aware of dull forms moving on the first floor. The occasional creaking board confirmed his impression. That would be the policewomen and the boys.

Peter's mind roamed till he reached the rafters, but found no trace of Bonnie. So he let his attention drift down the derelict stairs to the basement. He could not see the place in his mind's eye, but he could sense the damp, suffocating atmosphere of constricted spaces.

Although he was sure she must be there, he was disappointed to find no sign of her. To make sure he searched the basement a second time and came to a halt in front of a fracture in the wall. There was a confined space beyond he hadn't yet explored. Pushing forward he immediately felt the presence of Bonnie.

Not waiting to verify his impressions, he opened his eyes saying, "She's in the basement."

Descending the staircase was tricky. The stairs were in bad shape and they had no light. Peter ran his hand along the wall, feeling his way down. He knew there was a narrow passage off to the right and was lucky to find it immediately. The corridor snaked around storerooms and laundry rooms until it came to a dead end.

Nobody spoke, but he sensed their worry. Had he got it wrong? Or had he too gone crazy? He tried to ignore their concern and concentrated, letting out his senses as he sought the opening he'd felt earlier. Yes. There it was. Holding on to that impression, he eased forward, arms outstretched, till his fingers discovered a narrow gap.

"She's here," he said quietly. "There's a way through, but I can't figure out how to open the door. Has anyone got a light?"

Nobody had. In Kate's world, he'd been able to create a light in his hand. As he seemed to be recovering some of his abilities, maybe he could make a light.

He remembered well enough what Kate'd said, 'Let the ball of light create itself.' It had to be effortless. Trying not to be troubled by the paradox, he held out his hand and opened his mind to the idea that a ball of light could create itself and sure enough a pale blue ball of light sprang up just above his outstretched palm.

The others gasped. "It's a trick Kate taught me," he said. Then he searched for the hidden door. As he did, the light began to wane. "Fi and Andie, there's a way through. Can you look for it? I need to concentrate on the light." Together they made quick work of the hidden door.

Holding the light out in front of him, Peter looked around. The room was little more than a cubbyhole. There, trussed up on a chair, sat Bonnie, her dress torn, her lips stained with dried blood. One of her eyes was half closed by a bruise. At first Peter thought she was unconscious, but abruptly her head jerked up and her eyes spread wide with fear. She let out a piercing scream that rang off the walls in the confined space almost deafening them.

"Bonnie," her gran said. "It's me, Nana. We've come to take you home."

Bonnie looked unbelieving from her gran to Peter and then to the others. Finally she relaxed as tears brimmed over and coursed down her cheeks. Her gran hurried forward to take the girl in her arms and with Fi's help they were able to undo her bonds. She couldn't walk on her own, but Fi and Andrew shored her up.

They were about to leave when Peter sensed the police coming, no doubt alerted by Bonnie's scream. Without thinking things over, Peter extinguished the light. "Close the door, Fi. The police are on their way. When they find us there'll be more interminable questions. If we stay quiet, they'll never find us."

He sensed the adults were uneasy, but no one objected. Outside he could hear the policewomen descending the stairs. He breathed deeply, then let his presence spread like a bubble around their little group. He had no idea if it would work, but he hoped to mask their presence. The police were so close, he could see rays of light from a torch dancing through the narrow slit under the door.

20.

Peter would have preferred to sleep, if only to escape his worries about the Bargeton police. But sleep refused to come. The four girls were squashed on the back seat with Bonnie fast asleep on Fi's lap. Both Fi and Andrew had nodded off too. Up front, Christina talked quietly to Bonnie's gran whose name, he'd discovered, was Maud.

"...we should never have run away from the police," Maud said.

"It does sound wrong, doesn't it?" Christina replied. "But if they'd found us with Bonnie, it would have taken a lot of explaining and we urgently needed to get her home." She glanced over her shoulder at the children and, seeing Peter watching her, nodded almost imperceptibly. He managed a tired smile. Then she added more quietly, "All of them were shaken up. I want to get them to the quiet and safety as quickly as possible..."

Peace and quiet would be very welcome. He let his mind drift. He thought of Kate and the crazy nun. He was afraid it had been more than a dream. The scene had been strikingly real. That she'd helped him fight the youths was reassuring. She must have survived the nun. As far as he could remember she'd been in a small hospital ward although most of the beds were empty. Could she have been ill? Apart from her fright, he'd felt a nagging pain.

He closed his eyes and pictured the place where he'd seen her. It was the smell of disinfectant that alerted him. He was no longer in the car. If he was with Kate, her eyes were closed. He could see nothing. One thing he could feel was the temperature. Last time the place had been bitterly cold, now the heat was uncomfortable.

He tried to stretch out in search of clues. Unlike his first visits to Kate's mind, this time his impressions were fuzzy and hard to grasp. Most of the heat came from behind Kate, as if she were lying with her back to a radiator. Abruptly an elbow dug into Kate's back startling him. Someone was lying behind her in bed. He felt a surge of jealousy. Could that be why she'd so suddenly left?

Then he heard Kate's voice in her head. *Stop that Tania. You woke me,* she groaned mentally and promptly went back to sleep.

So it was a girl. The knowledge didn't appease his jealousy. On the contrary. Had he not spent ages pining over Fi who only had eyes for girls? Stop being silly, he told himself. You've found Kate. Be pleased, you idiot. What use if she's got someone else? You're daft, his other half told him. The more he argued the more he became delirious, as if the heat was getting to his brain.

Whoever it was lying behind Kate slid an arm around her and clutched her close. The movement woke Kate. *Quit that Tania. I need to sleep.* Turning uneasily in her bed, Kate took hold of Tania's hand and was about to push it away, when she stopped.

Hey, she said, sounding worried. *You're red hot.*

It was then that she opened her eyes and Peter was able to see Tania, a slender girl with a dark bruise under her eye and scratches on her neck and arms. Scantily dressed in a filthy pinafore dress, she looked to be about Peter's age.

Kate began examining Tania's face and arms. In the dim light, he could just make out tiny red blotches on her neck and shoulders.

You've got it, Kate told her.

Tania replied, at least Peter saw her mouth move, but he heard nothing.

I know, Kate replied. Clearly she had heard something, but why was she talking mind-to-mind? *I'll get you some medicine,* she told Tania and got to her feet. The moment she was out of the bed a wall of icy air struck her, making her shiver violently. Picking up one of the blankets heaped on the bed, she flung it round her shoulders and pulled it tight.

Kate, he called mind-to-mind, but she didn't seem to hear. *Kate,* he said again. No response. He was so used to talking to her, it was alarming not to have her respond. Could she be deaf? That might explain why he hadn't been able to hear Tania's words. That would also explain why Kate communicated with Tania via thoughts. But her being deaf shouldn't stop their exchange mind-to-mind.

In a small workroom, Kate was pouring a mixture into a cup while jotting down a list of ingredients. *Oh, and thyme,* he heard her think as she added the word to the list.

The pen and paper gave Peter an idea. If only he could take control of her hand, he could write her a message and let her know he was there. There was a time when doing so would have been easy, but being in her head felt so different. He tried to will her hand to write his name, to no avail. From past experience he knew the harder he tried the less likely he was to succeed, but being so close was frustrating. He tried again concentrating his efforts on Kate's right hand.

Two things happened simultaneously.

He heard Kate's voice, distant now, call out: *Peter?* and his hand snaked out and dug into Andrew's ribs awaking the boy.

"Ouch! Why did you do that?" Andrew asked.

It took Peter a moment to settle his wildly beating heart. "Sorry. I was with Kate. She couldn't hear me so I tried to use her hand to write a message."

"What a lame excuse," Andrew complained.

"Who's Kate?" a sleepy voice asked. Damn! They'd woken Bonnie.

"A friend," Peter said, hoping she hadn't heard the rest.

"Is she deaf?" Bonnie asked, beginning to sound more awake.

"She wasn't," Peter said. "But she may have become so."

"I don't understand," Bonnie said. "How could you use her hand when she's not here? Is this some sort of game."

Peter jumped at the cue. "You've found us out," he said, trying to sound despondent. "It was our secret."

"Can I play?" Bonnie asked.

"It's good that you are all awake," Fi's mum said. "We've arrived."

Glancing out, Peter could just distinguish the outlines of the bakery. Bonnie groaned. "Can't I spend the night with Fi?" she asked.

"If Fi agrees, I'm sure you can some other time, but tonight I want you in your bed," Maud said. "You need a good night's sleep."

Peter expected the girl to kick up a stink, but instead she kissed Fi goodnight, then waving a tired hand to everyone, she said, "See you tomorrow" and followed her gran meekly into the house. Whatever had been in the pills, it had transformed her.

At their own place, hardly had they opened the front door than the phone rang. Peter had horrible visions of it being the police from Bargeton. "They can't possibly have traced us yet," he said.

"Maybe it's Dr Grant," Fi suggested.

Despite that reassuring thought, no one made a move to answer. Finally it was Fi's mum who answered. "Mrs Grant," she replied. It always surprised Peter to hear Christina's new name. He had been in the coma when they'd married.

For a long time, Christina stood unmoving, listening, a haggard look on her face. Finally she said, "When was this?" her voice barely a whisper. Another long silence followed. "What should we do?" When she hung up, three pairs of worried eyes fixed her.

"It was the inspector in Tallford," she explained, heading for the kitchen. "They had located Brian," she told Andrew, "but your brother was armed and managed to escape. The inspector doesn't think the youth knows where we are, but we have to be especially careful." She put on a kettle and began making a pot of Earl Grey.

"How can we possibly be more careful?" Fi asked.

"I'm not sure," Christina admitted.

Half an hour later the three were gathered in Andrew and Peter's bedroom. Fi lay sprawled on his bed, Andrew was sitting in the only armchair, his knees bunched up under his chin, his face pinched in worry and Peter paced the tiny space between the bed and the window.

"So what was that about Kate?" Fi asked.

"She's in some sort of hospital. I found her in bed with another girl ..."

"Good for her!" Fi exclaimed.

"... who was ill," Peter continued, annoyed at Fi's self-centred view of the world. "Kate was trying to cure her, but not with minds, as we used to do, but with medicine."

"What do you mean 'with minds'?" Andrew asked.

"I'll explain another time," Peter said, at which Andrew promptly pouted. "We go into people's bodies with our minds and heal them," Peter added.

Andrew was about to reply but Fi beat him to it. "Where was this hospital?"

"No idea. I saw a nun, so maybe it was in a convent. The nun was a real monster. She tried to kill Kate." The thought had Peter shuddering.

"How did you manage to travel to Kate?" Fi asked. "I thought you'd lost the knack."

"I thought about the place I saw her in and suddenly I was there."

"Can we all go?" Andrew asked.

"I'm not sure I can manage that," Peter replied. "Everything is so blurred and unfamiliar. And going might not be such a good idea. She's trying to care for that girl who looked like she had the measles, or something similar. The girl - Tania's her name - was burning up with fever. Kate may well be ill herself. Being in her head made me feverish."

A knock came at the door and Christina poked her head into the room. "You three would do well to go to bed. After all that's happened today you need a good night's sleep."

The cries of an angry crowd awoke Peter. For a terrible moment he thought the police had found them, then he saw the empty beds in the dancing crisscross of torchlights. Kate was standing by the bed in which Tania lay awake, clearly terrified. Gripping the iron bed frame for support, Kate had a blanket wrapped around her shoulders. It was hardly necessary, her body was aglow with fever like Tania's had been earlier.

The mob surge into the ward only to stop short when they saw her. "That's her," Sister Helga called out, elbowing her way through the crowd till she reached the front. "Don't let her mislead you. The brat is possessed. I heard her speak with the voice of the devil. Let's kill her now."

Despite Helga's invective and the fact that they were armed with makeshift weapons, the crowd held back. Maybe they were afraid of contagion, Peter thought, wondering why Kate did not send them away. Instead the girl just stared at them, shivering violently as she tried not to collapse.

"I don't like this," one old woman muttered.

"Look at those spots," another exclaimed, taking a step back. "It's the pox."

The whole mob followed her lead, leaving Helga alone to confront Kate. The nun's fists were clenched and her face twisted in rage. She seemed unaware her supporters were slinking off into the darkness.

"We're going to settle your score, witch," Helga spat, taking a cautious step forward.

I told you you were not welcome in my house, a deep rumbling voice rang out.

Look behind you, the voice went on, *the mob you brought has already fled.*

Helga glanced nervously over her shoulder. Clearly alarmed at finding herself alone, she took a nervous step backwards.

Never enter my house again, the voice boomed.

Helga hesitated a moment, then spun round and took to her heals, careering down the corridor, bouncing wildly off the walls till she disappeared out the front door.

Exhausted by the effort, Kate collapsed onto the bed next to Tania and was engulfed in throbbing redness.

21.

Peter yawned and rubbed his eyes. He'd awoken in the middle of the night disturbed by his visit to Kate, sweating from the girls' fever. He grappled with his covers, battling to smooth the creases that made them so uncomfortable, before he finally drifted off to sleep. When daylight awoke him, he struggled to get up only to find Andrew's bed empty. The boy must have gone down to breakfast.

Peter's eyes smarted from the makeup. He'd forgotten to remove it the night before. Peering into the mirror, a wad of cotton wool grasped between his fingers, he was about to remove the makeup when he halted at the sight of a dull shadow across his upper lip. It looked like a dirty smudge but when he tried to rub it away, he was shocked to feel stubble. He was growing a moustache! He stared at himself in horror.

He might not want to go all the way to being a girl, had that been possible, but he certainly didn't want to become a man. Of course, a part of him knew it would happen some day, but it'd seemed so far off. He sat down heavily on his bed unsure what to do. Weren't there creams to rid him of facial hair? In his despondency, he was sure it wouldn't suffice.

He ran his fingertip over his upper lip, hoping there'd been a mistake. But gone was his peachy smooth skin, replaced by a roughness that refused to be ignored. He stared absently at himself in the mirror not daring to go down and face the others.

When he couldn't wait any longer, he was the last to arrive at breakfast. Christina had made porridge which she served with thick cream and Demerara sugar. Andrew and Fi sat shoulder to shoulder, hunched over a newspaper. The sight irritated him. He could not remember ever seeing them so close.

"What's got into you two?" he asked by way of greeting, keeping one hand protectively over his upper lip.

The worried looks they gave him had him worried too.

"What?" Peter asked, taking a seat at the table.

Fi slid the paper across to him. The front page headline of the local newspaper read: Girl bests six older boys in fight then disappears.

"That's torn it," Peter said.

"It has indeed," Christina said, handing him a steaming bowl of porridge along with a jug of cream.

He sprinkled sugar abundantly on a lake of cream in the middle of his porridge and spooned the mixture into his mouth as he read. The description of the fight was worthy of a Hollywood film and when the journalist likened the girl to a superhero who had the power to become invisible right under the noses of the police, Peter would have laughed had the situation not been so dire. Apparently the police were looking for a young girl whose description was remarkably accurate considering the rest of the fabulation.

"What do we do?" he asked.

"We should phone the inspector," Christina said. "He won't be happy."

"What about John? When's he due?" Fi asked.

John would be furious. Hadn't he warned them?

"He had meetings and wasn't sure he could get away," Christina told them. "If he can, he'll join us this evening. If not, he'll come tomorrow. I think I'll wait till then to tell him."

Although Peter feared the man's reaction, if anyone knew what to do, it would be Dr Grant.

"I'm not sure which is the biggest threat, the Bargeton police or your brother, Andrew," Christina continued. "Maybe we should get clothes for you two, so you can revert to dressing as boys."

Peter was reluctant. He'd got so used to dressing as a girl. It'd become second nature. He felt much better like that, as if he'd recuperated a key part of himself. The idea of donning boys' clothes didn't appeal to him. Not only were the colours tern, but the material was less soft and appealing.

Peter glanced across the table at Andrew who was absently twirling his spoon in his empty bowl. Judging from his face, his friend didn't relish the idea either. Andrew might have been traumatised about dressing as a girl when Fi first suggested it, not wanting to follow the path his uncle had forced on him, but he did so willingly now and seemed to enjoy it.

"I don't think either of us is willing to dress as a boy," Peter said. "Not now. Once the holidays are over, we'll probably have no choice."

Christina laughed nervously. "John is very open-minded, but, as headmaster, I doubt he'd be happy if his adopted son arrived at school dressed as a girl," she said. "Maybe some time that'll be possible, but in this day and age it's better to keep public and private separate."

"But surely walking through the village dressed as girls is public, isn't it?" Andrew asked.

"You're right," Christina said. "But nobody knows you here. They don't know that biologically you're boys."

"Biological boys," Fi echoed, making a face at Peter. "Sounds like the title of a book. A comic tragedy."

"Prod her in the ribs for me, Andie, would you. She's too far for me to reach," Peter said.

Andrew and Fi tussled briefly, but the mood was not playful and the two didn't have that kind of relationship.

"Well we are definitely not biological girls," Peter mused. "And I'm pretty sure I don't want to be one. But we are partly girls all the same. At least, that's how I feel."

"Girlie boys," Andrew said, sticking his tongue out at Fi who was making a face at him.

"Biologically there are two possibilities," Peter said. "But mentally there are many more. I remember you telling me that

Fi. I didn't really understand at the time."

"In fact, there are more than two biological possibilities," Christina pointed out. "Some people are born in between, although I gather there are few of them."

"You mean they have both a willie and a vagina?" Fi asked, clearly excited at the prospect. "That could be useful."

"Fiona!" her mother exclaimed. "Sometimes I wonder about you."

"She's a hopeless case," Andrew said, jumping out of reach.

"You're all intolerant!" Fi complained. "You accept girlie boys, but not girls who like girls."

"I'm a girl who likes girls," Peter said blowing Fi a kiss.

Fi got to her feet and curtseyed to Peter. "You'd better hurry up to my bed, then," she said.

"Fiona!" her mum exploded. "You're impossible. What did I do wrong in your education?"

"You did an excellent job," Peter hastened to say. "She's just trying to provoke. Some teenage girls are like that."

"Enough," Christina said. "You lot need a brisk walk and it's time for your singing lesson, Peter."

"So do we go as girls or boys or girlie boys or girlie girls?" Andrew asked. Everyone burst out laughing.

Peter laughed so much, he had to wipe the tears from his eyes. It was only then that he remembered his moustache.

"Something terrible has happened..." he announced, feeling like a wanted criminal.

All heads turned to him, the smiles fading from their lips.

"What?" Andrew and Fi asked together.

He rubbed his index finger nervously over his upper lip, but couldn't bring himself to say the words. Instead he burst into tears.

Both Fi and Andrew came to comfort him, but he pushed them away and buried his head in his hands, sobbing.

"What's the matter, Peter?" Christina asked. He was relieved she kept her distance.

"I'm growing a moustache," he blurted out.

Andrew gasped in shock, but Fi burst out laughing.

Unable to bear her reaction, he got to his feet and fled, seeking sanctuary in his bedroom. Half way up the stairs, he heard Christina scold Fi. "That was quite uncalled for Fiona."

He closed the door and flung himself on his bed, burying his face in the pillow. He didn't want to grow up and be a man. Most older boys in his school were ugly, coarse, ill-mannered brutes who stank of sweat. He despised them. Why couldn't he remain soft and gentle? How could he dress as a girl and have a moustache?

He heard the door open then close, but did not respond. Whoever it was sat on his bed but remained silent. He recognised the perfume. It must be Christina. After a while she spoke. "Sometimes Fi speaks without thinking."

"You can't imagine how terrible it is," Peter said, almost choking on the words. He turned over on his side, keeping his back to Fi's mum. "I don't want to grow up and become a man."

He appreciated that Christina didn't try to argue or console him. She just listened.

"All that roughness and hardness and fighting is not me," he said. "The very thought of it makes me sick. I want to be soft inside and curved at the edges and surrounded by pretty pastel colours and smooth, silky materials and delightful perfumes. I know now I don't want to become a girl, even if I had a magic wand that made it possible, but I want to be... What was Andrew's word for it? A girlie boy. How can I be a girlie boy when my face is sprouting a beard?"

He began crying again.

"I understand your despair, Peter. True, I have never experienced your situation, but I can imagine how terrible it must be..."

"My body is betraying me! How can I possibly live with myself?"

Christina ran fingers gently through his hair.

"I would be telling a lie if I promised we'd find a solution. But I do promise we'll do everything we can to help you be who you want to be."

Peter turned over and smiled weakly. "I appreciate that."

"And the first step," Christina said, getting to her feet and offering him a hand, "is to go and see Dr Tchensenko and work on your voice."

"I see you've been crying, Petrovitch. I told you this wouldn't be easy," Dr Tchensenko said as he ushered Peter in. Christina, Fi and Andrew had gone for a walk along the cliffs leaving Peter to attend the lesson alone.

"It's not the singing," Peter replied, in no mood to go into details.

The doctor leaned closer and studied Peter's face. "Ah! I see. Well at least there's something we can do about that."

How could the man make fun of him so cruelly?

"You don't believe me," the man said. "Despair is a ugly thing. It refuses hope."

"Well?" Peter said, petulantly. "If you have a solution, how long are you going to torture me before you reveal it?"

"My country is renowned for its gymnasts; young girls who vault, spring, spin and cartwheel as if they were gifted with magic. To be able to do so they need to stay small and agile. The moment they enter womanhood the magic is over. The hormones, the breasts, the filling out of their bodies, all get in the way. At first their trainers thought of giving them male hormones, but that had effects that even an idiot could see. What's more, both you and I know that men are rarely small and agile." He chuckled at his joke. "So they hit on using hormones to block the onset of puberty. It was an experimental technique secretly developed in laboratories somewhere in the heart of Russia. Well it worked and nobody suspected."

"So you are suggesting I take these hormones?"

"Exactly."

"Isn't it risky."

"For those girls it was. They took them too long. It stunted their growth. But you can safely take them for a couple of years."

"What happens when you stop?"
"Puberty sets in."
"So it buys time?"
"Exactly."

22.

What blithering idiot painted the walls red? Whoever it was needed her head seeing to. Kate knelt to examine the paint. It pulsated. When the floor started to slope, she lost her balance and rolled down a side corridor that also began to slope. She dug her nails in to slow her descent. A distant scream warned her that somewhere, somehow, someone was suffering from what she was doing.

The pulsing grew, sending shock waves rattling through her tiny frame till she thought she'd be shaken apart. She dug her nails even deeper into the red walls that were now slick with a ruby-red liquid. The scream took a step closer. The sticky red liquid clung to her fingers and as it did, she could feel an itchiness spreading like wild fire through the walls. She clawed at the redness, begging it to stop, but the more she scratched, the stronger it got, till it threatened to have her explode in tiny itchy lumps.

This can't be, she thought, fighting a desperate battle to gain control. Stop scratching, she ordered. Her fingers laughed at her and continued clawing. Could people die from the pain and pleasure of scratching? Don't ask such stupid questions, a voice barked. Breathe deeply, she countered as she tried to still her raking fingers.

A deep shuddering breath hissed into her lungs then staggered back out through a sore throat and parched lips. Again, she ordered, like a general rallying her troops in the face of imminent rout. Air rushed in then flowed out, repeatedly, till finally she got her fingers under control and they stilled. The itching continued to rage, like a crackling fire, but she held it at a distance.

In that triumph she felt it, clear as crystal. Something had changed. She was lighter, less blurred, more present. Keeping the itching at bay, she examined the world around her. She was inside her body. She knew the feeling well although it had been a long time since she'd felt that way. She roamed her new-found self, realising what had changed. She'd been cut off, as if someone had thrown a wall between her and herself. The red hot fire of illness had burnt up that divide. Now she was whole again. She would be able to work from within, helping her body heal.

She set to work on the many cuts and scratches she'd inflicted then drove out the fever and calmed the itching. When she'd set most right, thirst and hunger beset her. She opened her eyes, meaning to go in search of food and drink when she saw a feverish Tania staring worriedly down at her. Christine, Eileen and Suzanne were at her side.

Her healing efforts, coming after a prolonged illness, had left her frail and weak. She had difficulty sitting up.

"Water," she croaked and burst out laughing, delighted to hear her voice. Laughter? More like an insane cackle.

All four girls stared at her, mouths fallen open in wonder.

"You can speak!" Tania said, unbelieving.

"Water," Kate repeated, her voice stronger this time.

Suzanne hurried away and brought back a flask of herbal tea. "I made it," she said proudly.

The others helped Kate sit up. Suzanne administered tea, a small sip at a time. Kate sighed, savouring the delicate aroma. It wetted her parched mouth and soothed her sore throat. Suzanne grinned in satisfaction.

A glance round the ward revealed that not a single bed was empty. Many even had two girls sleeping together. So they hadn't been able to contain the illness.

"How long have I been out?" she asked.

"Three days," Christine told her.

"Three days! No wonder I'm starving. Is there any of that porridge left?"

Suzanne grinned and got up. "I'll fetch you some." She'd donned a white apron. Had it not been for the stains, she might have been mistaken for an apprentice nurse.

"Suzanne's porridge is much better than the slop the nuns served up," Tania said. Her face was covered in spots, some of which were infected. If she stayed like that her face would be marred for ever.

"Come closer," Kate said. "Sit next to me and give me your hand."

Tania must have taken it as an invitation for hugs and kisses because she tried to embrace Kate. "Not now. Keep still, close your eyes and do not speak," she told the girl. "I need to concentrate."

Tania clearly had no intention of remaining still and quiet, but Kate insisted.

You remember I healed your back, she explained mind-to-mind so the other girls could not hear. *Well I want to heal those spots. We can't have you growing up all spotty, can we?*

She took Tania's hand and, closing her eyes, slipped into Tania's body. Although it appeared to have receded, the disease was still virulent. Weakened by the prolonged illness, a renewed outburst could carry Tania off at any moment. Kate helped the body counteract the infection and eliminate the toxins. Once the way was clear she set about healing the many small hives of infection that dotted the girl's skin.

When she'd finished she opened her eyes only to have the world fade abruptly from view. The effort had drained her. Had it not been for Christine who caught her before she toppled off the bed she'd have hurt herself badly. With Eileen's help, Christine settled Kate back in bed with several large pillows behind her, then Suzanne began feeding her tiny spoonfuls of porridge. It really did taste good.

"You're appointed head cook," Kate said once she'd got a

little strength back. "This is heavenly."

"And you are our miracle worker," Suzanne replied, looking at Tania who was feeling her face in wonder. "All her spots have gone! How did you do that?"

Might as well tell them, Kate thought. They'll only pester me to know. "I used to know how to heal. A close friend taught me. However I lost the ability when I lost my voice and hearing. Now it's back."

"Not too much healing for the moment. You almost fainted," Christine warned her. Wasn't it typical of her, sensitive as she was, to immediately grasp what was wrong. Kate really liked the girl. "Let's get your strength back first," Christine continued. "Fetch her some more porridge, Suzanne."

"So what happened while I was out?" Kate asked.

"You couldn't possibly imagine," Christine said, grinning. "We have the convent to ourselves."

Kate was unsure that was good news. "How come?"

"Well a lot of nuns left with Sister Helga, terrified you might be possessed by the devil. Her madness was infectious. The Abbess managed to control the few remaining nuns till they realised more and more of us were ill. There were so many ill we decided to move into the infirmary. I think it was then that most of the other nuns left, although we never saw them go. When the Abbess brought us the keys saying she was leaving in search of the others we realised they'd all fled."

"That she gave you the keys was a kind act," Kate mused. It wasn't easy to see the Abbess as anything other than a monster. "She could just as easily have left with them." It sounded like she didn't plan to come back any time soon.

Suzanne arrived at that moment with a tray and several bowls of porridge.

"The nuns always rang the bells for the services throughout the day," Eileen said. "The silence is unnerving. As soon as we are better, I want us to ring the bells again." The others agreed.

"Have you been to see what supplies we have?" Kate asked.

"While you've been resting," Eileen said making a grimace,

"we've been a little busy."

Kate smiled. It felt good to be able to smile. It felt great to be alive. A thought crossed her mind. "Is Clara sick?"

"No. She's been lucky so far," Eileen said. "Do you want to see her? I sent her to the kitchen to fetch more oats."

"As soon as she gets back, I'd love to have a word with her."

When Clara returned she hurried to see Kate. "You look so much better," the girl exclaimed, clearly delighted. "All the spots have gone." Seeing Tania she added, "You too."

"It was Kate," Tania said, clearly proud of her friend. "And she's got her voice back."

"Clara," Kate said. "I want you to help us sing."

"Here and now?" Clara asked.

"Here and now. Nothing will do these girls more good than the joy of singing."

Clara put down the sack of oats and began a lullaby as she ambled between the beds. Clara was such a slight girl, Kate was always amazed at the power and beauty of her voice. It was the same lullaby they'd sung for Teresa. Everyone who could joined in, Kate too.

Looking round Kate wondered where Teresa was. There were no signs of her. Helga's attack had almost pushed the nun over the edge. If she'd recovered, it seemed unlikely she'd have fled with the others. Where could she be? Kate just hoped she'd survived.

Once the strains of the song stilled and those who were ill lay back in bed, Kate thanked Clara. Then she turned to Christine, asking, "What happened to Teresa?"

The smile that had been on Christine's face faded. "She didn't make it. She passed away this morning shortly before you recovered." Christine glanced at Eileen then turned back to Kate. "Do you think you can walk a short way?"

Kate nodded and they helped her to her feet. Supported by Christine on one side and Eileen on the other, closely followed by Tania and Clara, she shuffled slowly out of the ward and into a tiny bedroom near the entrance. The curtains were drawn and the only light came from several candles burning next to the bed. There lay Teresa on her back, her eyes closed, her hands crossed over her chest. She looked peaceful despite the mass of spots and blotches that littered her face.

Kate stood in silence for a long moment as she studied the nun's face, remembering the many things that had happened in the short time she'd known the nun. She had been the only one to recognise Kate's abilities as a herbalist and a healer. She'd embraced Kate's suggestions about clothing for the girls and had had the courage to present the idea to the Abbess despite Helga's virulent opposition. Tears welled up in Kate's eyes. If only she'd recovered earlier, she might have saved Teresa. Now she was gone for ever.

"She had our interests at heart," Kate finally said. "She was both brave and kind. She was a good woman. I'll miss her."

She could hear the others crying. "We must give her a warm farewell before we bury her."

"What do you suggest?" Christine asked.

"I'm not sure. Something in the church. But not one of their dreary services. Not a solemn event. Rather a joyful celebration. With lots of music and beautiful songs. And our fond memories of her."

23.

"I have spoken to Dr Tchensenko," Dr Grant began, addressing Peter and Andrew who were seated on the settee in their best dresses. Fi and her mother were also there.

Knowing that John Grant could be trusted and confided in, didn't alleviate Peter's discomfort at being dressed as a girl. Surely he should have got used to it. John had arrived several days earlier and Peter had been wearing girl's clothes all the time.

It was at such moments he wondered how his father would have reacted. Peter liked to think he'd have been understanding if not encouraging, but he couldn't be sure. His father had died when he was so young. He hardly remembered the man.

"Dr Tchensenko is a very persuasive fellow. He reassured me," Dr Grant went on. "I believe these hormones will do no lasting harm if used for a short time. The key question is: what do you two want?"

"What do you mean, Sir?" Andrew asked. He'd had little chance to get to know Dr Grant and was clearly intimidated.

"Taking this treatment will make it easier for you to be seen as girls. But you won't be able to remain on the verge of adulthood for ever. Peter, you once explained that you liked dressing as a girl but didn't want to physically be one. Does that still hold true? And what about you Andrew? How do both of you plan to continue this exploration of girlhood?"

"Lots of questions," Peter commented, blushing. He didn't like being the centre of attention, even less so when it came to such intimate questions. "To be honest, I've tried to put off thinking about it. When I discovered I was growing a moustache it was a terrible shock. The same goes for my voice breaking. Life seems set on reminding me these changes are inevitable. You're right, though. I don't want to become a fully fledged girl and lose my ..." He hesitated about saying the word. "You know what I mean. I believe I want to stay in between, both boy and girl."

"It's a bit like the garden of Eden," Fi's mum put in. "Puberty marks the end of your stay in paradise where you could readily be either girl or boy."

"Maybe that's why Peter Pan didn't want to grow up," Fi chuckled.

Peter had to smile at Fi's reference to his namesake. "You may be right," Peter said. "But JM Barrie was very discreet about the subject if that were ..." Peter halted, embarrassed, aware that he was avoiding the question.

Turning to Fi's mum, he sighed, saying: "I wish I could stay longer in that garden."

"Unlike Peter," Andrew said, "I was forced to dress up. I have mixed feeling about doing so. I enjoy it, but I can't rid myself of the guilt. I doubt anything will ever change that. I don't want to live between girl and boy. So I only need these hormones as long as I have to hide."

Andrew's answer disappointed Peter. He felt let down. Their ways had abruptly parted leaving him alone on a tricky journey.

"Is it enough for you to be dressed as a girl?" Christina asked Peter. "Or do you also need to look and sound like a girl?"

"I'm not sure I follow," Peter replied.

"Well, up to now you could easily be taken for a girl, but as your body changes it'll become more difficult. But that shouldn't necessarily stop you dressing in girl's clothes."

"I don't know," Peter had to admit. "I'll take these hormones during the Summer. That'll give me time to think. And anyway, I'll have to decide before I go back to school."

"A wise decision," Dr Grant said, sitting down in an armchair across from the boys. "If you can, it's always good to take time to make up your mind."

"I wish I could talk to Kate," Peter said. "I miss not being able to confide in her."

"Fi tells me you have managed to contact her," Dr Grant said.

"Sort of. I'm sure it was her, but we couldn't communicate and everything was unclear, as if there was a veil between us."

"Would practice help?" Dr Grant asked.

Peter shrugged. "I was wondering if Kate and I loosing a part of ourselves when she ..." He couldn't bring himself to say the word. The memory of the death of her body and the loss of his spirit still gave him nightmares. "Maybe that's why we can't reach each other properly."

"If we travelled together, it would be easier," Fi put in, enthusiastic.

They'd often done so before, but now he felt hesitant. It wasn't that he didn't trust Fi, but, since Andrew had been there, they'd drifted apart.

"Unlike you, I lost nothing when Kate was beheaded," Fi added.

She could be so insensitive. Peter cringed. "Thanks, but I have to do this myself."

Fi made a face and was about to reply when the phone rang. It rang so rarely that its strident tone was like a warning bell. Peter shuddered. He had an intuition that it brought bad news. John went into the hall to answer. Judging from Dr Grant's face when he returned, Peter's premonition must have been right.

John went to sit next to Andrew and taking hold of the boy's hand, he said: "I have bad news. Your uncle is dead."

Andrew's face turned pale and tears welled up in his eyes, but he didn't cry. Peter wanted to put an arm round him, but he wasn't sure it'd be welcome.

Dr Grant must have also sensed Andrew's reticence because he let go of the boy's hand. "He was shot as he left his home. According to eye witnesses, the gunman was a stocky youth.

The police are convinced it was your brother."

"Oh my God!" Andrew said, his voice strangled. "I hated my uncle. I'll probably always hate him. He did atrocious things to me. I could have killed him at those moments. But I never wanted him dead. It was him that brought me music and taught me to play piano..."

Andrew sat stiff and unmoving, staring into empty space, his jaw tense, his fists clenched. Nobody spoke for long moment.

It was Dr Grant that broke the silence. "The funeral will take place tomorrow afternoon. The police inspector advised against attending. They have not been able to trace your brother and are concerned about your safety."

Andrew looked at the headmaster as if he were an alien.

"You don't need to decide now," Christina pointed out.

"I have to go," Andrew finally said, his voice alarmingly calm. "I have to finish with this man or he'll haunt me all my life."

"You'll need proper clothes," Fi's mum said. "You can't go dressed like that."

"Oh yes I can and I will."

Christina looked surprised if not disconcerted at Andrew's sudden decisiveness.

Dr Grant got to his feet and went to stand next to Christina, laying a restraining hand on her shoulder.

"It may sound strange, but your uncle's death is a real opportunity," John said.

Andrew nodded, but didn't seem inclined to speak. He sat unmoving, his hands cupped in his lap, almost lost in the folds of his dress.

"If you want to wear a dress to the funeral, maybe we should make sure it is clean and ironed," Christina said.

Andrew did not immediately respond. He seemed caught up in his own thoughts. "It's only appropriate I should say my last words to him dressed as a girl. He hardly knew me any other way." Andrew turned to Peter. "Would you sing if I play piano?" he asked, adding as an after thought, "I'd very much like you to be dressed as a girl like me."

Peter was hesitant. The idea of appearing as a girl in front of a larger number of people many of whom might know him was worrying. But his main concern was his voice. He wasn't sure it would hold. The work with Dr Tchensenko was going well, but there was a lot still to be done.

"OK," Peter replied. "But I need time to work through the pieces we sing with Dr Tchensenko and you'd better come to accompany me."

"I'm not sure it's wise for you both to go to the funeral dressed as girls," Fi's mum said. "It could spark off all sorts of reactions, some of which might be uncontrollable. What do you think, John?"

John's face was creased with worry. "You just want to play and sing?" he asked.

"I want to speak first and then Peter would sing," Andrew said.

Andrews' words had John looking even more concerned. "I understand you want to settle an old score, and get justice, as it were," he said. "But in doing so I am afraid you might create a situation that will be far worse, not just for you, but for all of us."

Andrew got to his feet and began to pace the room. Peter wondered if he was going to fly off the handle but he remained calm. "I will find a way. Trust me. If you agree, Dr Grant, I would like your help in getting my thoughts in order."

Fi who had been silent all this time, spoke up. "I will not come. This funeral has nothing to do with me. I want to stay here. I'll get Bonnie to come over and keep me company."

Christina looked like she was about to disagree, but checked herself. "If you stay in Lettup," she said, "you should go to the bakery rather than be in this house alone with Bonnie. It's not that I don't trust you, but I'm worried Andrew's brother might find his way here. I know it's unlikely, but I'd feel happier if you were with Bonnie's grandparents."

A wave of giddiness swept over Peter causing him to clutch

the armrest to stop him falling. Voices in the room moved further and further away and everything around him swayed then blurred. A force tugged at his stomach, yanking him sideways. It got stronger and stronger till he felt like he was being dragged backwards out of the world. With a resounding "pop" he found himself looking down at the face of an elderly nun, her arms crossed over her chest, flowers grasped between her gnarled fingers. Tears were running down his cheeks

It couldn't have been the pull of another world that made him giddy because the feeling persisted. What's more, he was beset by an unpleasant stench. Try as he would, he couldn't block it. The effort exhausted him and his head swayed even more. He felt dreadfully weak.

"Kate," a girl's voice said as hands gripped his arms, supporting him. "You need to lie down and have a rest. Don't forget you were dreadfully ill for several days."

"I know," he heard Kate say weakly as his vision blurred yet again and the world turned first grey then sooty black. When he came too, he was lying on the carpet in the front room of the cottage.

"Peter," Christina was saying, his hand held in hers. "Are you alright?"

Opening his eyes he looked up perplexed at the tight group of worried faces peering down at him.

"You fainted," Fi said, chuckling. "It was spectacular. You sank forward like in one of those slow motion films till you landed on the floor."

"Here, drink this," Dr Grant said offering Peter a steaming mug. "It's tea."

Christina helped Peter sit with his back propped against the settee. Something of the nasty smell from Kate's world clung to his nose and throat that not even the sweet tea could dispel.

"Kate dragged me away," he finally said when he felt a little better. "I don't think she did it deliberately. She's been poorly..."

24.

Arthur W. Yong laid down his pen at the end of the sole sentence he had written that morning and sighed. He who had so easily slipped in and out of his stories now stood in the middle of a wordless wasteland. He re-read the first sentence: Kate hobbled disconsolate, her bare feet stinging on the freezing flagstones, her head bowed, enclosed in a world of silent misery... He'd read the damn thing so many times, it sickened him.

Something was not right. Try as he would, the story remained tantalizingly just out of reach. The words wouldn't flow. He took a long shuddery breath. In that strangled whoosh of air he could have sworn he heard time dashing by. His prolonged stay in hospital had left him frail and disconnected. He looked around seeking reassurance. As always, the young Queen smiled down at him from her portrait, he knew he could count on her support, but Prince Philip looked more dubitative, his brow furrowed in concern.

The three volumes of The Strange History of Syvatoy and Drailong lay on his desk, a little tattered. To think that if ever people remembered him, it would be for those books. How many times had he journeyed to the islands, preparing his army of priests then marshalling them to defeat the rebellious magicians of Drailong? Now even a peek at the worlds he'd created was barred him.

How had an insignificant boy and girl been able to ruin so much with such flippant ease? He shoved the thought aside and got unsteadily to his feet, almost upsetting the desk as his legs threatened to give way under him. His walking stick, that he'd propped against his desk, slid the length of the writing surface and clattered to the floor. Drat. There was no way he'd be able to recover the blasted thing.

He let go of the desktop and took a tentative step towards the table where the kettle and teapot lay waiting. When a second step followed the first, then a third, he began to feel more confident. It was at that moment that his legs buckled under him pitching him forward. His head narrowly missed the table but his right knee hit the floor with a sickening crunch causing a sharp pain to shoot up his leg.

He shifted his damaged leg a minute distance at a time till he managed to roll onto his back. He lay there panting as he stared up at the ceiling. Was this the end? How ignominious. He who had been so powerful and creative couldn't even think himself up off the floor. He closed his eyes for shame.

"Ah Baron, greetings," the nun said, a tired smile on her face. "You find us somewhat out of sorts."

He looked at the woman perplexed as he struggled to remember who she was. Her nuns habit looked like she'd slept in it and her face was clearly unwashed.

"I'm Abbess Johannes," she reminded him. "You brought us that deaf girl with the limp."

Of course! She'd seemed taller, more imposing, last time he'd seen her. No wonder he hadn't recognised her.

"Do take a seat," she said.

Joining her on an uneven bench behind a table, he made the mistake of touching the plastic cloth pinned to the table. His fingers came away greasy. Disgusted, he wiped them on a handkerchief he found in his pocket as he glanced about the room. Light from the one curtained window was not enough to dispel the gloom. He could just make out several tables, filled with nuns who all looked shabby and down-trodden. A sleazy tavern was hardly the place you'd expect to find such a group.

"Would you like a drink?" the Abbess asked, beckoning to a waiter who lounged behind the bar, looking as neglected as the tavern.

Surely his own miserable state couldn't have rubbed off on his characters. "What happened to you?" he asked, taking the glass the waiter handed him. Lifting it cautiously to his lips, he was startled to find it contained Schnapps.

"You remember that girl you brought us?" she began.

At the mention of her, he was filled with foreboding. What had the brat done now? He took a hasty swig of his drink and almost choked as it burnt its way down his throat. He coughed violently, his lungs struggling to breathe through the fire as the world around him faded. He strained to hear the rest of the story but the nun's words faded too.

When he opened his eyes, a familiar ceiling stared down at him. He was once again lying on the floor of his study. Furious, he struggled to get up causing a vicious pain to shoot through his leg and darkness enveloped him.

"... So you see, Baron," the Abbess concluded, "we were chased out of our home. This miserable tavern was the only refuge we could find." A couple of nuns looked up and nodded in agreement, but most seemed oblivious to their discussion.

He was about to take another swig of schnapps to mask his frustration, when he remembered the effect it had had.

"You wouldn't have somewhere to put up twenty nuns?" the Abbess asked wistfully.

If only she knew, he thought. "I'm going to visit that convent of yours," he announced, getting to his feet.

"I wouldn't do that," the nun said, reaching out to restrain him. "Did you not hear what I said? They have some dreadful disease. One of our sisters who remained behind died of it, so we've heard."

He slowly eased himself back onto the bench under the weight of the revelation, cautious not to touch the filthy plastic tablecloth. Disease? He looked the Abbess squarely in the face. She would not lie to him and she didn't seem the sort to believe fanciful stories.

"You look almost as tired and worn as us," she said, her

smile weak, but full of compassion. "There are rooms upstairs. Why don't you rest a while? It's a long walk to the convent and you'll need all your strength if you persist in going there."

The last thing he wanted was to hang around that flea pit, but her words had sapped his remaining resolve. He got to his feet and followed her meekly up the two flights of stairs, to a tiny attic room in which lay a narrow single bed covered with a filthy blanket.

The nun bid him a good sleep and left, closing the door. The room, which had no window, was haunted by the rank memories of former inhabitants. He lay atop the bed fully clothed, cringing from any contact with the blanket, and closed his eyes. Steeling himself for the pain in his leg as he shifted back to his world he was surprised to find himself drifting off to sleep.

The road was long indeed, so long he couldn't remember how far he'd already walked nor how long it had been since he left the inn. There were no signposts along the way, no turnings either and the sky was overcast. His legs were unused to such exercise and he could feel the blisters sprouting on his feet. Dust covered his clothes and stole up his nose and down his throat causing him to cough frequently. Maybe he should have stayed longer at the inn. Had not the Abbess advised him to rest?

The thought that that horrible girl was causing havoc made him quicken his pace. There was no way he was going to let her ruin another of his stories. Had he not started this new one deliberately to punish her?

The air swirled listlessly around him, calling up a mist that oozed from the ground at his feet. He battled forward, alarmed that he had still seen no sign of the convent. He should have reached it long ago. As if to taunt him, the mist carried with it the distant clang of a church bell and faint strains of a girls' choir.

At moments the voices swam closer as if his goal were only yards away, though he could see nothing of it. Then the voices retreated till they were almost inaudible. Some mean quirk of nature was playing tricks on him. He longed to be back in the tavern with the nuns, if only to rest. His face and clothes were soaked, but his throat was parched, his eyes stung and his lungs rasped as they fought to suck in air.

He was thinking how wonderful it would be to find a bench when he stumbled on one by the roadside. Despite his longing to sit down, he hesitated. The bench looked none too steady. Made of wrought iron, one leg was bent at an odd angle, as if some giant had played at twisting it, and the other legs were red with rust.

He gingerly prodded the seat with his foot. It rocked slightly but did not collapse. Cautiously he lowered himself onto the bench till he was sure it would hold his weight. He closed his eyes and breathed a sigh of relief as he leaned back against the few remaining iron bars that made up its back. What a mistake! The rusted structured shuddered as if it were alive, then keeled over backwards, flinging him headlong into a ditch.

Loud hammering jerked him back to the present. Had the convent been transformed into a workhouse?

The hammering ceased a moment and a voice cried out: "Mr Wong?"

He must be back home. He tried to move his leg and, sure enough, a stabbing pain confirmed his suspicions. "It's not locked," he called out, his voice sounding strange to his ears. Forcing his eyes open he saw the postman enter followed by several of what must have been his neighbours. He rarely saw them.

"What do you want?" he croaked.

"You hurt?" the postman asked, hurrying to kneel at his side. In his hand he held a small packet that he placed on the floor next to him. "It's for you," he explained.

"What happened?" a skinny woman with protruding eyes asked, leaning over the postman. He'd never seen her before. She must have seen his questioning look because she added, "I'm your new neighbour."

"It's nothing," he replied. "I just fell."

"You look dreadfully pale," the woman pointed out. "And

your leg is twisted at an odd angle." She slipped down next to
the postman, her skirts billowing out around her, her pungent
perfume making him cough. She laid a hand on his broken leg
at which he screamed and promptly blacked out.

The mist lingered on as did the tantalising sound of girls
singing. If anything, their voices were much closer. He struggled
to his feet and peered around. A gust of wind lifted part of the
veil revealing the west porch of the church, but the moment he
set off in that direction the mist wound its tendrils around him
concealing all from view.

He halted. "Think, goddamn you," he told himself.
"Something is amiss." His imagination stirred. It was as if
someone or something was hindering him reaching the convent.
A surge of fear sent cold shivers rippling up his spine. Could she
be doing that? Surely not. He was the author. Not her.

As if fate were goading him, the voices stopped and he
distinctly heard a girl say: "That was beautiful. Teach us another
one, Clara." He recognized her voice immediately. It was exactly
the same one he'd heard all those years ago at the concert. The
same mixture of soft-spoken self-assurance.

But how could she possibly speak? Had he not rendered
her deaf and dumb? The song of a solitary girl's voice rang out
around him. If he hadn't been so furious, he would have had to
admit she had a most beautiful voice. He could even hear the
girls of the choir shifting in their seats as they prepared to sing.
He was right amongst them, yet he couldn't quite reach them.

"Mr Wong, can you hear me?" a woman's voice asked.

That blasted new neighbour again! Women were such a
plague. Always meddling in things that didn't concern them.
The clumsy woman had pulled him back just when he was about
to reach his goal.

"Mr Wong," the female voice said again, insistent.

Why couldn't she let him be? He had things to do.

He wanted to protest but when he tried to speak no sound
came from his mouth. The irony of the situation struck him,
followed immediately by deep-seated fear shot through with

anger. It wasn't possible! She couldn't have turned the tables on him.

Meanwhile, the woman began pulling off his pullover, much to his distress. He wasn't sure his shirt was as clean as it should be. He'd tended to neglect such things since he'd got back from hospital. Hospital? That smell. Oh no! Was he back there again? He blinked open his eyes only to see a nurse dressed as a sister with a large cross hanging round her neck. Seeing his eyes open, she nodded to him and continued unbuttoning his shirt.

25.

Suzanne and Claudia led the way along the deserted drive. They passed their school and the library, their slender arms brimming with sprigs of herbs and bouquets of flowers gathered from Sister Teresa's garden. Close behind marched Eileen and Christine, solemnly pushing a low cart that bore the Sister. The girls had decided to cover the nun with a linen cloth found in the stores. The undyed flax, which was both rough and pure and gave off a light of its own, seemed particularly fitting for the person they'd known.

Clara came next, a few paces behind, a book of songs clasped in her hand, her face beaming. The remaining girls came two by two, hand in hand, wearing their new cloaks, each adorned with a flower of their choice. Some wore flowers woven into their hair. Only Jane dragged her feet, apparently uninterested in the ceremony. She frequently peered off down the drive, as if expecting rescue to arrive. Kate brought up the rear with Tania who held her by the arm in case she stumbled. They too wore cloaks that Claudia had finished while Kate had been ill.

The procession turned at the west entrance to the church and Suzanne and Claudia stepped into the porch, the doors of which had been thrown open in welcome, bringing a breeze of fresh air into the musty church. The moment Clara entered the nave, she burst into song, her voice soaring amongst the rafters. It reminded Kate of Peter singing in his church and with it a yearning to be at his side tugged at her heart. His voice too had magic in it. For all its force and beauty, Clara's singing couldn't completely mask the complaints of the rusty cart creaking its way into the church.

As they strode up the central aisle between the empty pews, the freshly cut blooms left a trail of delicate scents that wove its way in and out of the procession. From the stained glass windows, brightly coloured saints peered down, aglow with a sudden ray of sun. Statues of former abbesses stared in surprise from the safety of their recesses.

The girls halted at the foot of the carved wooden screen that divided the church in two. Beyond lay the altar and that part of the church reserved for nuns and priests. The girls had no wish to venture further.

Suzanne and Claudia stepped aside and the cart was pushed forward till Teresa came to rest at the foot of a carving of the Virgin Mary. The two young girls festooned the shrouded figure with flowers.

Taking up her position next to the flower-covered body, Clara opened her book and raised a hand to attract the girls' attention. She gave the note and then beat the time. Kate wanted to sing with them but a wave of exhaustion swept over her causing her to sway precariously. Tania guided her to a nearby pew, helped her sit and joined her, putting a comforting arm around her shoulder.

Kate glanced at the girls singing. It made her happy to see how they threw themselves into what they were doing. Only days before they had cowered under the brutal hand of Sister Helga, uninterested in the slightest thing.

At that moment, Jane looked in Kate's direction and made a face seeing her seated in the arms of Tania. They'd have to do something about the girl. Kate's eyelids were heavy and sleep called. She closed her eyes and drifted with the music.

Music? The transition was subtle, but it had changed. A young girl was playing piano. No, not a girl, a boy wearing a pretty dress. When he looked in her direction she immediately recognised Andrew.

Although she hadn't been in Peter's head for a while, she

was certain she was back with him. He was singing to Andrew's accompaniment. Concern troubled his pleasure at singing. She gathered that he too was to attend a funeral, but there was some kind of risk she couldn't identify.

Peter? she whispered.

He broke off singing in mid phrase.

Kate? Is that you? he asked astonished.

Silly boy, she said, her voice laced with affection. *How could it possibly be anyone else?*

To her surprise he burst into tears and buried his head in his hands. *What's the matter?* she asked, but he didn't reply. Had she done something wrong?

Andrew came to console him. He put an arm round Peter, just as Tania had with her. "Is it the stress?" Andrew asked. "We don't have to go through with this. We could simply let my uncle die in peace."

"No..." Peter replied, his voice trembling with emotion. "It's Kate. She's back."

"Kate?" Andrew said, drawing back, confused emotions clouding his face.

He's worried I'm going to steal you, Kate commented. She remembered the fears of Fi who'd convinced herself that Andrew was spiriting Peter away. Now it was her turn to doubt.

No, he doesn't, Peter insisted. *He loves you.*

The news embarrassed her. Of course she liked Andrew. Had she not flirted with him while Peter slept? But she was with Peter. Even now she had her own body she was still deeply attached to him. Her own body! How things had changed. Now she had a place of her own and good friends. Even in her home world she'd never had friends like Tania or Eileen or Christine or Suzanne.

When she didn't reply, Peter asked. *Are you still there?* Apparently he couldn't feel her presence.

Yes.

Where have you been?

She was about to reply when Andrew interrupted them. "If

you two want to talk, I'll wait outside."

"No," Peter replied. "Kate, say hallo to Andrew. I taught him to speak mind-to-mind."

Hallo Andrew, Kate said.

She didn't hear his answer because Tania shook her. "It's time to say goodbye," the girl said. "I thought you wouldn't want to miss that."

Kate was still aglow from being with Peter. It took her a moment to adjust. Tania helped her to her feet and she hobbled forward till she stood next to the flower-bedecked sister. Kate stood there in silence, her hands clasped in front of her, looking at the flowers for a long moment. She leaned forward and picked up a sprig of sage. Holding it to her nose, she breathed deeply.

"Sage," she said, holding the sprig up for everyone to see. "It's used to heal many things. Sister Teresa knew it well. She was a skilful healer and was well versed in herbs and other remedies. In the short time I spent with her, she taught me many things."

Kate paused a moment to look from girl to girl, wondering what would become of them. Without Sister Teresa, their future was a lot less certain.

"Despite her knowledge, she could not completely heal her own heart. When she was abandoned as a child, she was brought up in this convent by one of the nuns who was very hard and harsh. Like many of us, she bore the marks of that sister's heavy hand."

A hiss went up from the girls as they realised who that woman must be. Kate laid the sage back on Teresa's chest and waited for silence.

"Yet despite her doubts, her fear and suffering, Sister Teresa had the courage to protect each and every one of us as best she could. She stood up to Sister Helga so that we could be warm in our cloaks. We have much to be grateful to her for, so, on behalf of us all, I'd like to say 'thank you'."

She undid the flower attached to her cloak and laid it amongst the many other flowers covering Teresa. Then, one by

one, each girl stepped forward and stood a brief moment by the
nun, head bowed, muttering a few words, before leaving behind
the flower they unhitched from their cloak.

When everyone had said goodbye, Eileen and Christine
took up the cart again and wheeled it back towards the porch,
heading for the tiny cemetery that lay outside the walls. Once
again Kate brought up the rear with Tania.

Next to the entrance stood the remains of a strange statue
that resembled none other in the building. It portrayed an old
man, bent over almost double clasping his leg. He was filthy.
He looked like a tramp. Kate had never noticed it before. As she
stared at the man, a searing pain shot through her bad leg and
she collapsed.

The pain was so sharp, Kate expected to black out. Instead
she remained acutely aware of everything around her. She heard
Tania's screams of alarm as the girl knelt next to her. She sensed
the worried chatter in Tania's head the moment the girl clasped
her hand. She could feel their deep-felt concern as the girls
gathered round.

One thing surprised her, though. She could no longer feel
the pain in her leg. It had come in a flash and had left almost
as immediately. In fact, she felt extremely good lying there. It
didn't make sense. Caution had her resist the temptation to test
her leg for fear she'd lost all sense of it.

Come off it, Kate, she told herself. They are worried about
you. Open your eyes and let them know you're alright. The
moment she did, she was inundated with questions. "What
happened?" "Are you alright?" "Does your leg hurt?" And even
one of the younger ones asked: "You're not going to die like
Sister Teresa, are you?"

"I'm OK," she reassured the girl and reached out to Tania
with whose help she got to her feet. She tentatively put more
weight on her bad leg only to discover it held. The absence of
any pain troubled her. Letting go of Tania's hand she hiked up
her cloak and dress and examined her leg. She had to look twice
to believe what she saw. All trace of the nasty red wheals and

the twisted bones had gone. Her leg was as straight as it should be and looked remarkably healthy. She took a few cautious steps unaided before she let her joy burst from her.

"It's a miracle," she heard Clara say.

All the girls thronged around, trying to touch her, albeit fleetingly, as if her miracle could rub off on them. Each finger tip on her shoulders or hands on her arms brought with it a wave of thoughts and emotions that threatened to overwhelm her. There was joy but also suffering, a great deal of suffering.

It was Eileen that put an end to the emotional flood. She shepherded the girls back till they formed a circle around Kate.

"What happened?" Christine asked, speaking for the whole group.

"I have no idea. I had this terrible pain. Then when it was gone, my leg was healed."

"Another miracle," Tania said awed, hardly daring to approach Kate as if she were a saint.

Glancing over their shoulders, Kate could see Sister Teresa's body abandoned in the porch, flowers fluttering in the breeze.

"We have work to do," Kate said, pointing to Teresa. "And when that's over, how about a feast."

The girls cheered at the idea and the younger ones jumped up and down in an improvised dance.

"Shhhh..." Eileen scolded, nodding in the direction of the waiting Sister. "Don't forget where you are."

Contrite, they turned as one to face the cart were Teresa lay, patient as ever, and reluctantly set off. Kate skipped along behind, delighting in her newfound form.

When she reached the porch, she halted and looked back into the church, wondering what could possibly have happened. She was startled to discover that the statue of the tramp had gone.

26.

"I'm scared," Andrew admitted as he paced the vestry, his hands clasped behind his back, his ankle-length dress flowing behind him. In the half light, the dark blue velvet might have been mistaken for a cassock, had it not been for the way it was taken in at the waist. Pinned to the dress with a broach, he wore a single cornflower, its brilliant blue contrasting with the soberness of his dress. Fi, who'd seen them off, had complimented Andrew on his dress. With a wicked gleam in her eyes, she'd threatened to move in with him if he continued dressing that way.

Peter had chosen a dark green dress that reached to just below his knees that, unlike Andrew's, hung loose, leaving him room to move and breath. He was glad of the long sleeves. They made him feel less exposed. And they kept him warm. The air was cold in the church. Around his neck, concealed beneath his dress, he wore his St. Nicholas pendant, the patron saint of choirboys. His hand clutched it now through the velvet. As former head chorister, it had always brought him good luck.

He glanced at the policeman posted next to the door. How did he feel playing nanny to two boys dressed as girls? The man looked unperturbed as he leant against the doorframe. Several of his colleagues were concealed around the church, just in case.

From behind the vestry door Peter could hear the shuffle of feet and the muffled murmur of voices. They were expecting a crowd. As a concert pianist, Andrew's uncle had been well known. At least it was reassuring to know Andrew's mother wouldn't be there. The police had made sure of that.

"I am scared too," Peter said. Being so tense wouldn't help his singing. Dr Tchensenko had insisted he relax. You'll break your voice if you don't, he'd warned. "Come sit next to me," Peter said, patting the bench. "You're making me even more nervous walking up and down like that."

Once Andrew had settled next to him, Peter took his hand and began gently massaging the fleshy part of his palm at the base of the thumb thinking it would help them relax. He made the most of the physical contact to slip into Andrew's mind. He'd planned to talk to Andrew unheard by the policeman, but the intensity of the boy's emotions made any other thought impossible.

Brightly coloured images of Andrew's uncle massaging the boy's hand tumbled unbidden into Peter's head. Large, muscular fingers skilfully lingered on the most sensitive points playing pitilessly with Andrew's mounting excitement. Desire was tightly bound with sickening guilt and revulsion, not to mention deep-seated shame. The powerful mix of emotions churned in the pit of Peter's stomach. The two boys groaned in unison. Peter immediately let Andrew's hand fall.

"I'm so sorry. I didn't know..." Peter said, embarrassed.

The confusion of emotions he'd felt was reflected in Andrew's eyes, as the boy held his gaze.

"I don't think I'll ever be rid of the man," Andrew whispered.

Both boys looked up in alarm as the door opened and Dr Grant entered.

"You ready?" John asked.

"Do you think anyone will recognise us?" Andrew asked, sounding nervous.

"I hope not. I'm banking on the fact your uncle was very secretive. Few people would have known his private life and even less his family. You were one of his only relatives." John glanced at his watch. "It's time."

They followed him out into the packed church. Many heads turned to stare at them as they made their way from the nearby vestry to seats reserved for them on the front pew. Fi's mum was waiting for them. She patted Peter on the knee, whispering "It'll be OK."

The first notes of the organ were the signal for everyone to stand. Behind them the massive main doors of the church creaked open and the congregation as one turned to watch death make its entrance. Peter nervously smoothed his dress and stared pointedly at the altar, not wanting to look back. Regular footfalls getting ever closer announced the arrival of the coffin. Six dour men dressed in black slid the shiny wooden box on a pedestal at the foot of the few steps that led up to the altar. A bright blue wreath lay at the head of the coffin. Cornflowers. Andrew had chosen them.

The vicar stepped forward and the funeral service began. Andrew was to speak last, once the main service was over, and then Peter would sing a hymn accompanied by Andrew on the organ.

Peter stared up at the stained glass window above the altar. A solitary ray of sun set a fragment of the window ablaze: Mary, her head surrounded by a halo of light, all smiles, benevolently watching over the congregation as if she accompanied them in their ordeal.

Beautiful, isn't she? a voice said in his head, startling him.

Kate?

Indeed. Oh Peter, I'm so happy to be with you again.

Me too. With you gone, a part of me was torn out.

He felt her smile.

You can't imagine all that has happened, she said. *But tell me, what's going on?*

It's Andrew's uncle. He was assassinated by Andrew's brother, the same one that tried to kill Andrew. This is his funeral.

I too was at a funeral, Kate told him. She explained where she was and how Sister Teresa had died. She was telling him about the funeral when Andrew got to his feet. *Let's talk later,* Peter said. *I have to concentrate.*

Andrew walked around the coffin, halting a moment to look

at it, then climbed the several steps till he stood with his back to the altar facing both the coffin and the congregation.

"Cornflowers," Andrew said, indicating the wreath of flowers. His voice carried well. Dr Tchensenko had taken a while to teach him how to project his words to a large audience.

"This beautiful flower is said to heal weak eyes but what is less known is that it is also a cure for the poison of scorpions."

People shifted uncomfortably in their seats. Andrew's words were troubling. Peter had no idea what his friend was going to say. Only Dr Grant had been privy to the speech.

"When I first met my uncle, I was seduced by the way he played piano. He was an excellent pianist, as many of you must know. At the time, I wanted only one thing: to be a pianist like him. I begged him to teach me and despite my mother's opposition, he accepted. But there was a heavy price that I continue to pay even today."

Andrew stared at the cornflowers.

"When I learnt that he'd died I was sad and angry and relieved."

The audience stirred a second time, one or two people muttering muffled words.

"I was sad because I'd lost the man who led me to discover music, in particular the piano. I'm deeply grateful for that. He taught me everything I know. He opened my eyes to many other things too, not all of which I wanted to see. Would that I'd had something like cornflowers to rinse my eyes of those sights that haunt me even today."

Andrew took a deep breath, his eyes distant as he fixed the rose window over the west entrance.

"Anger? It doesn't seem right to mention such a word in a church during a funeral. Yet I am sure I'm not the first to feel angry. Words remain unsaid, deeds undone. Whether it be love or clarification or revenge. We feel cheated."

Andrew raised his voice at the word 'cheated', almost spitting it out. Peter was worried he might give way to anger. However, when he continued, his tone was once again measured.

"How dare he go without giving us a chance to set things right? Not that going was his fault. No more than our not speaking out. That's not strictly true. As a child I'd never have dared say what I thought or felt. I'm not sure I'd have been able to, had anyone given me the chance. And who'd have believed a child?"

He paused to stare at the wreath.

"They say that cornflowers blunt the blade of the reaper. Is not the reaper the figure of death? Yet no cornflowers can blunt the anger that comes when someone dies."

He took a deep shuddery breath.

"Why was I relieved? Because my uncle, like the scorpion, dug his sting deep inside me, releasing a poison I may never be able to rid myself of..."

Several people gasped. Many shifted uncomfortably at the words. Andrew's whole frame shuddered and tears began flowing down his cheeks.

"But he has left us," he continued, rubbing the back of his hand across his eyes to dry them. "It is hard, very hard, but I have to let him go, both the good and the bad. That's why I want to say farewell to this man in the only way possible, by playing music. To do so, I want to enlist the help of my friend Wendy who will sing while I play the organ."

He beckoned to Peter who got to his feet and went to join him. The boy embraced him then took hold of his hand.

"Uncle. This is for you. May you be forgiven all the wrong you did and remembered for all the good. God speed." Andrew stepped forward, unclasped the sprig of cornflower he wore attached to his dress and laid it solemnly next to the wreath then turned and headed for the organ console.

Left alone at the top of the steps facing the congregation, Peter took a deep breath. Andrew's words had moved him so deeply he wasn't sure he'd be able to sing. He clasped his St Nicholas pendant through his dress and stilled his heart.

The first notes of Jerusalem sounded on the organ, an awakening call of trumpets blowing. Peter took a deep breath and sang: "And did those feet in ancient times ..."

As the last notes ceased echoing off the walls, the church was ripe with intense silence. Nobody moved. When the six coffin bearers made their way down the central aisle to fetch Andrew's uncle, their footfalls came as a shock, awakening the congregation. Andrew and Peter, holding hands, followed the coffin and row by row the congregation filed out and shuffled along behind them.

Once they reached the porch, they halted. Peter stood close to Andrew, silently watching people's faces as they moved slowly by. They offered words of condolence. Many spoke of his speech. Fortunately, none questioned details.

Peter knew a number of the people, though none recognised him. Everyone had eyes only for Andrew. Until, that is, a small, chubby girl dressed in the green and yellow uniform of his school halted with her parents in front of Andrew. She paid no attention to Andrew. Instead, she kept glancing in Peter's direction. He held his breath hoping she'd move on. No such luck. The parents were engaged in a conversation about music with Andrew. The girl sidled over to Peter, her eyes now fixed on him as if trying to get beyond his disguise. "I loved your singing," she said in a squeaky, high-pitched voice.

Peter thanked her, unable to keep himself from blushing. He struggled to recall her name. Then it came to him. Margery. Of course. One of Witless's cronies.

"Your voice reminds me of someone...," Margery said, making a show of trying to remember who. "Are you any relation to Peter McCloud? You look remarkably like him. You even have the same voice."

She took a step closer. "Good Lord!" she exclaimed in a whisper. "Priscilla was right. You are a pansy."

Peter was at a loss what to do.

I could knock her out for you, Kate suggested.

That would be helpful, he muttered, hoping Kate understood sarcasm.

"You must be mistaken," Peter said. "My name is Wendy. I

have no idea who this Peter is."

Margery took a step even closer. She was so close he got an unpleasant whiff of antiseptic which he guessed had something to do with the rash of spots around her podgy nose. Peter had visions of her hiking up his dress to prove he was a boy. Instinctively he took a step back.

"I won't tell anyone," she said.

He didn't believe a word. Margery was one of the worst gossips in school.

Their conversation was interrupted when a scuffle broke out nearby. Someone shouted, "Look out!" as a shot rang out.

27.

Peter was hurled forward, knocking Andrew to the floor. People screamed. Kids wailed. Many flung themselves to the floor. Others pelted for the door. He and Andrew were caught in a maelstrom of panicking feet. Several people tumbled over them, knees and elbows taking their toll, till their owners clawed free. In the distance more shots rang out.

Keep down, Kate ordered, rolling Peter and Andrew out of the way. When she relinquished her hold, Peter was trembling violently. The smell of blood filled his nostrils. His hands were slick with it. Someone had been hit. But not him.

Disentangling himself from Andrew, he saw the boy grasping his shoulder, his hand red with blood. The boy's whimper was almost inaudible in the eddies of panic that swirled around them.

"Oh Andrew," he said, brushing his fingers lightly across his friend's forehead as if that could smooth away the pain.

You have to heal him, Kate insisted.

But I can't, he replied, tears in his eyes.

Yes you can.

Laying a shaking hand over Andrew's bloody hand, he let his mind flow into the wound. The shock of pain that greeted him almost drove him back.

You can do this, Kate encouraged.

The bullet was lodged in the bone.

I have no experience with gunshot wounds.

Help the body drive it out, Kate said.

I'm so sorry, Peter apologised to Andrew. *This is going to hurt.*

The boy drifted on the verge of consciousness barely aware of his surroundings. Peter's first attempt to rally the tissues around the bullet, had Andrew black out. Gently pulling Andrew's hand from the wound, Peter replaced it with his own.

He had to be quick if he was to stem the blood. Getting the bone to push the bullet out was not easy. Bones had their own sedate rhythm. He vaguely sensed a crowd gathering as people returned. In the distance an ambulance siren wailed. Kate joined her force to his as they urged Andrew's body to hurry. Once the bullet was free of the bone, pushing it out was much easier.

Just as the bullet eased out into his hand followed by a renewed flow of blood, a strong hand pulled him off Andrew.

"Let go!" he shouted, struggling to wrench free of the policeman. "Let go!" Furious that anyone should stop him healing his friend, he wanted to punch and kick the stupid man.

"Calm down girl," the policeman said. "The ambulance'll be here in a trice. They'll take care of her. She'll be alright."

What rubbish! He had no confidence in hospitals or doctors. He needed to staunch the flow of blood which darkened Andrew's dress.

Stop fighting, Kate advised. *He can't understand. The more you fight the less he'll let you close to Andrew. Remember what you told me: only experts are allowed to heal here.*

"What's the matter?" he heard Dr Grant ask.

"She's hysterical," the policeman replied. "She's likely to hurt the wounded girl."

I need just a minute, Peter pleaded in Dr Grant's head, startling the man. Seeing his hesitation, Peter said, *Hold out your hand.* When Dr Grant did, he laid the bloody bullet in it. *Just a minute,* he repeated.

Dr Grant glanced at the object in his hand. His face turned pale and he hastily closed his fingers over the bullet. Looking up, his eyes snapped to Peter's and he nodded. "Officer," he began, taking a firm grip on the man's arm. "I need to ask you a question," he said, looking meaningfully in the direction of the two girls, "in private."

The policeman reluctantly let himself be led away. Peter knelt next to Andrew and laid his hand on the wound from which blood continued to flow, albeit sluggishly, and encouraged the tissues to knit together.

When he was satisfied his work was done, he slumped down at Andrew's side, leaning his back against a bench. A wave of exhaustion swept over him. What with the tension of the funeral, the attack and healing Andrew, he was drained. When one of the ambulance men helped him up, he offered no resistance. Seated on the bench, he drifted off to sleep. It was the sound of the ambulance men arguing that awoke him.

"The bullet must have just grazed her," one said.

"Come off it. Look at all that blood. That's no graze," the other replied.

"But there's hardly a mark."

"Maybe it was the other girl that got hit."

The word 'girl' roused Peter from his stupor. They couldn't let the ambulance men take them to hospital. They'd discover Andrew was no girl. He opened his eyes and looked around for Dr Grant. The man was nowhere to be seen, but Fi's mum knelt nearby, a look of concern on her face.

Christina, he called mind-to-mind. Like Dr Grant, she was startled, more so than John. *Christina, we need to stop the ambulance men taking Andrew.* He didn't need to say more. He could see she understood, although she hesitated.

Remember when Andrew arrived at our home all covered in blood, he reminded her, *John persuaded the ambulance people to let him stay.*

She had to agree, although she was still reluctant. *Can you wake Andrew?* she thought.

I'll try. He's exhausted. He's lost a lot of blood.

The moment he spoke, he realised he'd said the wrong thing. His words had her hesitating again. *Maybe he'd be better off in hospital,* she thought.

He'll be OK, if he gets some rest.

Both of you should go, she decided. *John and I will ensure there's no trouble.*

Peter had only vague memories of the trip to hospital. Apparently John had secured a private room and a guard at the door. Fi's mum helped him out of his blood soaked dress and pulled a nightie over his head. They'd come prepared, if ever they had to stay over night. He was so tired, the moment Fi's mum tucked him in, he barely managed to mumble "thanks" before he fell asleep.

When Peter awoke he felt much better. People were talking quietly around him. He kept still and listened.

"...she came twice this morning," Christina said. "Such a charming girl and so full of solicitude. If you hadn't told me to turn every visitor away, John, I'd have let her in."

"What's her name?" John asked.

"Margery, I think."

Peter shuddered. Of course the likes of Margery wouldn't give up so easily.

"Yes. I know her," John said. "She's not very well liked. I'm not quite sure why."

"I can tell you," Peter said opening his eyes and propping himself up on one elbow. "She's the worst gossip in school. When she's on to something she won't let go. She's guessed who I am and wants to tell everyone she's seen me dressed as a girl."

"Well I'm glad I told you not to let anyone in, although I had no idea that a gossip would be the major danger," John said.

"She was one of Witless's cronies," Peter said. "She'd be delighted to prove Witless right."

A knock sounded at the door. Peter would have scrambled to hide under the covers, had not Dr Grant reassured him. "That'll be the inspector. He said he'd drop by." John rose and went to answer the door, returning accompanied by the inspector.

"You look much better after a night's sleep," the inspector said to Peter. "And your disguise is excellent. Although it may no longer work. Your friend's brother has seen you two dressed as girls."

It was only then Peter remembered Andrew. "Where's Andie?"

"Gone for an X-ray," Dr Grant said. "The doctors are puzzled by his wound. Or rather lack of it. They want to make sure there is no internal damage."

"I too am puzzled," the inspector said, pulling up a chair. "The absence of a wound is only one of the troubling things." He paused as if wondering what to say next. "How did you know? Do you have a sixth sense? You pushed your friend out of the way just in time. Had you not done so, he would surely be dead."

"I had no idea," he told the inspector. "I flung myself forward instinctively." He was content to tell the truth for once and relieved to know Kate had saved Andrew's life.

"And the wound? I saw the blood. The boy was hit in the shoulder. We searched everywhere for the bullet. There was no trace of it."

"This one, you mean?" Dr Grant asked pulling the bullet from his pocket.

"How the hell...?" the inspector began. He shook his head and took the bullet, examining it closely. "There's blood on it."

Should I tell him? Peter asked Dr Grant mind-to-mind.

Dr Grant nodded almost imperceptibly.

He's not going to like it, Peter replied mind-to-mind.

"Are you sure you really want to know?" Peter asked.

"What a silly question," the inspector replied, visibly irritated.

"You may not find it silly when you've heard my answer," Peter said. Enough, Peter thought. Quit beating about the bush. "The bullet was lodged in Andie's shoulder blade. I removed it and healed the wound before we were taken away in the ambulance."

The inspector burst out laughing. "You've been reading too many wild stories," he said. "Now tell me the truth."

Peter was about to reply when the door opened and Andrew stepped in, followed by a doctor and a nurse. His friend looked tired but otherwise well enough. The nurse helped Andrew into bed from where he gave Peter a weak smile.

"Well Doctor?" Dr Grant asked.

The doctor looked perplexed. He stared a long moment at Andrew before replying. "It's hard to believe. On the X-ray there was a faint shadow in the shoulder blade about the size of a bullet but there was no bullet."

"What could have caused that?" the Inspector asked.

"Well..." The doctor seemed reluctant to go on. "If a bullet had been extracted from there six months or a year ago, it might have left such a trace. There's also a faint scar where the bullet might have entered. It corresponded with the hole in the dress and all the blood. But it can't have happened yesterday."

The poor man looked like he'd seen a ghost.

"What a mystery!" Dr Grant exclaimed. "Were you shot six months ago, Andie?"

Andrew shook his head. "Not that I remember."

There was a scuffle at the door and a young girl burst into the room closely followed by a policewoman. It was Margery, of course. She managed to snap a picture of Peter with her little Brownie camera before the policewoman caught up with her. Peter shuddered to think what the girl might do with a picture of him in a nightie.

Dr Grant must have been thinking the same thing, because he went over to the girl who was struggling to get free. "Fighting will only make things worse, Margery," he said. "Now why don't you give me that camera?"

"It's mine," she spluttered in her unpleasant voice, cradling the little box in her podgy arms. "I won't give it to you."

Dr Grant hesitated, but the police inspector had no qualms. He wrested the camera from her paunchy fingers. "There's been a crime, young lady, and this..." he brandished the camera in the air "...is evidence. You can have it back as soon as we've finished our investigation."

"My Dad is friends with important people," she said, crossing her arms over her chest. "You're not going to get away with this."

The inspector gave her one of those knowing looks that was almost a smile. "I know your father quite well, Margery," he said. "I'm sure he'll understand when I tell him you could be arrested as an accomplice to attempted murder."

"But I had nothing to do with that," she whined, a frightened look on her face.

"Probably not, but by making your photo public, you would clearly be assisting the murderer to track these two." He nodded towards Peter and Andrew. "I'm sure you understand. Any mention of what you have seen here could be construed as a crime. It'd be a shame to have to arrest you. The cells at the station aren't made for young girls like you."

Margery screwed up her face, clearly unsure what to do. Then she stared at Peter, pure hatred in her eyes. "Of course, Sir. I hadn't understood. I meant no harm. Just a prank. I would never do anything against Peter."

What a liar! She's still fishing for confirmation that it's really me, Peter thought.

"Off you go," the inspector said. "I'll pay your father a visit later."

"She'll never keep her trap shut," Peter said furious, once she'd left. "She was buddies with Witless, the girl who gave us so much trouble earlier this year."

28.

"At last!" Tania exclaimed the moment Kate opened her eyes.

"What happened?" Kate asked, freeing herself from Tania's embrace. A quick glance around the room told her she was seated on her bed in the girls' dormitory.

"We were on our way to the refectory when you sank to the floor like a puppet with its strings cut," Tania said, snuggling close to Kate. "You just lay there in a heap."

"We couldn't wake you," Christine added, full of concern.

Kate found it hard to concentrate as memories of Peter and Andrew and the bullet overwhelmed her. She had no idea what instinct had drawn her to Peter, but it'd been a close shave. A moment earlier or later and either Peter or Andrew would've been killed. The thought had her trembling so violently she would have collapsed again had not Tania had her arms around her.

"You're trembling," Tania said. "You're not going to have another attack, are you?"

"No, no," Kate reassured her, getting unsteadily to her feet. "It's just the memory of what happened."

"The burial of Sister Teresa must have been a shock," Christine said, tears forming in her eyes. "It was for me."

At first, Kate had no idea what the girl was talking about. Then she remembered. The sight of the nun's form sinking into the ground then covered with clods of earth had upset the girls much more than the ceremony in the church. Perhaps they should have sent the younger ones away.

"No it wasn't that," Kate said. "It was the bullet."

She didn't miss the worried look Tania and Christine exchanged.

"It's a long story," she added.

"Why don't you tell us over dinner," Christine suggested. "The meal should be ready."

At the mention of food, Kate hastened her step. The day's adventures had left her ravenous. A delicious bouquet of odours greeted them as they entered the refectory. Someone had shifted the trestle tables to form a large rectangle in the middle with chairs placed around it. A winding path of flowers ran the length of the tables bringing light and colour to the room. Candles flickered here and there between plates and bowls.

The moment the girls caught sight of her they crowded round, some cheering others applauding, while many reached out trying to touch her. Their warm welcome had her feeling both wanted and embarrassed. Tania guided her between the girls to the table and sat her in the middle while she and Christine sat on either side. The other girls took their places around the giant table.

Once they were seated, Suzanne strode in carrying a bowl of soup. Other girls carried different dishes to the table placing them at the four corners. Despite the enticing smell, nobody ate. Instead all turned to Kate. What was she supposed to do?

"Grace," Christine whispered.

Kate got to her feet, pushing back her chair. She raised her hands in prayer as she'd seen others do. All followed suit, bowing their heads. Then, after a moment's hesitation, she spoke. "For what we are about to receive, but also for all that has happened today, both good and bad, may we be truly grateful."

"Amen," the girls chimed,

A joyous chorus of laughter and happy voices mingled with the sound of spoons on plates. Girls called out, congratulating Suzanne on her cooking as she carried in dishes with her helpers.

Kate stood surveying the group. This must have been

the first time the convent had been blessed by such a happy gathering. Ignoring Tania's insistent request to sit and eat, Kate walked around the table exchanging a few words with each girl. It was only when she returned to her place and sat down that she realised someone was missing. Glancing from girl to girl it took her a moment to realise who.

"Where's Jane?" she asked Christine and Tania.

Both girls turned pale and hurriedly got to their feet to check.

"Where's Jane?" Christine asked, raising her voice so everyone could hear.

"She said she felt ill and went to lie down," one girl told them

"There was no one in the dormitory," Kate pointed out.

Several people got to their feet, no doubt intending to search for the lost girl.

"Finish your meal," Kate said. "It would be a shame to let Suzanne's good cooking get cold. We can search afterwards."

She began to eat, trying to enjoy the meal, but much of the festive spirit had fled. Although the girls continued to chatter quietly, the smiles had faded.

"Where could she have gone?" Kate asked Tania and Christine.

"Hiding somewhere," Tania suggested.

"I doubt it," Christine said. "She probably ran to her beloved Helga."

The idea had already crossed Kate's mind, but she'd dismissed it. If Jane had joined Helga they'd be in for trouble. Who knew what lies the girl might tell? Jane knew enough about Sister Helga to fan her rage.

"Weren't you going to tell us your story?" Tania asked.

If Jane brought Helga back, it would be unwise for everyone to know how Kate got there and what happened to her. "Another time," Kate said, taking a bite of the chocolate cake Suzanne had baked. When Tania looked disappointed, Kate added, "I'm worried about Jane."

"Hey Suzanne," Kate called out, shifting attention elsewhere.

"Your cake is delicious."

Suzanne smiled as she began clearing away the dishes.

"Let us do that," Kate said. "You did the cooking. Rest while we tidy up." Suzanne protested, but Kate wouldn't take no for an answer. "Who'll help me do the dishes?" Kate asked. Hands went up around the room. Kate grinned. "You organise them, Eileen. You are so good at it. I'll be in the kitchen," Kate said.

Once the dishes were done, Kate left most of the girls with Clara and Claudia to sing and sew while she, Christine, Tania, Eileen and Suzanne went to explore. Once they were alone, Kate voiced her fears. "It's not safe here. I think we should move."

"Why?" Suzanne asked sounding disappointed. "Just when we've made our room more comfortable."

"If Jane tells Helga what we're doing, I wouldn't put it past the nun to return. She might even come during the night," Kate replied, "catching us off guard. If she finds no one, that'll stall her."

"Where should we go?" Tania asked.

"I'm not sure?" Kate replied. "I thought of the infirmary, but it'd probably be too small."

While they talked, they made their way round the cloister till they stood in front of that part used by the nuns. Kate had no wish to enter, neither had the others. Despite the daylight, the place was spooky, as if the spirit of the nuns still clung to the walls. The girls continued past the entrance to the church until they reached the door to Abbess's rooms.

Kate tried the door. Unsurprisingly, it was locked. None of the Abbess's keys fit.

"Here," Suzanne said, grinning as she pulled a key from her pocket. "When she told me I no longer worked for her, I kept the key."

Suzanne opened the door and showed them in. Switching on the light, she led them from room to room. A small reception room lay off the entrance hall, furnished only with dingy armchairs grouped around a low table. Although it was still daytime, Suzanne pulled the curtains, shutting out prying eyes.

Next came the bedroom. They crowded in the doorway, but no one wanted to enter. There was also a small kitchen and storage cupboards.

"This is her study," Suzanne said. "I was never allowed in."

Stepping inside, Kate saw a large desk littered with papers behind which stood a swivel chair with wooden armrests. Suzanne drew the curtains there too and switched on the light. There were no bookshelves or cupboards and the walls were bare except for a large map pinned behind the desk.

Examining it, Kate realised it depicted the convent.

"What's that?" Tania asked joining her while the others rummaged though the papers on the desk and peered into the drawers.

"It's the convent," Kate told her. "Look, here's the church and this is the cloister."

"And that's our dormitory," Tania said.

"What this over here?" Christine asked pointing to a building some distance from the convent.

"According to what is written here, it says Schola," Kate told them. "Have any of you ever been there?"

"I went once, but I didn't go inside." Suzanne said, brandishing a large stick in her fist.

"What have you got there?" Kate asked. She'd never seen the thing before.

"You're lucky you don't know," Christine said. "The Abbess used it to punish us."

Kate shuddered at the thought. Thicker than a cane, it looked heavy and deadly.

Suzanne managed to bend it a little but was unable to break it. They took it in turns trying to smash the thing, without success.

"Is there a fireplace?" Kate asked.

There was, Suzanne informed them.

"Use it to light a fire," Kate suggested.

Pleased at the idea, Suzanne and Tania hurried off to burn it.

Turning back to the map, Kate continued to study it. Judging from the contours, the "Schola" looked like a farm. Set on higher ground, it was surrounded by open fields. Anyone trying to approach would be easy to see. The farm itself was a sprawling building with a nearby barn and what might have been stalls for animals.

When Suzanne and Tania returned, their faces and hands sooty, Kate tapped the map with her index finger, asking. "Tell me, Suzanne, does anyone live there?"

"I don't think so. Nobody came to greet me. The door was locked, the shutters closed and cobwebs were everywhere."

"You thinking of going there?" Christine asked.

"Yes," Kate said. "I'd like to check it out before it gets dark."

"As a hiding place?" Eileen asked.

"Maybe," Kate replied.

"Off we go then," Tania said, eager to leave.

"We should tell the others," Kate said much to Tania's disappointment.

Once Kate had spoken to the girls about the farm, everyone wanted to go.

"Listen," she said. "We may be safer in the farm than here, but first we have to size up the place to see if it's suitable. If we all go, someone might see us and tip off the nuns. That's why I want you to stay here with Clara and Claudia. But don't think you won't be doing your part. I want you to prepare clothes and blankets and food to take, should we move to the farm. And you'll have to find some way to transport everything."

Waiting till the girls began their work, Kate finally set off with the four girls who'd been with her earlier. Before they could head for the farm, they had to find a way out the back of the convent. It wouldn't do to be seen leaving by the main entrance, but the walls surrounding the rest of the convent were too high to scale. Across the far side of the church, in a corner of the north transept, they discovered a small door. It was locked, but one of the Abbess's keys did the trick. Once through they found themselves outside the walls. A path led away that soon expanded into a dirt track. It wound its way between overgrown hedgerows from which thorn branches hung seeking to snag the girls.

At least they wouldn't be seen while they remained on the track, Kate thought as she dodged yet another treacherous branch. If they used it at night, they'd have to be careful. To her delight the sheltered way led almost up to the farm.

Shortly before the end of the track, Kate heard a snuffling behind them. Signalling the others to stop, she strained to hear, but whoever it was that followed them also stopped. They eased forward as stealthily as they could, only to hear noise of movement again. This time when they stopped, the noise continued. Putting the girls behind her, Kate steeled herself for a fight as she turned to face their adversary.

Their situation was all the more frightening as frequent bends made it impossible to catch a glimpse of their pursuer. Whoever it was let out an unearthly grunt and the footsteps sped up till a solitary sheep came into view. Trotting up to them, it nuzzled Tania. She laughed, but the other girls let out a sigh of relief.

29.

"You had us really worried, Baron," a female voice said. "What possessed you to wander off like that? You were supposed to be resting. Imagine our surprise when we discovered you'd gone. We searched all over. It was quite by chance we found you in a ditch not far from here. You were half hidden under an overturned bench, your clothes filthy and in tatters as if you'd been in a fight and, excuse me for saying so, you stank of cheap wine. At first, we took you for a tramp or a drunk. It's all very well having a vocation to be charitable, but these days you have to be careful. The world is not what it used to be." She sighed. "Imagine our relief when we realised it was you. But what an effort to get you back, you could hardly stand, let-alone walk..."

Did he really have to suffer the woman's senseless prattling? He squeezed his eyes shut and turned his back, wishing he could shove his fingers in his ears.

"This will not do at all, Mr Wong," a female voice said with a London accent. Someone grasped him firmly by the wrist. "If you want to recover, you need to eat. Look at all that food untouched. What a waste! Continue like this and I'll ask the doctor to have a serious word." Whoever it was let go of his wrist, his hand falling limp onto the bed, and prized open his mouth, sliding something smooth, cold and unpleasant between his lips.

He was about to bite the intruding object when the woman jerked it out of his mouth saying, "I wouldn't do that if I were you. Bite the thermometer and you'll cut your mouth. You can't imagine how much extra work that'd give us. There's nothing worse than picking glass splinters from someone's lips and tongue. What's more, you'd probably be poisoned by the mercury. Imagine being unable to hear or speak. And that would only be the first symptoms."

Deaf and dumb. He shuddered. Just like Kate.

So he was back in hospital! That would explain the smell. Keeping his eyes shut, he tried to flex his right leg. To his delight it didn't hurt, but despite repeated efforts, it wouldn't budge.

"We had to operate," a male voice said. "There were some ... er ... complications." The man sounded embarrassed.

Wong slid his hand discreetly under the covers, hoping no one would notice, and, snaking down to his knee, he sought to reassure himself that his wild imaginings were unfounded. Rotten luck! The path was blocked by some sort of metal contraption that encased his leg from the thigh down.

"... Yes! The girls called it a miracle," a young girl was saying in a grating, high-pitched voice. "More like the devil's work."

"And her leg was healed?" he heard the Abbess ask. She sounded sceptical.

"Completely. Before she couldn't walk without the help of that pest Tania." The girl paused a moment, for effect, before continuing. "There's something unnatural about the way those two cling to each other." She paused again, no doubt letting her insinuations take their toll. She'd make a good little actress, he thought, if ever she could resist overdoing it. "I saw her skip and dance, in the church of all places. She even cried out and sang for joy."

Healed? How could that be? Her leg was mangled, he'd made sure of that. And she shouldn't be able to sing. Something had gone terribly wrong with his story.

"Don't touch your knee, Mr Wong. We spent a lot of time and energy piecing it back together," he heard what he guessed to be the doctor say.

Piecing? What the hell had happened? Sure, he'd fallen

roughly, but not that his knee would be broken into pieces.

"It was very strange," the doctor continued. "As if an earthquake had shaken your knee apart, although none of us felt anything. One minute we were carrying out a routine operation, the next the bones were fractured in multiple places. I've never seen anything like it ..." The doctor's voice trailed off in confusion.

"What were they doing in the church, Jane?" a woman asked.

"Holding some sort of pagan rite for Sister Teresa," Jane replied. "At least that's what I think it was."

"Pagan?" Sister Helga asked, her voice raised in outrage.

"Yes. Flowers and herbs and folk songs and wild dances, all with that Kate prancing around like a priestess."

"It's a scandal!" Helga exclaimed. He heard a chair scrape as she got to her feet.

"Shhh! You'll wake the Baron," the Abbess whispered. "So Teresa is dead?"

"Oh yes," Jane said quietly. "The nun died shortly after that Kate administered a concoction of flowers and roots and berries. Wouldn't surprise me if that didn't kill her. It smelt foul."

He heard both women gasp. Surely they must realise the girl was taking them for a ride. Jane? Was that her name? She intrigued him. He would have liked to open his eyes, to size her up, she might prove useful, but he didn't want to attract attention.

"Oh, Mr Wong," a melodious female voice said. Not only was he enveloped in the woman's sickly-sweet perfume, but he could hear the rustle of her skirts as she sat down on the edge of his bed, her bony backside jabbing him in the ribs.

"Are you his wife?" the doctor enquired.

The woman snorted like a wild pig. "No. No. I'm his new neighbour." She must have leaned closer because the smell of perfume threatened to suffocate him. "He looks a little better, don't you think?" She brushed his hair from his forehead, making him cringe. She didn't seem to notice. Instead, he heard the woman rummaging through her bag. He shifted as far from her as possible, which wasn't far with his leg fixed to the bed.

"I've baked a cake," she announced. The familiar smell of candied peel had bile rising in Wong's throat. "He can eat cake, can't he?" she asked, doubtful.

The doctor sighed. "Yes, he can eat cake," he replied pronouncing each word separately, with exaggerated patience, as if talking to the village idiot.

"I'll leave you with your visitor, Mr Wong. Enjoy the cake," the doctor said.

Wong was miserable. He'd give anything to be whisked away to another world, a world without smelly neighbours with bony intentions and poisonous cake.

"A feast?" the Abbess exclaimed.

"Yes." Jane was speaking again. "Ham and bacon and sausages and vegetables and fresh bread and butter and fruit and cream and wine... Wouldn't surprise me if they hadn't emptied the larder. And they've moved everything round in the refectory. The nuns' table is gone. I saw them through the window. All sitting at one big table in the middle. And that Kate girl saying grace..."

"I told you that girl was in league with the devil," Helga said, spluttering with rage. "We should march up there and teach her a lesson."

He heard the door creak as if she were about to leave. Who knew what the idiot might do? She'd already caused the nuns to flee, making a complete mess of his plans. He struggled to open his eyes. For a moment he panicked, thinking they were glued together, but then the lids popped open and he was blinded by the unaccustomed light.

The first thing he saw, once his eyes adjusted, was a young girl crouched next to his bed, her short dress concealing nothing of the disgustingly filthy state of her legs and feet. Seeing him staring at her, she scrambled to her feet, pulling her dress down as far as it would reach, then folded her hands demurely across her lap.

"I wouldn't go running to the convent if I were you," he said, his voice broken and rough, startling the two nuns, who hadn't noticed he was awake.

"Why not, Baron?" the Abbess asked, once she'd recovered from her fright.

"It's far too dangerous. The illness that carried Sister Teresa off may still be lingering. We wouldn't want any more of you good nuns dying, would we?"

"But none of the girls got ill," Helga pointed out.

"Oh, but they did," the girl said. At which Helga gave her a filthy look. No doubt regretting she'd contradicted Helga, the girl added, "I mean, they did, a little, but then they recovered."

"There are illnesses that kill only older people," he said, making every effort to sound knowledgeable.

He was pleased to see Helga step back into the room and let the door close, frustration etched on her face.

"What do you propose?" the Abbess asked.

"I'll go and check..." he replied.

"You shouldn't take the risk," the Abbess said, sounding worried.

"It's the least I can do. And this girl will go with me as a guide."

It was the girl's turn to look alarmed. He wondered why. But then she said, "They mustn't see me. They'll kill me if they do."

He smiled, in what he hoped was a winning way. "They won't see either of us, young lady," he reassured her. "By the time we get there, night will have fallen and we'll keep well out of sight. As soon as we have a clear idea what's going on, we'll return and report."

He saw the girl relax, but both nuns remained sceptical.

"I still think I should go," Helga said.

"Your time will come," he replied, swinging his legs round till his bare feet touched the cold floor. He had planned to leave immediately, but the moment he let the blanket fall he discovered he was stark naked. A furtive glance in the direction of the girl revealed her ogling him, a look of morbid fascination on her face. She immediately looked away, making an exaggerated show of brushing dirt from her dress. He hastily wrapped a blanket around his shivering body.

"Where are my clothes?" he asked, trying to sound as if nothing out of the ordinary had just happened. He couldn't help shuddering at the thought that one of the nuns must have undressed him.

"They were beyond repair," the Abbess said. "Luckily the innkeeper was able to loan us clothes." She handed him a neat pile.

He examined the clothes: an off-white shirt, freshly washed and stiff with starch, brown corduroy trousers stained on one knee and frayed at the hem and a cheap waistcoat in matching material.

He glanced around to see what had changed in his absence. He was no longer in the tiny bedroom. Instead, he sat on a cot in a corner of the tavern. The tables had been pushed back to make room for him. None of the other nuns were there. Just the Abbess, Sister Helga and the young girl. Between the half drawn curtains, sunlight streamed into the room. What time could it be? He glanced at the clock over the fireplace: four-thirty.

"How long was I out?"

"More than a day," the Abbess replied. "You must be hungry. Get dressed and we'll fetch food."

The contents of the two large jerry cans slopped noisily as they lugged them up the hill. Luckily the road was deserted. He'd done well to send the girl to buy the petrol, you could never be too cautious, even if he'd had to put up with her sulking ever since.

Confronted with the impressive walls of the convent, he wondered how they'd get in. Then he remembered the tiny door he and the Abbess had used. Surely it'd be locked. He glanced up at the windows of the gymnasium. If anyone were in the school, the two would hardly go unnoticed, lugging their load up the hill. But all was dark as they stole in amongst the trees.

Happy to put the jerry can down, he rubbed his hands hoping to soothe the sores that had formed in his palms. He tried the door which, to his surprise, was unlocked. Hustling the girl inside, he hurried in after her. The dark passage stank of rot and mould and, each time they paused, it was alive with alarming rustling and scratching sounds. He hastened his pace frequently bumping his leg against the weighty can. When they emerged into the convent gardens, dusk had fallen and light flooded from a row of convent windows, illuminating patches of roses.

"What's that?" he whispered, pointing to the windows.

"The refectory."

"Where do the girls sleep?"

"There," she said pointing back over her shoulder at the first floor of building they'd just passed under. The place looked deserted.

Beckoning her to follow, they crept along a covered walkway that ran the length of the wall, till they could crouch next to the Guest House. He hid the cans behind a low bush and signed for her to come closer, which she did with great reluctance. He whispered, "I want to have look. Wait for me."

As he went to move off, she clamped onto his waistcoat. He was about to swear, when she hissed, "I'm coming too."

He wasn't sure he could trust her. But she was adamant, gripping on to his waistcoat with both hands. The two picked their way cautiously across the gardens till they reached the main building. Skirting storage rooms and the kitchen, all shroud in darkness, they made it to the lighted windows. The closer they got, the tighter she clung to the hem of his waistcoat almost throwing him off balance.

He peered cautiously around the window frame. Seated at a large table, he counted five girls, each draped in a blanket. Or was it a cape? He recognised Kate immediately, proud and full of herself. She was doing most of the talking. When she rose to fetch a water pitcher, he had to admit that none of the handicaps he'd inflicted had stuck. Could she have been a more powerful magician than he thought? The sooner he got rid of her, the better.

Now that night had fallen it was bitterly cold. He wished the nuns had given him a coat. The girl must have been cold too. He could hear her teeth chattering. He drew her back into the shadows.

"We'll wait till they go to bed," he whispered, trying not to get too close. The girl stank. "How long before lights out?"

Between chattering teeth, her whispered answer was incomprehensible. "Let's find a place to shelter," he whispered.

They set off for the guesthouse, the going slow. Several times he had to heave her up by her bare arms. Her skin was icy. If he didn't get her to shelter, she'd die of exposure, which wouldn't suit his plans at all.

30.

Kate poured water into her glass and drank deeply. She longed to lay her head on her arms and rest, but they had to get back. It was getting late. The others'd be worrying. Her little group had walked between the farm and the convent at least ten times that day, ferrying girls and goods as they did. It'd been hot, thirsty work and she was no longer accustomed to such exercise.

Finding the farm had been a stroke of good luck. At some distant epoch, it'd been converted into a boarding house, maybe housing pupils. Given the demise of the Gymnasium, that might explain why the house had long since been abandoned.

They'd discovered a host of small bedrooms on the first floor and under the rafters, along with rudimentary washing facilities on each floor. On the ground floor there was a common room, a small kitchen and a couple of offices.

In some bedrooms they found half-read books folded open on bedside tables along with stubs of crayons and crumpled notepads full of scribbled homework. There was even a sizable amount of abandoned clothes hanging amongst cobwebs in cupboards. The girls who'd lived there had left in a hurry. Kate couldn't help suspecting something sinister had happened. She tried to ignore the foreboding the place inspired. They had no alternative.

There was no electricity, but they found a good stock of candles and storm lamps in one of the cupboards. The place was heated by a wood-fired stove which also served as a range. Water came from a nearby well and was both clear and clean.

The wooden walls were solid, the roof in good repair and, as far as Kate could judge, there was no damp.

Eileen set some of the girls to work cleaning the house, while others helped Suzanne scrub the kitchen and, once they'd fetched plates and cutlery and kitchen utensils and a cart load of food, they set about preparing a meal.

"We need to get back," Eileen said, putting her glass down on the large table in the middle of the refectory. "Dinner'll be ready and I don't like leaving the young ones alone now it's nearly dark."

This was their last trip of the day. They hadn't planned to return, but Suzanne had run out of herbs and Kate had decided it would be good to transfer some of the salves and simples from the infirmary to the farm, just in case.

"We should leave a few lights on," Christine suggested. "If anyone is prowling around they'll think we're still here."

Swinging the rucksack onto her shoulders, Kate trudged after the others, her feet sore, her legs weary. The jars and bottles weighed her down, but at least they made no noise, wrapped as they were in cloth.

Taking the shortcut through the choir stalls, a dreadfully eerie place in the dying light, they headed for the north transept and the small door. Once outside, they made their way diagonally across an expanse of grass to the track that led to the farm.

Kate looked back one last time at the dark buildings rearing against the skyline, aglow with the distant lights of the town. The road that led down from the other side of the convent to the town was hidden from view. They walked in silence, Christine taking the lead, followed by Eileen and Suzanne, with Tania and Kate bringing up the rear.

They'd just reached the half-way mark, a large, flat stone set by the side of the track, when Kate was overcome by a wave of fatigue. Her vision blurred and she felt giddy. Was she getting ill again? Now really wasn't the time.

Tania led her to the stone, unhooked the bag from her shoulders and helped her sit. The others crouched in the dark, waiting silently for her to recover. She felt her eyes close and her head and shoulders sagged, but it was only when she began to fall that alarm gripped her, too late. Sound and sight faded leaving her floating in an empty no-man's-land.

The strident ring of a telephone brought her back to herself. She opened her eyes to find she was in a hospital bed, but not at all one from the infirmary. Disoriented, she struggled to understand where she was. Then she noticed Andrew in the next bed. The phone must have woken him because he was rubbing his eyes.

"Yes," she heard Dr Grant say, then he fell silent.

Peter, she whispered, nudging him mentally. *I'm back.*

She felt his delight.

Where have you been? he asked. But she had no time to reply.

"That was the police," Dr Grant told them, his face grave. "They have found Brian's hiding place."

"Did they nab him?" Peter asked, hopeful.

"No. He hadn't been there for several days."

Kate was trying to recall who Brian was when Peter whispered mind-to-mind, *Andrew's brother.*

"The police did find one thing," Dr Grant continued, a sour look on his face. "Press cuttings from a local newspaper about two girls giving an improvised concert in a church in the seaside village of Lettup Cove. There was even a picture of the two, one playing piano and the other singing…"

"How the hell did we get in the newspaper?" Andrew asked.

"Never mind that," Peter replied, scrambling to get out of bed and put on his clothes. "It's Fi I'm worried about."

I don't understand, Kate said.

Fi's there on her own. If Brian goes looking for us, he'll find her…

He didn't need to finish his sentence, she could smell blood and gunshot as Peter remember what happened at the funeral.

"Not so fast," Dr Grant said as Andrew climbed from his bed and pulled his nightie over his head, meaning to get dressed.

Kate was embarrassed to see the near-naked boy.

Don't look then, Peter said.

You're a joker, was her reply. *It's you that's looking not me. I just see what you see.* It was his turn to be embarrassed.

"The police are on their way to Lettup. If you go it could be dangerous."

"I don't care," Peter said, hastily pulling on a blouse, pants and a skirt. "She's my half-sister and my friend and I'm going to help save her."

"That may be exactly what Andrew's brother wants," Dr Grant said.

"Dr Grant is right," Andrew added. Kate could hear the fear in his voice.

"Of course he is," Peter snapped. "But we can do things the police can't … and that might just save her."

Dr Grant looked like he wanted to argue but in the end he just sighed. "Well, I hope we've got it all wrong and we are panicking for nothing. I will drive you. I know how courageous you can be, Peter, but I implore you to be careful. I'd hate to see any of you harmed."

"What about Fi's mum?" Andrew asked. "Surely we should let her know."

"She'll be back in a moment. As soon as she gets here, we'll leave," Dr Grant said, getting to his feet. "I'll let the doctor know."

Kate awoke to find herself cold and stiff, lying at the feet of the girls on the damp grass under the night sky. An owl hooted nearby, startling her. She must have fallen asleep in the back of the car while she told Peter what'd happened to her.

"Some people use any excuse to have a rest," Tania whispered, helping Kate to her feet.

"If you're jealous, be my guest. It's hard and damp. I'd much prefer a bed," Kate retorted, giving Tania a playful shove. When Tania responded in kind, Kate almost toppled over.

"Enough," Christine exclaimed, catching hold of Kate's arm to stop her falling. "Can you walk?"

Kate nodded.

Tania pushed past Christine and gave Kate her arm, while Eileen picked up Kate's rucksack and swung it onto her back. "God! It's heavy," she exclaimed. "No wonder you felt woozy."

The five set off towards the farm with Eileen taking the lead. They'd hardly walked ten yards when a strange red glow sprang up along the tops of the hedgerows. It spread rapidly making the countryside around jump and start as if they'd awakened some ruddy demon. Something was terribly wrong.

She halted and turned, as did the others, in search of the source.

Christine gasped. Eileen swore, "Oh my God!" Kate and Tania hurried back to the stone and clambered up to get a better view.

"It's the convent," Suzanne spoke for them all. "The school is on fire."

"Did we leave something alight?" Christine asked, sounding worried.

"No. I checked," Suzanne reassured her.

"Thank heavens we moved everyone out," Christine said, her voice trembling.

Kate couldn't rid herself of the suspicion that someone had deliberately set fire to the school. The thought was so horrible it left a tight knot in her gut.

"We should go and have a look," Tania said, excited at the prospect. "Maybe we can stop the fire destroying the rest of the buildings."

The girl would have hurried back to the convent, had Kate not placed a restraining hand on her shoulder.

"Wait," Kate said. "My guess is that someone set fire to the place, hoping to catch us inside."

"But that's horrible," protested Christine, her stricken expression further distorted by the dancing light of the fire.

"Who would possibly do that?" Suzanne asked. "They'd have to be diabolic."

"Sister Helga!" Tania exclaimed.

"If it was Sister Helga," Kate said, emphasising the word 'if', "it would be just like her to hang around in case any of us escaped."

Several girls groaned, staring at each other's flushed faces, horrified.

"I think we should go and have a look," Eileen said calmly. "If we keep to the hedges on this side of the church, we could get close enough without being seen."

Kate was torn. She wanted to hurry back to the rest of the girls. They must be in a panic. For all they knew, the five of them could have perished in the blaze. At the same time, Kate wanted to know what'd happened. She had a bad feeling. Something was not right. Sister Helga's might have been an abominable monster, but Kate couldn't imagine her doing such a thing.

"Christine and Suzanne, you should return to the farm. Someone has to reassure the girls and make sure nobody approaches the building. Eileen and Tania, come with me. We will skirt the convent and try to find out what happened."

Kate would have preferred to continue alone. Despite her affection for Tania, the girl was impetuous and could be a liability. The trouble was that she clung to Kate and would never accept being separated. As for Eileen, her skill at organising would have been better employed at the farm. However, having her along meant she could deal with Tania if ever the worse came to the worse.

Eileen handed Kate's bag to Suzanne and, after hasty goodbyes, the three slipped through a break in the hedge and cautiously followed the edge of the field. Their cover took them to some twenty yards north of the church where, just beyond the main entrance, the hedge veered north and away from the convent.

From that point, through a narrow gap in the hedge, they had a clear view of the fire. Flames roared skyward from the roof of their dormitory and the adjacent store rooms. The walls of the Abbess's quarters resisted, made as they were of stone, but the roof had caught fire.

Kate scanned the grounds. The leaping flames caused shadows to shift and swirl, constantly transfiguring the scene. Shapes appeared and disappeared confusing her, but she was pretty sure no one was there. Whoever had started the fire was long gone.

Do you not have people to put out fires? Kate asked.

The fire brigade, Eileen said. *I'm surprised they're not here.*

We'd hear them, Tania added. *They have a bell on their fire engine. I heard it once all the way from town.*

Kate was about to suggest they return, when she spotted a glint by the guest house. She fixed the point for a long time, but nothing more was to be seen. She must have been mistaken. Then the flash came again and she was able to make out a dark form leaning against the wall.

Kate tapped Tania and Eileen on the shoulder and pointed to the source of light, then put her finger to her lips for silence. A silly precaution, really. Even if they did talk, they wouldn't be heard, the fire was making so much noise.

See that? she asked mind-to-mind.

Eileen nodded mentally

What's going on? a boy's voice asked.

Both Tania and Eileen spun around searching for the source of the voice. Kate immediately recognised Peter, although she was surprised the others could hear him.

Don't panic, Kate said. *It's my friend Peter. Peter, meet Tania and Eileen.*

"Get out of my head" Tania shouted, clawing her fingers through her hair as if that could drive Peter from her mind.

Kate placed a hand on Tania's arm, hoping to reassure her, but the girl shoved her away. "Don't touch me. You brought him here. I don't want no filthy boy in my head."

Peter is not filthy, Kate tried to reason with her. *He's a good person. He saved my life.* As she said it, she was unable to conceal the affection she felt for him.

"I trusted you," Tania said, her lip quivering, tears springing to her eyes. Then she lurched forward and shoved her way through the hedge, blundering out into full view, heading for the fire.

Once Kate got over her shock, she wanted to run after Tania and drag her back, but Eileen held onto her. *She'll get us all in trouble,* she said.

I'm really sorry, Peter said. *I thought I was just talking to you, Kate.*

They had no time to discuss. A man had come out from behind the Guest House and was striding towards Tania. Trailing behind him they could just make out a second figure.

"That's Jane," Eileen exclaimed.

The fact didn't surprise Kate, although it made her sad that the girl had gone to such lengths to get revenge.

Peter suddenly gasped.

What's the matter? Kate asked.

That's Old Man God, Peter exclaimed. *He looks older, but I'm sure it's him.*

Who's Old Man God? Eileen asked, perplexed

A very nasty person, Peter replied.

We've got to stop him, Kate said, pushing between the bushes. It was at that moment that they heard the distant clang of fire engines.

31.

"Keep your distance!" the man snarled, raising his voice to be heard over the spitting and crackling of the fire and the cacophony of the approaching fire engines. "You've done enough damage."

Although Peter had talked of Old Man God, Kate'd never seen him. In the glow of the fire, he could have been anywhere between forty-five and sixty, possibly even more. He was nondescript, his shoulders were slightly rounded, he had the beginnings of a paunch, there was stubble on his chin and his hairline had begun to recede. It was hard to believe that this pathetic man, in worn corduroy trousers and a tatty waistcoat, had ordered the execution of both her and her father.

The man's hand snaked out and grabbed Tania by the wrist. Yanking her closer, he twisted her arm behind her back. She screamed and struggled but he forced her to the ground, silencing her with a kick in the stomach.

"Bring that rope," he shouted to Jane who hung back, clearly scared of Kate and the others. When she continued to stare at the girls, unmoving, he shouted, "Hurry up, girl. Now's the time to get your revenge."

Stay out of this, Jane, Kate said.

Unused to speaking mind-to-mind, Jane cast about, a terrified look on her face made all the more lurid by the glow of the fire.

Seeing she wasn't going to obey, the man took several paces in her direction, dragging Tania behind him. The girl screamed in pain, lashing out with her free hand trying to hit him.

Eileen, who'd been holding back, dashed forward to free Tania. It was then that the man pulled a knife from his pocket. "I wouldn't if I were you," he said, waving the blade close to Tania's face. Tania immediately stopped struggling and Eileen froze mid-step.

"That's better," he said. "Now let's finish this. Get the rope from that stupid girl," he told Eileen.

Eileen glanced at Kate. *Go ahead,* Kate said mind-to-mind. *Do as he says.*

Can you jump to his mind? Kate asked Peter.

I doubt it. I can't even control when I travel to your head. But I might be able to if you were to touch him.

He'll never let me close, Kate replied.

Then I'll have to travel via someone else.

Eileen went to Jane, who held the coil of rope at arms length, clearly terrified. At her side stood a large metal can.

It's a jerrycan, Peter told Kate. *We use it to transport petrol.*

Eileen took the rope and returned to the man.

"Now tie her hands behind her back," he said, pointing to Kate. "And make sure the knots are tight. For every knot that works loose, I'll slice her face."

Place your hand on my wrist, Kate instructed Eileen, *and keep it there as long as you can without arousing suspicion. My friend is going to jump to your mind. He'll explain what you have to do once he's managed.*

Peter made several attempts. Each time he bounced back getting ever more frustrated. *I'm not going to make it.*

"Stop dithering, girl and get on with it," the man shouted, pressing his knife on Tania's cheek.

Peter, Kate called out. *Take over my body, I'll jump.* She felt her body sag as she left him in control. She was relieved how effortlessly she flowed from her body to Eileen's. Once there, she noted that Peter had also succeeded and was now in control of her body.

Eileen, Kate said. *It's me, not Peter.* The girl took her voice for granted, thinking Kate was talking mind-to-mind. *I'm really in your head,* Kate told her.

I'm no good at knots, Eileen groaned, terrified. *And he'll hurt Tania if I mess up.*

I'll do it, Kate said. Just relax I'm going to take control for a moment. She felt Eileen tense then giggle mentally as Kate used her body to tie a knot. *It looks solid enough,* Kate explained, *but it can be slipped off very easily.*

You must find a way to touch that man's skin, Kate told Eileen, relinquishing control, *so I can get into his mind.*

"What should I do with her?" Eileen asked.

He dragged Tania to her feet and forced her to walk in front of him, his knife in the small of her back. "Follow me," he said. When Jane hung back, he shouted. "Bring that jerrycan." She stumbled after lugging the heavy weight.

The door to a narrow passage under the school hung precariously from its hinges. The man shoved it aside and forced the girls inside, following closely behind, keeping a tight hold on Tania as he did. Peter, who was still in control of Kate's body, stumbled several times in the dark and Jane, dragging the jerrycan after her, fell twice. When the man kicked her, she yelped and scurried to her feet trying to get out of reach.

Use his distraction to undo the knots, Kate sent.

Already done, Peter replied.

Once in the gardens, Kate could see the fire had not yet reached the kitchens, although it was lapping up the roof of the far side of the stores. As they neared the kitchen, Kate could hear the urgent clang of bells, but there was no way the firemen would find them any time soon, hidden as they were by the high wall enclosing that side of the convent.

He's got petrol, Peter said to Kate. *You need to hurry before he starts another fire.*

Old Man God herded them into the kitchen. Glancing back to check Tania was OK, Kate momentarily locked eyes with the man who was muttering to himself, his eyes ablaze with hatred.

"Watch where you're going!" he shouted, as she stumbled

over a stool.

Once they reached the refectory, he shoved Tania inside and took a swing at her, hitting her over the head. She crumpled senseless to the floor. Eileen wanted to rush the man, but Kate held her back. *He's still got that knife,* she said. *You'll get hurt.*

The man shoved Tania's limp body out of the way with his foot. Pocketing his knife, he busied himself dragging a table across the room, grunting as he did. He rammed it against the door, blocking all escape. Striding back to Jane, who was cringing in a corner, he wrenched the jerrycan from her fingers. When he moved to knock her out, she fell to the floor before he'd even touched her. Unscrewing the can, he poured petrol over her. She let out a high-pitched scream. Ignoring her, he splashed the stuff on the tables and over Tania.

We're not going to make it, Peter said, terrified.

When Eileen tried to sidle closer, the man snarled at her, whipping out his knife and brandishing it at arm's length, his features twisted in a horrific mask.

He's completely insane, Peter shouted. *Time's run out. Jump, Kate.*

Kate didn't jump. Instead she seized control of Eileen's body and flung herself forward in a double roll that brought her up behind the man. The ground was slick with petrol and she slipped and slithered too far. Twisting and turning to get into a better position, she swung her leg in a low, rapid ark cutting the legs from under him. His knife flew out of his hand and skidded under a table. Using her bent elbow as a weapon, she brought it down on his ribs. He collapsed beside her groaning. Fury gripped Kate. This man had done so much evil. She was temped to finish him off, once and for all, but Peter's voice stopped her.

Don't, he said. *No time for that.*

She got to her feet and, when Old Man God struggled to get up, she pushed him with her foot, sending him slithering across the room through puddles of petrol.

"You won't get away," he screamed, pulling an old-fashioned lighter from his pocket. His fingers trembled with rage, so much so he couldn't get it to light.

"You don't want to do this," Peter said using Kate's body.

"At last!" the man cackled, still struggling to get the lighter to ignite. "I get rid of you."

"No you don't," Peter said, trying to sound convinced. "You know the story can't end like this."

"Course it can!" the man shouted, one hand clutching his ribs, the other fumbling with the lighter. "I'm the author!"

Let him be, he's crazy, Kate said to Peter. *Grab Jane. Eileen and I will take Tania.*

But the door is blocked.

The man, who'd finally got his lighter to work, dashed it down on a nearby table, sending flames racing across the floor. Kate shouldered open the food hatch and shoved the unconscious Tania through, diving after her. Peter did the same with Jane. All four fell in a jumble amongst plates and saucepans. Behind them, they heard the terrifying wail of the man as the fire caught him. Hearing his agony was unbearable. It lasted only seconds but it seemed an eternity till the roar of the fire finally silenced him.

The flames already licked at the hatch and an intense wave of heat greeted them as they dragged the two unconscious girls out into the cloister.

Follow me, Kate said, swinging Tania over Eileen's shoulder. Her hands and clothes were sodden with petrol. The slightest spark and it'd be the end. Thank heavens the cloister walls were made of stone, although the slate roof was built on thick wooden beams. Smoke swirled around them as they staggered towards the back entrance to the church. That and the stench of petrol made it hard to breathe.

I can't go much farther, Peter gasped. *Your body is exhausted. I keep healing it, but that's not enough.*

Just a little bit more, she coaxed. *Through the church and out the back and we'll be safe.*

Christine, Kate called out, mind-to-mind.

Yes. Christine asked, alarmed. *Where are you? What's*

happening?

No time to explain. Bring the handcart and blankets. Wait at the end of the path behind the church. Keep out of sight.

Just you and Suzanne, Eileen added. *It could be dangerous.*

Peter tripped and fell as they entered the church, Jane's unconscious body collapsing on top of him. Kate helped him up and used the occasion to return to own body and relinquish control of Eileen.

Eileen shook herself and stretched her arms tentatively. *That was weird,* said, lugging Tania onto her shoulders.

Kate took a deep breath and tried to pick up Jane, but couldn't manage. Her arms and legs were spent.

Rest, Eileen said. *I'll come back for you and Jane in a moment.*

Kate thanked her weakly and stared around. *We can't stay here,* she told Peter. *Anyone entering will see us.* She tugged Jane's unconscious form till she was sprawled at the top of steps. Sitting with her back to one of the legs of the altar, she struggled to breathe.

The flicker of flames through the stained glass windows peopled the shadows with ghostly figures. The fire bell had ceased, but there was a constant patter like heavy rain and the fire hissed and coughed as water fought to extinguish it.

Kate must have drifted off, because it was Peter's voice that awoke her. *Someone's coming.*

He was right. She could hear gruff voices from the far end of the nave.

If they find you, there'll be trouble, Peter said.

Kate looked around. She'd never make it to the exit with Jane on her back.

Behind the altar cloth, Peter said.

Kate heaved Jane's unconscious body into the recess under the altar and followed herself. The cloth fell back into place just as two men appeared round the rood screen. Trying to make as little noise as possible, Kate peered through a crack between two parts of the altar cloth, but could see very little.

I hope she doesn't awake while they're here, Peter said.

His words reminded her of Eileen. *Eileen,* Kate called out.

Yes. Be there in a moment.

No. Stay where you are. There are two firemen. We don't want them to see you.

What about you?

We're under the altar. With any luck they won't find us.

"You smell that petrol?" one of the men asked, as they approached the altar.

"Nope. With all that smoke I can't smell a blinkin' thing."

"But it's really strong," the other insisted, moving even closer.

The smell is going to give us away, Peter said. *If only we could scare them away. Doesn't this church have a ghost or two?*

Kate grinned.

Don't take a step closer, her voice rang out in the two men's heads.

The one who was sniffing his way around the altar halted and took a step back. "What's that?" he asked.

The only reply the other man gave was a whimper.

How dare you disturb the peace of the dead, Kate continued, her voice growling in their heads.

The man who'd whimpered screamed and pelted down the aisle heading for the exit. The other was quaking with fear, but lingered in front of the altar.

He who committed this sin lies burnt in the refectory, Kate whispered in the man's head. *Make sure his remains are removed from this holy place. Now go.*

She wasn't sure he'd obey, but he turned and ran after his colleague.

Kate waited a while till she was sure they'd gone, then called Eileen.

32.

"Peter," an anxious woman's voice said. "We're almost there."

He blinked open his eyes only to slam them shut, wishing he could sink back into oblivion. But try as he would, he couldn't rid himself of the smell of smoke and petrol. It wasn't enough to tell himself he was safe, sitting in the back of a car with Andrew, and that Dr Grant was driving with Christine at his side. He couldn't silence the sinister cackle of Old Man God or the man's terrifying scream as the fire claimed him. The man had been pouring petrol over Jane and Tania, for god's sake! He shuddered at the thought, feeling his stomach heave in revolt.

"Are you alright?" Christine asked. "You look terribly pale."

Peter didn't dare reply for fear he'd throw up.

Christine leaned back and placed a cool hand on his forehead. Having ascertained he wasn't running a fever, she let her fingers stray absently through his hair, pushing it back from his eyes. Her evident affection was too much. Tears welled in his eyes, but he fought them back, gritting his teeth. He was there for Fi and needed to be strong.

"I'm OK," Peter said, his voice coming out shakier than he wanted. "Kate's going through a rough patch." He hoped they wouldn't want to know more, but of course they did.

"What's wrong?" Andrew asked.

"It's too horrible." He paused to swallow the bile that rose in his throat. "Suffice it to say, she escaped and is OK." At least, he hoped she was.

"Have you tried contacting Fi?" Dr Grant asked.

Drat! He'd completely forgotten. He was supposed to locate her and talk mind-to-mind. Being wrenched into Kate's story had driven all else from his mind.

"Sorry. I was rather busy," he mumbled. "I'll try."

He shut his eyes and breathed deeply. Fi, he thought. Not calling her, not yet. But trying to evoke her presence. Fiona. An image sprang to mind: Fi with her green beret aslant on her head, a broad smile on her face. She hadn't smiled much recently.

Fi? he called out.

No answer. He tried again. Still no answer.

She could be asleep… or unconscious. He pushed that nasty thought away and tried again.

"I can't reach her," he said. "But that doesn't mean anything."

Peter looked up to see why Dr Grant had brought the car to a halt. The road was blocked just where it wound down into the village. To one side of the road, Peter spotted the familiar inspector in a heated discussion with a group of police constables. John got out to greet him.

"If any of those are from Bargeton," Andrew whispered in Peter's ear, "they might recognise us."

Christina must have heard, because she leaned back and whispered, "Stay in the car and pretend to be asleep."

Both turned their heads, half concealing their faces as they dug down into the car's padded seats, but their ploy was to no avail. The same tall policewoman who'd come to the derelict house in Bargeton peered through the window of the car, then wrenched open the back passenger door. "Well, if it isn't our mysterious supergirls. Are you going to disappear again?" she asked, grabbing Peter by the shoulder.

"Leave him alone, constable," the inspector said. "He is one of the people we are here to protect."

"He?" the woman said. She drew a torch from her pocket with a flourish, as if it were a gun, and shone it at point blank range into Peter's face, blinding him. Wrinkling her nose in disgust and shaking her head, she switched off the light plunging him in absolute darkness and let go of his shoulder.

"Could have fooled me," she muttered as she stepped away.

"That's the point," the inspector said, sounding irritated.

Peter, Andrew and Christina got out and greeted the inspector.

"You couldn't follow orders, could you?" the inspector complained. "I meant it when I said you shouldn't come."

Peter ignored the comment. "Is Fi OK?" he asked.

The man shook his head. His sombre expression had Peter fearing the worst. "We haven't managed to locate her yet."

"And Bonnie?" Andrew asked.

"Disappeared too."

"Just like you two," the tall policewoman said accusingly.

"There's no comparison," Peter snapped, unable to rein in his anger. "We chose to disappear. Fi and Bonnie had no choice."

"Enough," the inspector said, raising a hand to silence the policewoman, who was about to reply. "You two should get inside," he added, talking to Peter and Andrew. "Your brother could be holed up anywhere around here."

"What about Bonnie's grandparents?" Christina asked. "They must be in an awful state."

"They were lucky," he replied, shaking his head. "Brian didn't shoot them out right. He left them lying on the floor of the bakery in a pool of blood."

Andrew's hand flew to his mouth in shock and shame. Christina gasped in horror. "But…" she began.

"They were rushed to hospital. The doctor says their lives are not in danger."

"It's not possible," Christina muttered, repeating the words over and over.

Dr Grant put a comforting arm round her shoulders and they walked slowly, accompanying the inspector, towards the cottage. Seeing Andrew trailing behind, his head bowed, Peter laid a hand on his shoulder.

"If I hadn't been here," Andrew began, shrugging off Peter's hand, "none of this would have happened."

"It isn't your fault. You can't blame yourself."

Andrew didn't reply.

"Remember when we talked about your uncle," Dr Grant said.

Andrew's shoulders slumped even further.

"Do you recall what you said?" Dr Grant asked.

"That I wasn't to blame for what my uncle did," Andrew repeated grudgingly.

"Exactly. And the same is true here," Dr Grant said.

Andrew shook his head. "This is different. I led Brian to you…"

Having unlocked the door, Christine was about to enter when the inspector stopped her. Silently he signaled to the two policewomen to go in first. Peter was surprised to see them draw a gun. The sight of firearms made him uneasy. He couldn't remember ever seeing a policewoman carrying one.

For a tense moment they stood in silence, each straining to hear what was happening. Doors opened, there was the sound of furniture shifting and then the creak of feet on the stairs. Finally, one of the policewomen strolled out and gave the all clear.

Hardly had they settled around the kitchen table and Dr Grant put the kettle on, than a quiet knock came at the kitchen door. Both policewomen, who were leaning against the larder door chatting quietly, stiffened, their hands flying to their guns. The inspector peered cautiously round the curtains that obscured the garden windows. "At ease," he said. "It's one of ours."

Unlocking the door to the back garden, he opened it just enough to let a tall policeman in, then locked it firmly after him.

"Curtis," the inspector greeted him.

"We've found them," Curtis said.

"Where?"

"In a shack at the far end of the cove. God knows how he managed to get both girls down there."

"Both?" Peter asked.

"Yes. They are inside with him, tied up."

"Are they OK?" Peter asked.

"Can't be sure. He's covered the only window with a piece of sacking, but we caught a glimpse of them when he let them out one at a time to pee. He had them on some sort of leash."

"Did he see you?" the inspector asked.

"No. He was too busy making sure the girls didn't make a run for it."

"Did they look hurt?" Christina asked.

"Cowering and scared, but not physically hurt."

"So what do you plan to do?" Dr Grant asked.

"Call for reinforcements," the inspector said. "There are too few of us to surround such an isolated spot.

"How long will that take?" Dr Grant asked.

"An hour or so."

"Then I think we should go upstairs and rest while we wait," he said.

Peter knew he wouldn't be able to rest, even if he wanted to. He was about to say so, when Dr Grant gave him a warning look.

"I don't like this," John said once they were crowded into Peter's room. "I don't like it at all."

"The longer we wait…" Peter began.

John interrupted. "They'll launch an attack." He was completely caught up in his preoccupations. "There will be casualties if they do."

"What do you suggest?" Christine asked. "Negotiation?"

John shook his head and looked questioningly at Peter.

Peter knew exactly what was wanted. "I'll try again," he said. He lay down on the bed and closed his eyes.

"We'll make sure nobody disturbs you," John said.

Kate, he called out, praying that for once it would work. *Kate,* he called again. Nothing. *Please, Kate. I need you. Now.* Only silence answered his pleas, but he refused to give up. *Kate,* he called again, putting his whole heart into the word.

You always did try too hard, he heard Kate say, laughter bubbling in her voice.

Kate, he said, overwhelmed with relief, but in no mood for humour. He hugged her mentally, then drawing back, he said, *I need your help.* He briefly explained what had happened to Fi and Bonnie while Kate listen soberly. *I haven't been able to locate Fi,* he added, *let alone jump to her head.*

Let's try together, Kate suggested.

What happened then was very strange. Peter had never experienced anything like it. Their thoughts curled around each other in a growing spiral drawing them ever closer till it was hard to tell which was Kate and which him. Was it we or I or both? When they thought of Fi, there was only one mind thinking it. And together they sprang across space in search of their friend and found her in a flash. It was as one that they spoke in Fi's head, which probably wasn't a good thing, because she had no idea who was talking. So they unravelled, much to their separate disappointment, and greeted Fi each in their own way.

Peter, Kate? Is that you? Fi asked, relief in her voice.

Yes, Peter told her. *I couldn't make it on my own, so we came together.*

Can you open your eyes? Kate asked. *We need to see.*

He's blindfolded us. Now that she mentioned it, Peter could feel the cloth bound tight around her eyes. He could smell the musty old sacking. He also felt Fi hands tied behind her back. A quick check revealed that she wasn't hurt, apart from a few bruises on her arms and around her wrists, but she was exhausted.

We're going to have to jump to his mind, Kate said to Peter.

The thought left Peter filled with dismay. He remember only too well battling with the executioner in Kate's world in a desperate attempt to stop him killing her. It hadn't worked. There were limits to how much you could influence brute force and determination. He was careful to keep those thoughts to himself.

We should try together, Peter suggested.

A mental nod from Kate was all it needed and their thoughts twined together again until they merged completely. In a trice they located Brian and jumped. Slipping into his head unnoticed,

234   Alan McCluskey

they looked out through his eyes only to be disappointed. His attention was riveted on the sacking that masked the window. Through a tiny rent he kept a tense watch on the police.

They set about coaxing him to look back at the girls. They didn't want to try to take full control, not yet, for fear he would instinctively sense it and react with violence. Making him move wasn't easy. His neck muscles were locked in place and his teeth clenched in a mix of fear and rage. Despite their coaxing, they were unable to force him.

They would have to go for his body. As healers they shied away from doing harm. But this was urgent. The police were sneaking closer. The assault was imminent.

Not wanting to get caught in his body if he were to die, they braced themselves to jump as they limited the flow of blood to his head, in particular his eyes. Black patches swam across his vision causing him to panic. Try as he would he couldn't counter the ever-growing darkness that obscured his sight. The police must be using nerve gas, Peter heard him think. Brian wasn't going to give himself up and he wasn't going to let them catch him alive. Whatever happened he'd take the two girls down with him.

He brandished the gun and turned towards the girls, leaving Peter and Kate no choice. They stomped on the artery in his neck, blocking the flow of blood to his brain, and in that split second they jumped back to safety in Fi's head, praying that Brian wouldn't get in a shot before he blacked out.

A deafening roar exploded in the shack, hurtling Fi against the wall. The impact dislodged Peter and Kate, flinging them out of Fi's mind.

Had the police attacked? Or had Brian managed to fire despite them? Were Fi and Bonnie unhurt? There was no time to spare.

Peter ripped himself from Kate's mental embrace and opened his eyes looking desperately around for Dr Grant. "John," he said in a forced whisper. "I was with Fi. We were unable to take control of Brian, so we knocked him out. I'm not sure what happened. But I think he managed to fire a shot. You have to stop the police attacking. They might hurt the girls."

33.

"No!" he screamed. "No! No! No!"

In vain. His screams were carried off by wave after wave of dark desolation. He went under, only to surface seconds later, gasping for air as he struggled to stay afloat. A hopeless combat. He went under again, this time not to resurface. He plunged deeper and deeper, till nothing was left but black despair.

In the absolute silence that engulfed him, he was cut adrift, severed from his own body, estranged from his thoughts, as if someone else thought them.

You don't even know who you are. You could be anyone. Or no one. If I were you, I'd panic. At least if you panicked, you'd be something.

Or you could just pop out of existence, like a bursting balloon. Pop! It's as easy as that. There's not much left, anyway. Why bother? At least then you'd have peace and quiet. Think of the relief.

Good Lord, no! I wouldn't do that. What you need is hope. Hope is like a lifeline...

Now who's talking rubbish? There's no hope in this place. And what would you cling on with? You haven't got a body, let alone hands...

The word 'body' left him perplexed. What could a body be?

And so it went, on and on and on.

With only contradictory thoughts to exist by, complete silence might indeed have been a solution, had he had a will of his own. Whenever he did have the beginnings of a thought, it was immediately taken up by other thoughts and spun away in an interminable meandering during which any feeling of "me" got completely lost.

Time, for example. How long had he been there? *No point worrying about that. Everyone knew time was an illusion. For all he knew, it could have been a flash of a second or a million years. What did it matter? Of course it mattered. Without time, there could be no action...*

And so the thoughts chattered on, until one word brought the discussion to an abrupt halt. One word? Peter. He heard it spoken from an immense distance, in a voice that was not that of the thoughts. So there might be something 'other'. As for the word, it meant something particular, that much he knew, even if he couldn't remember what. The thoughts began again, but he fought them as he struggled to remember what 'Peter' meant. The sound brought with it a substance that was unfamiliar, as if the word had solidity.

Peter, the voice called out again. The voice had a tug to it that the other thoughts did not. Something other than thoughts responded to it, yearning to move closer. How come he hadn't noticed that other before? Whatever it was, it was called Peter.

Another word formed: Kate.

Kate was calling Peter.

Kate? he thought, savouring the sound. It asked something, although he knew not what.

Peter, the voice that was Kate responded. No question there. More of an affirmation, as if it was tightly bound with a 'yes'.

In that instant, the very 'yesness' of the word 'Peter' caused the jumble of thoughts to fall away and he shot upwards out of the gloom and into the light, breaking the surface in a blinding rush. And as he did, memory came flooding back. He remembered why he'd taken refuge and immediately wished himself back in the black depths.

No you don't, Kate said, as he began to sink. *You stay with me.*

Her words did battle with the suffering that dragged him

down.

Fi was dead! Dead! He'd known. Of course he'd known. But he hadn't realised. And now he had, her death hit him so hard he floundered.

Hold on, Kate said, flinging mental arms around him in a desperate embrace.

He clenched his fists as tears sprang to his eyes and let out a cry of anguish that sparked a flurry of movement around him.

"Peter?" several voices asked.

He felt hands grasp his. He felt a soft hand wipe the tears from his cheeks. He felt fingers running through his hair. But all he could think was that Fi had gone. He'd never see her again. His chest heaved as an immense sob burst from his lips.

"Fi," he wailed. "I'm so sorry…" He couldn't say more. His body was wracked by a storm of sobs that threatened to wrench him apart. Only when he could sob no more, did he hear Christina crying too. It must have been her hand that held his, because it was trembling and wet with tears. Keeping his eyes closed, he pulled her close, taking her in his arms, and hugged her tight. Wet cheek against wet cheek, her chest heaving in time with his, they cried together.

"My lovely, lovely daughter," Christine finally whispered.

"My best friend," Peter replied softly, his heart in every word. *My boyish girl,* he thought.

Christina disengaged from his arms and sat back, but kept a hand firmly clasped in his.

He could feel Kate waiting silently, sharing his sadness and regret. He reached out mentally and took her in his arms and felt her shuddered as she too cried.

She was a good friend, Kate said. *With her gone, something will forever be missing in my life.*

Peter opened his eyes and looked round the tiny room, darkened now, with curtains drawn. He puzzled over the pile of dirty clothes abandoned in one corner and the suit on a hanger by the bed. This was not his room. It was Fi's. How cruel! To force him to sleep on her bed after what had happened. He opened his mouth to berate Dr Grant, when he saw the man's eyes red and puffy. Reining in his anger, he asked, "Why am I here?"

Dr Grant glanced at Christina, then replied, "It's Andrew. He's not well. We thought it better if he were alone."

John was reluctant to say more.

"What happened?" Peter asked.

John drew in a deep shuddery breath, tears flowing down his cheeks. "Brian is dead. The doctors think he had a heart attack, but before he died, he shot Fi at point blank range." His voice caught and he paused a long moment to regain control of his emotions. "As for Bonnie, the shock drove her over the edge."

"When is the funeral?"

Dr Grant looked pained and took a long time to reply. "Two days ago."

"Two days! How long have I been out?"

"Four days."

"Where was the funeral?" He remembered Andrew's uncle's with all those depressing people, shuffling past as they muttered their condolences. Fi might have been extravagant and out-going, but deep down, she was herself only in private. He hoped Fi had had a more intimate ceremony.

"Here, in the village. She's buried next to the church."

Peter shuddered at the image of Fi being lowered into the cold, damp earth. He wanted to cry, in anger this time. It was unjust. What had Fi done to deserve such an end? He struggled to think of something else.

"And Andrew?"

"He blames himself for …" John couldn't bring himself to say the words. Christina got to her feet and joined him, putting her arms around her husband as the two cried quietly together.

Peter blamed himself. Had he not killed Brian, and in so doing, caused the death of Fi?

We couldn't have known, Kate pointed out.

It was true they'd taken a risk. At least they'd saved one of the girls, he just wished it'd been Fi. He thought of Bonnie. He'd heard that those who survived generally felt awful. She was all alone, what with her grandparents being in hospital. And Andrew. He'd surely be convinced it was his fault. With Brian gone, who else could take the blame?

"I want to see Andrew," Peter said, making a move to get up.

"Better not," Dr Grant said, his voice still shaky. "The doctor said he should rest and gave him sleeping tablets."

"I'll go all the same," Peter said.

He got unsteadily to his feet and crossed the narrow corridor to Andrew's room. Pushing the door, he found the boy curled up on his bed with one hand across his face. Someone had spread an eiderdown over his sleeping body, but it had slipped to the floor. Peter bent down and set it back in place.

Pulling up a chair, he sat down, placed his elbows on his knees and cupped his head in his hands, studying Andrew's half-hidden face.

The boy had always been frail. He appeared even more so now. Dark shadows had formed under his eyes and his slender face was furrowed with wrinkles, especially round his eyes. His full lips lay slightly open, breath hissing gently in an out. There seemed to be no rest for him, even in sleep.

One of Andrew's hands lay cupped over an eye, his fingers splayed across his forehead, their tips dug deep into his hair. The long fingers of a born pianist, both fragile and beautiful, moved involuntarily now in sleep and, as they twitched, Andrew's eyes popped open. He spotted Peter, snapped his eyes closed and turned his back.

"Come off it, Andy," Peter said, not moving from his position.

The boy remained walled in silence.

"I want to go for a walk. Come with me."

Andrew continued to ignore him.

"I am going to visit Fi's grave…" He broke off, unable to free his mind of an image; a mound of earth under which she lay. "I want to say goodbye." He stumbled over the words as tears sprung to his eyes.

"Andy, I need you to come," he said, his voice almost a

whisper. "Please."

Peter waited, hoping, but Andrew wouldn't budge. Finally he got to his feet and, gently laying a hand on Andrew's unmoving shoulder, took his leave.

Back out in the corridor, he found Christina leaning against the top of the bannisters. Dark shadows had formed beneath her eyes and wrinkles he'd never noticed had hewn deep creases around her mouth and eyes. She looked old and weary. He had always thought of her as Fi's mum, an older version of Fi. What was she now?

"You must be hungry and thirsty," she said, her voice flat and emotionless. "You haven't eaten for days. Let me prepare something."

"Thank you, Christina, but I have something I must do first."

Her disappointment was plain to see as her shoulders slumped, making her look even older and more tired.

"Ok," he replied. "Maybe it would be wise to eat. Thank you."

She turned, descended the stairs slowly, one step at a time, and disappeared into the kitchen, with Peter following her down. He sat across the kitchen table as she pulled bread from the bread bin and butter and ham from the fridge. As she took down a jar of pickles, she looked at him questioningly.

"Sure," he said, hoping to reassure her, and got up to put the kettle on.

She set a plate in front of his place, with a knife and a mug, then carefully laid the food around it.

Once he'd emptied the hot water that warmed the tea pot and poured more hot water over the tea leaves, instead of sitting down, he skirted the table till he stood in front of her. She looked like a lost child, incapable of fending for herself. He felt an urge to care for her, to protect her. Cautiously taking her in his arms, he hugged her. Unlike Andrew, whose shoulder had been hard and unyielding, Christina was soft and unresisting. She laid her head on his shoulder and cried softly.

In similar situations, he'd seen people pat others gently

on the back, as if that would comfort them. Instead, he laid a hand on the small of her back, channelling feelings of comfort and love through his unmoving fingers. He recalled the strange circumstances of their first meeting. He'd unwittingly discovered she'd lost her second child at birth, a boy she so much wanted. Now she'd lost her first born, a beautiful girl called Fi. He let his silent tears mingle with hers, as they clung to each other, two lost children together.

Her crying finally ceased and she sighed. Pulling free, she said, "You should eat. You must be starving."

34.

The cemetery in Lettup, which crouched in the shadow of the chapel, was even tinier than the church. Apprehensive, Peter pushed open the rusty gate and stepped inside. The place was deserted, as had been the village.

Finding Fi's grave was not difficult. The graveyard had not been tended for years and weeds rivalled each other to smother the tombstones. Fi's resting place lay in the only part of the jungle that had been cleared. A narrow path of flattened grass led to a long mound of earth at the head of which was planted a plain wooden cross. On it, a small inscription read: Fiona Tanner, the joy of our lives. On top of the cross, someone had hung Fi's green beret, even now aslant as it always had been.

Peter ran his fingers along the rim of her beret. The roughness of the ribbing against his fingertips sparked a rush of memories. He remembered Fi hurrying up her drive, late after Guides. She'd had to take one of the younger girls to hospital. It was their first meeting at her home. She always looked so good in that navy blue skirt with her shirt sleeves rolled up to her elbows. He remembered sitting with her on the banks of the river Frayne in Tallford, hiding from the prying eyes of fellow pupils. They'd shared a helping of greasy fish and chips. He remembered her being bullied by the Rake, their local vicar, who'd caught her in the church during choir practice. Peter had sung for her then, holding her in his arms, singing like he had never sung before. "The voice of an angel," the choirmaster had said. He remembered kissing her in the school playground out of sheer defiance... So many happy moments. That was how he wanted to remember her.

He crouched down and touched the fresh sods of earth that covered her grave. The dew lingered in the shade making the soil moist on his fingers. Mingled with the odour of earth, the air was rich with the smell of wet grass and the scents of a riot of wild flowers blossoming in every corner of the cemetery. Nearby, on a hawthorn bush that clung stubbornly to the cemetery wall, a thrush burst into song only to be answered by the cries of seagulls circling overhead. Life went on. That was what Fi would have wanted. He was sure. She was indeed a joy, like life itself.

Brushing the soil from his fingers, he got to his feet and stood, head bowed, hands clasped in prayer and meditation. He thought of that last moment in her head. At first, she hadn't recognised them, entwined as they'd been. He remembered her relief when she realised he and Kate had come to rescue her. Would that it'd worked out otherwise, that they'd had the knowledge to stop the madman. Peter halted that train of thoughts, not wanting to plunge into those depths.

Fi, he thought, please forgive me. I couldn't always follow you in your wild escapades, just like I can't follow you now. But then as now, my thoughts and heart go with you. I hope that you finally meet the love of your life in Paradise. Try not to tease the angels. He imagined her perplexed at the sight of them, unsure whether to call them pretty boys or handsome girls. He smiled at the thought.

She'd taught him a couple of camp songs from the Guides. One in particular had stuck in his mind. She always sang it with such relish. He was sure it had been written specially for her.

This is for you, Fi, he thought with a smile. Then taking a deep breath, he began to sing, softly.

> I wear my pink pyjamas in the summer when it's hot
> I wear my flannel nightie in winter when it's not
> And sometimes in the springtime,
> And sometimes in the fall,

I jump into my little bed with nothing on at all!

He'd finished the first stanza and was about to launch into the chorus, when quiet applause behind him had him stop. He turned to see the vicar leaning against the cemetery gate.

"Not the song I would have chosen," the man said. "But beautifully sung."

"Fi was in the Guides," Peter explained, turning back to the grave. "It was one of her favourites." He'd planned to sing the whole song, but the moment was gone. He bowed his head, by way of farewell, and turned towards the vicar. "If we stay on a few weeks," he said, wending his way between the weeds, "I'd really like to sing in the church again. In memory of Fi. No press. No cameras. Simply for the people of Lettup, at a normal service."

"That would be wonderful," the vicar enthused. "I promise there'll be no press or radio or television. Do forgive me," he said, opening the gate for Peter. "It's not easy, you know, living in such a tiny village. I was brought up in London. I miss the hustle and bustle. Sometimes the quietness of this place drives me..." He hesitated a moment. "To BIG ideas," he added, grinning, "and, a bit like a storm at sea, they threaten to carry me away."

The vicar shook his hand as they parted in front of the vicarage, saying "Let me know when you are ready to sing."

"I will."

Instead of returning home, Peter set out along the path that bordered the beach, heading for Viktor's cottage. He hadn't seen his singing teacher for over a week. So much for twice-daily lessons.

His teacher's cottage was not small, but it was half hidden in the scrub scattered across the windswept seashore. A trail of smoke rose from the chimney, only to be dispersed by the blustery wind that blew in off the sea. Squares of brightly coloured cloth, suspended on a makeshift line, flapped noisily in the wind. Tibetan prayer flags, Viktor had called them.

Peter knocked.

"Ah, young man," Viktor welcomed him as he opened the door. As always, the man paid no heed to Peter's disguise. With Brian gone, it was true, Peter no longer had an excuse to dress up, but he had no boy's clothes with him and dressing as a girl had become natural.

"I was wondering when you'd wake," the man continued.

As usual, Viktor was extremely well informed. "Just now," Peter explained.

"Tea?" the man asked, heading for the kitchen.

"Yes, please," Peter said, remaining in the living room. Over the fireplace, amongst a motley collection of objects on the mantlepiece, stood a small photo of a young woman, yellowed with time. He picked it up and examined it closely. Her hair was cropped short, barely reaching her ears. She reminded him of a boy, but the curves of her face, the arch of her brows and the fullness of her lips were decidedly feminine. He was struck by her beauty, in fact, there was something about her that fairly took his breath away.

"I see you've met Beth," Viktor said, carrying in a tray with tea and biscuits.

"Beth?" Peter said, startled by the name as if it hadn't been what he expected.

"The love of my life," he said.

Peter wondered why Viktor would confide in him about such a personal matter. He turned the photo over and read: Beth, 1930, scrawled in generous letters. "A long time ago," Peter said putting the photo back on the mantlepiece.

"It was indeed." Viktor replied. "How's your friend Andy?"

Peter sat in the armchair across from Viktor and picked up his mug of tea. "I haven't been able to talk to him. He seems very upset."

"And so he should be."

Peter was surprised at the sharpness of Viktor's words. What right had he to blame Andrew? "It's not his fault," Peter insisted.

"Who said anything about fault?"

"You did."

"Did I?"

"You said Andy should be upset."

"And I meant it. Anyone in his circumstances would be terribly upset. Let me tell you what happened to Beth. Maybe you'll understand." Viktor tugged at his goatee as he leaned back in his chair, a distant look on his face.

"From the first moment I met her, I was smitten. It wasn't just her looks. Oh she was beautiful all right. Don't get me wrong. It wasn't her wit, either, even though conversations with her were brilliant. No, above all, it was because she was so full of life and joy, it literally shone through her."

Peter glanced in the direction of the photo on the mantlepiece. Yes. He would have been smitten too.

"She lived in Luzern, in the German-speaking part of Switzerland. Imagine a fairly large city nestling in the mountains, at one end of a lake, a city of churches and sumptuous hotels, a city where tolling bells are constant companions. Her parents had a mansion down by the lake with its own little port where they moored their yachts. They had several. Life was a formal affair, with organised salons which only the best families attended, carefully planned meals prepared by first class chefs and servants that waited on the family at all hours. I was never invited. She didn't care too much for that life, but obedience was a virtue in her family, especially in women."

He paused a long moment as he sipped his tea, apparently savouring some far off memory.

"We met in secret in the rolling foothills above town. Her family had a rambling chalet. It was uninhabited and we were relatively safe. They never used the place, despite the magnificent view over the lake. I think it was too lowly for them. Not for her though. She loved its garden which she tended with great affection. She would be driven out there by the family chauffeur, who would drop her off for an hour or two."

"That fateful day, a bitterly cold wind blew off the lake and the line of snow had sunk so low it was only a short distance from the chalet. She had wrapped a bright red scarf around her neck and wore a cloth cap over her short hair. I was late. My car had broken down and a friend generously loaned me his new-fangled sports car. It was a Martini NF built in the French speaking part of Switzerland and could reach the colossal speed of 130 km. an hour."

"Beth didn't like being kept waiting, but the moment she saw the car she forgot all else. She climbed eagerly in and begged me to take her for a ride. I didn't want to. I was unsure of the car and the roads were icy. But no one, least of all me, could say no to Beth when she got an idea in her head.

So we headed off, taking a road that wound its way just below the snow line. At one point, the road straightened out for more than a kilometer. There were no other cars on the road. She urged me to take the car through its paces. She badgered me till I got the speed up to a hundred, the cutting wind howling around us. 'Faster' she shouted. It was then that we hit the patch of black ice and the car spun out of control. I heard her scream as the car shot up the bank and rammed into a giant tree. I was flung out of the car and lost consciousness. It was only much later that I learnt she'd been killed by the impact."

Viktor got to his feet and fetched the photo of Beth from the mantelpiece. Seated once again, he studied her face at length, in silence. Thinking of Fi, Peter wondered how he'd feel in Viktor's place. It wouldn't be enough to tell himself he'd tried to persuade her not to go or that he couldn't have known there was black ice on the road. He shouldn't have driven so fast in such a powerful car. Suffering and regret would probably have submerged Viktor as it had Peter when he realised Fi was gone.

"While I lay shroud in misery in the hospital, the family tried to have me arrested, they stirred up the local papers and many a politician, but the inquest showed I wasn't at fault. I didn't care. I was plunged in despair. Nothing mattered. Beth was gone and I was to blame."

He fell silent and brooded over the photo, periodically turning it over to re-read the inscription on its back.

"You see what I mean about the inevitability of being upset?" Viktor finally said.

Peter nodded. "How long were you lost to the world?"

"A year or more."

"And how did you get out?

"I would never have managed. It was one of my music teachers that saved me. I'm truly grateful to her. She used the only thing that could reach me. Music. At first I resisted. Melody and harmony, all was bland and tasteless. But little by little the notes worked their way through and, although I would never be the same, they brought me back to life."

35.

What was that squeak? It tugged at Kate's nerves till she wanted to scream. First it came closer, then it moved away, over and over again. She lay on her back, eyes closed, struggling to shut out the noise. It didn't make sense. Had she not been with Peter in his world? Yet this was clearly somewhere else. It smelt different. It felt different. In her world, there'd been a terrible fire. She remembered that vividly enough, too vividly, but afterwards her memories blurred. Had she made it to the farm and the other girls?

The squeaking abruptly stopped, there was a whispered exchange, then the squeaking took up again. Shoes! That was it. Someone was pacing up and down. She opened her eyes, and once they'd adjusted to the light streaming in the window, she saw she was lying in a bed in a small room. The white walls were bare, barring a large wooden cross nailed at head-height such that anyone lying in the bed couldn't miss it. There was one metal chair, also painted white, and next to it a small table on which someone had placed a colourful bouquet in a plain vase. She immediately recognised the flowers from Sister Teresa's garden.

The squeak, she realised, was coming from the other side of a door. A dull pain in her right arm just above her wrist had her looking for its cause. A tube cascaded down from a bottle suspended above her and disappeared under a bandage around her lower arm. She was about to examine it, when the door opened and a nurse stepped in wheeling a small trolley. The woman was slightly built, with tiny delicate hands and dark brown hair tied up in a bun. Yet, for all her size, she moved and acted with authority.

"Ah! You're awake. That's good," the nurse said, pushing the trolley to the side of the bed. Noticing Kate's hand on her wrist, she added, "You shouldn't touch that, my dear. It was the only way to feed you while you were unconscious. Now you're awake, we'll be able to remove it."

"Unconscious? How long?"

"Four days." The woman busied herself with the metal containers on the trolley. Kate could smell food. She should have been hungry, but the smell left her nauseous. Instead of giving her something to eat, the nun handed her a cup of herbal tea saying, "Drink this. It'll do you good."

Kate sniffed the mixture. "Camomile and elder flowers," she said.

The nurse nodded, looking surprised.

Kate had no time to explain. The door opened and the squeaky shoes walked in. They belonged to a tall, wiry man in a dark suit who had a permanent stoop, as if he were afraid he'd hit his head on the doorframe. He stared at Kate through the long black locks that hung in front of his eyes, then he raked his fingers through his hair to free his face.

"Young lady, I'm Detective Inspector Schmidt. I urgently need to ask you some questions." His voice was high pitched and nasal, a sound that was as annoying as the squeak of his shoes. His chin, nose and cheek bones along with his forehead protruded from his face making him look like a skeleton that had hastily been covered with skin.

"Yes," Kate said, sipping her tea, in an attempt to conceal her disgust and misgiving.

The inspector turned to the nurse. "Maybe you have other patients to attend to while I ask my questions."

"Of course," the nurse said, looking put out at being dismissed. She cast a worried glance at Kate, before scurrying from the room, abandoning her trolley by the bedside.

The man drew a spiral notebook from his pocket, pulled out a pen and leaned against the wall. He made Kate think of a beanpole desperately trying to avoid something growing up it.

"Why did you move the girls out of the convent?"

"I didn't."

"The other girls said you did."

Of course they would. In the short time she'd been amongst them, they'd come to look on her as their leader. "The nuns had abandoned us, but we were afraid one of them would return and do us harm."

He dismissed her explanation with a wave of his bony hand. "Why would the nuns want to harm you?"

"Have you seen the cuts and bruises on the girls' bodies? Do you think they did that to themselves?"

The man shook his head, causing his hair to flop across his face. "Why did you return to the convent that evening?"

"To fetch needed supplies."

"And to set fire to the building."

"Why would I do that?" Kate asked, indignant.

"To get revenge."

"What nonsense!" Kate could contain her irritation no longer. "We were hiding from one of the nuns who badly mistreated many of the girls. Starting a fire would make no sense. It would immediately attract attention."

"That's what you say. But then how do you explain that you stank of petrol?"

"Because the man who started the fire took us hostage. He was completely mad. He poured petrol over some of us..." Kate couldn't help it, she burst into tears at the horror of the memory. "He planned to set fire to us and nearly succeeded."

He shook his head in disbelief, as if she were raving. Pushing off from the wall, he pocketed his notebook and knocked loudly on the door. "They'll probably lock you up in a special institution." he said, tapping his index finger against his temple several times. "If you want my opinion..."

"I don't," Kate said firmly.

The door opened and a man in a white coat entered, closely followed by the nurse.

"Problem?" the man asked, dismissing the nurse away with a wave of his hand.

"She's been making a fuss," the inspector said. "I'm afraid she might be a danger to herself and others. If I were you, I'd give her something to calm her."

"What nonsense!" Kate exclaimed.

"You see what I mean?" the inspector said.

"I do indeed," the man in the white coat replied. He pulled a long thin tube from his jacket pocket and, uncovering a needle at its end, he began flicking it with his fingernail. Kate tensed, in case he attacked her. Instead, he plunged the needle into the tube attached to her arm and emptied its contents inside. Almost immediately Kate felt strange, as if her feet were drifting away from beneath her. Then little by little the whole world floated away and she floated with it.

She slipped in an out of sleep but, despite her struggle to remain awake, she couldn't make sense of the world. On several occasions she thought she heard Tania, but dismissed it as a dream, until finally she surfaced and realised that Tania really was there, sitting by her bed.

Seeing her awake, Tania immediately embraced her. Kate noted that she smelt much cleaner that she had in the convent. "We were so worried about you," Tania said. "You know, they've shipped everyone off to another orphanage ..."

As Tania told her about the place she'd been sent to, a special boarding school for unruly young girls, Kate caught sight of the policeman hovering outside the door. He probably hoped Kate would let something slip while she talked to a friend.

Tania, Kate said, mind-to-mind. *I've got to get out of here. They think I set fire to the convent and they are drugging me.*

Tania halted mid sentence, her mouth falling open in shock. Then she whispered "What should I do?"

The inspector must have sensed something was wrong, because the door opened and he entered, calling out as he did,

"We need you doctor."

The doctor bustled in already brandishing his syringe.

That's the drug, Kate thought to Tania. *Talk to the others and get me out of here...* the moment the needle entered the tube, her thoughts became jumbled and she lost contact with Tania.

When she resurfaced Tania was no longer there. The policeman wouldn't try that trick a second time. Seeing she was awake, the man interrogated her again. "Where did you get the petrol from?"

"I have no idea where he got the petrol from," Kate replied.

"Don't you mean she?"

"He! The man who started the fire." His mind seemed made up. She was guilty and there was no way she'd alter his stubborn conclusions.

"We know that several girls were your accomplices. Tell us which ones and the judge will be less harsh on you."

"Dim wit," she muttered.

"Do you want to sleep again?"

"No," she added hastily. Each time she awoke, she found it more and more difficult to gather her thoughts. She was afraid she might drift away permanently if they continued drugging her.

"You have a visitor," he said.

So Tania had come back. What a relief. Maybe she'd devised a way to get her out.

The door opened and in stepped Sister Helga. Kate felt an icy grip tighten around her heart as she met the hate-filled eyes of the nun.

"Yes that's her," Helga said without bothering to greet Kate. "She's the one who poisoned dear Sister Teresa."

"Dear?" Kate spluttered. "You lie! Your treatment of Teresa was vile, far worse than the horrors you inflicted on the girls."

The situation exasperated her and, at the same time, she was frightened. They were leaguing up against her: Helga, the doctor and the inspector. How could she possibly escape? It was worse than being executed. Was that possible? At least she had

Peter on her side. Peter. He'd know what to do.

Peter, she called out. What would she do if he didn't respond? He'd been finding it difficult to reach her. Maybe he couldn't hear her. She called again. No answer.

Her insolence had been too much. The doctor was back with his syringe. With one desperate last call to Peter she sank into oblivion.

When she next resurfaced, she felt weak and promptly sank under again. As she feared, the drug was having a wider effect. Her mind was filled with fears and doubts. Maybe they were right. Their story made so much sense. As for hers, she couldn't remember it so well. Maybe she had set fire to the place. Thank heavens nobody had been hurt. Or had they? A wave of horror shook her body.

Get a grip, she told herself, desperately struggling to stop trembling. This is the effect of the drugs. She lay as still as she could and concentrated. Breathe, she told herself, and she went through the mental exercises her marshal arts master had taught her. The fear and doubt receded, but she was still no closer to escaping. Next time they drugged her, she might not get off so lightly. Let them think I'm still asleep, she told herself as she called out to Peter.

The door opened quietly and closed again. Was it the inspector back to continue his accusations? Or the doctor with his dreaded needle? Despite her fear, she lay unmoving. To her surprise, a cool, damp cloth wiped her forehead several times.

"Poor thing," she heard a voice whisper.

Cracking open her eyes, she saw the nurse leaning over her.

This might be her only chance. "You've got to get me out of here," Kate whispered. "If this continues, I really will go mad."

The nurse wiped her forehead once more, saying "I want to help, but it's too difficult."

Kate's mind was racing. "How long before they come back?"

"Don't know. Five minutes. Maybe more."

Kate knew she wouldn't be able to walk, let alone run. She

was far too weak from lack of food and too many drugs. "Can you get a wheelchair and a bathrobe?"

The woman seemed torn with indecision. "I don't like what they're doing to you, but helping you escape would be too risky." She cast about as if someone were watching.

"Please. You know what they're doing is wrong."

The woman shook her head, more as if she wanted to free her thoughts than in denial. "OK."

"You're wonderful." The woman turned to leave when Kate added, "Before you go, could you remove the tube from my arm."

The nurse unwrapped the bandage and gingerly pulled the needle from her arm. "Here," the nurse said, handing Kate the bandage. "Hold this where the needle was to staunch the flow of blood."

"What's your name?" Kate asked.

"Lydia," the nurse said.

"Thank you Lydia."

Lydia hurried away.

Kate tossed off the blankets and swung her feet to the floor. For a long time, much too long, she sat there shivering. Where had Lydia got to? Surely she wouldn't tell the doctor or inspector. Maybe she'd got caught. Kate cautiously got to her feet but, feeling her legs about to give way, hastily sat down.

It was at that moment that the door flew open and Lydia pushed in a wheelchair on which was a dull brown bathrobe. Helping Kate to wrap the thick woollen bathrobe round her, Lydia took hold of the girl and eased her into the wheelchair. Having pulled the door shut, they were off.

Lydia careered down a deserted corridor, running behind the wheelchair. The soles of the nurses sandals on the tiled floor made an alarming slapping sound. They rushed down a ramp, almost crashing into the wall as they veered off to the left and along another corridor. When they reached the fork at the end, the nurse slowed her pace. There were people about, nurses and doctors as well as visitors.

"Let your head slump forward as if you're asleep," Lydia whispered.

Kate did as she was told, but kept an eye open just in case there was trouble. Luckily no one paid any attention. So far so good. But how where they to get out of the hospital and away? Outside, they'd be far too conspicuous.

Speeding down another long corridor which, to Kate's relief was deserted, the nurse finally halted at a small door. Opening it, Kate saw a short ramp that led to a road where several delivery trucks were parked. It was at that moment they heard the wailing of police sirens.

"They've found out," Kate said in a panicked whisper.

"It'll be alright," Lydia said. "You're safe now."

Kate was not reassured.

As they neared the trucks, a burly man with a bright red, round face, stepped out from behind a baker's van and blocked their path. His hands were enormous and his arms muscular. Kate tensed to make a run for it.

"Meet my husband, Klaus," the nurse said, giving him a hasty hug. "I phoned him. He's come to drive you to safety."

36.

Peter paced the empty kitchen, clearing away breakfast things as he did. Yet another day closeted with Andrew moping upstairs! He had to get out or he'd suffocate. John had gone to Tallford and would be away for several days preparing the new school year. Christina had left just after breakfast to drive Bonnie's grandparents to town. She often went with them to visit their unhinged granddaughter, who was in a psychiatric clinic not far from Bargeton.

Being alone with Andrew was no fun. He'd tried coaxing the boy out, but Andrew rarely left his room, except at meal times, and even then he sat walled in silence. The rest of the time, the boy stared blankly out his bedroom window or lay curled up on his bed, asleep most of the time. All Peter's efforts to get him to play piano had failed. He'd even tried singing. To no avail.

Peter hadn't heard from Kate either. It was days since she'd last been in his head. Her absence worried him. He tried calling as he strolled down the road to the small square at the centre of Lettup and beyond to the harbour and beach. Such was his preoccupation that he didn't see the clergyman and almost bumped into him.

"Do we need to set up a kitty to collect for your new glasses, young lady?" he asked, maintaining an exaggerated look of concern.

Peter chuckled, both at the idea of the villagers collecting money, but also that the vicar continued to act as if he were a girl. When the news broke about the death of Fi, it'd made the headlines in all the papers, although the press had not revealed that he and Andrew were boys disguised. All the same, the fact was now common knowledge in the village. Pretending was maybe the vicar's way of avoiding embarrassment.

"Sorry. I was lost in my thoughts," Peter replied.

The vicar made a show of being disappointed. "There was me hoping you were silently rehearsing the songs for the concert in the church."

Peter chuckled again. "I haven't forgotten. It's just that Andie is very upset about what happened and can't seem to find the will to shake off the sadness."

"Maybe a little prayer might help, or possibly even a visit," the vicar wondered.

"You could try. It would be a miracle if you could do something. None of us have managed."

"OK. Let's go for a miracle," the vicar said, taking his leave. "I'll drop by at about four. Is that all right?"

"Sure. See you then."

Peter walked on down to the harbour, where he stood watching two fishing vessels chug out to sea. Gulls swirled above as the boats rounded the headland and disappeared into the open sea.

The wind had veered and clouds were scudding across the sky obscuring the sun. Peter shivered. He was not dressed for bad weather. He turned his back to the harbour and the cold wind, hesitating about whether to return home for a coat. But finally he set out along the path that boarded the beach as he made his way to Viktor's cottage.

Before it curved up to his teacher's house, the path ran beside the wooden hut where Fi had met her end. The lingering smell of creosote was enough to plunge Peter in a dismal mood. He halted a moment, leaning on the rough wooden walls, his head bowed, finding it hard to proceed. At his feet was a tiny posy of faded flowers, no doubt left in memory of Fi. The wind had blown over the jar, scattering the flowers across the path. He bent down and, anchoring the glass with a few pebbles, he picked up the flowers and rearranged them.

It would soon be time for his lesson. To his surprise, the door was closed when he arrived and no one answered his knock. He tried again but got no reply. Worried that something might have happened, Peter turned the handle. The door was not locked.

Taking a cautious step inside, he called out, "Viktor? Are you there?" Only the echo of his own voice answered. Not wanting to leave the front door ajar with the buffeting wind, he pulled it shut. Walking down the hall and into the main room, he found it empty.

"Viktor?" he called out again. Getting no answer, he strode across the room and hastily glanced into the kitchen and the bathroom and finally into Viktor's bedroom, a room he'd never been into before.

The bedroom was very plain with just a large bed and an oil painting hanging on the wall above it. A life-size portrait of Beth. Peter glanced around to make sure he was alone, then skirted the bed to get a closer look. Unlike the photo, the painting went far beyond the visible appearance, portraying the vibrancy and vitality of the young girl.

He could have stood there for hours, constantly discovering new facets of Beth, but he was embarrassed at having penetrated such a private space and retreated to the doorway, from where he continued to study the painting.

He knew he should wait outside, but he didn't fancy standing in the cold wind. As he crossed the main room, the front door slammed, startling Peter. He was sure he'd closed it, but maybe he hadn't. The sound of Viktor whistling softly had Peter wanting to hide, but instead he called out, "Viktor, is that you?"

"Sorry I'm late. I couldn't get away from that chatterbox of a vicar," Viktor said, as he strode into the main room and dumped his leather satchel on the table. "You did well to come in. The wind is getting up and the temperature is dropping. I wouldn't be surprised to see it rain."

Peter mumbled a greeting, still embarrassed at being caught

snooping. "Put the kettle on, will you?" Viktor said, pulling off his coat. "I'll be with you in a moment."

As they sat to drink their tea, Peter couldn't help feeling there was a change in Viktor. The man was generally quite tense. He had a way of tugging at his moustache when something troubled him. He hadn't touched it once since he got back. Instead, he was all smiles and seemed remarkably relaxed as he leant back in his chair savouring the tea with his large hands wrapped round the mug.

"I went to the village to make a call," Viktor explained.

Few of the houses had phones. Their cottage was an exception. Most people went to the bakers or the pub to call. Peter wondered why Viktor was telling him. It didn't concern him.

"I had an idea," Viktor went on. "A way of getting your Andie out of the dumps."

So that was why he was acting like a gleeful child.

"Now that would interest me," Peter said. It was a game which he had to play along with.

"A concert tour," Viktor said, getting to his feet and pacing the kitchen.

"A what?" Peter asked, startled and not a little worried.

"Yes. I plan to organise a concert tour for you and Andie on the continent."

"But surely we're not good enough," Peter said. "And where would we go and who would pay?" Peter had never travelled beyond England. The thought of crossing the channel was both appealing and alarming.

"I phoned a friend in Switzerland. She likes the idea. She suggested you sing in Geneva, Fribourg, Bern and Luzern. She's prepared to organise things…" From the tone of Viktor's voice, Peter could hear he was excited.

"But how would we pay for it?" Peter asked.

"That's no problem. My friend had several ideas for funding. There's an exchange scheme for young musicians, for example. And, don't forget, people will pay to listen. If ever it's not enough, I have plenty of money set aside..."

"You have been generous enough already," Peter said. "There's no way we could accept your paying for such a trip."

"It probably won't be necessary."

Peter couldn't help being excited. He loved singing and the idea of travelling from town to town to sing appealed to him. It was then that stern voice of reality spoke up.

"But what about school?"

"For such an adventure, I'm sure your headmaster-father would agree to a couple of weeks absence."

"John and Christina still have to agree to let us go and we'll have to convince Andie. That's not going to be easy."

"I'd better come and talk to them."

"John's away on school business for a couple of days and Christina's gone with Bonnie's grandparents to visit the girl. There's only Andie in the cottage and he's moping."

"All the more reason to start with him."

"So there's to be no lesson today?" Peter asked, trying to conceal his hopefulness. He would've readily shirked the lesson. It wasn't that he was lazy, but working with Viktor was so demanding.

"Course there is. Lesson first. Persuasion afterwards."

An hour later, Peter was exhausted. Viktor had never pushed him so hard. With Viktor it wasn't so much a question of singing right, of course that counted. Rather it was being aware of what you were doing, where the sounds were coming from, what emotions they sprang from. And how your breath gave birth to the sounds. Much of what Peter sang that day, most people would have called noise. That didn't bother Viktor. It was the authenticity and the discovery that counted. Peter had to agree, those rales and squeaks could be extraordinarily beautiful.

"I hope I don't sing like that in the concerts," Peter commented as they made their way through the steady rain to the village. Viktor had loaned him an umbrella, but it was of little use against the blustery winds.

By the time they reached the cottage, Peter was soaked.

Showing Viktor where to find material to light a fire, he hurried upstairs to change. He had difficulty pulling off the wet dress and underwear, his fingers were so cold and he was shivering violently. He finally managed and hung his dress on a hanger to dry. Dressed in a full length skirt and blouse, he pulled on woollen tights and wrapped a shawl around his shoulders.

Out on the landing, he knocked on Andrew's door. "Andie," he called out before entering. "Viktor is here. He has a wonderful plan for us."

Pushing open the door, he found Andrew curled up on the bed, his back turned. "Andie," Peter said. The boy did not respond.

As he entered, Peter sensed an unfamiliar smell, a bit like rust. He rounded the bed only to discover that, concealed by Andrew's body, the covers were red with blood seeping from Andrew's slashed wrists.

"Viktor!" Peter screamed. "Come quick!"

Not sure what to do, Peter placed a hand on Andrew's chest to see if his heart was still beating. It was, but only just. He heard Viktor bustle into the room behind him.

"Oh my god!" was all Viktor could say.

"He's still alive," Peter said, his voice shaky.

"Have you got any bandages? We need to staunch the flow of blood."

Peter hurried downstairs to fetch the first aid kit from the kitchen, then watched on as Viktor bound up Andrew's wrist.

"We must call an ambulance," Viktor said, shaking his head. "It'll take them at least half an hour, that might not be soon enough."

Peter sat down on the bed next to Andrew and placed a hand lightly on his shoulder. "I'll try to heal him."

Viktor looked dubious, but said nothing.

"I removed a bullet from his shoulder and healed the wound..."

"Not that I don't believe you, but I'll still call an ambulance, just in case."

"Good. Hurry back. I'd welcome you being here."

The man nodded and hurried away.

Peter turned to Andrew and, closing his eyes, he called out to Kate.

To his relief, she responded immediately. *What's up?*

Peter showed her Andie's wrist.

Ok, she thought, as calm and determined as she had been before that dreadful day. *Let's get to work.*

Once again their spirits wound together and it was together that they jumped into Andrew's body and headed for the wounds. They staunched the flow of blood, helped the body clean out any possible infection then encouraged the skin to grow over the wound. It was much easier than extracting a bullet. In no time, the wounds were healed over.

They knew, however, that their work was not finished. They also had to heal Andrew's spirit. That wasn't going to be so easy. They could try talking to him, but that avenue seemed firmly closed. It was together they thought of singing. Peter had used it before to cure a man dying of cancer.

Each body had its own fundamental chord that resonated in every living cell. By identifying that chord and singing it within the person, he'd been able to quell the growth that threatened the man.

Here there was no growth, but a dark shadow that threatened Andrew's life. If they could reinforce the fundamental chord of life, maybe it'd help drive away the depression. Together they listened, homing in on nearby cells, till they sensed what sounds were needed. Tentatively humming the notes, they shifted slightly till the cells began to vibrate in resonance.

As their humming grew stronger and more confident all the cells responded. He had the impression the sun had come out. There might be no extra light or warmth, but the feeling was akin to the relief after a dreadful storm when the clouds part letting down the first rays of sun.

They withdrew into Peter's body, untwined reluctantly, then hugged each other mentally, such was the strength of the emotions they felt.

I have to go, Kate said. *I promise I'll be back soon.*

Peter opened his eyes and saw Viktor standing in the doorway staring at him. His face was elated despite his evident incomprehension.

"What was that?" Viktor whispered as if he were afraid to scare away an angel.

"We healed the wound but it wasn't enough. We had to heal…" He hesitated about the word to use. "Andrew's soul. Only music could do that."

"I know. I heard," Viktor said, his face transfigured. "I've never heard anything like it. As if the boy's whole body was singing, but not alone, with other people, a bodily choir… I can't explain…" Tears were running down his cheeks. "It was so beautiful."

37.

"My parents were lucky," Klaus said, as he cut slices of bread. The delicious smell of freshly baked bread filled the room, making Kate's mouth water. On their way to Klaus and Lydia's chalet in the hills above town, they'd dropped by his bakery. Kate had kept well out of sight, while he hurried to fetch several loaves.

"They had very little in the way of savings," Klaus continued, as he busied himself heating water on the range, "so when a good customer told them a family urgently wanted to sell a chalet, they dismissed the idea, thinking it'd be far too expensive. When the customer insisted, they enquired." He fetched butter and jam from the larder and poured Kate a cup of tea from an earthenware pot.

Kate sat at the large wooden kitchen table, wrapped in an elegant, embroidered housecoat. It was one of a whole roomful of girl's clothes, an unbelievable treasure trove, leftovers from a former owner. Running her fingers over the exquisite material, she basked in the warmth of the cooking range. It seemed years since she'd last been warm. The kitchen, which was spotlessly clean, had glossy red tiles on the floor and the walls were painted a warm yellow. Yellow curtains hung at the windows and outside pine trees swayed in the wind.

"Although the chalet was in bad repair, they were enchanted. In addition, there was a series of outhouses and a rambling garden with lots of flowers gone wild, many of them healing herbs. My mother was delighted. She worked for an old-fashioned pharmacist in town and knew a lot about herbal remedies.”

“They hardly dared ask the price as the estate agent finished the visit. When they plucked up the courage, they were dumbfounded how little the owners wanted. Apparently the family were eager to get rid of the property, but didn’t want it to fall into the hands of promoters. It’d been the favourite haunt of their daughter before she was badly injured. They wanted nothing more to do with it. Later, once my parents had bought the chalet and settled in, they learnt from local people that it was thought to be cursed. The prospect didn’t bother them. They were enthralled by the house and garden.”

The sound of a telephone ringing startled her. Getting up to answer, Klaus explained, “We had it installed because of the business.”

Alone, Kate wondered what’d happened in the delivery van. She’d drifted off and dreamt she’d visited Peter. Little remained. Pain. Suffering. A lot of blood and an intense sense of joy. It was the latter that reassured her. Peter couldn’t be hurt. At least she hoped so.

When Klaus returned, he was shaking his head and looked worried. “That was Lydia. The police questioned her. They couldn’t prove it, but they suspect her of helping you. She’s afraid they’ll come here.” He busied himself clearing away the breakfast things. “Luckily we have a good place to hide.”

He piled a loaf of bread, a hunk of cheese, some shiny red apples and a flask of water in a wicker basket. Carrying it in one hand, he held her arm to support her as he led her outside. Taking their time, they followed a narrow path between dense bushes to a long, low building all made of wood, half hidden amongst the trees. The tiles on the roof looked as if they were also made of wood and there were many small windows.

“My parents dreamed of converting this into a guest house, but, what with the bakery and my mother’s work, they never had the time.”

Kate would have liked to ask what it’d been used for before, but her shaky legs forced her to concentrate on not falling.

Ignoring the main door, he led her round the back and, pulling a bunch of keys from his pocket, unlocked a small door. She had expected dust and cobwebs, but the place was spotlessly clean and smelt pleasantly of dried herbs. "Lydia insists on keeping this tidy. She always says, you never know when we might need it."

He led her down a short corridor, picked up a folded blanket from a chair and placed it in the basket with the food. Then he unlocked a door and reached into the dark in search of the switch. When he flipped it on, she could see a steep flight of stairs.

"The basement is the best place to hide," he said. "It's dry and clean and there are plenty of secret corners that are not easy to find. I'll just put this at the bottom," he said pointing to the basket, "then I'll come back and help you down."

At the bottom of the stairs, she discovered row upon row of shelves from floor to ceiling, many of which were laden with bottles of dried herbs, each carefully labelled and arranged by name. Kate was fascinated and leant forward to have a closer look. Her father, who was an accomplished herbalist as well as a first-class magician, would have been jealous. His storeroom on the ground floor of their house paled in comparison.

"Does Lydia use these herbs in her work?"

"No. She wanted to. That's why she became a nurse. But she quickly realised doctors get upset if nurses suggest what to do."

He wound his way between the shelves, penetrating ever deeper. She was beginning to wonder whether the basement extended beyond the building when he halted in front of a large wardrobe. In a bedroom, you probably wouldn't have given it a second thought. But there, in the basement, it looked a bit forlorn standing on its own against the wall.

Klaus chuckled. "It was Lydia's idea. She got it from a book."

When Kate looked perplexed, Klaus added, "You'll see. Do you think you can take a few steps on your own?"

She nodded. The breakfast she'd eaten and the thought of

being free in the company of such good people made her feel much better.

"I could help you through, but it is more fun if you discover for yourself."

He opened the door, letting out a distinct smell of moth balls, and stepped inside amongst the fur coats hanging there. "I'll go first. Wait a moment till I'm through, then follow. Make sure you close this door behind you or it won't work."

He pulled the door shut, leaving Kate standing alone in the basement. All of a sudden the place felt creepy. Tiny noises she hadn't noticed before caught her attention. For all she knew, these people, kind though they seemed, might find it funny to leave her stranded. Try as she would, she couldn't completely allay her fears.

Not wanting to wait any longer, she pulled open the door, squeezed in amongst the coats and pulled the door closed behind her. Once inside, the smell of moth balls was overpowering. She had a horrible suspicion that Klaus might be hiding there, waiting to jump out and surprise her. She took a deep breath, trying to calm her hammering heart, then listened carefully. She was alone.

With the door closed, she was plunged in complete darkness. If Klaus was not inside, there must be another way out. Easing her way from the door till her outstretched fingers collided with the back of the wardrobe, she began searching for an opening. She found none, but when she pushed against the wood, a part of it gave way revealing a well-lit room beyond.

A beaming Klaus was waiting to help her out. "Smart, hey?" he said, clearly proud of his wife's invention.

Kate was now standing in a large room, sparsely furnished with a couple of beds in one corner, a large table in the centre and several wooden chairs arranged around it. She pulled out one of the chairs, which was surprisingly heavy, and sat down. The adventure had exhausted her.

Stacked on the shelves of a small bookcase were piles of books, the flimsy kind that told stories. She'd already seen such things in Peter's world. She'd never been able to understand why people found them so absorbing. No such thing existed in her world.

She pulled off the sandals Lydia had given her and dug her toes into the thick carpet. Similar carpets had been fixed to the walls. Seeing the way she looked at them, Klaus explained, "To stop the sound travelling."

Kate was astonished at such elaborate preparations. "Do you often have to use this room?"

Klaus chuckled. "Only in our imaginations so far." He set the basket on the table. "I have to go back. Just in case the police turn up. They'll probably want to search the basement, but they'll never get through Lydia's wardrobe." He took the blanket out of the basket and tossed it onto one of the beds. "You've got food and drink for a while and Lydia or I will fetch you as soon as the coast is clear."

He turned to go then changed his mind. Hurrying to the bookshelf he rummaged through the books and pulled one out. "You might like to read this," he said, handing her a book with a giant yellow lion on the cover. "It's the story that inspired the wardrobe idea." And he left.

Kate walked gingerly from the bed to the table and back, feeling caged. These last days she'd been stuck indoors. She longed to get out and roam the gardens and woods around Lydia and Klaus's house. From time to time she halted, clinging to the table to steady herself, and listened carefully. All was quiet.

Encouraged by her ability to walk unaided, she debated whether to try some exercises. Since she'd recovered full use of her leg, she hadn't once gone through the exercises she used to do regularly to keep up her combat skills.

Even though she took things gently, she still worked up a good sweat and was hungry after only a few exercises. She sat at the table and broke off a chunk of bread which she ate with a piece cheese.

The book with the lion on the cover stared at her, lying as it was on the table next to her. She opened it and began reading. It was only when she glanced at the page number that she realised she'd already read over fifty pages. How strange. In her world, stories were never written down. They were always told. That she could get lost in something she read was a completely new experience.

She wanted to read on, but a faint noise broke the silence. Could that be barking? Surely not. Would the police bring a dog to sniff her out? The bark came again, more clearly this time. With any luck the moth balls would throw it off the scent. How clever of Lydia to think of such a thing. Hardly daring to breathe or move, she listened for any sign they'd found the entrance.

The sound of claws scratching on the wooden door had Kate on the verge of panic. *Peter,* she thought, *I need you, NOW!*

Peter to the rescue, she heard him say, a broad grin in his thoughts.

Thank heavens this mind travelling works when we really need it, she said. She looked around the room to let Peter see where she was as she explained that the police were after her and there was a dog scratching at the other side of the door to hideaway. *You who were once in the head of a lion cub ... how about trying a dog?*

Peter's doubts were palpable. *I was much better at mind travelling then.*

A loud scratching had Kate swinging round in alarm to face the door.

Put your hand on the door, Peter ordered.

It was odd to feel his presence shifting to her outstretched fingers. He must have made several attempts to jump because she felt a strange tingling in her fingertips. Then, abruptly, he was gone. Had he succeeded, or had something drawn him back to his world? The scratching had not ceased.

Despite her heaving heart, she obstinately held her hand against the door. Peter might need to jump back. She had to be there for him. With each scratch of the animal's claws she felt the door tremble under her fingers. She wondered if she shouldn't push the table against the door, but that would make a noise.

Then just as abruptly as he'd left, Peter was back. She felt him shuddered mentally and she caught a glimpse of what it felt like to be in the head of a dog, especially one trained by the police. She waited patiently for him to recuperate. At least the scratching had ceased. Maybe he'd succeeded.

I hate dogs, Peter thought, shuddering again. *They are servile and stubborn. The lion cub was so much more intelligent. At least it reacted to the images I sent. The dog just ignored them. I had to wrench control from its paws and drive it out of the wardrobe. Neat system that, you'll have to tell me how it works.*

But surely the police knew I was in the wardrobe.

Luckily the dog handler had been called away. That was why the dog was frantic to let them know it'd found a scent. I suppose it wasn't its fault. But I was so annoyed, I made it knock over a flask of alcohol and pull the cork out with its teeth. Once I'd made it lap up the stinky liquid, it sagged to the ground and rolled over on its back. I was lucky to be able to jump back before I became as drunk as it was.

38.

Kate must have fallen asleep because the squeak of a door opening startled her. In a moment of extreme alertness, panic ran hot through her veins. The sight of Klaus and Lydia stepping into the underground room allayed much of her fear, but it took longer for her heart to settle and her stomach to return to its rightful place.

"I thought you were the police," she said, her voice shaking as she got to her feet. Klaus no longer wore his flour-spattered apron, but Lydia looked like she had hurried straight from the ward. Her starched, white pinafore over her sober, dark blue dress, was creased from working long hours at the hospital.

"They left a while ago," Klaus reassured her.

"Down here is so stuffy. Let's go upstairs," Lydia said, taking Kate by the arm and helping her to the door. "We'll tell you all about it."

Once they were in the kitchen and Lydia had drawn the curtains, Klaus opened a cardboard box and gingerly eased a cake from inside. "We call it Black Forest," Klaus told her, cutting generous slices.

He spooned a piece onto a dainty china plate and offered it to Kate with a small spoon. The cake looked delicious with tiny flakes of chocolate clinging to it. As she bit into it, she couldn't help sighing with pleasure. There were successive layers of cake and whipped cream that melted in her mouth. For a chocolate cake, it was surprisingly light. There were even candied cherries. "Delicious," she mumbled, helping herself to another spoonful.

Once they'd finished eating and Lydia had served tea, conversation turned to the police.

"It would seem my moth balls did the trick," Lydia said, chucking. "Their dog couldn't sniff you out."

"A neat idea, those moth balls," Kate said, wondering if she should tell them what really happened.

"What I don't understand," Klaus said, "is why they had to carry the dog out? It looked sick. Its head and legs were flopping all over the place. Could moth balls have poisoned it?"

Kate had to smile. She was tempted to tell them. It would have made such a good story. But they might not take kindly to the idea of traveling to minds. "That seems unlikely," she said, instead.

"You remember that young girl who came to visit you?" Lydia said. "Well, she came back."

Tania!

"We were lucky the police had left," Lydia added.

"Did you talk to her?" Kate asked.

"Briefly. I was afraid she might lead the police here."

"So what did you tell her?"

"I fixed a meeting near the bakery."

Kate was delighted. She missed Tania and her friends. "When do we go?"

"I don't think you should go. It's too dangerous. The police will be watching," Klaus said. "We'll bring the girl here, if it's safe."

Lydia fetched a large tube from a draw in the kitchen and placed it on the table. Kate glanced at the label. "Arnica?" she asked.

"We'll need it if the girl comes here," Lydia said. "She's peppered with bruises."

"In the convent the nuns weren't very kind," Kate explained.

"These looked recent," Lydia said, sounding concerned.

"She told me they split the group, sending her to a 'special boarding school for troublesome girls'. Sounds like it was even worse than the convent. I wonder how she managed to get out."

"It wouldn't surprise me if she wasn't on the run," Lydia said. "She looked starving and exhausted, and she didn't smell very clean either."

"When are you to see her?"

Lydia glanced at the watch pinned to her uniform. "In half an hour. We should go."

"I want to come," Kate said. "I might be able to help. I know her better than you…"

"That's not a good idea," Klaus insisted.

"I could go disguised. Is there not something in the clothes room upstairs to make me look like a boy?"

"Are you sure you have the strength?" Lydia asked.

"I'll be alright."

"Ok. Let's get you kitted up," Lydia said, putting her arm around Klaus to reassure him.

Klaus parked the van a couple of blocks from the bakery and the three made their way in silence along back streets, till they were in sight of the bistro where Tania was to meet them. Lydia had chosen a venue that was very small. From her vantage point behind a large bush across the road, Kate could see only four tables in front of a low counter. Two were empty. A man sat at one, the server sat at the other chatting with him. Apart from the occasional passer-by, the place was quiet.

"Could that be a policeman?" Kate whispered, pointing to the man in the bistro.

"I doubt it," Klaus replied. "They'd have to follow her to know where she was going, unless of course they interrogated her."

"There she is," Lydia said, drawing their attention back to the bistro.

Kate wanted to hurry and greet her friend, but Klaus placed a cautioning hand on her shoulder. "Wait a moment," he said. "Let's see if she was followed."

In her new home, she must have received new clothes, because Tania was wearing a pleated, blue skirt that looked new and a grey blouse that was a little too big for her. Slung over her shoulders, the girl had draped the cloak they had made at the convent. She seemed reluctant to enter and spent a long moment staring at the menu in the window, glancing for time to time furtively around.

"She probably has no money. That's why she can't go in," Lydia whispered.

"I'm going…" Kate began to say, but Klaus placed a large hand over her mouth, silencing her. When she looked to him for an explanation, he just nodded in the direction of Tania. Some twenty yards away, unseen by Tania, stood a policeman and a policewoman watching her.

"We have to leave," Lydia whispered. "If they see you, we'll all be in for trouble."

"No," Kate said. "Let me talk to Tania."

"I won't let you go," Lydia insisted.

"I don't need to," Kate whispered. "I can do it from here."

Klaus and Lydia looked perplexed, but neither said anything. Finding a large stone, Kate sat, making sure she was concealed, but still able to see Tania. *Tania,* she called, mind-to-mind. *Don't be startled. It's me.*

Kate, Tania replied, spinning round in search of her friend despite Kate's warning.

Keep calm, Kate told her. *You're being watched. Look back at the shop window as if nothing were happening.*

Where are you? Tania asked, her thoughts bubbling over with excitement.

Close. But we have to be very careful.

What should I do?

Hold on. Lydia is with me, with her husband. I need to ask them a question. I'll relay their answers to you.

"Lydia, Klaus," Kate whispered. "Is there any way Tania can get out the back of the building?"

"Yes. The toilet is out back. There's an alley leading away. It goes past the bakery."

"Good. Could you hurry to the bakery, Klaus, to help Tania

when she arrives?"

He didn't bother to reply, but set off down the road on the opposite side to the police, heading for his bakery. The policeman and woman were so absorbed watching Tania they didn't notice him.

Tania, did you hear that?

Yes. But how can I get to the toilet. I can't just walk in and asked to go.

Go inside. Order a drink. Point to a table. Tell them to put the drink there. Then ask where the toilet is. If they want you to pay, say you'll do so immediately you get back. Once outside hurry down that alley and look for the back of the baker's place. Klaus will be waiting there. You'll recognise him. He's a big, burly fellow with large hands and a bright red face. He'll be wearing an apron all covered in flour. Call me if there's a problem.

When she looked up, Kate saw Tania enter the bistro. All seemed to be going well. Tania had just slipped out the back door when the police couple moved closer and Kate heard Tania call out in her head, *There's a policeman waiting in the alley.*

OK. Kate said. *Lock yourself in the toilet for a moment. I'm going to ask Lydia if she has an idea.*

"I sent her out back," Kate whispered to Lydia. "I wanted her to go down that alley to meet Klaus, but there's a policeman. Got any ideas what she can do?"

"Give me your hat and coat," Lydia said. To disguise as a boy, Kate had found a smart suit that almost fit her. Over the top, she was wearing a long trench coat with a cloth cap. Lydia took the clothes and hastily wrapped them into a bundle. "Tell your friend I'm coming. Wait for me here and keep out of sight."

It was surprisingly cold without the coat. Kate crouched down and hugged herself to keep warm. *Tania,* she called. *Lydia is coming. She'll bring a disguise. Let her in when she knocks.*

Glancing across the road, Kate saw Lydia disappear into the bistro. It would seem she knew the server, because they exchanged a few words before Lydia disappeared out back. The police couple posted outside were getting impatient. They peered into the window several times to see if Tania had returned. Finally, one of them stepped into the bistro and questioned the server. Kate could see the young woman shaking her head and shrugging.

Lydia's here, she heard Tania say mind-to-mind, *and I'm all dressed up. We're going to try to get round the man. Oh. And Lydia says to make your way back to the van.*

Seeing that the two police officers were busy with the server, Kate got to her feet and cautiously crept out from behind the bush and headed off down the road.

"And where would you be going?" a familiar voice said. She looked up to see the tall, wiry man who'd interrogated her in the hospital.

Did you make it? She hastily asked Tania.

Yes. The policeman was suspicious, but Lydia was very convincing.

Listen. I've got a problem. It's the police inspector. I'm going to have to use force. I won't be able to make it to Klaus' van. I'll call you later and tell you where to meet me.

She broke the contact, her time was up. Hoping her strength would hold out, she took a deep breath just as the inspector made a move to grab her. She stepped aside, using his momentum to catch him off balance and sent him flying into the bush. She had to act quickly now he knew what she was capable of. As he struggled to get up, she swung her leg in a low arc, and knocked his feet from under him, following through with a sharp blow to the back of his head. It was a move her arms master, Zhuru, had taught her. The inspector crumpled in a heap at her feet.

Kate, Tania called out, anxious. *Are you all right?*

Yes.

The baker says you stand no chance alone with the police hunting you. Go to the van and we'll be waiting.

OK, was all she replied, walking as fast as she could. She rubbed her fist trying to ease the ache from hitting the inspector. She really was out of practice, her legs and arms trembled and her heart was beating far too fast. She wasn't sure she'd make it to the van. Her vision was clouding and dark patches swam before her eyes.

She was about to lean against a wall when she spotted Klaus standing next to the van beckoning. She drew on the last of her force and stumbled to join him.

He helped her inside and hastily closed the back door. In the half light, amongst the sacks of flour, Kate was immediately assailed by Tania who seemed bent on catching up on all the hugs and kisses she'd missed. The van surged forward as Klaus put it in gear and let out the clutch, pitching the two girls backwards amongst the sacks.

"Are you two all right?" Lydia called out from the front, sounding worried.

"Sure," Kate replied, struggling to catch her breath. "If Tania doesn't kill me with her affection."

39.

Peter crawled from under the table and heaved himself to his feet. Brushing off his knees, he straightened his skirt which had ridden up around his thighs while he'd searched on all fours.

"I've found it," he said, handing the ring to Viktor who sat at the kitchen table in their cottage at Lettup.

"Beth gave it to me, all those years ago, in a stolen moment, concealed in the crowds of concertgoers," Viktor told Peter as he slipped the ring back on his finger. It was good to see the man smile again. His despair at the loss of the ring had taken Peter by surprise. Despite his strange behaviour, his teacher was normally level-headed.

"We'd just attended a concert," Viktor continued, caught up, as he always was when he spoke of his lost love. "Of course, we couldn't go together. But we exchanged stolen glances across the audience."

"Concert?"

"Yes. I remember it as if it were yesterday. Choral music, including Fauré's Messe Basse. Magnificent!" A broad grin lit up his face. "There's a very strong choral tradition in Luzern. You should go."

Andrew entered at that moment. Taking his place at the table, pale and taciturn, he sat silently watching.

"Viktor was talking about Fauré's Messe Basse," Peter told Andrew. "Do you know it?"

"The women's mass," Andrew commented laconically.

"Women's?" Peter asked.

"Because it was scored only for upper voices. No tenor or bass."

"It's just the sort of music that would fit this village," Viktor said, completely forgetting to finish his tale about Beth. "It requires a small setting. Lettup church would be ideal. Instead of an organ, you could use a harmonium. And the closeness of the sea. I don't know why, but I imagine it being sung before an audience of fishermen, their wives and children fresh from the sea."

He sang them a short extract from the beginning of the Agnus Dei. Peter had often heard Viktor sing. He had a beautiful, rich tenor, but this countertenor was quite unexpected. Something about it made Peter want to grin.

"Sound's wonderful," Peter said, not sure if he meant the man's voice or the idea of singing the composition in Lettup. "What do you think Andy?"

He and Kate might have pulled Andrew back from the brink, but the boy was still tern and unresponsive. Andrew had always been reserved, but with the death of his uncle, the attempt on his own life and the tragic death of Fi, not to mention his brother, he'd clammed up. What he needed, he imagined Fi saying, was a pretty boy to warm his heart. On careful reflexion, such a solution would just make things worse. No. What Andrew needed was a purpose in life.

"But where would you get the choir from?" Andrew asked, his voice flat and unemotional.

"You'd be surprised. There are a number of women in the village who sing well. Maybe we could find the rest in Bargeton," Viktor said.

"I'll ask the vicar. He'd be delighted to have us perform and maybe he knows people who could sing," Peter said. "How many would we need?"

"Well, if you sing the solo part and Andrew plays the harmonium we'd need at least four sopranos and four altos."

The sound of a key turning in the front door interrupted their discussion. "It's open!" Peter called out, supposing it was

Christina.

To their surprise, the door opened and Dr Grant walked in. He was wearing a smart grey suit with a white shirt unbuttoned at the neck. Under his arm, he carried a newspaper folded up. Despite his dapper appearance, he look frayed, as if he'd just been through a trying ordeal. He shrugged out of his jacket, hung it on the back of a chair and came to join them at the table.

"You folks got any tea? I'm parched," he said, as he sat down and discarded the newspaper.

To Peter's ears, he sounded more weary and worried than thirsty. Peter got to his feet and put the kettle on, saying: "You know Viktor, don't you?"

John nodded greetings and then, noticing the pink marks around Andrew's wrists, starred at them, his eyes wide in horror. Andrew hastily hid his hands under the table, an embarrassed look on his face. Too late. The damage was done. Nobody spoke till the cheerful whistle of the kettle broke the silence.

"We had a little problem..." Peter began, but then faltered, unsure how to go on.

"Everything's all right now," Viktor told Dr Grant. "Thanks to Peter. But what about you? Are you all right?"

Peter was glad Viktor dared ask. He couldn't bring himself to do so. His heart sank at the thought of what John might reply.

John glanced at Peter then wiped his hand across his face, sighing as he did. "Priscilla Wit killed herself yesterday."

There was a time when Peter might have been relieved. The girl had caused him so much trouble. But she'd been removed from his life a while back, shut away in a mental institution, like his own sister and mother. So much had happened in the mean time, he felt little at the news. He certainly didn't wish her dead. If anything, he felt sorry for her aunt with whom Witless had stayed when her mother was unable to care for her.

"She hung herself," John told them, his voice heavy with sadness and not a little anger. "She wrote a note…"

Peter was unsure whether the man would break down and cry or shout in fury. He did neither. Fists clenched, jaw tight, he continued.

"It was addressed to you, Peter."

Peter suddenly felt fear grip him. Had the monster reached out on the verge of death to deal him a fatal blow? It was the sort of thing she was capable of. Her father too had hung himself in spectacular circumstances. Priscilla had been the first to find him dangling in the stairwell. She'd also discovered the note. It had poisoned her life, unhinging her mind. Priscilla had tried to pass on that poison to Peter.

John pulled a folded piece of paper from his pocket. "This is a copy. The police kept the original."

Peter wanted nothing to do with it. Maybe if he refused to touch it or read it, he'd be spared the venom Priscilla had intended for him.

Rather than hold the note out to Peter, John crumpled it in his hand. "I would understand if you refused to read it," John said. "I certainly won't force you."

When Peter made no move to take the paper, it was Viktor that leaned across the table and extracted the crumpled note from John's clenched fist. Carefully unfolding it, he smoothed it out on the table. Then he lifted it close to his eyes and read, as if it were written in an unintelligible hand. Once he'd finished, he read it a second time, then just as carefully folded it once then twice then three times. He went to hand the small square back to John, but the headmaster withdrew his hand, refusing the responsibility, so Viktor laid the letter on the table.

It lay there a long time, a tight white rectangle on the varnished wooden tabletop, a foreign body in their daily life. To Peter, it felt like the note was taunting him. He dug his hands deep in the pockets of his dress as if they might defy him and reach out to take the message of their own accord. He knew he wouldn't be able to resist very long. Witless had cornered him, yet again, and he was powerless to fight her off. He remembered the time she'd rammed him against a shop window, her hands clasped around his throat. She'd spat in his face and the wet slime had dribbled over his eyes and down his cheeks. He'd been terrified and humiliated. The same feeling surged as he stretched out and picked up the paper.

"You don't have to," Andrew said, some of his earlier colour and emotion returning to his voice.

"Oh, but I do. That's the thing about Priscilla Wit, you can't ignore her."

He began to unfold the note, bile rising in his throat. Like Viktor, he turned the note face down and smoothed it out on the table. What point in putting it off? He turned the paper over. No wonder Viktor had found it difficult to decipher. The words were a jumble of ill-formed characters that jostled their way angrily across the page. Peter read:

To Peter McCloud.

With this note I publicly denounce you for the filthy fairy you are. Your disgusting habits leave behind the stench of rotting flesh. Your perverted presence contaminates all those who surround you. Such vermin as you should be exterminated. The world has no place for pansies like you. You will always be a mistake, a miscarriage, a miscreant. You and your sort have ruined my life. You killed my father. The only person in the world who loved me. You drove my mother mad. You had me locked up when it was you who should have been put away. And now you have murdered me and everyone will know it was you. They'll lock you away, for ever. May you rot in your own squalor. May lice and cockroaches consume you, one filthy lump at a time...

The writing trailed off in wild, enraged squiggles that made no sense. There was no signature. Yet the whole message spoke of Witless. Signing would have been superfluous.

The force of her words battered him. Their violence had him staggering. He grasped the edge of the table for support. So much hate. For a moment he thought he might succumb, then her words rolled on and away, till they were little more than distant rumbles of thunder, leaving him standing there shaking but unscathed.

He released his death grip on the table and carefully folded the note, placing it back on the table. A glance around the room showed that everyone was watching, apprehensive, waiting for his reaction. What did he feel? He wasn't sure. One thing was certain, he no longer felt frightened. Sad. That was it. He felt sad. Deep sadness at the girl's tragic tale. Frequent misreadings of the world and misplaced religious fervour had driven her over the brink.

She had tried to drag others into that black hole. With some she'd succeeded. But, despite all his failings and weaknesses, despite the guilt and doubts he'd felt, he'd managed to resist and, now that she was dead and gone, her note had none of the effect she'd no doubt hoped for. As with many other things in her life, she'd misjudged the people around her, him in particular.

"Poor girl," Peter said, meaning no irony with his words. "She really was unhinged." He got to his feet and refilled the kettle. "Anyone for tea?" As he said so, he felt the atmosphere in the room relax.

"Is this going to cause problems for you?" he asked John.

"Probably not. She was known to be crazy and this note proves it. Neither you nor I, even indirectly, will be in any way held responsible for her death." He handed his empty cup to Peter, then turned to Andrew. "What happened to you?"

"I came unhinged too," Andrew admitted, taking the cup of tea Peter offered, winding his fingers around it in search of warmth. "It was a long time in the making but it came to a head this afternoon. After all that had happened, I couldn't bear to go on. Alone and useless, harmful even, there seemed no point in continuing." His voice broke and he paused a moment, struggling to get a grip. "I felt unloved and unwanted. So I slashed my wrists. The pain was terrible, but it all happened so quickly that when I realised my life was seeping away, it was too late to regret. I was in reach of the other side when Peter and Kate brought me back." He held out his wrists for John to examine. Only a faint pink line remained where the bloody gashes had once been. "But more than heal my cuts, the two healed my soul. I don't know how they did it. But I am profoundly grateful."

He got to his feet, cautiously placing the cup of tea on the table, and put his arms around Peter, hugging him tight. Peter felt Andrew's breath on his neck as the boy laid his head on Peter's shoulder. Running his fingers through the boy's hair, Peter couldn't help remembering the stirring moment when he and Kate had sung life back in a chorus of health and well-being.

40.

Peter cleared away the dishes and cutlery, piling them up in the sink and, running the water, he left them to soak. He had the kitchen to himself. Andrew had gone for a nap, exhausted after his ordeal. Viktor had returned home, excited about working on a performance of Fauré, and John had driven into Bargeton to fetch food for the weekend.

Outside the weather had cleared and rays of sun were slanting through the kitchen window. Peter pulled up a chair and sat down at the table, pulling over the newspaper John had brought from home. He thumbed through the pages paying little attention to what was written. He thought of Witless and her despair and hatred. He thought of Brian determined to kill Andrew. He thought of Margery, the chubby girl from school, who'd wanted to follow in Witless's footsteps. Why did some people get so set on an idea that they were prepared to kill for it?

His musing was interrupted by tiny headlines at the bottom of one of the last pages. Mysterious death of Arthur W. Yong. He knew that name. Good lord! It was Old Man God, the author of the story about Kate.

Only a few paragraphs long, he wondered how he'd spotted it. He read on. Little known author Arthur W. Yong (a footnote mentioned his trilogy: The Strange History of Syvatoy and Drailong) was admitted to a hospital in South London after a bad fall in his flat in Balham. During a routine operation on his leg, which was broken in several places, the bones suddenly shattered in many tiny pieces. He died unexpectedly while recuperating from the operation. Nothing indicated his life was in danger. Questioned about the accident, Dr Mbabwe, who operated on Mr Yong, pointed out that they hadn't even been touching the man's leg when the incident occurred. "It was like a mini earthquake," the doctor reported. "The phenomenon had us baffled." A specialist from the NHS, who wishes to remain anonymous, said such an incident was quite unheard of. The hospital board refused to comment, saying only that there would be an inquest.

Perplexed, Peter put down the paper and stared unseeing out the window. If the author of Kate's story was dead, what did that mean? Would she die too? Surely characters outlived their authors, didn't they? He'd always imagined they did, but then he'd never met any in real life, before he met Kate. Or would she be trapped forever in that last story, unable to find a way out?

An idea formed in his head. He got to his feet and hurried out into the hall. Pulling a cloak around his shoulders and donning a pair of sandals, he hurried outside and set off for the centre of the village. He was in luck, the pub was still open. The last customers were downing beers and preparing to leave. He'd never been in the pub before, he'd had no call to. But he knew they had a public phone and might have telephone directories.

"Excuse me," he said to the girl behind the counter.

"Yes, ducky. It's closing time, you know. What can I do for you?" she asked.

"Have you got London phone directories?" he asked.

"Sorry luv. No we ain't. That's far too new fer us 'ere." She continued wiping down the bar. "Try the operator."

"I didn't bring my purse," Peter admitted. "Does it cost anything?"

"Nope," she replied, pointing to the phone in the corridor. "If yer quick, yer can phone before we close."

Peter hurried out back and picked up the receiver. The dialling tone took a while to come. He dialled 100 and listened.

"Good afternoon. What can I do for you?" a woman's crisp

voice asked.

"I'm looking for the address of Arthur W. Yong who lives in Balham," Peter told her.

"Hold the line caller."

After a long wait, the woman came back saying, "The gentleman lives in Balham High Road." And she gave him the number.

Having thanked her and the girl behind the bar, he hurried out, please to be free of the stale pub air. Rather than return to the cottage, he headed for the harbour and sat on the low wall that bordered the ramp leading into the water. Most of the fishing boats were out so he had the place to himself.

Beyond the bay, he could see waves crashing against the rocks where the cliffs dived into the sea. Even at that distance, he could feel the mass of water pressing against the rocks, as if it were exerting its force against him. He watched the gulls gathering along the far end of the wall on which he sat. From time to time, one would take off lazily and, catching an up-draught, would soar up and away.

Maybe if he could get into Old Man God's place, he'd be able to find clues to where Kate was. But he'd have to hurry. People would soon clear out his belongings. Maybe the inquest would buy him time, but he couldn't be sure. Resolved to go to London as soon as possible, he got to his feet and hurried back through the village to their cottage.

Christina had returned. John too. Vegetables, butter, bottles of beer, milk, syrup, a hunk of cheese, a side of bacon, several loaves of bread, even a couple of rolls of toilet paper lay higgledy-piggledy on the kitchen table. John and Christina were busy putting away food in the larder. Andrew sat at the kitchen table .sipping a cup of tea watching the adults bustle around.

"Old Man God is dead," Peter announced. Christina and John knew about the man who'd invented Kaitlin. Only Andrew looked perplexed. "Kate was part of a story written by a man called Arthur W. Yong," Peter explained. "We called him Old Man God because he reigned over Kate's world like a god. Well, he's dead."

"How do you know?" Christina asked.

"An article in the newspaper. Apparently his death was strange. There's to be an enquiry."

The grown-ups had finally finished tidying away and Christina set about toasting crumpets while John made tea.

"I want to go to London to see his flat," Peter told them. "Maybe we can find a clue to where Kate is."

"Do you know his address?" John asked, putting the tea pot and a set of mugs on the table.

"Yes. I phoned directory enquiries. He lived in Balham."

"We could drive up on Saturday," Christina suggested.

Anything could happen in the two days to the weekend. "That may be too late," Peter said. "Who knows when they'll clear out his flat?"

"Why don't we go now," Andrew said, surprising them with his enthusiasm. "I'd welcome a change of scenery. I haven't been to London for ages."

"Would you let these go to waste?" Christina asked, placing a large plate of crumpets on the table along with the butter dish, plates and knives.

By way of answer both Peter and Andrew set about buttering several crumpets. John had the foresight to give them napkins.

"It'll take at least three hours to drive to London. We're likely to get there right in the rush hour," John said, as they planned their trip. "Balham is to the South West so, coming from the coast, we might avoid the worst traffic."

All four were to go and they'd overnight at John's house in Talford before returning to the coast. They quickly packed their nighties and a toothbrush, while Christina prepared sandwiches for the trip and John plotted the route.

The journey was uneventful. Peter slept much of the way, as did Andrew. Peter had wondered if he'd travel to Kate's world, but that hadn't happened.

The High Road in Balham was surprisingly wide, the pavement too, with rows of redbrick buildings on either side, two, three or four storeys high, often ending in strange towers or larger windows stretching up beyond the rest of the roof, all coiffed with regimented chimney stacks. The ground floor generally housed shop windows or store fronts, most of which were already shut or shutting down.

It could have been majestic, but despite it's size, the street struck Peter as shabby. Here and there, papers blew across the pavement. Cardboard boxes were stacked outside shops and piles of rubbish overflowed dustbins in corners and down blind alleys. The people, who hurried on their way, looked shabby too. Their clothes were mostly grey and worn, their faces surly and downcast. They looked tired after a long day's work.

The house in which Old Man God had lodged had a greengrocer's on the ground floor. Access to floors above was via a narrow door, to one side of the shop. The door was locked. Peter, who was to go in on his own, hailed the greengrocer, as he shifted crates of potatoes and carrots back inside the shop.

"We're closed," the man snapped.

"I am a friend of Mr Wong," Peter explained, trying to smile winningly, despite the unpleasant smell of rotting cabbage. "He lived here, I believe. I'd like to visit his flat before everything is moved out."

"Don't ask me. Never heard of the bloke. Ring Mrs Smythe's bell. She'll know." On which the man turned his back and continued his work.

Next to the door Peter found a row of door bells. Only one had a name: Mrs Smythe. He rang. Nothing happened. He rang again, and then a third time. He was about to give up when the door cracked open and an old lady peered out, huffing and puffing as if she'd been up or down several flights of stairs.

"Yes?" she asked. Then seeing Peter, still dressed as a girl, the woman said. "What is it ducky. I've got work to do."

"I'm a friend of Mr Wong, the writer. I wondered if I could visit his flat, one last time, before they clear out his things."

"Poor bloke," the woman said, making no move to let Peter in. "All happened so sudden. Such an elegant gent. Always paid his rent on time. You never can know where it'll strike next."

"He wrote such fascinating books," Peter added for fear the woman would forget him, lost as she was in her memories. "Would you mind letting me in?"

"I suppose it wouldn't do any harm. The police've finished. Tomorrow the removals men come 'n clear everything out."

Peter heaved a sigh of relief when Mrs Smythe finally eased back, leaving just enough room to slip inside. "You know your way," she said. "The door's open. I'll be on the first floor if you need me."

Peter guessed the flat must be further up, so he went on ahead of Mrs Smythe who laboured up, one step at a time, puffing and groaning like an abandoned train.

Peter halted at the second floor and quietly tried the doors. They were all locked. The third floor was the same. Reaching the fourth floor, he realised it was the last. If none of the doors opened here, he'd be in a mess. He was about to try one door when he heard a radio inside. He hastily tried the other. It wouldn't budge.

"It's always been stiff," a woman said behind him.

Spinning round, his cheeks colouring with embarrassment, he saw a skinny woman with protruding eyes peering down at him. An overpowering wave of scent preceded her as she moved towards him across the landing.

"You have to push with your shoulder, luv," she explained.

He did and the door flew open with a sudden rush that almost flung him to the floor. The woman burst out laughing. "It did the same to me." She followed him in, dashing any hopes of searching for clues. "I tidied up a bit. He wasn't very orderly," she said, pushing passed him in the corridor and on into the main room.

From the door, Peter spotted the poster of the Queen and Prince Philip that he remember so well. The one time he'd been in the flat, he'd been in Old Man God's head. The poster had been a clue that Old Man God lived in Peter's world.

Peter looked around. There were two small windows high in

the walls, devoid of curtains, out of which he could see only the sky and the corner of a chimney pot. Against one wall, stood a wooden table cluttered with papers, pens and a large bottle of ink. Apparently the man didn't use a typewriter. Leaning at an angle against the table was a carved walking stick. There was only one chair in the room, a straight-backed wooden chair with a hard seat that looked none too comfortable. It stood forlorn next to the table.

Across the room below the royal poster was a second table, with an off-green Formica surface, on which was an electric kettle, a tea pot, a bowl of sugar, various spoons and a single mug.

"He wrote books, you know," the woman said, absent-mindedly riffling through the man's papers.

"Can I have a look?" Peter asked, taking hold of the pile of papers, afraid she'd damage them before he got a chance to look.

"I've been reading them," she told him.

"The papers?"

"No, his books. There were three. About two islands and a lot of priests and magicians. It's a bit complicated. But I persisted. I reckon I owe him that."

"Where are the books now?"

"I took them to an antique dealer, thinking they might be worth something. The man told me they were worthless. The books were pretty badly made. He showed me where the binding was coming apart. Shoddy work, he called it. He reckoned Mr Wong had a cheap copy printed just for himself. And there was me thinking he was a famous author. Goes to show."

Indeed. Yet those books, however insignificant they might seem in London in 1960, had created Kate's world, in which she had almost died and many others had been tortured and killed. Peter glanced at the papers in his hand. He shuddered. He didn't want to read them. The handwriting on the first page was tiny and clumsy with several ink smudges. If that was the beginning of the man's novel about Kate, he didn't get very far. He glanced at the last sentence, and caught his breath. *Kate hobbled disconsolate, her bare feet stinging on the freezing flagstones, her head bowed, enclosed in a world of silent misery...*

41.

"Are you all right, Ducky?" a woman asked.

Peter scratched his head, confused. Who was this lady leaning over him, surrounded by a cascade of perfumed frills and lace? And, more important, why was he lying at her feet? Then, round her voluminous dress, he caught sight of the royal couple starring down at him and whole chunks of his memory chugged back into place.

The monster! Old Man God had deliberately hurt Kate and imprisoned her in some miserable place, all because the withered runt wanted revenge. And why? Because Kate had dared defend her life and those of the people she loved. None of which explained why he was lying on the floor.

"What happened?" he asked, as she helped him to his feet and brushed down his dress for him. He hated it when people touched him like that, especially people he didn't know. As if being a child gave adults a right to all kinds of excesses. It wasn't just that he was afraid of being unmasked for what he was or wasn't. He felt threatened when strangers got too close.

"You fainted, luv," she said, handing him a wad of papers. "You dropped these."

"Thank you. Do you think anyone would mind if I took them?" he asked, indicating the papers. "As a souvenir."

"No. Go ahead. They'll only get burnt with the rest when the men clean up. It's such a shame." She sighed. "That's life. Next week someone else'll live here."

"Did you know him well?"

She shook her head. "I only met him once, quite by chance, the day he collapsed. It was just after I moved in. Ah! If I'd arrived earlier, maybe I could have saved him. Where was I? Oh yes. I saw the postman knocking at his door. No one answered, but we heard a terrible crash and a groan. So the postman forced the door. And there he was, lying on the floor, and him such a gentleman and so well dressed, lying exactly where you were just now, his leg broken." She made a dramatic gesture, one hand pointing to the floor, the other to the ceiling, that Peter had a hard time interpreting.

"Someone called an ambulance, I would have done so myself, but I don't have a phone, and they whisked him off to hospital. I climbed into the ambulance with him, swept along by the action. Funny really. The ambulance men took me for his wife." She giggled. "There was me, sitting like a lemon, with the cake I'd baked on my lap. I tried offering Mr Wong a slice, but he'd have nothing of it. I don't think he could figure out who I was." She plumped down on the only chair, her dress billowing out around her, and rested her head in her hands.

"That's when things went skew-whiff. Of course, the doctors said nothing. You know how doctors are. But they couldn't fool me. I saw it in their eyes. Something was dreadfully wrong. I overheard two nurses chatting. One minute they were saying his leg was broken, I mean, like you or I if we broke our leg. And him lying there peacefully on the operating table doing no harm to a soul. The next thing you know, his leg was all mangled and he was screaming with pain. A nurse said he looked like he'd been hit by a car gone wild. A real mess."

Peter shuddered at the horror of it. All the same, this was the man who'd readily mangled Kate's leg for his story and his own vengeance. What would the woman think, if she knew what a monster he was?

"Took them hours to find all the bits. And many more hours to piece them together. Worse than one of those puzzles with five hundred parts. The shock must have driven him mad. He kept mumbling that it was his story, not hers. He was furious.

How dare she turn on him like that. I began to wonder if he hadn't been bewitched. From then on, its was all down hill."

Had he been talking about Kate? Had she managed to turn the tables on the man who'd created her, gifting him the poison he'd meant for her? All the better for Kate, but the idea that characters in books could get revenge on their authors was more than alarming.

A knock came at the door and in stepped John. "We need to be going," he said, visibly relieved to see Peter okay.

"Sorry I kept you waiting," Peter apologised. Turning to the woman he said. "I didn't catch your name."

"Margaret," she said smiling at Dr Grant.

"Margaret," Peter said, "let me present Dr Grant, my..." There was a short hesitation while Peter weighed up what to say. "... my father."

John came forward and shook hands with the woman. "Pleased to meet you, Margaret. I trust..." and it was his turn to hesitate, "Wendy didn't keep you chatting too long."

"Not at all," Margaret said. "Your daughter's charming."

The word 'daughter' sent a delicious shiver through Peter, the sort of secret pleasure he hadn't experienced for ages. So much had happened, he'd had little time to indulge in thoughts of being a girl. Three months earlier, the idea of being taken for the headmaster's daughter would have probably given him vertigo, if not deep-seated guilt. That John played along, despite his obvious reticence, continued to amaze Peter, but it also left him troubled.

"Are you ready, Wendy?" John asked, no hesitation this time.

"I think so. Many thanks Margaret. I hope your new neighbours are charming."

Clasping Peter by the hand, the woman pulled him into a strongly-scented embrace, crushing his head against her bony bosom. Then, freeing him abruptly from her grasp, he almost collapsed a second time while she shook hands with Dr Grant.

Nothing was said as they trudged down the stairs. It was

only when all four were settled in the car and John had driven in the direction of Talford that Peter told them what had happened.

"So maybe Kate managed to get the better of him," Peter concluded.

"Show me those papers," Christina asked. Daylight was fading, making reading difficult. Luckily there was a torch in the glove compartment. "He didn't get very far," she said. "It's probably better that way. If he'd managed to write what he intended, judging from these notes, Kate would have been far worse off."

"Maybe that's why she managed to hit back and get the upper hand," Peter said. "He hadn't written enough to trap her."

"Does anyone know German?" Christina asked.

"No. Why?" John replied.

"Here, tucked in amongst the papers, I've found a newspaper clipping in German."

None of them had learnt German.

"We should ask Viktor. I believe he's fluent in German," Peter said.

The conversation turned to other things as they got closer to Talford.

"We've been pretty open about you two dressing up," John began.

Peter immediately felt his heart sink. Here we go, he thought.

It's only normal, Kate thought in his head.

Kate! he said, greeting her warmly. Travelling between minds had become so unpredictable, he was always startled when she turned up.

I mean, he's got his reputation to think of, she said.

Peter changed the subject and told Kate that Old Man God was dead. She was delighted. Peter explained that he had visited the man's flat. When he told her about the papers she was thoughtful a moment. Then she said, *I guessed as much. My leg was a complete mess. I tried healing it, but nothing worked. It was when I saw that filthy tramp in the church that the miracle happened. Could that have been him? From the moment I saw him, I was cured. Maybe the affliction that was meant for me bounced back on him. How strange.*

Well at least you're OK now.

Things are finally getting better. But I have to go. I'll tell you later.

"Peter? Are you listening?" Christina was saying, her voice raised. "Did you hear what John said about dressing up?"

No. I didn't."

"It was important,..." she said, sounding irritated.

"I was talking to Kate," Peter interrupted. "All that business about Old Man God's knee breaking makes more sense now. Apparently Kate had been injured in a car accident and she could hardly walk. Then, when she was in a church and she saw a filthy tramp crouching there, she was suddenly cured." When Kate had explained it, everything had made sense. Now, as he told it, he had to admit the explanation was hardly convincing.

The car came to a halt and Peter realised they'd arrived.

"Let's go in. You can tell us the rest later," John said, sounding tense as he hurried them indoors.

Hardly had they entered, than the phone rang. John dashed into his study to reply, Christina headed for the kitchen to make something to eat while Peter and Andrew plodded upstairs to prepare their beds for the night.

"So what has happened to Kate?" Andrew asked.

Peter had no time to reply as John called up. "Peter, Andrew, could you come down."

John stood waiting in the hall. Christina, who had joined him, had one arm round his shoulder. He looked even more tense than before.

"That was Mrs Greengage," John told them.

Peter knew the woman well. She was his English teacher and had sided with him against the horrible Sanson who'd temporarily replaced John as headmaster.

"She'll be here in a short while. Apparently there's a problem at school."

Peter hadn't seen John so worried since the time when

Sanson had tried to discredit him.

"So I have an urgent request," John said.

Peter knew immediately what was coming next. Reality had caught up with him and he and Andrew would have to change into boys' clothes.

"You want us to dress as boys," Peter said.

"No. It's even more serious than that," John said. "I want you, Christina, to drive the three of you back to the coast."

"What's going on?" Christina asked.

"I don't want to bother you with my problems," John replied.

"Listen, John," Christina began. "Since we met, we've been sharing everything. Why should we change now, just because the situation is more difficult?"

John looked miserable as he glanced at Peter. Whatever it was, he didn't want to admit to it.

"Let's sit down," John said. "It will be easier.

In the living room, Christina sat next to John on the settee, her arm laced around his shoulder. Peter and Andrew took the two armchairs. A low table separated them.

"It would appear that Pricilla Wit made a copy of her suicide note and had it sent to Margery."

Peter's heart sank. The Witless girl was set on doing him harm even if it meant doing so from beyond the grave.

"When is she going to leave me in peace?" Peter asked.

"Apparently the note was not the same as the one we've seen. You are not the only person attacked," John said, sounding old and weary. "It says that I took you in as my…" He ran his hand across his face, hesitating to go on. "My toy thing."

"But that's absurd," Christina burst out.

"It's not," John replied, sounding defeated. "Margery has been busy collecting evidence. With the help of friends she has managed to get together a rather convincing case."

"How can that be?" Peter asked, unbelieving.

"She found out about Bonnie."

Both Christina and Andrew gasped.

"But…" Peter began.

"It was in all the newspapers when Fi was killed. Apparently Margery bullied or coaxed Bonnie into giving evidence that you and Andrew dressed as girls. Bonnie is not very strong emotionally at the moment. If she thought Margery would befriend her, she might well do whatever Margery wanted."

Peter had to admit John was right. Bonnie would have given anything to be loved and appreciated by another girl. He only had to think how she'd behaved with him and Fi.

"Well," John continued. "Margery got Bonnie to admit that I slept with you two boys…"

Peter had the impression that John was crumpling before his eyes. Christina tried to console him, but to no avail. It made Peter furious to think that such a good and generous man, who had helped many a student, could be so easily destroyed by malicious gossip.

He could see the nightmare unfolding. Hadn't Christina told them most people wouldn't understand the way they lived and they'd get very angry if they knew. He imagined how newspapers would turn the story, pandering to people's delight in scandals. Little heed would be paid to the fact that both Witless and Bonnie were unhinged. No consideration would be given to who John really was and the work he'd done as headmaster. Only wild, slavering imagination would triumph.

"What do you plan to do?" Peter asked, quashing the fury he felt against Margery.

"First, I will resign as headmaster," John said.

"No!" the others said in chorus.

The doorbell rang at that moment.

"We're not leaving," Peter said, suddenly finding strength and resolve. "We will change into boys' clothes and we'll take part in your conversation. We have our word to say. No Margery is going to ruin our lives. We'll fight back."

42.

"That's awful," Klaus exclaimed, piling soup bowls in the sink.

Kate and Tania were seated at the large kitchen table. Nothing remained of Lydia's delicious vegetable soup. Tania had been famished. Between mouthfuls and sometimes during them, she'd explained how she managed to escape the special school where she was being held. She'd been so badly beaten they'd had to put her in the infirmary where the nurse was less vigilant. Apparently the infirmary had a service door. Tania had been on the run ever since and had hardly slept or eaten in that time.

"How could they possibly treat young girls so badly?" Klaus continued.

Kate was worried about the other girls. They'd come to depend on each other, with the younger girls looking for support and guidance from Christine and Eileen, not to mention Clara, Claudia and Suzanne. Being split up would make life much harder.

"What about the others?" Kate asked.

"Suzanne, Clara and Claudia were at the same place as me. Clara has had the worst of it. She was in the infirmary like me, but didn't have the strength to escape when I did. I have no idea where Christine and Eileen went."

Kate told Lydia and Klaus about life in the convent once the nuns had left, in particular about the role of her little group of friends: Christine, Eileen, Suzanne and Tania.

"So you see," she concluded, "we organised our own lives. You should meet Suzanne. I taught her the rudiments of healing and herbs. She'd make a good assistant."

"And Claudia is a wizard with sewing," Tania added, barely able to stay seated such was her enthusiasm. "Then there's Clara who has such a beautiful voice and led our choir…"

Lydia glanced at her husband then smiled knowingly at Kate. "Maybe you should go lie down for a while," Lydia suggested to Tania. "You must be exhausted."

Tania yawned as if to confirm it.

"Show Tania the bathroom, Kate. She'll need a good wash before she goes to bed," Lydia continued. "Leave her old clothes in the bathroom. Give her a nightshirt from the clothes room. She can sleep in your bedroom till we find a better place. Once you've done that, come down, I'd like to talk to you."

Tania wanted Kate to cuddle up in bed once she was thoroughly washed, hair and all.

"I can't," Kate told her. "Lydia wants to talk."

"That can wait," Tania said, pouting.

As a compromise, Kate sat on the edge of the bed and placed a hand on Tania's shoulder with the girl lying next to her. Not satisfied, Tania curled up around Kate and slung an arm across Kate's lap, nuzzling her nose against Kate's thigh. In no time, her movements calmed, her breathing became regular and she drifted off. The first time Kate tried to get away the girl groaned and gripped on tighter. But soon enough Kate was able to work free.

"Sorry I took so long," she said when she found Lydia waiting in the kitchen. "Tania wouldn't let me go."

"Let's take a walk in the garden," Lydia suggested, holding the kitchen door open. Kate followed Lydia down the same narrow path to the long wooden building where she'd hidden from the police. Although the sky was overcast, the sun was struggling to break through and the early afternoon was warm and humid. Kate pulled off her jacket and hung it over her arm, delighting in the smell of all manner of flowers.

They rounded the end of the building and, stepping through a line of majestic oaks, Kate discovered row upon row of flowers and bushes in a well tended garden. For a herbalist, it was akin to walking into paradise. So many familiar plants greeted her. She was kean to explore, but Lydia began talking.

"We must do something for those girls."

"Will you complain to the authorities?" Kate asked.

"We discussed that with Klaus. But that'd take far too long and could make the situation worse."

"So?"

"I have an idea, but its completely crazy."

Lydia's voice trembled with excitement and uncertainty. That strange mixture sparked a growing anticipation in Kate as she waited for Lydia to find the courage to speak.

"I want to bring the girls here," Lydia finally said, her words coming out in a rush. Pointing to the wooden building, she added, "We can convert that into a comfortable place for them to live."

The idea pleased Kate immensely, but she didn't want to cause Lydia and Klaus hardship. "But you surely can't afford to keep so many girls."

"That's one of the good things about the idea," Lydia explained. "We will teach them to do different jobs and they can help us in our work."

"The herbs, you mean?"

"Sure, and we could teach some healing. Others could make clothes. And there could be a choir…." The more Lydia talked, the more the woman allowed herself to show her excitement.

Kate too was enthusiastic. The pieces of the puzzle fit together in way that pleased her immensely. It'd make the girls very happy. "But what about the police and the authorities. How will they react?"

"I haven't managed to think that part out yet," Lydia admitted. "Let's get the girls to safety first. We can figure out how to legalise the situation later."

"What does Klaus say?"

"He agrees. He's shocked and upset and wants to do something."

"You realise you could get into a lot of trouble..."

"Somebody's got to do something. It's like saving you from that horrible policeman. I couldn't let him and that doctor drug you till you went mad."

"But how are we to get them out?"

"Klaus has gone to reconnoitre."

"Surely he can't just walk in and look round."

Lydia grinned. "He's taken a box of tiny loaves. He's going to insist he gives them to the girls personally."

Kate had to chuckle. The idea was ingenious, and might well work, providing the nuns weren't too stubborn.

"We should return, just in case your friend wakes. She could be frightened if she finds herself alone. And anyway, Klaus should be back soon."

Kate cast a longing glance at the herbs.

"Don't worry," Lydia said, "there'll be plenty of time to explore."

As they were about to enter the house, they heard a vehicle pulling up on the other side of the house. Kate was afraid it might be the police, but Lydia reassured her it was Klaus. "I'd know that sound anywhere."

All three sat around the kitchen table tasting buns Klaus had brought.

"In a few weeks I won't be able to fend off a fly," Kate said.

Both Klaus and Lydia looked at her strangely.

"I am an expert in unarmed combat," she explained, wondering how to explain she came from another world. "It's a long story, but to cut it short, I had a very good arms master." She wondered if she should tell them how she beat the police inspector.

Lydia was looking at her with admiration, but Klaus was grinning.

"I wondered how that inspector got those bruises and the broken arm," he said.

"How do you know that?" Kate asked, surprised.

"The girl who serves in the bistro told me he came hobbling in with a policeman supporting him on either side. You didn't just slip round him as you hinted. You thrashed him." The idea seemed to appeal to him.

"I didn't "thrash" him, as you put it. I just helped him let me escape. Anyway, it was easy. He wasn't expecting a girl to resist. A big man like him is at a disadvantage against a smaller opponent. I'm faster and more agile. But I won't be much longer if you keep feeding me such delicious cake."

"You should teach those poor girls to defend themselves," Klaus said, his face serious now. "Maybe then people will stop mistreating them. Those who did it ought to be punished."

Klaus seemed set on justice. Kate would have been satisfied seeing all the girls safe and happy.

"I started teaching them, but we didn't get very far. Learning combat skills takes time and practice"

"We have a small, unused barn we could convert into a gym," Lydia said.

"At the speed you develop ideas," Klaus said to his wife, taking her tiny hands in his massive fingers, "it's surprising there's no smoke rising from the top of your head."

She made a show of shoving him, but it was clear there was a great deal of affection between them.

"Did you find the girls?" Kate asked. "And did they let you in?"

"Oh yes, I found them alright. And a sorry state they're in," he said, his face grim, his fists clenched.

The news worried Kate. The girls had already been so badly treated they didn't need further abuse. "So how are we going to get them out?" she asked.

Klaus got to his feet and fetched a wad of paper and a pencil. With broad gestures, he sketched a rough outline of the boarding school. "This is the main entrance," he said pointing to a door to the street. With his index finger, he traced a roundabout route to a large room. "This the classroom."

"How did you get to see all this? Kate asked.

"The superintendent showed me around. She must have thought she'd found a new benefactor, because she was charming. Apparently they have serious money problems."

Turning back to his improvised map, he pointed to another large room not far from the classroom. "This is the dormitory and here," he pointed to a series or smaller rooms, "are the kitchens and the refectory."

"Where's the infirmary?" Kate asked.

"The woman didn't show me that."

"We need to know. That's where Clara is. We can't leave her behind."

"I did manage one thing," Klaus said. "I told them I knew a rich woman with a young daughter who might donate money."

"Who's that?" Lydia asked, intrigued.

"You," he replied with a grin. "You and Kate."

When both of them stared at him, uncomprehending, he explained. "With clothes from upstairs, both of you could be made to look like a rich dowager and her daughter. I'll act as chauffeur."

"Why should we do that?" Kate asked, still perplexed.

"To get inside and lead the girls out."

"Surely it wouldn't be as easy as that," Lydia said.

"Imagine you arrive with a small bus early afternoon and offer to take some of the girls to visit your house in the country…"

"But what about Clara?" Kate asked.

"A wheel chair," was Klaus's answer.

"Maybe Tania could play the nurse," Kate suggested.

"There are one or two people missing from this expedition," Lydia said, taking up the idea with enthusiasm, weaving in new ideas of her own.

Both Kate and Klaus waited for her to break the suspense.

"A photographer and a journalist."

"Why? Don't we want to stir up as little trouble as possible?" Kate asked.

"To bear witness," Lydia said, triumphantly. "If we're to get away with this, we need guarantees that the authorities won't lock us away for kidnapping. That's why we need people to document conditions in this school and collect evidence. We need someone who can question the girls and write a report about the hell they've been through. Someone who can get articles in the press about the outrageous conditions the girls were in."

"And I know exactly who," Klaus said grinning.

43.

Peter yanked at his shorts. The rough material was unpleasant, the form unfamiliar. They'd agreed to dress as boys, but that didn't mean he had to like it. He felt more conspicuous walking into the room and greeting Mrs Greengage dressed as a boy than decked out in a dress and tights.

Luckily he could count on Greengage, his English teacher, for understanding and support. She was seated on the settee, her immense form taking up most of the space. She was normally the sort of person who remained unruffled even in the worst of crises, so the tenseness of her smile surprised him.

John and Christina had taken the remaining armchairs, so he and Andrew fetched chairs from the dining-room.

"I asked Peter and Andrew to leave for the country," John began, glancing at the two who'd set their chairs on either side of Christina. "I didn't want them to get involved, but they insisted on staying."

"I'm just as concerned as you," Peter burst out, irritated at John for not being more decisive. He got to his feet and paced the room. "It's just like Witless and her attacks," he said. "Must we stand by and be the defenceless victims of the imaginings of a sick mind."

Unbidden, his own father sprang to mind. Would he have reacted so? Peter wasn't sure. One thing was certain, he was angry and disappointed. He wanted to hit out. "How can you sit there and let them sully our relationship?" Peter burst into tears. "Why are they always picking on us?"

"Come and sit next to me," Christina said, shifting to make room for him on the cushioned armrest. She wound an arm around his waist and pulled him close, running her free hand through his hair.

"Wasn't it enough to deal with one mad girl," Peter said, "and then that impostor Sanson who imagined he could be headmaster instead of you."

"Life's like that," Greengage said. "One victory is generally not enough to win a war. Not that this is a war."

"Well there are casualties," Christina pointed out, looking at Andrew. "Even if we prove Margery lied, her words will hang in the air like doubts that niggle at people."

Peter glanced at John, hoping he'd take the lead, but the man seemed downtrodden and defeated. "Who knows about this?" Peter asked.

"Anyone who read the local newspaper," Greengage replied, sounding mournful. She rummaged in a leather satchel at her feet, pulled out the local newspaper and laid it on the low table between them. Splashed across the front page were the headlines: Headmaster suspected of abuse.

The sight made Peter furious. "Is family life so fragile that it can be destroyed by a slur?" he spluttered. "Where's the proof?"

"People are not interested in evidence," John said. "A hint of misconduct is enough to trigger imaginations."

"I can vouch for the truth," Andrew said.

"They'll say you're young and influenceable," Christina pointed out.

"What is Margery, if she's not young and influenceable," Andrew retorted, getting angry too.

"Hold on," Peter said, getting to his feet again. Pacing helped him think. "Who's influencing Margery? She can't be doing this alone."

"Good question," Greengage said, brightening a little. "As you can imagine, I tried to see her, but was told she'd been taken to a safe place for fear someone might influence or even hurt her. When I asked, it would seem Priscilla Wit's generous aunt had taken Margery under her wing. Nobody knew where she was. Or if they knew, they weren't telling me, knowing I was a good friend of yours, John."

"We need to find Margery. If we can get her to admit it was all lies and that Witless's aunt forced her, maybe we can put an end to this," Peter said. "Remember last time. We found evidence that Witless's aunt had been feeding false information to the school board."

"That's all very well," John said wearily, his head rested on his upturned hands, "but we only had to win over the board. Here it's a question of public opinion. People are not so easy to convince."

"That may be so," Greengage said. "But Peter's right. We should get our hands on Margery…"

"They'll only say we put pressure on her to recant," John replied, his words trailing off.

Something bubbled over in Peter's mind. He'd had enough. "In this very room, not so long ago, a young girl stood right here, proud like a Celtic warrior woman. She berated her mother for her behaviour saying that she no longer recognised her. That her mother would never have said such things. And Fi was right."

At the mention of her name, several people winced. By evoking her, it was as if Peter had called up her presence. He could feel her there, although nothing like when Kate was with him. She brought him strength.

"And now I stand here, just like she did, and say to you, John, you aren't the father I thought I had. That father was a brave, steadfast man who remained level-headed and solid in a storm and wouldn't let himself be bowled over. We can deal with this. But we need your help. So let's get this mess sorted out."

John raised his head to look at Peter, pain and suffering etched on his face but also pride. Tears welled in his eyes as a faint smile crossed his lips. "Like Christina said to Fi, it is not always easy to live up to the expectations of our children. But I agree to do my best. So let's go find this Margery and get the truth out of her."

Saying so was easy enough, but they had no idea where she might be.

"If Witless's aunt's got her, maybe Margery will be in a house or a flat belonging to her. How can we find out what places she owns or rents?" Peter suggested.

"Directory enquiries," Christina said.

"There's one more thing we should do before we go hunting for Margery," Greengage said. "Journalists will be on the look out for you two," she nodded to Peter and Andrew, "in the hope of getting a photo of you with Dr Grant."

Peter picked up the newspaper and quickly read the article. It contained no mention of them dressing as girls. Margery must have kept that to herself.

"We've got an easy solution to that," he said, heading for the door, trailing Andrew behind him.

"I wouldn't do that," John said, stopping them with his words. "It could backfire terribly."

Greengage looked questioningly at John then Christina.

"It's a long story," Christina said, sighing. "Andrew's brother threatened to kill him and almost succeeded. To escape, the boys were disguised as girls and have been so ever since. I imagine Peter's plan is to dress up once again."

"If people figured out that the two girls living with you, John, were really boys," Greengage said, "that would probably put the cap on everything."

Andrew groaned, no doubt thinking of his uncle's behaviour, and returned to his seat.

"I have nothing against boys dressing as girls," Greengage said. He was sure she was sincere, but coming from his English teacher it sounded strange. "But in the circumstances, I don't think it'd be a good idea."

If he'd thought his idea through, maybe he wouldn't have suggested it, but a part of him longed to be dressed as a girl again and any excuse would do. The more he thought about it, the less there seemed to be a way out. Whether they be dressed as boys or girls, their presence with John was a problem.

He came to a decision. "Our presence is not helpful. I suggest we return to the cottage."

Christina and John looked at him, startled. "Why did you change your mind? Are you that upset?" Christina asked, concern in her voice.

"No. It's true I do enjoy dressing as a girl." He glanced at Greengage, but no reaction was visible on her face. "It's just that I think John was right. We're more a liability than a help in the present circumstances." He turned to John. "I'm not abandoning you. I'd never do that. But we can be of more help at a distance. For that I need a photo of Margery."

"You're not planning on black magic?" Greengage asked. It was meant to be a joke, but, judging from the look on her face, she was clearly worried.

"I wouldn't know how to begin," Peter said. "If I'm to locate her, I need something that reminds me what she looks like."

"Locate?" Greengage asked.

"You remember during that business with Sanson you wondered how I got the information, well I have my ways. But as I said then, it's probably better if you don't know how."

Greengage looked to John and Christina for reassurance.

"It's OK," John told her with a sigh, then he added, "Margery is in the girls' hockey team. There may be a photo of her in the yearbook." He got to his feet and went to the bookshelf where he pulled out the last of a line of gilded volumes. Flipping through the pages, he quickly found what he was looking for. "Here she is," he said, showing Peter the photo.

"When will you leave?" Greengage asked. "Presumably you'll be going with them," she said to Christina.

"Yes," Christina replied. "But I'll come back to help John. It's late now. We'll probably leave early tomorrow morning."

A ring at the front door startled them.

"That could be the press," Greengage said.

"Or the police," Peter said, hoping he was wrong.

He and Andrew were about to hurry upstairs to hide, when

John stopped them.

"No. Not up there. If the worst comes to the worst, and you need to escape, the basement would be a better choice. There are several ways out. Christina, go with them. Here are the car keys."

They crossed the hall and were about to head into the basement when Peter remembered the girls' clothes lying upstairs on their bed. "Can you wait a moment before replying?" he whispered.

John nodded.

Peter ran up the stairs two at a time, scooped up the dresses and tights lying on his and Andrew's bed, stuffed them in the small holdalls that contained their girls' clothes and hurried back down the stairs with one in each hand.

"You don't need that," Christina growled.

"Evidence," Peter whispered, opening the basement door and disappearing into the dark. Andrew and Christina followed.

Luckily Peter had explored the basement, because he might have broken his neck going down those steep stairs in the dark. Andrew followed, cat like. Christina had more difficulty. Peter helped her down. Once on the hard stone floor, they set off between the many storerooms, heading for one of the exits at the back of the house. Peter held Christina's hand, leading her and Andrew brought up the rear, holding Christina's other hand.

As they halted near a ladder leading to a hatchway into the garden, Peter strained to hear any movement outside. All was quiet. But that meant nothing.

When they'd saved Bonnie in Bargeton, he'd been able to reach out with his senses and locate the girl in the building. He needed to do something similar. He warned the others what he was up to and closed his eyes to concentrate.

Instead of venturing cautiously outside with his mind, he landed in a small room filled with luxurious clothes for young women. He glimpsed exquisite dresses, blouses, skirts, jackets, and cloaks, tightly packed on row after row of hangers.

At first he thought he was dreaming, but the familiar pull of another presence rapidly told him he'd travelled to Kate's mind. Someone else was with Kate, a young girl, trying on clothes. The girl might have been pretty had it not been for the myriad bruises.

Kate, he spoke in her head.

Peter, she replied, delighted. *You can help us chose.*

No time. There's an emergency.

He hurriedly explained.

"Tania," Kate said. "I have to leave for a moment, but I'll be back."

Tania didn't seem happy. She flung her arms around Kate's neck and tried to hold on.

Kate unlaced her fingers saying, "I'll be back. Chose clothes for me. I need to look like the daughter of a rich woman."

Kate hastily retreated and went to a nearby room. Shutting the door, she lay on the bed and closed her eyes. *Take us to your place maestro.*

In no time, they were back in Peter's body at the foot of the ladder. The place smelt moldy compared with the freshly scented rooms in Kate's house.

Let's check if anyone is about, Kate thought.

Peter expected to stretch out his attention as if listening with finely attuned ears. But instead, he felt the two of them lurch out of his body, only to be projected into the head of a policewoman standing guard over the hatchway. The shock of being in someone else's body reminded him of his tragic stay in Brian's head just before Fi got shot. The memory would probably have overwhelmed him had not Kate come to his aid.

Let it go, she said. *It wasn't your fault. We've other things to do.*

She flicked through the woman's memories like the pages of a book. Apparently there was a policeman posted out front, near the car. That was all. Peter was amused to see the woman fancied the policeman.

Kate was about to take control of the woman, but Peter stopped her. *We can't. The police'll figure out we can manipulate minds. Then even if Margery goes back on her word, they'll believe we forced her.*

He felt Kate grin as she said, *There are other ways to control people without them knowing.*

In their work with healing they'd learnt how to stimulate different functions in the body. Kate must have set off hormones in the woman's body, because Peter was disturbed to find himself aroused. He could have sworn he heard the woman groan.

Now let's persuade her to declare her passion for the policeman. Peter would have willingly turned his attention away while Kate coaxed the woman with the most salacious thoughts. At first he was embarrassed and then shocked to find the thoughts stirred something deep inside him.

Leaving her post without the slightest glance back, the woman made her way to the policeman lounging against the car.

"What yer doin' 'ere Betty?" he asked, surprised but not displeased to see her.

"Came to check on you," Betty purred. "Thought maybe you were being a naughty boy."

She sidled up to the man and planted her lips on his, forcing her tongue into his mouth. To his merit, he struggled, but even if he'd wanted to complain, he'd have had a hard time. She wound an arm around his neck, pulling him in a tight embrace. Her other hand lingered on his chest, then slithered over his belly till it reached his groin. Peter heard the man groan.

Jump back, Kate told him. *I'll just see these two off into the bushes.*

Back in his own body, Peter had to pause a moment, waiting for his hammering heart to calm, then he whispered, "Time to go. Don't worry about the police, they're busy."

He unbolted the hatch, pushed it open and clambered up the ladder. The other two followed. They moved cautiously round the house in the direction of the car. No policemen were in sight.

"You'd better not start the car here," Peter whispered. "Get in. Andy and I will push."

Peter dumped the holdall in the car, making as little noise as possible. Somewhere off behind him he could hear the crashing of branches and the sound of animal-like grunts coming from the bushes.

Christina sat in the driver's seat with the key in the ignition. Once she'd released the clutch and the hand brake, he and Andy pushed the car along the drive. They were lucky it was pointing the right way. When the car was out of earshot, they climbed in, Christina turned the ignition and the car jerked forward.

44.

"Meet Regina," Klaus said. "She's the journalist I told you about."

Both Kate and Tania stood to shake hands with the young woman who smiled winningly. Petite, with short brown hair, Regina looked to be in her early twenties. She was casually dressed in a pleated skirt and blouse over which she wore a light sweater. Her shoes were flat-healed but elegant. Her blue eyes were bright, intelligent and attentive. Kate decided she liked her.

"You must be Kate," she said, as she sat down. They were in a tea-house not far from the reform school. "Klaus told me something about you. I must admit your disguise is convincing. No one would ever guess you'd recently been locked up in an orphanage and were constantly mistreated."

From amongst the stock of clothes, Kate had picked a sober black dress that reached to below her knees, with wrist-length elegant sleeves, trimmed with black lace. Black stockings concealed the bruises on her legs. She'd even found a red wig with ringlets that made her look considerably older. Lydia had chosen similar clothes as they were to play mother and daughter.

"And you must be Tania," Regina said.

They'd had a hard time disguising Tania. As she was to push Claudia in a wheel chair during the pretend outing, they'd opted to disguise her as a nurse. She hadn't liked the idea, which explained the sour face. She'd wanted to be decked out in fancy clothes like Kate and had kicked up a stink, but they'd finally convinced her she was to play a key role. The ankle-length, dark blue skirt concealed the marks on her legs and the white blouse had long sleeves, but even makeup couldn't conceal her black eye.

Regina studied her for a moment, then said, "I'd like to interview you. Your story must be fascinating."

Kate wasn't sure 'fascinating' was the right word, but at least, in showing such interest, she'd made the girl perk up, a little.

"What's the name of your friend, the photographer?" Lydia asked.

"Heinz. He should've been here by now," Regina told them, peering out the window. "Ah, there he is."

Looking out, Kate saw a tall, spindly man with his hair cropped short hurrying across the road, a camera bag slung over his shoulder.

Once inside, he spotted Regina and joined them. "Sorry I'm late," he said. "There was a problem with the trams."

Like Regina, he too was casually dressed with trousers, a brightly coloured shirt and a grey pullover. Regina presented all four to Heinz, explaining that he did freelance work for the same newspaper as her.

"I specialise in coverage of complicated, in-depth reports," Heinz explained. "I just published a book of photos about gypsies and how they are mistreated. Regina wrote the text."

The subject intrigued Kate. "What's a gypsy?" she asked.

Her question surprised the others. Apparently it was a common word. "We don't use that word where I come from," she explained.

"Gypsies don't live in any one place," Regina explained. "They wander the countryside in tiny houses on wheels often pulled by horses or cars. They have a bad reputation. People are convinced they're thieves. I suspect people are afraid of them because they're different."

"Ah! Nomads," Kate exclaimed, understanding.

"The authorities decided to take gypsy children away from their parents and put them in special schools, rather like the one you attended," Regina explained.

"Why ever did they do that?" Kate asked.

"Life here is very much influenced by the church and priests don't like gypsies. They never go to church. Instead, they play wild music and dance half the night, at least, that's what people think. There's a lot of promiscuity and girls often get married and have children as early as your age. Most can't read or write. I'm not sure which is the bigger sin," Regina said with a smile. "So the church convinced the authorities to take away the children."

"That's awful," Kate said, shocked that children could be forced to leave their mother and father. "It would seem it's not just our friends that need help."

"One thing at a time," Klaus said.

Kate wondered if he was afraid she'd lumber him with a load of gypsies in addition to all her friends. "Don't worry," she said. "I'm not going to force you to look after gypsies as well. You have been generous enough already. But maybe your example will inspire others."

"Well spoken," Regina said. "You hardly sound like a girl who lived all her life in an orphanage."

"I didn't. My father was one of the top leaders where I lived. I was educated to follow in his footsteps. But then he and many others were murdered by an army of warmongering priests."

A glance at Tania, who was fidgeting with her nurses cap, her eyes downcast, showed the girl was completely deflated. She resembled someone who'd dreamed she was a princess only to discover someone else had been cast in the role.

Outside, Kate could hear a church clock strike ten. The sky was overcast but it seemed unlikely it would rain, a good day for an outing.

"Time to go," Klaus said.

Kate wanted to have a word with Tania, but the two were separated in the small coach Klaus had hired. Kate was to sit up front between Lydia and Klaus, while Tania was sent to sit behind with Regina and Heinz. She sat as far back as she could, pouting as she stared out the window.

"Let me tell you our cover story," Klaus said as he put the coach into gear and drove out into the traffic. "Lydia is a rich woman come with her daughter, Kate, to visit the reform school. She's thinking of offering them her patronage. There'll be a visit and Lydia will suggest her daughter Kate select some girls to visit to her mansion. Regina and Heinz, you're preparing an article about Lydia for a newspaper and are here to cover her visit. As for Tania, you're here to help Clara, whom we gather is bed ridden, so she can join us on the visit and subsequent trip."

Kate closed her eyes and concentrated on Suzanne. She chose to contact the slim girl because she was very reliable and level headed. *Suzanne,* Kate called out mind-to-mind. She had to call several times before she got an answer.

Kate? Is that you? She sounded dubious.

Yes.

Where are you? Are you coming to stay?

I'm coming, but not to stay, rather to rescue you all.

Suzanne let out a silent cry of joy. *I knew you'd do something for us,* she said, her words laced with such warmth and gratitude that Kate found it deeply moving.

Kate quickly explained what was planned. *How many of you are there?*

Eighteen. They moved Christine and Eileen back, so now all of us are here, except you and Tania.

Tania is with me. How is Clara? Is she still in the infirmary?

She's a little better, but she's still in the infirmary.

We'll fetch her first. We've got a wheelchair for her. Can you warn her we'll be coming?

Yes. I was planing to visit her.

It is very important that none of you show you know us. Is Jane with you?

No. She never came here. I think they took her to a hospital. She was a bit wrong in the head, after the fire.

Are the other girls in your school likely to give you trouble if we say we're taking you on a visit?

No. They'll be glad to be rid of us.

Kate could hear Klaus saying they'd arrived.

We've just arrived. Hurry to tell the others, but be sure they're quiet about all this.

She broke off the conversation and opened her eyes. "There are eighteen of them," she announced. "All the girls are back together, including Christine and Eileen who were originally in another school. They'll be expecting us, but I've told them to pretend they don't know us."

Both Regina and Heinz looked at her strangely. "Do you have a hidden telephone?" Heinz asked.

"You could put it like that," Kate replied, as she climbed out of the coach. "Do we have enough room for eighteen?" she asked Klaus.

"Without the wheelchair it should be OK."

"Apparently Clara is a little better. Maybe she can travel without the chair and we can fold it up?"

They were greeted at the main entrance by the superintendent who waited at the top of the steps, her feet planted a good distance apart, as if ready for combat. She was a mass of muscle, those in her arms bulging visibly through her blouse, and her hands were like hams.

The sight sent a shiver down Kate's back. The moment the woman boomed a greeting, Kate couldn't help feeling afraid. No wonder the girls had fared even worst than at the convent. The woman seemed more of a monster than Sister Helga, if that was possible.

"You must be Frau Junker," the woman said, fawning over Lydia with such insincerity that it disgusted Kate. Junker was the name of a rich family in the city, which they'd agreed Lydia would use, so as not to reveal her real name.

"And you must be her daughter. You look so much like your mother." The superintendent leaned forward and pinched Kate's cheek in what was supposed to be a friendly gesture. It took all Kate's self control not to pitch the woman down the steps. The superintendent nodded a greeting to Klaus, but ignored the others.

Klaus briefly explained who Regina, Heinz and Tania were and then the woman ushered them inside. "Would you like refreshments, Frau Junker?" she asked.

"I'd prefer to visit the school first," Lydia said, "and meet some of the girls."

The woman led them down a winding corridor that was deserted, as if staff had been warned to keep out of the way. All the better, Kate thought.

They passed one room, the door of which was closed, but the strong smell of chemicals made Kate think it was the infirmary. Lydia must have had the same idea.

"Is that the infirmary?" she asked.

The superintendent looked put out. She clearly hadn't intend them to visit that part. "Yes, Frau Junker," she replied. "But it isn't very interesting."

"Please indulge me," Lydia said, sounding every inch a noble lady. "In my work with the poor, I often visit hospitals and infirmaries."

The woman reluctantly opened the door and they entered. The room contained only four beds. The tiny windows, high in the walls, made Kate think of a prison rather than a place for sick people. Only one bed was occupied. Clara peered out at them from below the covers, clearly terrified.

"What's your name?" Lydia asked.

"Clara."

"Would you like to come for a walk with us?" Lydia asked.

"Frau Junker, I don't think that would be a good idea," the superintendent hastened to say. "The girl's been quite ill."

Heinz chose that moment to take a picture of Clara. The superintendent didn't seem pleased her school be the subject of a newspaper article, but the presence of Frau Junker and the lure of money, were apparently enough to keep her quiet.

"We have a wheelchair in our vehicle for just such cases," Lydia commented, making it sound as if that was a normal thing to carry around. "Klaus and the nurse can go and fetch it while we continue our visit."

The woman was not at all happy, as if leaving the infirmary would be letting Clara off a punishment. "Ok," she said, a sour look on her face. "Providing she remains within the building."

As Klaus and Tania hurried off, Lydia and Kate followed the superintendent towards the classrooms while Heinz took a few more pictures in the infirmary and Regina chatted quietly with Clara. The superintendent marched silently in front of them, her back stiff, her head held high. Heinz and Regina had just caught up with them when the woman opened a door and showed them in.

Row upon row of small wooden desks were each occupied by girls carefully decked out in uniforms that looked new, or at least recently washed and pressed. Not a girl moved, each frozen as if terrified the slightest movement would bring a punishment. To Kate's horror, she recognised none of them.

45.

No one spoke as they drove out of town, as if for fear the police might hear them. The pause gave Peter time to think. He could probably locate Margery from any distance, but if they were to get their hands on her, they needed to stay close. But how were they to convince her to admit to her lies? Barring taking control of her, which he dared not do, no solution sprang to mind.

Christina was about to turn onto the main trunk road south when Peter stopped her. "Surely the cottage'll be the first place they'll look for us," he said. "Let's pull over for a drink. We need to talk."

The cafe was both smoky and noisy as groups of truck drivers exchanged stories or let off steam on a pinball game. Andrew found them a small terrace out back away from the bustle. Christina bought them tea and a plate of doughnuts.

"Have you got that map?" he asked Andrew.

The boy set their mugs and the plate on a neighbouring table, opened the map and spread it out.

"The further we travel," Peter said, "the more difficult it'll become to reach Margery." He bit into the doughnut, causing strawberry jam to dribble down his chin. Christina handed him a napkin.

"If I can find out what's going on," he went on, once he'd wiped his mouth, "that'll help us decide what to do. But I have no idea how to proceed after that."

"Why don't you just take control?" Andrew asked. "Did you

not tell me you could?"

"That wouldn't work," Peter replied. "We need her to confess of her own free will."

"I'm not sure we should run after Margery," Christina said, sounding worried. "The last thing we want is to create more trouble."

"You're right," Peter said. "But for the moment all I'm going to do is find out where she is and what happened."

Christina was ferociously and unwaveringly opposed to prying into other people's minds. She was very vocal about it. But when Peter explained what he wanted to do, limiting as much as possible his invasion of the girl's mind, Christina finally gave her consent.

Peter took out the yearbook and studied the photo of Margery. Dressed in her hockey clothes, she really didn't look the part. He could hardly imagine her running with her short stubby legs. How ever had she been selected? On closer examination, he wondered how the photographer had managed to remove all the spots that dotted the girl's face. She looked tense, her lips pinched and her fists clenched. Had someone forced her to play hockey? Was that why she was so angry?

He wedged himself in a corner and closed his eyes. Calling up the picture of Margery, he hoped he'd be able to travel directly to her mind. Nothing happened. After several attempts, he resolved to call Kate for help, but he couldn't reach her either. He tried looking at the photo again, but that didn't help. Finally he let himself drift. The moment he did, he found himself in Margery's head.

The girl was miserable. She sat on the edge of a double bed in the corner of large, rather shabby room, her head bowed, her hands clasped tight in her lap. The curtains had been drawn back and light flooded in, but nothing of the gaiety of the sunny day or the joyous chatter of bird's reached her, cloaked as she was in her misery.

Peter took stock of her body, to be sure she hadn't been drugged. She was tired and hungry, she'd been crying and her whole body was tense. Her face stung because she'd been picking her spots, but otherwise she was unhurt. Should he help her relax? If he did, she'd probably fall asleep and he might need her awake.

He could do one thing for her, rid her of the eczema. It was not something he'd already done, but that was no problem. By tapping into the body's blueprint and encouraging the body to heal, most common illness could be cured rapidly.

It was a real delight focussing on the blueprint, rather like contemplating the source of all life and wellbeing. Only the slightest nudge and Margery's body righted the hormone imbalance and healed the sores and marks on her face. He stood back, as it were, and marvelled at the simplicity and strength of such healing. The next time she looked at herself she wouldn't recognise the face looking back.

Now her memories. It didn't surprise him that Witless's aunt put the idea of Dr Grant and boys in her head. He'd been expecting as much. What he didn't understand was why Margery so readily agreed to bear witness, when she hated being in the limelight.

He continued flicking through her memories, wondering if something had turned the girl against the headmaster. Even returning to before her first day at school threw no light on the matter. Turning round, he threaded forward, taking more time as he searched for some explanation of her anger, for it was clear she was angry. He searched for bad marks, a half forgotten reprimand, a cautionary look, a careless comment. He found nothing.

One thing did attract his attention: the memory of the first time she'd seen him. He knew it was unwise to dig into what people thought about him. But he was intrigued, mainly because she'd tried to bury the memory deep amongst other memories as if she wanted to forget it. Of course, the way the mind worked, that only made it stand out all the more.

He was waiting in line for class. He'd been eying Fi, as he often did, not thinking anyone was watching. But she was.

She'd seen his interest and Margery hated Fi for it. God lord! The girl had a crush on him. He skipped over the hours she spent looking out for him and her wild fantasies of kissing him on the far side of the playing field.

He hurried forward till Margery met Witless. Cunning as she was, Witless immediately cottoned on to Margery's weakness for Peter and saw how she could exploit it. She repeatedly pointed out that Peter might seem to only have eyes for Fi but in reality he wasn't interested in girls at all. Margery came to depend on Witless, who took her under her wing, alternately flattering her or putting her down. Any other friendships the girl might have had were soon neglected.

When Witless finally came unhinged, it had profoundly upset Margery who found herself alone. She blamed Peter. Rather like her niece, Witless's aunt had perceived Margery's violent feelings for Peter and also saw how she could make use of them. So that was how Margery had been convinced to speak out against Dr Grant, to get back at Peter.

Peter needed to know where the girl was, but unfortunately she didn't know herself. She'd slept on the journey. He would have to force her to find out. Although he could do such things, he didn't like it. A wild idea crossed his mind. It involved talking to her mind-to-mind. He hesitated a long moment, knowing the whole thing could easily turn sour.

Margery, he said softly in her head.

She spun round, terrified, wondering who'd spoken. "Who's that?" she asked.

Don't be frightened, he said, mentally kicking himself for being so stupid. Telling a terrified person not be frightened was futile. *It's me, Peter. I'm talking to you in your head.*

As he could have anticipated, fear escalated to terror, as she was convinced she was going mad like Priscilla.

"Leave me alone!" she pleaded.

You are not going mad, he said firmly, using his healing ability to allay some of her fear.

"Get out of my head," she screamed. If anyone else was in

the house, they'd be there in a trice. But no one came.

If you want proof of my goodwill, look at your face in the mirror.

That troubled her. "You're just mocking me as you always do."

I've never mocked you, Margery. Do as I say. Look at your face.

"What have you done to me?"

I have healed your spots.

"That's nonsense. None of the creams I ever used had any effect. I'm stuck with the blasted things."

If you are so sure, it won't hurt to have a look. He felt her waver. She desperately wanted to be free of the spots.

She got to her feet reluctantly and went to the dresser. At first she didn't want to look, knowing the mess she'd made of her face with her nails. He said nothing. When she finally looked, all she could do was gape. She didn't exactly look pretty, her eyes were red from crying, but her skin was healthy again. Only faint marks showed where the spots must have been.

"Have you bewitched me?" she asked.

I am no witch. I am a healer. But unlike doctors, I heal from within, with the help of your body.

She gingerly touched her face in disbelief.

Whatever anybody said, I don't and never have meant you harm, he said.

She longed to believe him, but she had mistrusted him for so long. She moved closer to the mirror and examined her skin. Seeing that the blemishes really had gone it finally dawned on her he was telling the truth and she burst into tears. "What have I done?" As he could hear her thoughts, he knew she was talking of the lies she'd told about Dr Grant. But he kept silent. "I'm so sorry," she said. After a last glance at her face, she sat down on her bed and plunged her head in her hands.

Don't give in to despair, Peter told her. *It won't help.*

"But what can I do?"

Do you really want to set things right?

"Yes."

Then you'll have to stand up to Priscilla's aunt and tell the truth to the police.

"I couldn't possibly do that."

Yes you can. You'd be surprised all you can do.

"Will you teach me that healing thing?" she asked.

That might not be easy, but if I can, I promise I will.

"Then I'll tell the truth." She thought for a moment. It was odd to be one step ahead of her, knowing her thoughts, but he kept silent. "But I am stuck here. We're out in the sticks. Priscilla's aunt had to leave and I'm stranded on my own."

If you can find out where you are, I'll come and fetch you.

She got to her feet and ran down stairs. The rest of the house was as dingy as her room. Wallpaper was peeling off the walls and the carpets were threadbare. The place smelt of damp and mould. An odd assortment of furniture filled the living room.

She began looking for clues. There was no telephone and a glance outside showed they were far from any other habitation.

Look in the drawers, Peter suggested, *there might be an electricity bill.*

Sure enough, an old electricity bill was stuffed under a load of rubbish in one of the drawers. Barton Farm, it said and gave the name of the area.

Listen, he said. *I'm not sure how far we are from you.*

"We?" she asked, wary again.

Andrew and Fi's mum.

"Always that bloody Fi," Margery burst out, her tone bitter.

Fi's dead, Margery. She was shot by a killer who wanted to kill Andrew and me.

Margery's rage came to an abrupt end. "Dead?" There was no triumph or gloating in her voice, just incredulity and then sadness.

Deep down, you liked her, didn't you?

The girl had begun to cry. "I loved her clothes," she said. "She had such good taste in colour and she always dressed so well. Yes, I did like her." She sounded astonished at her admission.

We'll come and fetch you as soon as possible. If ever the aunt comes back…

"She won't. She told me she wouldn't be back before tomorrow."

Have you got food?

"Yes. She left things in the larder."

OK. We'll hurry.

46.

Kate looked at Lydia aghast. "What have they done with them?" she whispered, terrified they'd hurt the girls so badly they couldn't show them.

The superintendent was talking quietly to the teacher. The teacher, who resembled the superintendent both in build and muscles, looked more like a prison warden than a teacher, with a wild mop of black hair and thick, knitted eyebrows. Just visible behind her desk was a yard stick. Kate was prepared to bet the woman didn't just use it to draw straight lines.

Lydia wandered around the room exchanging a few words with the children, accompanied by Regina and Heinz, while Kate slipped into a corner and spoke to Suzanne. *Where are you? We're in the classroom, but none of you are here.*

They must have thought we'd cause trouble, Suzanne replied. *We're locked in the dormitory.*

How do I get there from the classrooms?

There's no point, Suzanne told her. *The door is locked.*

Is there no other way out?

No.

Get the girls ready to leave in a hurry, Kate told her.

She broke the communication and called out to Tania. *Where are you?*

We've got Clara into the bus…

Listen, Kate said. *The others are locked in the dormitory and we're stuck here with the superintendent. Can you and Klaus get them into the bus? I'll send Heinz and Regina to help. We'll keep the others occupied. Let me know when you've finished.*

Kate could feel Tania's excitement and pleasure, delighted to play such a key role.

A glance at the superintendent reassured her the woman was still in deep whispered conversation with the teacher. Kate went to join the little group around Lydia, and taking hold of Heinz's sleeve drew him away. When Regina looked at her, Kate beckoned for her to join them. She led them to the door, making signs as if it would be a good vantage point from which to take photos.

Once the three stood in the entrance, out of sight of the superintendent, she whispered, "Can you help Klaus and Tania get the children into the coach? The girls are locked in the dormitory."

"Good," Heinz said. "I was looking for an excuse to get photos of the dormitory."

Seeing Klaus and Tania hurrying along the corridor from the entrance, the journalist and the photographer went to join them. Kate quietly closed the door behind her and returned to Lydia's side.

"We need to buy time," she whispered. "The others are getting the girls out."

Kate looked around the class for a way to hold the superintendent's attention. Pinned on the wall she found a series of rudimentary drawings. Having the children draw wouldn't be enough. Then she saw the words and music of a song Clara had taught them. It was a moving song about a mother's love for her child. Kate wondered how the song had ended up there. Such a school hardly seemed the place for the sentiment expressed in it. Carefully unpinning it, she walked casually over to one of the older girls at the back and asked her if she knew the song.

The girl was as thin as a rake, like all the other girls, but there was a look in her eyes that made Kate think she might, at times, have authority over the others. Now she was cowering like the rest of them, too frightened to reply. Apparently they'd been ordered to keep their mouths shut. Staring at her desk, the girl finally whispered, "Yes."

"Do all the girls know it?"

The girl nodded almost imperceptibly, her eyes shooting up to glance at the superintendent, who'd stopped talking and was looking sternly at her.

Moving away, Kate wound her way between the desks till she was nearer the front. "Do any of you know this song?" she asked, and she sang the first few bars.

Most of the girls looked down, but a few looked back at her blankly, some had even turned pale.

"Don't be shy," Kate said. "I'm sure your teacher will let you sing." With which she smiled winningly at the teacher and the superintendent. The women looked at her coldly, as if to say: Who are you to do such things in my school?

"Oh yes!" Lydia joined in. "I do love music."

Lydia's interest tipped the balance. "Go ahead," the teacher conceded, although her tone sounded more like she'd prefer Kate to stick her head in bucket of water.

"Do you remember the words?" Kate asked.

Still no reply. Kate read the first lines out loud. When she asked them to repeat the words, only silence greeted her. She walked to the back of the class and going to the girl she'd spoken to earlier, she helped her to her feet, then slipping an arm gently around the girl's waist for fear of hurting any bruises or cuts she might have, Kate asked quietly: "What's your name?"

"Sandra," the girl whispered.

"Pick two friends to accompany you, Sandra."

Sandra pointed to two girls, who were about the same age as her. Both sat stiffly, gripping their desks as if afraid someone might drag them off at any moment. They were clearly not happy about being chosen. "Get them to join us," Kate said.

To her credit, Sandra managed to get the girls to follow. As she watched, Kate wondered how Tania and the others were faring. No time to ask.

"Well done, Sandra," Kate said, taking the girl by the arm. She linked arms with one of the other two and indicated they should all do so, to form a tight circle facing inwards.

"Now let's sing," Kate said quietly. "Very softly at first." She began singing and the others soon joined her. It was as if the ring protected them. Little by little she had them sing louder till they reached the end of the first verse.

"Now," she said to all three, "each of you chose a girl and bring her here."

They did as they were told. Singing seemed to have given them courage. Arm in arm, they returned with their choice and once again they formed a ring. This time it was easier, although many a voice was still shy. Kate repeated the procedure till she had the whole class in a huddle, backs turned to the outside world, singing together. Kate glanced at the superintendent to make sure their activities still held her attention. Lydia had joined the teacher and the superintendent and was talking quietly to them. She was doing an excellent job of being Frau Junker.

"Now let's try the second voice," Kate told the girls. She picked out several of the older girls who had lower voices and sang the second voice. Thank heavens Clara had taught her so well.

Getting them to sing the two voices together was difficult, but when the girls heard what it sounded like with the two voices intertwined, they improved immensely and began to sing with real pleasure. The words were moving and the girls found the emotion with which to sing them.

It crossed Kate's mind that these girls might well get the brunt of the teachers' anger when they discovered the other girls had escaped. There was not much she could do about it. But the thought upset her.

When the song was almost over, Tania spoke in her head. *We've got everybody out and are waiting in the coach.*

Send Heinz to take a few photos, then drive round the block and wait for us.

While she waited for Heinz to arrive, she had the girls huddle as close together as they could and she spoke into their heads. Most of them would probably think she was talking out loud so it wouldn't matter.

You sing beautifully, she told them. *I thank you. You have given me a wonderful gift. Treasure this moment. You're strong when you sing. If people try to frighten you, remember what it's like to sing together. I know how terrible it is to live in such a place. I too have lived in one. I promise I'll do my best to get you out. You deserve better. Do not despair. Stick together. They'll try to divide you. They'll try to blame me for what happens to you. Don't let them. And when they try to put you down, use song to raise your spirits.*

Glancing over her shoulder she saw Heinz standing in the entrance, his camera at the ready. *OK,* she said the girls. *Now let's turn to face the world and show them we have the courage to do what we want.*

The tight circle of girls unfurled till they formed a row that stretched across the back of the class, facing the teacher, the superintendent and Lydia. Kate gave them the beat and they sang with all their hearts. Lydia burst into applause when they finished. Neither the teacher nor the superintendent joined her. They stood there, looking furious at such defiance.

"Thank you," Kate said, hugging each girl in turn. Then she joined Lydia who was promising to get in contact in the very near future. That future contact would surely not be to the woman's liking. Kate did not shake hands with the superintendent. Instead, she said mind-to-mind in that deep voice she called the voice-of-god: *If ever I learn you've hurt these girls or any of your staff have hurt them, I assure you I'll make your life hell.*

The woman gasped, her hand flying to her mouth and she went dreadfully pale. Kate turned, waved goodbye to the girls and left.

When Kate clambered onto the coach, a roar of greeting went up. She moved through the coach hugging each in turn. They were so excited they chatted noisily. Kate raised a hand for silence. "We've not got away yet," she said. "You need to be very quiet until we get to your new home. And even there you'll probably have to hide for a while."

Returning to the front of the coach with Klaus, Lydia and the others, she was eager to know how they'd managed.

"It wasn't easy," Tania burst out, excited at her adventure. "We couldn't open the door. You should've seen us. Klaus tried everything."

"I couldn't just break the door down," Klaus said, finally getting a word in.

"Luckily," Tania continued. "Some friendly teachers unlocked the door."

Kate had some trouble imagining friendly teachers in such a dump.

Klaus laughed. "I'm not sure they were friendly. But we told them the superintendent sent us to fetch the girls because Frau Junker wanted to see them. They seemed as frightened of the superintendent as the girls."

"I'm glad I was there," Heinz added. "The place was filthier than a pigsty and I was able to get some very striking pictures. Would you believe the teachers even agreed to pose for me?"

"They let Heinz and I visit other rooms while Klaus and Tania led the children out," Regina said. "I'm glad they did, because they were so occupied, they had no idea where the girls were going."

"You'd be amazed what we found," Heinz said. "You wait till you see the photos, you won't believe it."

Their conversation came to an abrupt halt when Klaus broke unexpectedly, jerking them all forward in their seats. With a screech of tyres, the coach slithered to an ungainly halt in front of a police car parked blocking the road. The familiar inspector stood next to the car, surrounded by several policemen.

47.

Peter couldn't imagine why anyone would stick a house in the middle of a field surrounded only by sheep and flies. The land was flat, stretching away into the distance, a wasteland of hedgerows and small fields, most gone wild with thistles, docks and great clumps of grass. This was no shepherd's shack, it was a four-up, four-down suburban house that had got lost. The track that led up to it hadn't even been covered with tarmac and ruts had formed where tractors had driven up and down in wet weather.

Christina drove slowly round the house trying to avoid the potholes. As they rounded a large bush, they were appalled to discover two cars, a mini and a police car, parked in front of the entrance. Christina braked. The track was too narrow to turn the car, but she could try reversing as far as the nearest gate. She was about to do so, when the inspector stepped out and beckoned for them to join him.

"How good of you to call," he said, beaming, once the car was parked. "Saves us running round the country looking for you."

Peter, Andrew and Christina trudged after him. So much for cleverly seeking to out do the police. If Witless's aunt and the police had got to Margery, there was little hope she'd admit to her lies.

The house was as run down as Peter had seen through Margery's eyes. What he hadn't noticed was the stink of mould. Then there was the overwhelming stench of dried dung that wafted in from outside. The hallway, which had no window, plunged him in darkness. The moment he emerged in the brilliant sunlight of the living room he missed his step and stumbled. When he recovered, he was astounded to find John and Christina sitting side by side on the settee.

He would have liked to judge how bad the situation was from their expressions, but both were being very cautious. They did look grim and didn't even offer a greeting. A stout elderly lady, who sat next to the table, her back stiffer than the chair she was sitting on, stared at him with eyes like daggers, her mouth curled down in disgust. It had to be Priscilla's aunt. Margery was cowering in a corner, her eyes red from crying. At least the spots were not back.

He wondered if he should go to her when she glanced up at him, her eyes pleading. *It'll be alright,* he said mind-to-mind. She jumped at his voice, then gave him a watery smile.

"Well, Peter," the inspector began, "what have we got this time?"

Peter didn't appreciate being made the centre of attention, especially not in such a tense situation. He took a deep breath and replied all the same. "A misunderstanding," he said, glancing at Margery, "ill-will," he looked pointedly at Witless's aunt, "and a good deal of imagination, if not a sprinkling of folly." Then he looked at John. "All of which led to a great deal of pain and unnecessary suffering."

"I'm so sorry," Margery burst out, tears welling over in her eyes. "It's all my fault."

"Keep quiet girl," the aunt snapped, getting to her feet to go to the girl. "You're clearly over wrought."

"Keep away from me," Margery said, somewhere between a plea and a warning.

"Sit down, please," the inspector said to the woman in his no-nonsense voice. "Your turn will come."

The woman huffed, clearly annoyed at being ordered about, but reluctantly did as she was told, glaring in Peter's direction as she returned to her seat.

"You were saying, Margery…." the inspector prompted.

Margery must have been intimidated by the aunt, because she had difficulty continuing. She clasped her face in both hands, her unbelieving fingers searching for signs of spots. Nobody spoke.

"I lied," she finally managed.

"You lied?" the inspector repeated.

"Yes. I had no proof that Dr Grant did anything…" She hesitated about venturing further, "…untoward with the boys."

"Where did you get the idea from?" the inspector asked.

Margery nodded almost imperceptibly at Witless's aunt. "She suggested it."

"What nonsense," the aunt burst out. "The girl's mad."

Peter wanted to say: If she's mad, it's you that made her so. But he held his tongue.

"Priscilla, her niece," Margery said, bolder now, pointing at the woman, "had always said Peter was a poof, I mean a homosexual." She said the word as if it might bite her. "Priscilla was obsessed with the idea. She talked about naught else. I came to believe her. So when that woman told me about Dr Grant, it seemed plausible."

"I don't understand," the inspector said. "Why go to all this trouble. Did you have a grudge against your headmaster?"

Margery shook her head and looked pleadingly at Peter, but there was no way he could help.

"It wasn't Dr Grant. It was Peter."

Everyone turned to look at Peter making him feel even more uncomfortable.

"What did he do to you?"

"Nothing," she said, her tears beginning again. "That was the problem."

A glance at Christina's face made Peter think she'd guessed what the problem was.

"You were in love with Peter," Christina said.

Margery nodded.

"And he paid no attention to you," Christina continued. "Instead you saw him with my daughter, Fi, and you were convinced he loved her."

Margery nodded again, tears rolling down her cheeks.

"Did you ever speak to him?" Christina asked.

Margery shook her head, shamefaced.

"It's not easy, is it," Christina said softly, getting to her feet and sitting next to Margery. "When you like someone but you think they only have eyes for someone else."

Margery leaned her head on Christina's shoulder and sobbed. The woman put an arm round the girl and rocked her gently back and forth.

"So you wanted to get revenge?" the inspector asked.

Margery looked up. "Priscilla always said Peter couldn't like me because he only had eyes for boys." She glanced nervously at Andrew.

"I'm not his boyfriend," Andrew said, blushing, as if there might be some doubt.

"To be honest, I never saw Peter with boys. If anything, he seemed to avoid them. I watched him a lot, you see. When he wasn't with Fi, he was often on his own. But Priscilla was convincing. Not only did she have lots of arguments, but she quickly became my only friend. I couldn't disagree for fear of loosing her."

"And you?" the inspector asked, turning to Pricilla's aunt. "What was your part in this?"

She looked at the inspector stonily. Peter though she was going to deny everything, but he was wrong.

"My brother was bent," she began.

"You mean Priscilla's father?" the inspector asked.

The woman didn't even bother to reply, caught up as she was in her story. "Already at school he was caught several times with younger boys, but our father managed to hush it up. We were a very devout family. Such a scandal would have ruined us. I was younger than him and didn't really understand. All I knew was that my parents were very unhappy. I heard them arguing often. Their marriage would probably have broken had it not been for a generous offer from the church to train my brother as a priest.

That didn't work out, but he became a theologian…"

Peter knew that part of the story. He'd read about it in Witless's medical files that he and FI had stolen from Priscilla's old school.

"…so he hung himself," the aunt concluded. "It was Priscilla that found him dead. I blame her mother for giving the girl free rein of his house. It unhinged her completely."

"I still don't understand," the Inspector said. "Why did you encouraged Margery to tell such lies?"

The woman sat up even straighter, her back completely unbending, her eyes flashing. She looked proud and angry. "I've always hated queers," she said with vehemence. "They're against nature."

Peter had heard the likes from Priscilla. Could it all have come from her aunt?

"My twisted brother almost destroyed our family. He drove his wife and daughter mad. From what Priscilla told me, this boy," she motioned in disgust at Peter, "was one of them. It didn't take much imagination to think this man who took young boys into his house was one of them too."

"What proof have you got?" the inspector asked.

"What proof do you need," she spluttered. "Just look a them. Isn't it self-evident?"

"Maybe you can explain," the inspector said, surprising Peter with his patience. He was seeing a completely different side to the man.

She shrugged. "If you can't see it, I can't imagine how I could explain it to you."

How could you possibly show someone that what they took for a certainty was not at all what other people saw or thought? Maybe if she knew the man better, she'd change her mind.

"Why don't you ask Dr Grant some questions," Peter suggested. "That way you can point out what you mean."

Christina held up her hand to stop Peter, but the inspector intervened. "That's a good idea."

"What sort of questions," the aunt asked, clearly irritated at having to do what she thought was unnecessary, especially at Peter's behest.

"Find out more about him," Peter suggested.

She turned to look at Dr Grant, staring at him a long time in silence before asking, "Are you attracted to boys?"

"No. I'm not."

She shrugged off his answer. She'd been expecting as much.

"Is that the only question you have?" Peter asked.

She glared at him.

"Why don't you ask him why he chose to make our school mixed?" Peter suggested.

Exasperated, she repeated Peter's question.

"Because it seems unnatural to separate boys and girls," Dr Grant replied without hesitation. "They are not separated in society, so why separate them when they are learning? Boys and girls have different ways of approaching things. I believe they have a lot to learn from each other."

His answer bothered her. She didn't seem to know what to make of it. "What do you think of homosexuals?" she asked, returning to familiar ground.

"Our society has cast out homosexuals, rather like it did at one time with wise women that the church falsely called witches…"

"But you yourself said separating boys and girls was unnatural… Aren't men who go only with men unnatural?"

"Suffice it to say, I find it wrong to lock men up and to subject them to the most horrendous treatment because they prefer men to women. That doesn't make me a homosexual. Would you have women subjected to electroshock treatment because they spend all day lounging with other women and saying bad things about men?"

The aunt scoffed. Peter was frustrated. His idea was getting them no closer to a solution. The woman refused to see things otherwise.

"I am prepared to go before the press and tell them I lied," Margery said, surprising them all. Now there was courage for you, Peter stared at her in admiration. "You can come with me," she said to Witless's aunt, "and explain your part in this charade. Or you can keep silent and pay the price."

"I won't be part of your lies," the aunt spluttered.

"Oh but you are," Margery said, clearly delighted at her new-found self. "I am not ashamed to admit I like Peter. He was our hero when he got rid of Sanson. He helped those who were younger and weaker protect themselves against the harsh prefects Sanson set on us. And Dr Grant sided with Peter. School was so much worse when he was not there. And now he's back, there have been many improvements. I must have been blind to want to destroy his reputation."

Priscilla's aunt got to her feet and stormed out of the house slamming the front door after her. They heard her car rev up and drive away.

On the road to the coast, John explained what had happened. The police couple that got lost in the woods had caused a stir and not a little embarrassment, but John didn't ask Peter if he'd had a hand in the farce. Instead he talked of Margery. "I must admit, you did a remarkable job convincing her to admit she lied."

"It was a question of spots," Peter told him.

"Spots?" John asked.

"Yes. She was in such a pitiful state I wanted to help her. So I cured her spots. I never dreamed doing so would be of any use. It turned out to be the main reason she trusted me."

"How did you manage to cure her spots?" Andrew asked. "She's had them for ages."

"Healing," Peter replied.

"You can heal people?" Andrew asked, amazed.

"How do you think your gunshot wound healed so quickly? Kate and I extracted the bullet and sealed the hole."

Andrew's eyes went wide with surprise. "But surely you have to study medicine first?" Andrew exclaimed.

Peter laughed. "That's the way it's done here. They come

at it with books and lessons in a classroom. That takes ages. But if you can travel to people's minds and bodies, you quickly discover that the body knows how to cure itself. Every single cell has a blueprint for the whole body. All it needs is a little nudge of encouragement."

"But if you can do that, why don't you do it more often. It's such a wonderful gift."

"Did you not say you need to study to be a doctor? Anyone who knows how to heal, however well, will be treated as a dangerous charlatan by those who studied all those years and who earn their living by clumsily hacking away at the body. John mentioned witches earlier. They got burnt because, amongst other things, they knew how to heal. If people knew I could heal, I too would get burnt at the stake."

48.

Inspector Schmidt, looking even more like a tall skeleton than in the hospital, seemed puzzled at the sight of the coach. It clearly wasn't what he expected.

He couldn't possibly know they'd smuggled the girls out. The police would never have had the time to get there. And how could they have guessed it was Lydia and Klaus that did it? This must be something else.

Kate expected Lydia and Klaus to take the situation in their stride. Hadn't they rescued Tania behind the backs of the police? Yet at the sight of the inspector, Klaus and Lydia looked as if they'd been caught redhanded. Their courage had crumbled. Kate'd have to take the lead.

Clara, she called out, *do you have the strength to get the girls to sing?*

Clara didn't answer, but behind her Kate heard the girls sing.

Good, Clara, she said mind-to-mind. *Don't stop when the police come on board.*

"Introduce us as Lady Junker and her daughter," Kate said hurriedly to Klaus. "Remember you've never seen him before. Make sure he knows we have a photographer and a journalist with us. Tell him the girls are rehearsing for a choir festival in town. I read somewhere there's going to be one very soon."

The inspector rapped on the door, his bony knuckles sounding almost metallic. Klaus took a deep breath and opened for him. "What can I do for you…?" Klaus asked.

"I'm looking for a runaway," the man said.

"Oh dear!" Lydia said, unable to conceal her nervousness. Luckily that might appear normal in the circumstance. "That sounds dreadfully dramatic."

"Let me present Lady Junker," Klaus said, gaining confidence as he spoke. "I imagine there's no need to tell you who she is."

When the inspector looked at him blankly, Klaus nudged his memory. "Patroness of the arts, amongst other things. And this is her daughter," he said, indicating Kate. "We have a reporter and a photographer from the newspaper with us. They're covering this outing generously sponsored by Lady Junker."

Heinz chose that moment to take a picture of the inspector, who glared at him. "Smile," Heinz said, looking up from behind his camera. "You want to look your best in the paper."

The inspector continued to glare. "You publish that photo and I'll have you arrested."

Heinz took the photo all the same and grinned at the inspector who turned back to Klaus and asked, "Who're these girls?"

"That's the Lost Girls Choir," Klaus replied, as if it were self-evident.

The name pleased Kate immensely. Lost and found.

"Surely you've heard of them," Regina chipped in. "They're the main attraction at next weekend's choir festival in town. We're planning a big spread about them. Would you like to say something for the newspaper?"

The inspector didn't bother to answer. He continued to eye the girls who'd begun a new song under Clara's guidance. He seemed set on uncovering his prey amongst them.

"If you don't mind," Klaus said, interrupting the man's scrutiny. "We have a tight schedule and need to be getting along. The choir has to give a concert in half an hour." He started up the motor and wished the policeman a good day. The inspector was furious, clearly realising he was being out-manoeuvred, but at a loss what to do.

"If you give us your name and address," Lydia said, in her most regal voice, "we'll send you an invitation for the concert next weekend."

The inspector thanked her, but declined. "I've got far too much work with this runaway," he said, stepping off the coach.

Klaus waited patiently for the police to remove their car, then drove on.

"Do you think we dare go home?" Lydia asked. "What if they call on us?"

"No," Klaus said, a wicked smile on his lips. "We'll do exactly what we told them. If the girls are up to it, we'll have a picnic, that's what was planned. Then, we'll take them to give an impromptu concert in that beautiful church a few miles from our home."

Kate got to her feet, gripping the rail of the seat behind her for support as the coach wound its way up the mountain roads. "You were wonderful," Kate told the girls. "Klaus has a suggestion. Do you feel up to eating a picnic?"

The girls cheered.

"And you Clara? How do you feel?"

"I'm OK. Just a little tired and hungry."

"Klaus also found a name for our choir," Kate told me. "The Lost Girls."

The idea delighted everybody. Several girls whistled their approval.

"After the picnic, if you still have the strength, he suggested you give an improvised concert in a small church higher up the mountain. It'd be the first concert of The Lost Girls."

"Who'd come to listen?" Suzanne asked.

"I'll drive up and prepare things," Klaus called out from the driver's seat, "and let people know you're coming."

The idea of a picnic pleased everyone. They were less enthusiastic about the concert. Talking to the girls as they picnicked on a grassy area amongst pine trees, Kate realised many thought they weren't good enough.

"What do you think, Clara?" she asked. "Are we good enough?"

The girl looked a little flushed. They'd have to be careful not to overstretch her.

"I'm sure we can do it," she said, then turning to the others, added, "You're better than you think."

So it was agreed they'd sing two songs. Clara chose a couple and they quickly ran through them before climbing back into the coach. It was a warm afternoon and, given the food they'd eaten, it was not surprising that the younger girls and even some of the older ones drifted off.

"We've plenty of time," Klaus said. "I told the people in the village you'd sing at three o'clock." He pulled off the road, parking the coach in the shade of some trees while the girls had a nap.

Seeing that Christine, Suzanne and Eileen weren't asleep, she waved them over and with Tania they left the bus and found a comfortable spot away from the road where they could talk.

"Lydia and Klaus's place will be really good for you," she told them. "It'll take some work to make it comfortable, but once that's done, life will be quite different." She explained about the long wooden house that would be their home and how they planned to convert it to suit their needs. "Lydia is full of good ideas. She wants to make a gym so we can do sport together and I'm sure we could also make a place to sing."

"How can they possibly pay for all this?" Suzanne asked, as down to earth as always.

"They're not rich. But there are plans for you to learn to do things that can bring in money. Suzanne, you could help Lydia with her herb garden and learn how to do healing from me. Some of the girls could help you." Suzanne was enchanted.

Tania listed some of the other ideas, not wanting to be left out. Through it all, the others looked on wide-eyed. They'd have to take it easy, Kate thought. Only that morning the girls had been locked away with zero future to look forward to.

"How about you?" Kate asked them. "How are you faring?"

"It hasn't been easy," Christine said. "They sent Eileen and I to another place were life was even worse. The girls were real criminals who took an instant dislike to us. Anything was an excuse to pick on us. It wasn't just words. They beat us, for no reason. Luckily the authorities moved us before those girls had time to finish us off..."

Her words trailed off as tears welled in her eyes. Kate knew no one so attached to peace and harmony as Christine. She would do anything to avoid conflict. Kate pulled the girl into her arms and rocked her gently from side to side. The others joined them forming a warm huddle under the trees. All cried, even Kate. Shedding some of the tension of the last few days.

The sound of Klaus honking the horn had them separating and wiping their eyes.

"Maybe you should lead the choir," Eileen said. "Clara is not as strong as she makes out. It might be too much for her."

Kate didn't want to steal Clara's glory. Maybe if she had a chair, she'd manage two songs.

The church was tiny, with hardly enough room to seat fifty people. Throughout the dimly lit nave, an odour of candles and incense hung thick in the musty air. To their surprise the rows of wooden pews were full of folk of all ages, eagerly craning their necks to get a better look at the girls. There were even people leaning against the grey-stone walls at the back. The only natural light came from above the altar where a brightly-coloured, stained-glass fresco depicted a gathering of saints and apostles who shone down on the congregation. It seemed appropriate that their little community of lost girls should be watched over by such a benevolent host.

That riot of colour contrasted with the dirty grey of the girls' dresses as they shuffled after Kate down the aisle. She wheeled Clara in her wheelchair, it'd seemed the best solution to spare the girl's energy, and lined up the others with their backs to the altar, keeping up a steady flow of encouraging words mind-to-mind. Once in place, she turned to face the congregation.

"Welcome," she began. "The Lost Girls Choir is very proud and pleased to be able to perform for you. Lost Girls? An odd name you might think. All these girls were lost from view, locked away in a school where they were regularly beaten and mistreated. All have bruises or burn marks to show for it. All have deeper scars, those in their minds, that may never be healed.”

Several people shook their heads, a few even muttered unintelligible words to their neighbour.

“The leader of our choir, Clara, was so brutally beaten that she lay for days in the infirmary unable to move. She should be in a hospital bed now, recuperating, but she insisted on being here. For today is the beginning of a new life. These girls come before you to share their hopes for the future; hopes they will express by their songs. Please give them a warm welcome.”

As Kate went to take her place in the choir, the audience responded with polite but restrained applause. Her words must have been hard to accept. Maybe they preferred to believe she was exaggerating.

The choir sang the two songs they’d prepared, but, despite the brevity of their concert, the moment they’d finished the audience was on its feet in its enthusiasm, applauding such that their hands must have hurt. Once the applause had died down, Kate helped Clara to her feet so she could take a bow. Everyone, choir and audience alike, applauded the girl whose face shone with delight, despite the tears that streamed down her cheeks.

“Singing here today is a dream Clara would never have dared believe in.” She helped Clara back to her wheelchair and then turned back to the audience.

“You can imagine it is very tiring, after all we’ve been through, to stand here and perform this afternoon. We had planned to perform only two songs. But your warm welcome was so touching, we will sing one more.”

She glanced questioningly at Clara who nodded.

“It would be wrong to say everybody was nasty to us. A few brave people tried to help. Sister Teresa was one of them. A shy, little woman, peppered with bruises and cuts like us, she knew what it meant to be cowered into silence by those bigger and stronger than her. Yet she stood up to them, despite her fears and misgivings, and spoke out for us. We sang this last song at her funeral, as she lay there bedecked with our flowers, abandoned by the adults, accompanied only by us girls."

Clara gave the note and the girls launched into the song, many with tears in their eyes. There was a long, reverent silence at the end, then the audience rose as one and applauded.

Klaus and Lydia helped the girls out, shielding them from the many people who wanted to congratulate them and above all ask questions. Tania had wheeled Clara out, leaving Kate the last to step out into the fresh late afternoon air. A smartly dressed woman stopped her, extending a gloved hand for Kate to shake. Kate did so, admiring the neat way the woman had tied her long brown hair in a bun, fixing it with a butterfly broach. The woman looked well-meaning and smiled encouragingly. But Kate was tired and was about to excuse herself, when the woman handed her a visiting card.

"I organise a choir festival in town. It is taking place next weekend. I would very much like your choir to sing at the closing event, if you agree. I know you're tired, so I won't keep you. Phone me and we'll settle everything then." She shook hands and left.

49.

"So you've decided to be a boy again," Viktor commented as Peter took his place at the kitchen table in Viktor's cottage.

Peter yearned for the soft silk of his dresses and the caress of the breeze as it blew around his legs. Above all he missed the feeling of being complete that wearing girl's clothes gave him. Despite that, he shrugged at Viktor's question. "There was a bit of a stir in the press," Peter said. "Being dressed up wasn't worth the trouble it caused to those I love."

Viktor raised his eyebrows, but said nothing.

"And you?" he asked Andrew, who'd borrowed some of Peter's clothes till they could go shopping.

"Never was so important to me, at least, not once my uncle was out of the way," Andrew said. "Does the change upset you?"

Viktor chuckled. "Why should it? Lest it be that we will no longer have an all-female line up for the Fauré."

Peter had completely forgotten the concert. "Good Lord! When is it?"

"This Sunday," Viktor reminded them.

"But that's the day after tomorrow!" Peter groaned.

"Dress rehearsal is tomorrow afternoon with the choir at 4 o'clock," Viktor said, clearly delighted at alarming them.

"We'll never make it," Peter exclaimed.

"Sure you will," Viktor replied, hesitating a moment before continuing, "if you practice day and night."

Peter glanced at the man only to see him grinning.

"You're joking," Peter said, unsure if that was true.

"Not about the date," Viktor said, still grinning as he tugged at his goatee. "But you both know the piece. It just needs some 'polishing'. The harmonium is already in place, so we'll practice in the church"

Viktor was about to get to his feet, but Peter said, "Before we go, I need your help with a translation." From his bag, he pulled the newspaper clipping they'd found at the author's flat. "It's in German. It is probably nothing. But we wanted to be sure. None of us can read German."

Viktor took the fragile piece of paper and unfolded it carefully. When he saw what was written on it, his face went ashen. Peter was afraid the man might have a stroke.

"What's the matter?" Peter asked.

"Are you alright?" Andrew added.

Viktor remained speechless as he scanned the article, a feverish look in his eyes.

"Mein Gott!" he exclaimed when he'd finished.

Both Andrew and Peter looked at Viktor in alarm.

"It's Beth," Viktor finally managed to say.

"What about her?" Peter asked, thinking of the attractive girl he'd seen in the photo and the painting. To be truthful, her image had haunted him ever since.

"She's not dead" Viktor said. "Or at least she didn't die in the accident as I was made to believe."

The man's hands were trembling as he clutched the paper.

"I have to go," he said, getting to his feet.

"Where?" Peter asked.

"To look for her."

"But we have a concert on Sunday," Andrew exclaimed. "You can't leave."

Viktor glanced at the calendar hanging on the kitchen wall. "July 15th," he muttered, then hurried off into his bedroom from where he emerged carrying a small cardboard box that he upended on the table. Rummaging through it's contents, he pulled out a tattered programme. "Here it is," he muttered.

Peter wondered if he'd gone mad. Could the discovery that

your long lost love was not dead do that to you?

Viktor had unfolded the programme and was searching through it. "I thought as much," he muttered.

"Can you tell us what's going on," Peter asked, amusement giving way to irritation.

"There's a music festival in Luzern every year mid-July," Viktor said as he hurried off again. This time he returned with a train timetable.

"We could sing the Fauré there," he said triumphantly.

Peter took that as a sign the man really had gone bonkers. There was no way they could get to Switzerland before the 15th. It was only a week away. And where would they get the money, even if John and Christina let them go? The choir might have been small, but it'd still cost a fortune. And anyway, the festival programme must have closed ages ago.

"How could we pay for the trip?" Andrew asked, dubious, but clearly excited at the prospect.

"That's no problem," Viktor said. "I have some savings."

"But you can't pay for the whole choir," Andrew pointed out.

"Let's check the times and prices," Viktor said, bent on making his dream materialise.

"Why is attending this festival so important?" Peter asked.

"Because Beth always attended. She was often in the jury as her family gave a generous donation each year."

Peter wasn't going to point out that Beth's parents might long be dead, as might well be Beth. Or she might live elsewhere. Or she might be confined to bed, unable to move because of the accident. Not to mention the fact that she might not want to see him after so many years. Peter didn't have the heart to discourage him. He truly hoped that none of his sombre imaginings were true, for Viktor's sake.

"Let's not forget we have a concert in two days," Peter said.

All the way across the scrub, Viktor continued making plans. He'd phone the leader of the choir to see if they could come. He'd contact a foundation that gave money to choirs. They'd ask people to put money in a hat at the concert. When he started talking of giving a concert in London to earn more money, Peter stopped him. "The schedule is already tight," he said. "If we have to give another concert, we'll be exhausted and no good in Luzern."

Viktor readily agreed as his mind chased after further details.

"You realise," Peter said, "we'll have to ask permission from John and Christina."

Viktor dismissed the idea, saying "Of course." He'd have continued his frenetic planning had they not arrived at the church and it was time to rehearse.

Several hours later, in the kitchen of their cottage, Viktor was explaining the idea to Christina and John. Neither seemed opposed. John actually said, "There's a very beautiful wooden footbridge that spans the end of the lake. It's well worth seeing, as is the old town. Maybe we'll join you for the weekend."

"Isn't it a bit far by train for a weekend?" Christina asked.

John agreed, taking hold of Christina's hands. "But let's do something crazy for once. As long as I am back on Monday for meetings at school… and you are on holiday," he reminded her.

"Do you mind if I use your phone?" Viktor asked. "I couldn't get the head of the choir earlier."

Once Viktor had gone, Christina asked quietly, "What's bitten him?"

"He just learnt his long lost girlfriend is not dead like he'd been led to believe," Peter said. He went on to tell the story in a heavily abridged version.

When Viktor returned, he beamed. "The members of the choir can all come," he informed them. "And their choir has a fund for travelling so that's one less worry." He sat back at the table before continuing. "I also got the president of Tscheheri Foundation. They offer grants to female choirs for attending just such festivals. They need a short written project and a budget, but seem willing to help us make the trip."

"Female choirs?" John said glancing at Peter.

"I thought one public performance wouldn't do any harm," Viktor said, trying to look innocent.

"Two, you mean," Peter corrected. "There'll be the performance here, too."

After a long, somewhat heated discussion, it was agreed that Andrew would be dressed as a boy and Peter as a girl, but only for the two performances. That conversation left Peter with a sinking feeling. He pleaded restlessness and went for a walk to think things over. Down by the harbour, out at the end of the breakwater, he found a dry stone to sit on.

Rationing his time to dress as a girl seemed like a big step backwards. He might be reasonable and agree not to cause trouble by dressing up, but the thought that the adults he loved might curtail his right to dress when he'd been doing so all summer left him feeling anxious. Sure, when the summer break was over, he'd have to go about as a boy, at school at least. He also knew he couldn't take the hormones indefinitely. Sooner or later, the inevitable would happen and he'd become a man.

He thought of Peter Pan. No wonder the boy had taken refuge in Never Never Land. He had to laugh at the name. He was astonished its true meaning had not struck him before. The place outside time where you never got old. As Peter McCloud, he had no such choice. There was no secret place he could fly away to, no place where he could continue to revel in the ambiguity that came before manhood or womanhood left their mark.

He got to his feet, ready to return. There seemed to be no satisfactory solution. Or if there was, he couldn't see it. At least he was grateful for the few weeks he'd been free to be who he was, although circumstances had kept his mind elsewhere most of the time. Talking about being whom he was, there was the healing too. He remember Margery's joy at being rid of her spots. It'd been so easy. There were so many people he could help. There were so many people he could teach. Yet he knew only too well that society wouldn't tolerate it. What was wrong with this world?

As he stared out over the waves, he toyed with the idea of writing a new version of Peter Pan. One in which it was Wendy, not Peter, that lived in joyous chaos on a magical island with a band of lost girls who never got old. In his imagination, the girl looked remarkably like Beth. Her hair was cropped short, boy-like, barely reaching her ears, but the curves of her face, the arch of her brows and the fullness of her lips were very feminine. She even wore the same old fashioned clothes Beth had worn in Viktor's photo. The thought of her stirred a deep-seated longing that had him yearning to move.

The only adults on the island were a band of bloodthirsty nuns, each one more ugly than the next. They lived behind high walls in joyless misery, hardly ever coming out except to snatch one of the girls in the hope of making her a nun. Wendy waged a continuous battle against the nuns to stop them luring girls into the nunnery, where they promptly became old and ugly.

It was Wendy that flew down to rescue Peter from the suburban house in which he was a prisoner, kept forever in the straight jacket of his boy's grey school uniform. She draped him in dresses of wild colours and wrapped him in delicate silks, then, armed with that magic, she whisked him away over unimaginable distances, so he could live forever with her and the other lost girls…

But that was only a dream. He sighed and wound his way back to the cottage where the table was set for the evening meal, and Viktor was in their kitchen making an improvised exotic eastern European dish. Seeing Peter arrive, Viktor handed him a mug of tea and raised his own in salute. "Here's to our trip to Switzerland!"

50.

The air was bright with laughter, chatter and joyous fragments of song as Kate made her way from the main house to the large annex where the girls were housed. Organised by Eileen, the girls had been split into groups. One was preparing beds with a carpenter friend of Klaus. Another was clearing a large room and shifting furniture to turn the place into a refectory under the supervision of Suzanne. Claudia aided by Tania was measuring the girls for clothes. They'd decided to keep most of the stock of clothes for special occasions but some were being measured as patterns to make new ones. Yet another group was helping Lydia pack dried herbs, then collect new ones and hang them up to dry.

Regina had set up a desk in a quiet corner under the shade of an oak a small distance from the Lost Girls House, as they called it. From there she went to fetch the girls for interviews and typed up her report. Heinz was roaming the property taking photos of the girls at work and doing portraits, as well as documenting the cuts, bruises and other injuries the girls had suffered. They were to prepare a full report but there would also be a shorter illustrated piece for publication in a special supplement to Saturday's newspaper. Heinz had contacted a rich benefactor who'd agreed to finance the work, although she wished to remain anonymous.

Kate had phoned the woman who organised the choir festival in town. It was all organised. Their group would close the festival on Saturday evening singing the same three songs they had in the church. It was to be a surprise. No mention would be made of them in the programme and the girls would arrive by a back door to the cathedral, just in time for their performance. The woman herself would announce them, insisting that Kate also speak as she'd done in the church. She wanted the girls to wear the worn-out clothes they had in the church, but Kate refused, arguing that the girls were turning a page and didn't need to put on a show to demonstrate their miserable past.

They also agreed that a special offprint of Regina's article about the Lost Girls, illustrated with Heinz's photos, would be handed out to the audience at the festival's expense. When Kate asked why she was doing all this, the woman simply replied, "I can't bear to see good young people hurt. It is our contribution against injustice. I have talked about it to one of our main sponsors and she thinks like me. She'll close the festival and will no doubt have a few words to say about your choir and the hope it represents."

Kate shared her news with Heinz and Regina who were delighted.

"There is so much material here," Regina said, enthusiastic, "I'm sure we'll be able to turn it into a book. If that works, Heinz and I have agreed to give the proceeds to you girls to help you on your way."

"Thank you," Kate said. "Any extra money will be welcome." She didn't want to further burden Lydia and Klaus.

"I've already lined up an exhibition in one of the most visited galleries in town," Heinz told them. Both seemed excited by the project and eager to get on. "I have to phone the printer. We'll need extra copies for the festival goers," Heinz said and hurried off.

Kate left Regina to her typing and walked from group to group talking to the girls, checking all was well and giving a helping hand when necessary. Lunch would soon be ready. She'd announce the news about the festival then.

Lydia, Klaus, Regina, Heinz and the carpenter joined the Lost Girls for lunch. The girls applauded Suzanne when she and her helpers brought in the food and cheered when Heinz announced there'd be a special supplement about them in the newspaper.

"Does that mean the police'll come and fetch us?" one of the youngest girls, Dee, asked, tears in her eyes. Christine went and sat next to her, putting an arm around her shoulders.

"No, little one," Regina said. "It means you'll be much safer and can stay here as long as you like. The police won't trouble you again."

"I'm glad," another little girl called Anita said. "I like it here and I don't want to return to Sister Helga."

Several of the girls hissed at the mention of the woman's name.

"Don't worry about her, Anita," Kate said. "She'll never bother you again."

Kate judged it was a good moment to tell them about the concert. "As you know, the woman who organises the Choir Festival this weekend offered us a chance to sing. I have spoken to her and she wants us to sing at the end of the final concert on Saturday evening. It is to be a big surprise. It'll be in the cathedral and they'll smuggle us in by a back door so no one knows."

Several girls squealed in delight.

"Why would she do that?" Suzanne asked. "What's it to her?"

"She told me she doesn't like to see talented girls so badly treated. She wants to do something to stop it. So she'll use her festival to let people know and to celebrate our new life here."

A lot of the girls cheered.

"As you know," Kate went on, "Regina and Heinz are preparing a long article for the newspaper about The Lost Girls. The organiser of the festival will have it distributed to the audience."

"I hope you don't put pictures of my cuts and bruises in the newspaper," Anita said, making a face. "They look horrible, despite all Lydia's creams."

"Me too," a younger girl said. Several others agreed.

"We won't do that," Regina said, getting to her feet. "The story for the newspaper is about you and how you escaped the horrible life you used to live and about your future here. Those photos of wounds are only for the official report. Don't worry, they're not for everybody. We need them all the same, to prove that those nasty people mistreated you."

"Will they get punished?" Christine asked. "I know they were horrible to us, but I wouldn't like them to be hurt."

Kate had to smile. That was Christine for you. All consideration for everyone, even her worst enemies.

"They may well get punished," Heinz said, getting to his feet. "That'd only be right. What they did was wrong. It's against the law. But the punishment they might get would in no way be comparable to what they did to you."

It was then that Clara got to her feet. "We'll have choir practice before the evening meal," she said shyly. Despite her growing role with the choir, she was still very unsure of herself. "But I wanted to ask another question. What about Jane? Have we had any news?"

A number of girls muttered. Some even hissed liked they had with Helga.

"I understand that some of you don't like Jane. She did something very wrong," Kate said. "Jane was Helga's favourite," Kate explained to the adults. "She ran away to help Helga and came back with that horrible man who set fire to the convent." Turning back to the girls, she went on, "But something terrible happened to Jane. Most of you know nothing about it." She had no intention of telling them. It'd give the younger ones nightmares. Goodness knows, it gave her them. "What happened to her at the hands of that man would have been punishment enough, if punished she should be. Now she's locked away in a special clinic, a place that might be far worse than the convent. So if I were you, I wouldn't hiss when her name is mentioned. She's a Lost Girl like us. Don't forget."

Later that afternoon, the festival organiser phoned and asked to meet Kate at the cathedral to finalise plans. It was Lydia, who'd taken several days off, that drove her into town. They parked in a narrow street at the back of the cathedral. Lydia led her along a cunning little path that bridged a street below then ventured into the grounds of the cathedral through an arched opening in the walls surrounding the building. The grounds were mostly taken up by tombs and gravestones, some sheltered by a roof that extended out from the wall making it look like a cloister. They followed the path round the church till they came to a tiny door. The woman was waiting for them there.

"Good to see you," she said, shaking Kate's hand then Lydia's. "This door is generally only used by the priests and the choir and is always kept locked. You'll get in here on Saturday evening. I'll make sure it's open."

They went inside, with the woman leading them into a room in which row upon row of robes hung. "You'll wait here till I fetch you. We're just behind one of the side altars, so be sure the girls make no noise." They went on into an enclosed area to each side of which were two parallel rows of benches facing each other. "This is the sacristy and these are the choir stalls. When I fetch you, you'll come and sit here on the left. Silence is essential. Any noise will be heard throughout the church. I'll bring you here when there's a pause between choirs and this part'll be in darkness. I don't think anyone will notice."

Kate turned to look through the intricate metal latticework that separated that part from the rest. The building was immense and full of light. In the distance, she could make out the banks of silvery organ pipes over the main entrance glinting in the sun's rays. Turning to look behind her, she saw a giant portrait framed by three marble columns on each side that took up most of the wall above the elaborate altar.

"It's Christ in the garden where he was betrayed," the woman explained.

Kate had heard of Christ although she was at a loss to understand why these people built a religion around betrayal, torture and death. At home, they had no religion, and death was less of a trauma because they believed in reincarnation.

"When I announce The Lost Girls, you'll come forward through this gate in screen," the organiser said, opening it and stepping through. Kate and Lydia followed, finding a second altar on a low dais in front of which, they were told, the choirs would sing.

"Could we sing part of the first song before we appear?" Kate asked. The idea of their identity remaining hidden at the beginning appealed to her. It'd be more dramatic. "Maybe you could even lower the lighting."

"Why not?" the woman said. "When would you speak?"

"At the end of the first piece. And like in the church I'll also speak before the third and last piece to explain about Sister Teresa."

"Excellent. Now come with me, I have someone I'd like you to meet."

She led them down a few steps and across the central aisle to where an elegantly dressed lady sat in a wheelchair.

"Meet the main sponsor of our festival," the organiser said.

Kate was surprised the name of the woman was not mentioned. Maybe she wanted to remain anonymous. The tasteful mixture of colours and textures of the woman's clothes impressed Kate. Here was someone who knew how to dress and had the means to do so, despite her handicap.

The woman sat there a long moment staring at Kate, making no move to greet her. Kate began to worry she'd done something wrong. She looked to the others for reassurance, but all eyes were on the woman. Then, as if a spell had been broken, the woman wheeled forward and held out her hand to Kate. "Pleased to meet you, Kate," she said, her voice melodious and welcoming. She also greeted Lydia before turning to the organiser and exclaiming, "It's remarkable! She looks exactly like I did before my accident." Turning back to Kate she said: "If I'd had a twin sister, she'd have looked exactly like you."

51.

Along the riverside, banners fluttered high in the breeze, announcing the choir festival. Spanning the river slantwise, was the low, wooden Chapel footbridge that John had mentioned. The air smelt of neither the sea nor the city, but of a large expanse of lake water mixed with the scents of flowers in baskets hung from the lamp posts. Peter breathed in deeply and promptly yawned. Viktor always told him yawning was good for him, it helped relax the jaw and neck muscles, making his voice better.

It was hardly surprising he yawned, Peter had slept badly. He'd shared a compartment with Andrew who took the upper bunk. According to Viktor there were normally three bunks in each compartment, but he'd paid extra so they could have a good night's sleep. Despite that, Peter hadn't slept well. Of course, they'd talked for a long time, with him listening to Andrew describe his dreams of being a pianist. He himself had been less forthcoming, despite Andrew's questions. He saw no radiant future he could be enthusiastic about.

Later, as he lay in his bunk, trying to shut out the constant clatter of the train as it crossed the points of Europe, Peter mulled over his new version of Peter Pan, adding details here and there. He resolved to write it up after the festival, especially now he'd found a title: The Lost Girls.

He and Andrew made their way along the riverside pavement, heading for the bridge that they'd have to cross to reach the church. Viktor had gone on ahead to organise rehearsals and the rest of the choir were visiting the town and would join them later. John and Christina were to arrive just before the concert.

In their absence, Peter had chosen to continue to dress as a girl. Andrew had tried to reason with him, but Peter was adamant. Their sponsors, the Tscheheri Foundation, were expecting a girl and, what's more, it was his last fling before it was too late. No one knew him in Luzern so there was little risk. He'd had the idea a while back when he packed his case, deliberately adding all his favourite dresses, blouses and skirts not to mention underwear and make-up.

"Why do you insist on dressing up?" Andrew asked, as they climbed a couple of stairs and stepped onto the Chapel bridge.

To Peter's surprise the planks were rough under his feet, as if the bridge wanted to remind him at every step that it was there. A fresco spanned the two hundred yards of the bridge, lodged every few yards on triangular boards wedged between the beams that supported the roof. From what he could judge, every scene had something to do with the church. There was a text in gothic script under each image, but he couldn't understand the German.

"You know it can't go on," Andrew added, giving Peter a nudge to get his attention. "You're going to have to make up your mind."

Peter ran his hand down his dress smoothing it as he halted to study the eight-sided tower that rose out of the water next to the bridge. He didn't want to answer. An argument was in the making and he didn't want to fight. Intuition told him this might be the last time they'd be together.

"It's part of me," he finally said, dodging a group of tourists who were pointing at the tower. "Removing that side of me would be like cutting off my nose. And cutting off people's noses is all this society is good for," he said, thinking of Alan Turing, a mathematician his English teacher had told him about.

"Someone forced you to dress up and, whether you liked it or not, dressing up was bound with sex." He lowered his voice. "No one forced me and dressing up has never been about sex. It's just how I am. I'm in between. I am both and neither." His decidedness surprised him. The situation had never seemed so clear. "Why should I have to be otherwise? Where is the crime in that?" He broke off, realising that his voice had risen and some of the tourists had turned to stare.

A debonair man in his early forties stopped Peter and asked in almost flawless English if he'd pose by the side of the bridge for a photo. The look in the man's eyes had Peter shuddering. He declined as politely he could, and taking Andrew by the arm, hurried away along the bridge.

Andrew chuckled. "I reckon he fancied you."

"It's not funny," Peter said pouting. He knew full well the man had seen a young girl, not a boy dressed as a girl, but that didn't make his accosting them any less repulsive.

"The question is going to be," Andrew continued, more serious now, "how you plan to fit in. You can't just shut yourself away on a desert island."

Peter thought of Wendy on her island with the lost girls. Was that not what they did in the story, shut themselves away? "I don't know," he finally said, as they reached the end of the bridge and stepped onto the pavement. "There must be an answer, but I can't find it."

Truth was, the situation made him want to scream. He might have been able to talk to Fi about it, although she hadn't really understood. She had her own agenda. John and Christina were no help. What he felt was beyond them. Not even Andrew, who should have been able to understand, was capable of it. Kate was probably the only person he could unreservedly confide in. She neither judged him nor had preconceived plans for him. Unfortunately Kate wasn't there.

They crossed the street that flanked the river and turned right in the direction of a major road a short distance away. The church they were heading for was called St. Leodegar. According to Viktor, it was the most important church in town and had once acted as a cathedral. That was where the festival was to be held.

They walked in an uncomfortable silence, following the

main road at the end of which the church was clearly visible. Peter wasn't sure if his arguments had convinced Andrew or if the boy had simply given up. Violent circumstances had flung them together, forcing them to share their most intimate secrets. They might have become close friends, but something had held Peter back. Ever since the death of Fi, and possibly even before, they'd begun to drift apart. Depending where Andrew lived once term began, they'd probably have little more to say to each other, lest it be about music or reminiscences of the past.

When they finally entered the narrow square in front of the cathedral, the bells began to toll the hour. Other bells elsewhere joined in, till the whole city resonated with their strident clangs. Peter couldn't help imagining they'd conspired to greet him.

He looked up, impressed by the majestic building that stood atop two steep but broad flights of steps. The main entrance was flanked by two towers that culminated in steeples each topped with a gold orb and a cross. The massive wooden door was beautifully carved with life-like figures that Peter took to be a lord and a bishop. He halted a moment in the entrance, delighting in the craftsmanship as he ran his fingers over the curves in the wood.

The interior of the cathedral surprised him. Not only did light stream in the many high windows free of stained glass, but the simplicity of the unadorned walls with their light grey stone gave an airiness to the place that came as a relief. Neither the weight of elaborate, gold-plated saints, nor the majestic crosses on the main altar and the side altars, nor even the ever-present scent of candles and incense could distract from the freshness and serenity that inhabited the place.

Viktor spotted them and hurried over, bringing with him a man with a jovial face and an abundant, greying beard he introduced as the cathedral's official organist. Andrew would be playing the organ for the Fauré. Talking in proficient English, the man led Andrew away to show him the organ, while Viktor walked Peter to the steps before the main altar. There were two main altars, one, raised up on a dais a few steps high, was in full sight of the congregation. The other lay half hidden behind an intricate wrought iron screen. It was there that he could just make out the choir stalls.

"You'll be singing here in front of the public altar," Viktor explained. "Try out the acoustics."

Peter climbed the two steps that ran the whole length of the dais, took a deep breath and sang the opening bars of his first solo. The acoustics were good and his voice carried well. Andrew must have reached the organ because he began playing the accompaniment, so Peter continued. Soon after the choir arrived and together they went through the first part of the Mass. Compared with their performance in the tiny chapel in Lettup, the piece sounded totally different. Gone were the colours and scents of the sea, the call of the gulls and the intimate atmosphere, to be replaced by a majestic but sober ode full of light and hope.

After rehearsals, the choir went off to visit a massive lion, sculptured in a rock nearby, while Andrew was invited to lunch with the organist and his family. Finding himself on his own, Peter opted to go with Viktor in search of Beth, and, with any luck, something to eat. He was famished. The breakfast of rolls and jam in their hotel, albeit delicious, had not sufficed.

Seeing that it was almost midday, Viktor took Peter through a side street till they reached a large square on one side of which was a sprawling, old-fashioned two-storey building called the Old Swiss House. Viktor explained that it was almost 120 years old and served some of the best food in Switzerland. Not having reserved a table, all was taken inside, but a small table for two was free out back in the garden. Someone had cancelled at the last minute.

Viktor advised him to order sliced veal with cream sauce which was served with rösti, a local speciality made of fried potatoes. Despite his hunger, Peter was not a big eater, but he did as Viktor suggested. While they waited to be served, Peter sipped ice-cold water and looked around the garden. He much preferred to be outside, especially as roses tumbled over the walls that boarded the garden, filling the air with their delicate perfume.

"I'd like to visit the house where Beth and I used to meet," Viktor said, his face alight with anticipation. "It's not far out of town. I'll hire a car. Maybe I can pick up her trail there. Will you come with me?"

Peter agreed, although later, in the twists and turns as the car wound it's way up out of town, after all the cream sauce and fried potatoes, he wondered if he wouldn't have been better off in his bed. When Viktor brought the car to a halt in front of a large wooden chalet, Peter was glad to get out and stretch his legs. The air was rich with the scents of a multitude of flowers and plants, as if someone nearby cultivated all manner of sweet smelling herbs. He liked the place. It was the sort of peaceful home he could imagine retreating to when the world outside was too much.

Viktor was looking around in search of familiar landmarks when a small lady with tiny delicate hands and dark brown hair tied up in a bun came out to greet them. She looked tense, no doubt unhappy to have them trespass on her property. Peter understood nothing of the conversation that ensued, although, judging from the tone, the woman seemed to become more and more friendly and finally invited them in for a drink.

He felt strange sitting at the large wooden table in that old fashioned kitchen listening to the two of them chattering away in German. It was almost as if he were drifting outside his own body in search of something. Maybe it was his stomach that was playing him up. When Viktor asked him what he wanted to drink, Peter refused, saying he thought the midday meal had disagreed with him. The woman nodded knowingly when Viktor translated and went in search of a sprig of camomile. Peter recognised it immediately. Kate had begun teaching him about medicinal herbs before she'd been stolen away.

On the table Peter found a couple of programmes for the Choir Festival. He wondered why they were there. Perhaps the woman liked choral music. He flicked through the programme as the two chatted. They were to perform on Saturday afternoon, in two days time, just before a final concert given early evening by a number of invited choirs. At the bottom of the programme he found a list of sponsors, most of them sounding like companies. There was no Beth amongst them.

"What was Beth's family name?" Peter asked, when he could get a word in their conversation.

Viktor didn't answer. Instead he pulled over one of the programmes and hunted through it for the list of sponsors. He must have found what he was looking for because he grinned. The grin transformed Viktor's face, making him look like a naughty boy who'd got his hands on a chocolate cake he was not supposed to eat. He got to his feet, shook hands with the woman and motioned Peter to follow.

Peter hesitated, unsure how to say goodbye. To his surprise she hugged him, kissing him lightly on each cheek. Then she handed him a small posy made of camomile. He thanked her in English and hurried after Viktor, clutching his present.

"Do people always kiss like that here?" Peter asked when they were in the car.

"It's because you're a girl and she's a woman, and you ate and drank in her house."

Peter found Viktor's explanation confusing, but let it go.

"Did you see how she reacted when I asked to visit the place?" Viktor asked. "She went all tense and tight lipped."

Peter shook his head. "How could I? I didn't understand a word."

"I bet she's hiding something," Viktor continued, like an eager dog after a bone. "I wonder if Beth's hidden there."

The idea seemed absurd, but Peter said nothing. How strange to discover this completely new facet to his teacher. He'd always been so wise and measured. It had Peter wondering how Viktor would react if ever he found Beth. Would he make a fool of himself?

52.

"Well," Peter said quietly, laying his hands in the lap of his dress as he settled in the front row next to Viktor, "that went well." He was still elated from the singing, so much so that he felt like he was floating. It was the first time he'd sung for such a large and knowledgeable audience. The Fauré had received an enthusiastic reception with people applauding for what seemed like ages as he stood with the choir and bowed.

The moment he was seated, people behind, recognising him, patted him on the shoulder to congratulate him. In broken English, they tried to share their appreciation. One young girl about his age even wanted him to sign her programme. He was about to write Peter, when he remembered. He was beginning to get a crick in his neck from turning to thank people when, at last, the woman who organised the festival walked out to announce the final part of the programme.

Peter just had time to wave to John and Christina who were seated several rows back with Andrew. They hadn't been able to get places together. Even in the side aisles, where people probably couldn't see very well, all seats were taken. The rest of their little choir was scattered throughout the audience. Thank heavens Viktor had the foresight to ask someone to reserve two seats for them up front.

He glanced at Viktor. His teacher's attention was fixed on the woman as she explained what was about to happen. The man had been pleased with the performance and had received a lot of praise, but he was clearly disappointed. He'd badly wanted to find his Beth. He'd been so close, but nothing had come of it. The woman might have had her name in the programme, but she'd not shown her face.

The first choir took its place, a local men's choir that had won a lot of prizes according to Viktor. They sang in Swiss German, a strange local dialect that fascinated Peter. The men had a striking way of forcing their voices to break on one note rather like a yodel. Viktor had talked about it. Peter was not one for men's choirs, but he liked the sound of the deep basses. They stood so close, their voices vibrated in his chest. Would he sing like that later? Probably not. He'd be a tenor.

Several more choirs followed, most of them small groups, all very proficient, appealing to the tastes of the local audience. It might have been an international festival, but it closed on a local note. When the final group had sung, he suddenly realised it was over. A wave of disappointment rolled over him. He'd been unaware he was hoping for a miracle to happen, but it hadn't. Tomorrow he'd exchange his dress for boy's clothes and would catch the train with John, Christina and Andrew. It was time to return to reality. How he hated the word.

The organiser was back before them. Whatever she was saying caused a stir. He leaned close to Viktor for an explanation. "There's to be one more group. It's a surprise. A group of local girls that have suffered great hardship and have been rescued, amongst other things by their singing." The woman continued to talk, but Peter told Viktor he needn't translate. Peter leaned back and closed his eyes. None of this had anything to do with him. Tears formed in his eyes and rolled down his cheeks. There might be a magical world for lost girls but it was lost to him.

The stir of wonder of those around him at the sound of distant voices singing had him open his eyes. The lights had been dimmed. Only the flicker of candles on the altar and on other altars around the church cast an eerie light that fit the music well. He could hear young girls' voices singing beautifully, but no one stood on the low platform. The combination of the girls voices and the absence of girls, had tears flowing anew down his cheeks. The lost girls were singing, he thought.

Then, one by one, lit only by the candles, the girls marched slowly into view. There must have been twenty of them, of all ages, their faces and hands pale, their feet bare, their dresses pitch black, as they swayed gently with the song they sang. They took up their places on the platform singing all the time. And with them wafted a mixture of wild herbs and plants that reminded him of the gardens around the house they'd visited that afternoon.

When the song came to an end, the audience broke into rapturous applause. As some of the lights came on, a tiny young girl who conducted the choir turned and bowed followed by all the others. When the applause went on and on, the girls looked at each other wondering what to do. Then one of their number came forward and raised a hand for silence.

And what Peter saw then was the shock of his life. There, before him, only feet away stood Beth, or at least how she must have looked all those years ago. The same hair cropped short, the same high cheek bones and arched eyebrows, the same intelligent smile. If he hadn't been clutching the pew on which he sat, he might have got up and rushed to embrace her. A glance at Viktor showed he too was alight with a yearning that spanned years. Who was this person?

All this time she'd been speaking. Whatever she said made the audience react. People were shocked. Many muttered. Others shook their heads. And throughout it all, the girl talked on, calm, firm, decided, sure of herself. The sight of her filled him with such longing that it almost broke his heart. He would have liked to know what she said, but Viktor was in a state of shock, his hand cupped over his mouth, his eyes wide in wonder.

Finally the girl ceased, and returning to the ranks of the choir, the little girl who conducted led the choir in a second song. Peter couldn't take his eyes of that beautiful girl, shifting slightly to keep her constantly in view. He trembled with excitement and anticipation. He'd been waiting for a miracle and now that it'd happened he could hardly believe it.

What would he do if she disappeared at the end of their performance leaving him no chance to talk? That would be unthinkable. But how silly of him. He couldn't talk to her, even if he wanted to, she spoke the local dialect which he didn't understand.

The song came to an end and once the applause died down, the girl came forward a second time and spoke again. Peter looked to Viktor but he was still in shock, frozen in place. A woman sitting behind Peter must have seen his dilemma because she leaned forward and translated quietly in broken English. So this was a song for a nun that had died while looking after them. At least that much Peter managed to understand. He thanked the woman, his eyes still riveted on the girl.

Once the song was over, the festival organiser strode out onto the platform, shook hands with the girl who'd conducted and beckoned forward the girl who'd spoken. Putting an arm round the girl's shoulders they both turned to bow to the audience. There was magic in the air, Peter could feel it. So could the audience. Everyone got to their feet, applauding again.

As the applause died down, the organiser, her arm still laced around the girl's shoulder beckoned to someone they couldn't see. Then, out of the shadows came an elegant lady in a wheel chair. Despite her age, the resemblance to the girl was striking. Peter was convinced it must be her mother. Could this woman in the wheelchair be Beth? He glanced at Viktor, as the woman began to speak. Viktor's face was a mixture of joy and alarm. There only yards away sat the love of his life, the woman he'd thought he'd lost for ever. Tears were streaming down his cheeks at the sight of her.

"Beth," Viktor said, unable to hold back the name.

The woman ceased talking and looked at him for a long moment in silence. People whispered in the audience, trying to understand what was happening.

"Viktor?" the woman asked, shifting her wheelchair a little closer.

Viktor got to his feet, took the few steps needed to join her and knelt at her feet. She laid a hand on his cheek, running her fingers up and through his hair. Then she turned to the audience and spoke. Peter was desperate to know what she said. He glanced back at the woman behind him. She shook her head, her smile apologetic. It was her neighbour that offered to translate. "This man was the love of my life. Tragic circumstances separated us. Both of us thought the other was dead. We have not seen each other since then." Tears were now streaming down her proud face.

People applauded one last time and when the applause died away, not wanting to pry on what was clearly a private moment, they got to their feet and turned to leave. The festival was over and a joyous ending it had been. Then abruptly the organ burst into life with a hiss of wind in its pipes and a fanfare. The audience stopped in its tracks staring up at the unseen console below the array of pipes over the main door.

Someone was improvising on the last song of the lost girls. Peter glanced in Andrew's direction, but he was no longer there. When the short piece came to an end, the audience, tightly packed in the aisles, applauded as the organist and Andrew appeared over the balcony, clasping hands held high in salute. People cheered and clapped, then slowly their appreciation gave way to chatter and laughter as one by one they made their way towards the exit.

Once his astonishment had subsided, Peter looked back at the girl who was still arm in arm with the organiser. To his surprise, her eyes were fixed on him. Her look was full of questions to which he had no answers.

Peter? a familiar voice said in his head.

Kate? Where are you?

Standing right in front of you, you silly thing.

Peter thought his heart would hammer its way out of his chest when he saw her smile at him. He had never seen anything so beautiful in all his life.

Don't be shy, she said, a grin in her voice.

He saw her turn toward the woman next to her and say

something, then she came to him and taking him by the hand pulled him to his feet. How good it was to feel her hand warm and inviting in his. In all the time he'd known Kate they'd never, never been able to be together like this, two separate people who loved each other, not just voices in each other's heads.

Keeping hold of his hand she led him to the organiser. There was no need for introductions, but Kate explained that they too had been lost to each other and now were found. He was able to understand thanks to Kate's thoughts. Kate presented him to Beth but the woman's whole attention was on Viktor. Then Kate took him to meet the Lost Girls. So many names and faces to remember!

Only one made him feel unwelcome. Her name was Tania. Peter had heard that name before. Wasn't she the jealous girl who wanted to keep Kate all to herself?

She'll get over it, Kate told him, their arms linked together.

More and more people surrounded them as members of the audience came to congratulate her not only on the singing but for all she'd done for the girls. One of the people handed her a newspaper supplement in which figured several photos of the girls. There was a portrait of Kate on the cover.

After a while they managed to give everyone the slip. Kate knew a secret way out through a back door. The cool evening air brought welcome freshness. They followed a path that led around the church till they found a quiet seat on a low wall. Nearby was a roofed walkway that surrounded the church. It reminded Peter of a cloister but with the church in the middle.

I saw a picture of you a while back, Peter said. *I didn't know it was you. Viktor told me it was Beth, his long lost love. But I treasured that photo and secretly, deep down, hoped it was you.*

He turned to look at her, her face only inches away. They leant forward till their lips touched. Something wild, immense, deep and profoundly quiet swept through his veins leaving him trembling.

I love you, he thought. He'd said it to her before, but never like this.

I love you, too, she thought.

The church bells began to ring, a deafening clamour that filled him with joy.

It's for the curfew, she told him. *An old tradition.*

They huddled back into the shadows, their arms laced around each other and kissed again.

Epilogue

Hand in hand, Peter sauntered into Lydia's kitchen with Kate. Both were wearing dresses borrowed from Beth's collection, not the frilly sort with all the lace trimmings for special occasions, but simple smocks that Beth must have worn when she tended her herb gardens. Peter felt buoyed up by all that had happened. Now that he'd finally found Kate, it was as if his questions had found answers.

John and Christina were seated at the large wooden table drinking tea, their heads close together, talking quietly. He regretted he'd seen so little of them, he'd been so busy with Kate and the festival.

"Kate's been showing me Lydia's herb garden," he said, when the two looked up to greet them. "There's so much to learn."

They took two seats next to each other, still holding hands, while Christina poured them herbal tea. "You need to change and pack your things, Peter," Christina said. "We're catching the two o'clock train. Andrew has already packed."

Peter looked at Kate, then at Christina and John. This wasn't going to be easy. "I'm not coming," he told her quietly, but firmly. "I'm staying with Kate."

"Talk about jumping out of the frying pan into the fire," Christina muttered. "Women don't even have the vote here, and let's not talk about homosexual rights with a catholic church at every street corner." She burst into tears. "I lost Fi and now I am to lose you. It's not fair." She put her head in her hands and sobbed.

John shifted closer and wrapped a comforting arm around her.

"I know it's hard," Peter began. "We'll come and see you during the holidays, I promise. But now I've found Kate…" He lifted her hand to his lips and kissed her fingers, at which she blinked her eyelashes at him. "I don't want to leave her. And here I can work on healing, something I could never do at home. I will work closely with Kate and Lydia, developing their business with medicinal plants. Viktor is going to live nearby with Beth, so I can continue my singing. And Beth has generously offered to pay for German lessons, amongst other things. Not to mention all the clothes I have to try out," he said grinning.

"I admire your courage, Peter," John said, his face serious. "I think you are making the right decision." He paused, thoughtfully pulling at his handlebar mustache. "I want you to know that both of you will have a place with us. Our home will always be your home, should you wish."

Peter thanked him.

Christina struggled to her feet and came to Peter's side. Hugging him, she kissed him on the cheek. "I love you like my son," she whispered in his ear. "I always will."

He knew how important having a son was for her, especially since she'd lost her own in childbirth. Not trusting himself to speak, he returned her kiss. Christina beckoned for John to join them and then held out an arm to Kate till all four huddled together.

Kate, who no longer knew much English, spoke into their heads so they could understand. Whenever she spoke that way, Peter felt her thoughts full of laughter and sunshine. *If Peter is good,* she said, *we might even let him be one of the The Lost Girls.*

Annexes

The Author

Alan McCluskey lives amid the vineyards in a small Swiss village between three lakes and a range of mountains. Nearby, several thousands of years earlier, lakeside villages housed a thriving Celtic community. The ever-present heart-beat of that world continues to fuel his long-standing fascination for magic and fantasy.

Whether it be about Sally, Brent and Keira in The Storyteller's Quest or Peter, Kaitling and Fi in Boy & Girl. In Search of Lost Girls or We Girls, all Alan McCluskey's novels tell the story of young people who, despite the immense difficulties that abound, discover and develop their own astounding talents and manage to do the exceptional.

We Girls is the third in the Boy & Girl Saga. The other two books are Boy & Girl and In Search of Lost Girls. Alan McCluskey has published three YA novels in The Storyteller's Quest series: The Reaches, The Keeper's Daughter and The Starless Square. The fourth book in the series, World o'Tales is awaiting publication. In addition, he has published two other novels, Chimera and Stories People Tell. The sequel to the latter, Local Voices, is awaiting publication.

Boy & Girl Saga Book 1
Boy & Girl
2020 edition
Alan McCluskey

Boy & Girl
The Boy & Girl Saga - Book 1

When Peter awakes in the head of a girl, he is both delighted and alarmed that his secret yearnings have become reality. Very quickly, however, his error is apparent; this girl is not him. Kaitling –that's her name– is twelve years old, like Peter. She's the daughter of a magician, a prominent figure in another world. Boy and girl travel back and forth from each other's minds, but have little time to get acquainted before Kaitling's island is overrun by warrior priests and she has to flee. At home, a conflict erupts in Peter's family forcing him to take refuge at a friend's place. Meanwhile at school, a haughty new girl goads him about his girlishness and, spitting in his face, vows to rid the earth of people like him. The stage seems set for a desperate struggle to survive, but will ingenuity and youthful fervour be enough against folly and fanaticism?.

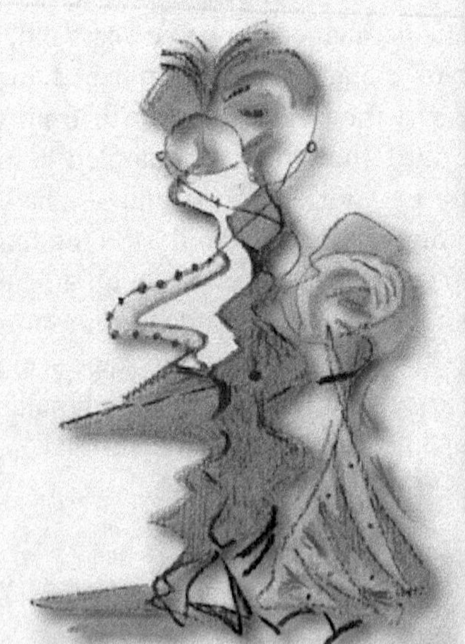

Boy & Girl Saga Book 3
We Girls
2020 edition
Alan McCluskey

We Girls
The Boy & Girl Saga - Book 3

Peter is beset by an existential choice, retain his androgynous ambiguity or say goodbye to his girlish self. Circumstances, however, force both him and Kate to take up other challenges. By straddling the line between child and adult, between carefree creativity and weighty responsibility, between play and work, they find imaginative ways to confront far-reaching problems on which adults persistently turn a blind eye.

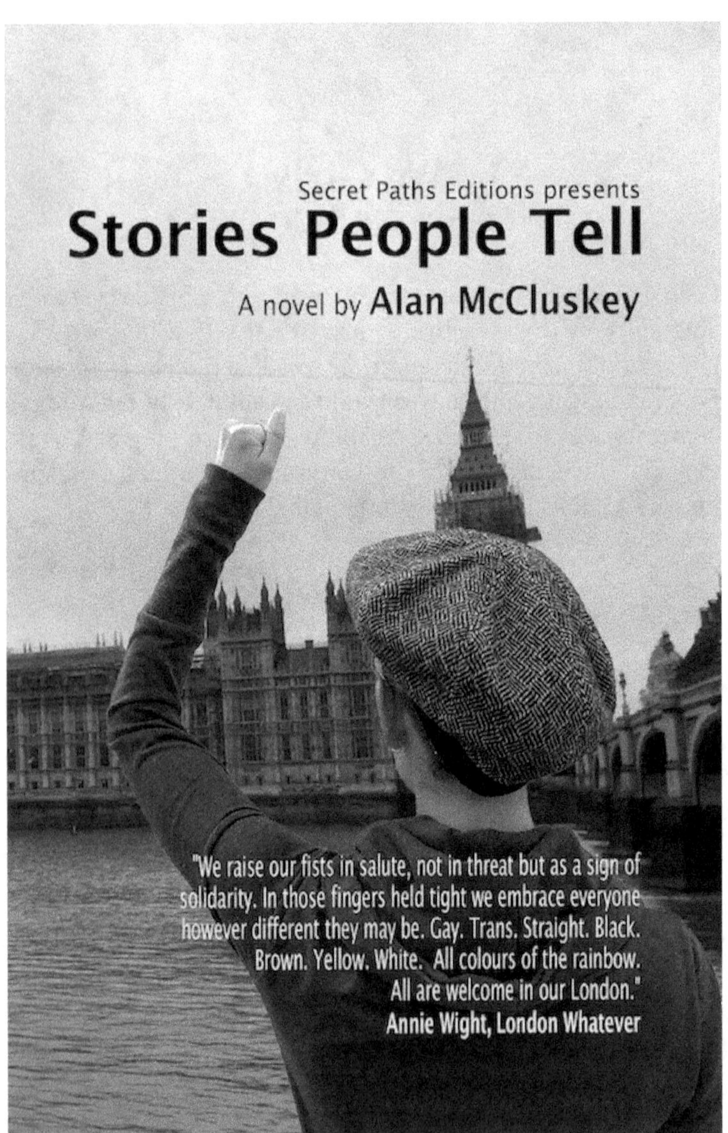

Secret Paths Editions presents
Stories People Tell
A novel by Alan McCluskey
"We raise our fists in salute, not in threat but as a sign of solidarity. In those fingers held tight we embrace everyone however different they may be. Gay. Trans. Straight. Black. Brown. Yellow. White. All colours of the rainbow. All are welcome in our London."
Annie Wight, London Whatever

Stories People Tell

Stories People Tell is a tale about Annie Wight, a shy school-girl who, despite sustained, cruel treatment and personal doubts, blossoms into a major voice in the grassroots movement 'London Whatever' celebrating gender diversity while struggling to end violence against women and care for the weak and marginalised.

Annie wasn't expecting to fall in love with a girl or to shoot to notoriety when she got swept up in 'London Whatever'. Nor could she have known that, right from the outset, she would become the number one target of Nolan Kard, the homophobic Lord Mayor of London. who was campaigning to 'Keep London Straight'. She bore the brunt of attacks from his rogue police, not to mention from a sinister gang of ghostwriters, the nightmare of all Kard's enemies.

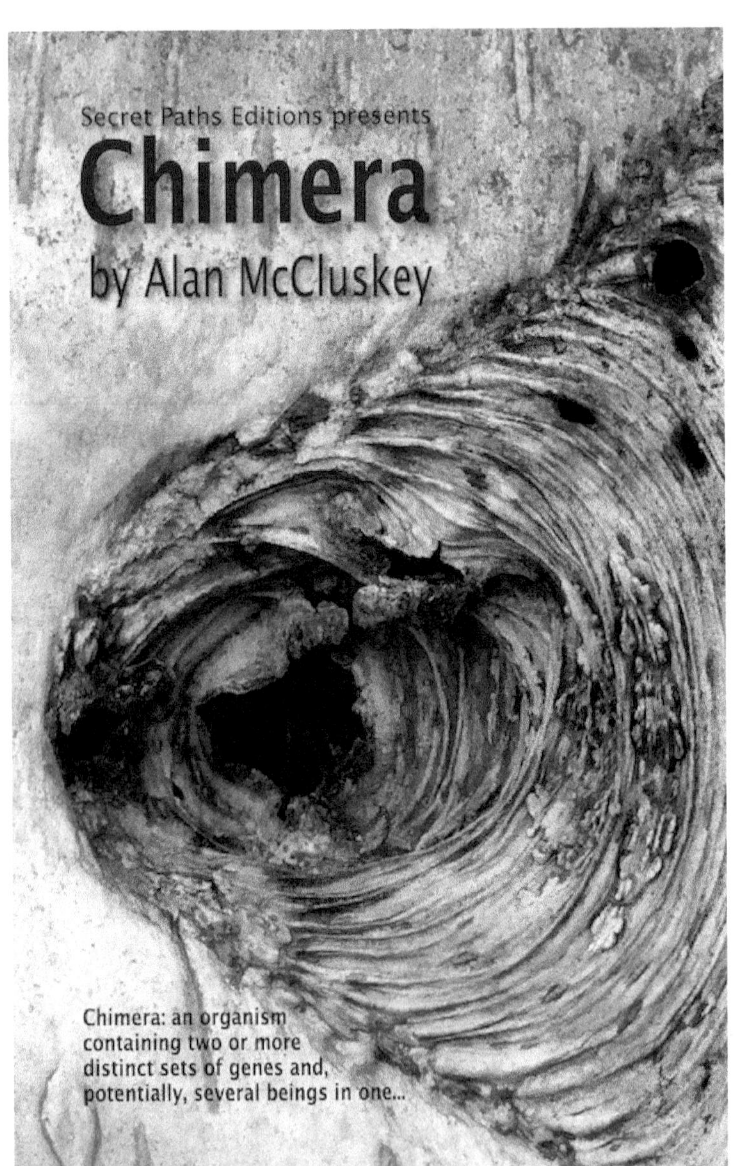

Secret Paths Editions presents
Chimera
by Alan McCluskey
Chimera: an organism
containing two or more
distinct sets of genes and,
potentially, several beings in one...

Chimera

A chimera is an organism containing two or more distinct sets of genes and, potentially, several beings in one. Sami and Sam are a chimera, two people in one, a girl and a boy, a leader and healer of people sharing a body with a brilliant but autistic child.

Sam talking to himself on discovering he is one half of a chimera...:
:: not being able to speak, to move - such was the price I had to pay - to cut out the chaos and confusion from a world run wild - a raw satisfaction - being barricaded in my head these past twelve years - all for nothing - that blasted girl has ruined everything - surging out of nowhere - pirating my body - bridging the gap between me and the others - letting chaos rush in - beguiling everyone with her codswallop - not me - I'm not impressed - some say she's destined to be our saviour - as if the block-head could save a fly - I just want her gone

Sami's first ever words to her teacher and her father...:
"I … need … to explain. Words come with … difficulty. I must … be brief. Sam and I are a … chimera ... there are two of us... Sam is the boy you know. New things terrify him. He cannot speak … out loud. He stumbles. He falls. I am new. I just awoke. I am a girl. I play piano I talk. I walk. As for that violence you just saw, that was Sam trying to kick me out"

The Storyteller's Quest ~ Book One
The Reaches
Alan McCluskey

The Reaches
The Storyteller's Quest Bk 1

The quiet town of Avan with its port, its provincial university and its conservative seafaring folk would hardly be the place you'd expect to run into an adventure and frankly neither Brent nor Sally nor Keira were going out of their way to have one. At least nothing more than the occasional torrid love affair and the awkward self-questioning typical of many young adults like themselves. Sally was finishing her studies in the Theosophy Department of the University hoping to become Professor Rafter's assistant, Keira, Sally's best friend and lover, was a young librarian who occasionally sang in a popular folk group and Brent was a would-be writer who couldn't quite get his act together and who spent hours wandering the streets and lanes of the town in search of inspiration. Yet unbeknown to them forces had long been at work that would throw them together in a series of adventures that were going to tax them to the extreme forcing them to develop abilities that went way beyond what would seem possible during a voyage from the real world to the realm of dreams and on into another world called the Reaches that at first sight looked deceptively like their own.

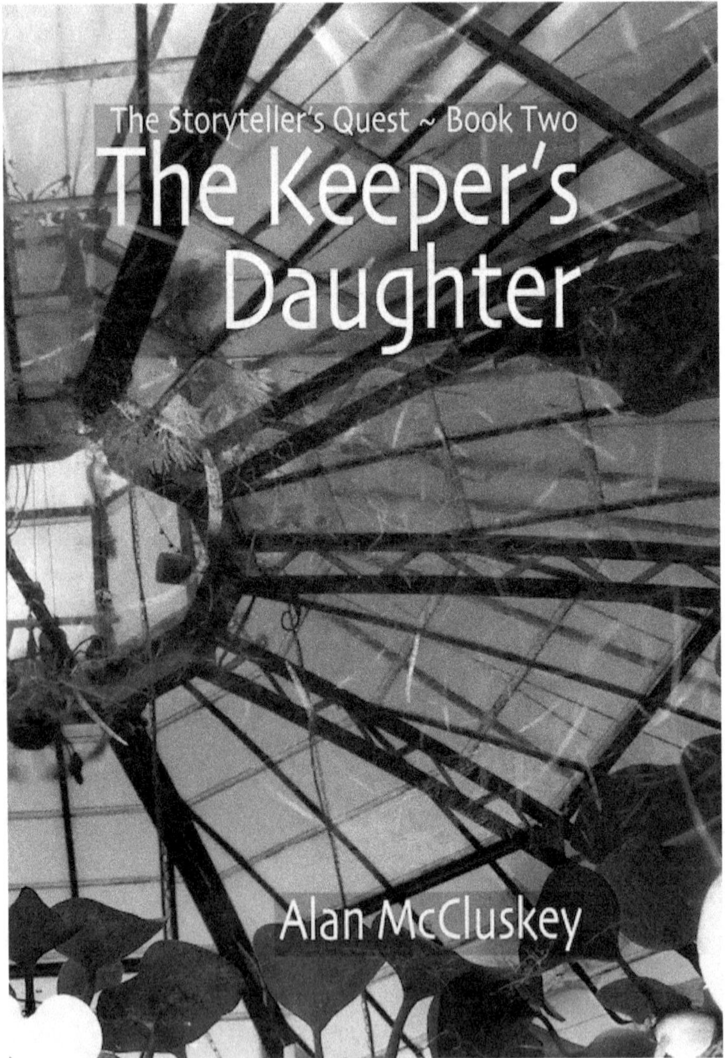

The Storyteller's Quest ~ Book Two
The Keeper's Daughter
Alan McCluskey

The Keeper's Daughter
The Storyteller's Quest - Book 2

It wasn't Brent's fault if he was stuck in the form of Jake the Owl, at least he didn't think it was as he sat on a branch preening despondently. The threads of all his stories had become inextricably muddled in his owlish head. To think that he'd once prided himself on being a storyteller. His stories had become adventures and some of those adventures had become nightmares, and now he was stuck with them. He'd flown in search of his friend and lover, Mia. She'd been dragged off by a band of thugs just when it was time for them all to return to their world. Only Sally, their mutual friend and lover, had made it back from the world of the Reaches to their hometown of Avan. Hearing her story, despite the dangers she'd had to face, her friends suggested Sally teach them to travel to the Dream Realm and beyond to the Reaches. The idea appealed to everybody. Not that Sally knew how to get back to the Reaches, but the idea of a 'dream class' as they called it pleased her and, above all, she wanted to return to the world where her newly-found half-sister lived and where her two friends had so abruptly disappeared.

The Storyteller's Quest ~ Book Three
The Starless
Square
Alan McCluskey

The Starless Square
The Storyteller's Quest - Book 3

A weekend of joyous festivities! Such was the Theosophy department's response to a group of fanatics bent on destroying their reputation and having them shut down. Theosophy? Professor Rafter, head of the department, calls it "the study of our direct relationship with that which is beyond and above the normal range of human experience". He could just as well have been describing the adventures of a group of young friends who have been called back from their travels in another world to defend their department with their new-found abilities. But how could entrancing singing or breath-taking storytelling or exquisite cooking possibly stand a chance when pitted against the evil black cloud that threatens to obscure the Starless Square?

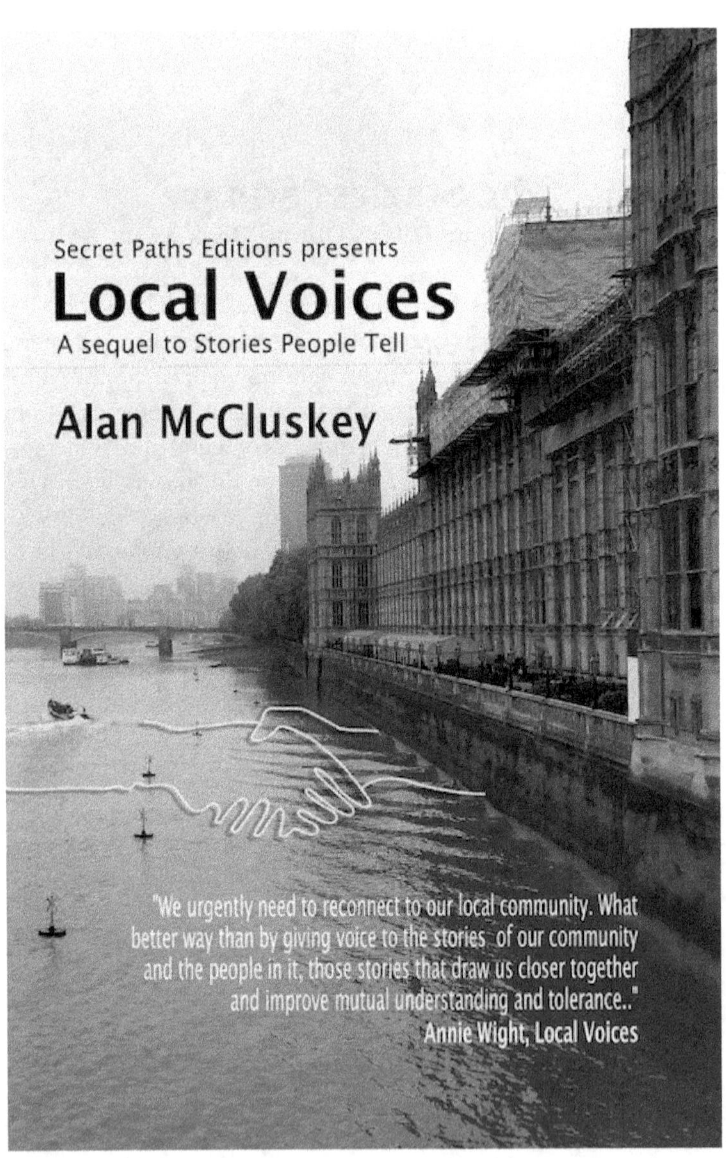

Secret Paths Editions presents
Local Voices
A sequel to Stories People Tell

Alan McCluskey

"We urgently need to reconnect to our local community. What better way than by giving voice to the stories of our community and the people in it, those stories that draw us closer together and improve mutual understanding and tolerance.."
Annie Wight, Local Voices

Local Voices
Coming soon: a sequel to Stories People Tell

In her campaign to re-assert and strengthen the role of women at the heart of hearthside healthcare, seventeen-year-old Annie Wight finds herself pitted against Health England, a conservative think-tank backed by pharmaceutical giants and private healthcare providers. Pretexting the defence of the National Health Service, they stop at nothing to stamp out Annie's efforts. They target not just her but those close to her, wreaking havoc in friendships and affairs of the heart. As part of her response, Annie launches a project to share the stories of those that never figure in the spotlight. By celebrating local voices, the project fights against isolation and disempowerment.

Online

Secret Paths: https://author.secret-paths.com
Facebook: https://www.faccbook.com/Secret.Paths
Instagram: https://www.instagram.com/secretpathseditions/
Twitter: https://www.twitter.com/Almacme